THE SEA HIDES ITS DEAD

MEGAN BONTRAGER

THE SEA HIDES ITS DEAD

A list of the Orbit imprint
orbit-books.co.uk

RUN FOR IT

First published in Great Britain in 2026 by Run For It
1 3 5 7 9 10 8 6 4 2

All characters and events in this publication, other than those clearly in the public domain, are fictitious and any resemblance to real persons, living or dead, is purely coincidental.

A CIP catalogue record for this book is available from the British Library.

HB ISBN 978-0-356-52960-8
C format ISBN 978-0-356-52961-5

Typeset in Adobe Caslon Pro by Aptara
Printed and bound in Great Britain by Clays Ltd, Elcograf, S.p.A.

Papers used by Run For It are from well-managed forests and other responsible sources.

Run For It is a list of the Orbit imprint.

Orbit
An imprint of
Little, Brown Book Group
Carmelite House
50 Victoria Embankment
London EC4Y 0DZ

The authorised representative
in the EEA is
Hachette Ireland
8 Castlecourt Centre, Dublin 15,
D15 XTP3, Ireland
(email: info@hbgi.ie)

An Hachette UK Company
www.hachette.co.uk

orbit-books.co.uk

For those still learning who they are. Take your time. No one has the answer but you.

And for Papa. Thank you for the stories. Because of them, and this, I know who I am.

Content Warnings

Emotional abuse, narcissistic abuse, suicidal ideation, animal death, sexual coercion, gore, blood

To see a World in a Grain of Sand
And a Heaven in a Wild Flower
Hold Infinity in the palm of your hand
And Eternity in an hour

"Auguries of Innocence" | William Blake

7

There was no ceremony in the anniversary of my mother's death. I bore the day like a rotten organ, one that had gotten stuck in its botched extraction. No one mourned her in the way that one might hope to be mourned, missed her in the way one might strive to be missed. The art of mourning was one that had always eluded me, an equation that I never quite got the answer to. No one teaches mourning. It just happens.

It takes no bravery to make the active choice *not* to mourn. This, too, just happens.

The date occurred to me only after the day had already come to its dark and watery conclusion. The flicker of a time and date across the dashboard of my car; a change of time on the phone in the passenger seat. I had more important things to tend to: a flight to catch, a paper to finish, a thesis to edit. The soaked-through backpack in the back seat and the useless poncho in the trunk didn't care what day it was, or what day it wasn't. I had work to do. Mourning had no space on the agenda.

The rain was endless, all the way from Maine to Ohio, and had been for nearly forty-eight hours. A thick swath of it, a heavy canopy that seemed to have been placed on purpose. The moment it had struck a thick line across the landscape, Professor Beck had stopped his lecture – *History of Religious Anthropology* – short, bustling from the hall and leaving a room full of undergrads in bewilderment. They'd all come to expect a certain level of strangeness from the infamous Edward Beck, but this was . . . different. More.

"The idea of judgment before the afterlife, or what we understand as the stage of being after material life," he said, "is an excellent place to start when building a case for an ethnocultural profile." Beck had gestured to me, and I'd dutifully flipped to the next slide. It was a thrilling post, and one best left to the professionals. "What do rites like the Duat or the Bridge of the Requiter teach us about these cultures?" Another nod, another slide. "Some might say that man mandates divinity. Others believe that divinity directs man. Which is more—"

A phone rang. For once, it was Beck's. He'd looked to the usual troublemaker at the back of the lecture hall, only to redden when he realized that it was his own ringtone coming from behind the projector desk. As he took the call, I did my best to fill the space.

He was gone before I could finish my speech about deadlines, leaving me no instructions. I'd flipped awkwardly through a few more slides before giving up. I distributed handouts, reminded them all of the homework, and had followed Beck's arrow-keen trajectory from the lecture hall and to the cloister of his office.

But when he informed me, once I'd caught up, that a monolith of limestone and dolomite had risen from the sea, I understood.

"A monolith?" I echoed. I could see it clearly in my mind's eye. Enough hours I'd spent entrenched in his work; I knew his theories, his notes, his crude drawings better than I knew my own phone number. "Like . . . just *out* there?"

He nodded, my incredulity washing off him like rain. "With a single opening in the rock face, turned right in toward the coast. It's an invitation." This was no question, no uncertain hypothesis.

The rain began shortly after he'd received the call from his colleagues at the University of Maine, and even sooner did he raise a toast to the fishing village on the coast that had all but been washed away. The rain stretched across the northeast like a hand reaching in good faith for Beck himself. *Come and see*, it said. *Come and be vindicated.*

"I need you with me, Caroline," he'd said, his lips hot against the hollow of my throat. The photograph of his wife sat downturned atop the stack of notes he had meticulously moved from the desk. This was practiced, routine; it didn't seem like the time to fuck in his office, but men were men. "Will you come?"

Historically, no.

Of course, that wasn't what he'd meant. "I'm just a grad student, Edward," I huffed, bracing my palms flat upon the mahogany desk top as he tore at the buttons of my blouse. "I would only be in the way."

"Bullshit." His pants hung round his thighs, just low enough. A tungsten band slipped from his pocket and rolled beneath the couch. A place for crying undergrads, mostly. We rarely used it. "*Need*, not want. I trust you more than anyone with this work. You believe in me. Don't you?"

I nodded, and wrapped my legs around his middle. For the briefest of moments, I couldn't pull my eyes from where the band had disappeared beneath Beck's designated *crying-for-better-grades* sofa. Had his wife heard the news? Did she know what the rain meant? Did she care?

But of course I believed in him. I always had, and always would. I believed in him as he believed in me: fervently, quietly, and against all odds. Whenever he asked me questions like this, I couldn't help but think of the very first time. He'd found me crying in the hall outside his office, fresh off a call with my father. My father, who *never* called. My father, who loved to talk about death. About belief, and how little of it he reserved for me.

Edward Beck was the very first person to believe in me, as far as I was concerned. And so I'd follow him anywhere. Even if I had to do so in secret.

His hand slipped to the slope of my neck, fingers playing in the loose tie of my hair. "*God*," he sighed. "It's finally happening. As if the earthquakes weren't enough; the cave, the islet, the *runes*. It's real. It's *there*." Beck lifted his head and met my gaze. Something fiercer than anything I'd ever seen roared in his eyes. It tugged at the hard knot in the pit of my stomach. I'd believed him before now, of course. But this . . . this was something else.

"What is it?" I'd asked.

Beck's face had slipped into a sly smile, the practiced curl of his lips like that of a fox, or a cat with claws poised above a mouse. "I have my theories," he said. It was always theory. Theory above everything. He needed to see it to believe it.

"A monster?"

"Maybe."

"A god?"

"Could be."

"An angel?"

A twitch of the lips, an invisible seam tugged taut. "We'll just have to wait and see. Theories and understanding; one feeds the other."

I didn't believe in any of those things. Not really. So where did that leave us?

He left me alone in his office, trusted to clean myself up and not touch anything important. Beck took his notes and left the ring, likely not even noticing that it had slipped out of his pocket. A weather alert lit my phone, the only glowing reminder in the midst of a room that had been left darkened by design. Another earthquake, and more rain. The sea was angry. I imagined the monolith in Maine to be no more than a raised middle finger.

I wondered idly if he only wanted me there so that he could fulfill some fetish. It wasn't every day that one found themselves alone in a cave with their *lover.*

Lover. What a stupid word.

Why else would he want me there? I was his assistant, sure. I'd heard all his rants and read all his papers – whether I wanted to or not. I knew what he believed, knew what haunted him. It didn't mean that I believed it, too. Hell, I'd only registered for his class in the first place, years ago, to fill an "undecided" credit. I was directionless. He had seen it as malleability.

No – it was unfair to ascribe that line of thinking to him. Beck valued me for my ideas. That we were actively sleeping together, that he told me that he loved me and that he chose me above all others, was a side benefit. Ours was a partnership born into the warmth of shared ideas, of belief in the impossible. I just had to work a little harder at the latter than he did.

Someone so sure of his purpose, his life's grand design, could no doubt smell my indecision on me like pheromones. Maybe this – this discovery, this research, and the notoriety that would come with it – would spur me toward something tangible. I couldn't work at the co-op for the rest of my life, wandering without aim or purpose. I hadn't come this far to *only* come this far. I had done too much, sacrificed too much, to settle for uncertainty. All I needed was a hard push off a sharp drop.

"What do you *want*, Caroline?" he'd asked me once. "What do you want your life to be?"

I had no answer for him. Even as he asked it a second time, and then a third, with every ounce of honesty in the world, I couldn't muster a response. I wanted him, but couldn't have all of him. I wanted purpose, but couldn't find the way. I was a collection of half-wants and maybes, where he had, no doubt, spawned into the world fully realized. And so I had shrugged, and let him do what he wished with me. I was good at being used, filled and molded and squashed and stretched to fill a need. An accessory. I existed for the negative space. I made people whole. That was enough. That was purpose.

For a while, anyway. And so today, on the anniversary of my mother's death, I decided to jump.

Beck paid for my plane ticket. A separate flight from his own, and that of the rest of the crew. Even the other graduate student, Mallory, was allowed to sit with the group. I took it in my stride; I lived on the Kentucky side of the river and worked a part-time job in addition to being in school and serving as Beck's teaching assistant. I was only ever invited to his brick townhouse in Hyde Park for school functions that would fill the room with enough people to force us onto opposite sides. The great divide between the Ohio and Kentucky sides of the Ohio River gave me enough plausible deniability that I could show up to the airport for a later flight and not be looked at sideways.

The university had offered him no stipend, no emergency grant, to travel from Ohio to Maine. Nor did they even think of funding his team, an assemblage of professionals from all walks of life, as they made their pilgrimage to Seal Harbor. They did nothing to intervene as the Coast Guard and Navy swarmed the place like they intended to blow it off the map. Beck himself made a call to the local authorities, demanding to be put on the phone with the Lieutenant Commander on site. He'd turned the worst shade of purple I'd ever seen when the man on the phone let it slip that they'd sent a SEAL team into the mouth of the cave, only to come back empty-handed. Their first inclination was to blow it up. As it always seemed to be, where the military was concerned.

There was no dissuading the Navy, I'd told him. But somehow, some way, he'd done it anyway. Getting the US military to do *anything* with measured patience was an act of something divine, I guessed. It seemed completely improbable. Amid the media circus, the keyboard conspiracy theories, the clamor for footage and on-site coverage of the strange *thing* that had risen out of the sea, Beck said with no reservation that we'd be in and out before the Navy got to work.

Hysteria was pervasive, touching every corner of every hole that the internet could take me down. Nearly every radio station, even the local chatters here on the Kentucky–Ohio border, wondered at the great stone monolith that had risen from the sea off the coast of Maine. Some seemed to be onboard with the Navy's line of thinking: blow it up first, and ask questions later. But some were like Beck. Some wanted to *know.* One man from Columbus, whose Reddit account I'd found with almost verbatim transcripts of what he posited on air, suggested that *someone* – anyone – should sneak in and get ahold of whatever was inside before the "red-pilled bureaucracy of the military" could ruin something so significant. I couldn't say that I disagreed. And maybe, it occurred to me, Beck didn't either.

I made a note to press him about the legitimacy of this "permission" we'd been given. Asking questions likely wasn't going to change his mind, but it would at least keep mine free from the worry of getting thrown in federal prison before graduation.

The only one who'd questioned my exclusion from the group at large was Mallory. She'd texted me a photo of the donut and green smoothie – "*Balance!*" – that she was bringing on the plane, along with an unflattering selfie and a picture of the back of Beck's head. All of it came with questions about my whereabouts, requests to bring an extra phone charger, and enough sparkly emojis to effectively hide the photo of Beck's cowlick. We grad students had to stick together, I figured. At least *she* knew what she wanted to do with her life. If she was willing to brave Beck's wild fantasies for the sake of a thesis, she could do anything.

I reached across the center console and turned my phone facedown. Any reminder of the day was unwelcome. I had work to do, and no phantom pain could be great enough to deter me from that. No matter how I wondered what my mother might make of the rain, what she might think of Beck's wild theories and his endless studies, mourning was no business of mine.

No texts, no calls, no condolences. Only silence.

I drowned it with a crank of the radio, turning the evening talk show higher than was strictly comfortable. Even the pair of radio hosts that pandered to truckers and rural-Kentucky ranchers had turned their attention skyward, theorizing that the great, immovable patch of rain over the northeastern US was some kind of biblical warning.

Not me, Rusty, said Darryl, the louder of the two. *Reckon it's punishment for that goddamn foul they called on Tennessee . . .*

They worshiped at the altar of beer, football, and Jesus Christ. I often wondered how someone like Beck, someone so secular and academic, ended up here. What a world to carry out his research in. No wonder he was met with skepticism and snide, sideways laughter. He spoke of old gods and cosmic knowledge. If it didn't guarantee a showing at church on Sundays, people here didn't want to know about it.

The rain hadn't let up for a week, almost like a wink and a nudge from up north. I could barely see the road ahead of me, the dark Kentucky back road that arrowed away from the highway and toward the cargo roads behind the terminal. There, I'd park in one of the free long-term lots and shuttle to the Cincinnati Airport – which, oddly enough, was just as Kentucky as I was. Windshield wipers whirring furiously and headlights cutting weakly through the deluge, I fiddled with the radio dials.

The steering wheel wobbled as I whipped around a curve, the wetness of the road threatening to pitch me into the steep ditch on the side of the road. Something small, something set apart from the endless, monotonous black of the woods on either side of the road, cut through the watery beam of the headlights. I gasped, slamming my foot down on the brake pedal. My suitcase toppled forward, slamming into the back of my seat. The car skidded, twisted, and thudded into the grass.

I flicked on the hazards. My phone had flown from the passenger seat, now face-up on the floor; my backpack had toppled, and my suitcase righted itself with a thud in the trunk. But I hardly noticed. My eyes, wide and watering at the corners, trained upon the body on the side of the road, the great lump of brown and white fur that I had just missed as I'd skidded around the turn.

A deer. Its side heaved with belabored breaths. And across its back, a great bloom of crimson that the rain simply couldn't wash out.

How long had it been left here? Had it been hit here, or had it struggled from far off to die in peace? It was alive, certainly; even through the rain, each breath puffed from its wet muzzle in a short burst of steam. For a long moment I could only watch it, dumbstruck, as its eyes wheeled wildly. Its front legs gave a great lurch, and the unbidden wetness in my eyes spilled over my cheek.

"*Shit*," I hissed, fumbling for my phone. "Shit, shit, *shit*."

I put the car in park and hoisted the door open before I could think otherwise. My boot sank into the muddy rut left behind by my tires, and I nearly slipped as I spilled from behind the wheel. The rain was a roar; I could hear nothing else. Door left wide, light swallowed by the darkness of the rural road, I stepped into the street. I was soaked through immediately, the denim of my jeans slick to my thighs. As best I could, I shielded the phone with my trembling hand as I did a quick search for the number for animal control.

I relayed to them our location and the state of the deer. "Someone just left it," I said. Spitting rainwater from my shivering lips, I looked down the road in one direction, and then the other. "It can't get up."

"You could do the humane thing and put it out of its misery," the man on dispatch said. "Or let nature take care of it."

Put it out of its misery. End its suffering. Take its pain. *Kill it.* I wouldn't. I couldn't. The deer's head had barely inclined to mark my approach, its shining eyes locked onto me as I eddied at the edge of the street. I could help it, I knew. It would be the humane thing. Anything to lessen a creature's suffering was worth doing. And the deer didn't deserve to suffer.

Foolishly, I wondered if it might be fixed. Healed. Rural veterinarians were tantamount to miracle workers. Animal control could come collect it, take it to the after-hours vet in Idlewild, and set it loose again with a stern talking-to about coming near the road in such heavy rain. They could even track down the bastard who'd done it. Only a real monster would simply leave such a creature, knowingly, to suffer.

But I couldn't kill it. I couldn't.

"I—absolutely *not.* I'm not a killer. It just . . . it just needs to see a vet is all."

A sigh, and then the clacking of fingers on a keyboard. "I'll send a truck along now, ma'am. Give it 'bout ten minutes. You have a blessed day."

The line went dead before I could say anything else. I watched the deer, the phone still pressed to my cheek, as it tried to move its legs again.

"Hold still!" I cried, my voice swallowed by the roaring of the rain. I tucked my waterlogged phone into my back pocket and wiped my hands futilely down the front of my soaked-through jacket.

The deer opened its mouth, then closed it again. I splashed into the road without thinking, crossing the warm headlight beam. Blood spilled from an open wound only to be washed away by the rain, running in watery crimson rivulets down the bloated curve of the deer's belly. A doe, and young by the looks of it; she had no antlers, faded spots on her rump, and a ring of white fur around her muzzle. Her eyes tracked me, alert and aware.

I stared down at her for a long moment, gaze darting from the wound, to her eyes, to the unnatural jut of her legs. No animal deserved to suffer. Humans had a more complicated relationship with the concept of anguish. But not animals. In a perfect world, they would know nothing of it.

As I stepped from the road, my boots slipping in the mud beneath me, the deer made an attempt at moving once more. I shushed her, holding out my hands like I might have done with a startled horse. Knees knocking and teeth chattering, I sank into the muddy grass beside the doe. She made no moves to squirm away from me, though her eyes followed me closely.

And then, with trembling fingers, I reached out. I let her get a whiff of me, her breath hot on my hand. Carefully, I wiped the mud from her muzzle, clearing her nose of muck and refuse. Hot tears spilled faster still over my cheeks, ruining what little remained of the makeup I'd put on early that morning.

The deer gave a great, heaving sigh. Her side billowed, then deflated at last with a heavy groan. I looked up and down the empty road again, searching for any sign of headlights. Nothing.

"Someone's on their way," I muttered, touching the deer's wet fur again. "Hold on a little bit longer. They're gonna fix you up real good."

I wanted the deer to hear it, to believe it, in any way an animal could. No matter how violently I shivered, no matter how warm the tears felt on my cheeks, I hoped that perhaps a moment of kindness might make her believe. If she could understand me at all.

Without thinking, I slid closer. Mud soaked through my jeans, slick and impossibly cold on the skin of my thighs. Surely my phone was ruined, but I couldn't find it in my heart to care.

As gently as I could manage, I tucked my hands beneath the doe's head and lifted. Gritting my teeth to quell the chattering, I slid my legs underneath and settled her back down atop my thighs.

"There," I said. I stroked her cheek, wiped mud, rain, and bits left over from the underbrush from her muzzle. Her body splayed weakly, angled down toward the quickly flooding ditch below us. I debated pulling her higher, further from the ditch and into the light of the headlights. But she was safer here, out of the road. I had almost hit her myself, skidding around the curve with no regard for what could be on the other side.

The deer blinked heavily. Wiping the mud from my palms on the front of my sodden jacket, I stroked her cheek. Her head was heavy in my lap, breath short. I spoke aloud, my voice drowned by the roar of the rain on the cracked blacktop. I hoped that I could comfort her, in a way one might comfort a loved one on their deathbed. There was no telling if the doe understood me, or if she even heard me at all, but her breathing was slow. Even.

And then, when the glare of the Animal Control truck's headlights curved around the bend, she was still. The doe's eyes were glassy, unseeing, and for ever fixed on the underside of my chin. My hands were cold, so numb that I could barely feel her fur beneath my fingertips. The rain had well and truly soaked through my clothes now, and my teeth chattered so harshly that I could barely speak to the man in uniform as he crossed the street to appraise me.

"You been sittin' out here with it since you called?" he barked.

It. I wanted to fling mud at him, but I couldn't feel my hands.

And so I nodded. "I couldn't leave her."

"She's dead, kiddo."

She was. It didn't matter. All things deserved gentleness in the end.

I sat behind the wheel of my car, still half-jutting from the ditch, as the man from Animal Control loaded the doe into the back of his truck. Mud and rainwater soaked into the seat and dripped from my legs and onto the floor beneath the pedals. I cranked the heat on high and sat with hands outstretched over the vents as the truck disappeared around the corner.

My phone buzzed in my back pocket. I startled, smacking the tops of my thighs on the steering wheel.

A text from Beck sat atop a stack of unopened email notifications. *Hope you have a good flight*, it said. *Let me know when you land.*

I blinked numbly at my phone. With the pad of my thumb, I wiped away the muck that had collected in the crevices. It was only then that I noticed the blood on my jeans. Barely visible, as muddled by the road-dirt and rainwater as it was, but it was there. All that remained of the deer I couldn't save.

This – *this* – was mourning. Maybe I did understand it.

I tabbed through the notifications on my phone's home screen, blinking away hot wetness from my eyes as the image jolted and stuttered against the water on the screen. Beck's text, a number of emails from the Anthropology department – and my plane ticket. I looked at the time. The gate was likely closing by now, last call for boarding coming and going in my absence. Beck would be furious.

That, more than anything, was tangible. A problem I could fix.

And so I shot off a text with a weak excuse. A flat tire, a wreck, something that he couldn't verify and couldn't blame. He wouldn't understand why I had taken the time to sit with a dying deer in the rain. He wouldn't understand the tears that still wet my cheeks, nor the feeling of acute hollowness in my chest. And so I wouldn't tell him.

I returned home to find another ticket in my inbox. First flight out; I would need to leave again in just a little under twelve hours. With little ceremony, I set about peeling off my muddy clothes and scrubbing the dirt from beneath my fingernails. Short brown and white hairs shook off my jacket when I stuffed it into the wash. I turned on the news simply for something to fill the silence. Another undersea earthquake, another record-breaking day of rain. Fishermen along the east coast presented buckets and buckets of dead fish – "*already dead when we pulled 'em out of the water*"– to begrudging reporters, and representatives from the Navy spoke at length about a stretch of Massachusetts waterfront that had simply been washed out to sea.

But it mattered little. As I slipped into bed, curling beneath a generous heap of blankets, I could think of only one thing.

The deer deserved more. Maybe I should have complied. I could have done it, put the doe out of its misery. It *would* have been the humane thing to do. But death was never humane. It was just death. And that, more than mourning, I understood.

By the time I arrived in Seal Harbor on the eleventh of April, the others had already assembled in the only pub in town. The Silver Fisher was devoid of all life, save Beck's assemblage of professionals and begrudging students. Even the place's owner, who stood behind the bar and polished the same glass for the entire duration of our debriefing, seemed as if he would rather be literally anywhere else. All four of the daily specials on the blackboard over the bar – some variation of fish on all counts – were messily scribbled out. Instead, the blackboard read "NO MEDIA" in thick, striking letters. Bits of chalk clung to the surface, like whoever had written the message had done so with a heavy hand and a clenched fist.

Even through the rain, I'd seen a great hulk of grey metal out in the bay, far beyond the monolith and down the coast. The Navy had already assembled by the looks of it, patrol boat bobbing like a hungry shark and a convoy of utility trucks gumming up the one exit off the interstate that led to this little corner of Maine. Between the soldiers and the news crews that buzzed like flies, it was strange that The Silver Fisher could stand to sit so empty. Maybe the people of this town hated the intrusion. Maybe they hated *us*. I couldn't blame them.

I decided that *my* ire would be solely reserved for the folks that amassed in RVs on the highway with signs declaring that Jesus had come, that the monolith in the bay was somehow a retributory warning sign. The fanatics on the *other* side of the highway who, instead, shouted at the Navy corpsmen about the undeniable proof of aliens within the rock, I could handle.

The place smelled of dead fish. Not only the pub, and the inn above, but the whole town and all along the waterfront. And not in the way one might expect a fishing town to smell; it was rotten, dead, and decayed, like a carcass left to the maggots.

And there, just barely visible through the rain and fog, the rugged monolith of stone and salt loomed in the bay. Not so close that I could make out the mouth of the cave at its base, our intended destination, but not so far that I could pretend it didn't exist. I pressed my face to the glass of the taxi's passenger window as we sped down the main street of Seal Harbor. A great shapeless darkness in the mist, watchful as a guardian.

On all sides, shop windows bore hand-written signage, all similar in message. *OUT OF FISH*, said one. *CALL DOLORES FOR CARCASS REMOVAL*, said another. A third sign felt significantly less subtle: *LEVITICUS. 26:18-20.* I didn't know a great deal about the Bible, but I could make an educated guess that this was fairly damning, given the circumstances.

"Hell of a time to come here," said the taxi driver. "You and the rest of the goddamn country."

"Any idea what it is?" I mused. Beck wouldn't like it that I'd asked a stranger for an opinion when *his* was so indisputable, and so very readily available, but I had to know.

The driver shrugged. "Far as I'm concerned, it's just a hunk of rock that's gettin' in the way of business as usual." He met my eye in the rearview. "This is a quiet town. Never asked for any of this ruckus."

I opened my mouth, then closed it again. Were archaeologists and graduate students the same shade of "unwelcome" as the rest? Or had Beck let it slip to their hosts, too, what he planned to do out in the bay? It didn't seem like the ideal time for tourism, certainly. So what had he done? What lies had he spun? Suddenly, "permission" felt like a faulty word. I felt like apologizing, but I didn't know what for.

The taxi driver left me on the curb before I could fish a tip from my bag. Alone on the sidewalk I stood, the sound of chatter audible from within. The eyes I felt upon me, however, came from elsewhere.

I hated being the center of attention. Needless to say, the sheer ferocity of the attention on me as I entered the pub with my sodden bags and slick-wet hair made me feel like I could very easily dissolve like sugar in a hot drink. Beck's spread of papers – maps, tide charts, and diagrams from his own long-suffering study – was momentarily forgotten as I eddied in the doorway, a puddle of rainwater pooling at my feet. I gave a nervous wave, then shuffled over to where the others had left their crates upon crates of survey and caving equipment, setting my suitcase aside as quietly as I could manage.

Not quietly enough, apparently. Mallory shot from her chair, one of many around a wide, round table, and rocketed across the creaking boards to meet me. A bright splash of pink and candy hearts, she looked wonderfully out of place among the damp, and dank, and gray. She waved with both hands as she approached, and I flushed a deeper crimson as every eye around the table followed her approach. She hugged me, smelling of vanilla and peony, the colorful clay of her dangling earrings snagging in the wet mess of my hair.

"Come sit by me!" she said, squeezing my arms and giving my shoulders a rub like she might chase away the cold by sheer force of will alone. She took my hand and I obliged, Beck's gaze following me keenly as I scuttled across the room to join the others. Maybe it made him jealous to see that someone was, in fact, capable of giving me the kind of attention I craved without needing to lock a door to do it. Or maybe I was projecting. Two of the others smiled noncommittally at me as I settled into the chair beside Mallory, scooting it closer to her with a scrape of wood on wood. The others . . . did not.

Mallory and Beck's were the only faces I recognized here. The woman closest to Beck picked furiously at the loose skin around her nails, her glasses slipping down the slope of her nose and the strap of her professional-grade camera sagging around her neck. Beside her sat a meticulously dressed woman too far hunched over her notebook, in which she scribbled furiously, to appraise. The more rugged man at her shoulder made no effort to conceal his curiosity, scratching at his generous beard as he leaned away from his own stack of paperwork to snoop. The stranger in the occupied seat beside me had round glasses that magnified her eyes – eyes which, to my dismay, had been trained on me from the moment I entered the room.

Notebook glanced up at me only once, as my chair scraped gratingly across the floor. She looked from the frizz at the top of my head to where my hands disappeared beneath the table, then added a new bullet point to whatever it was she was recording in her book. Somehow I knew that it wasn't complimentary.

"As you can see," Beck said, clearing his throat, "the tide patterns have completely changed. Where we might have had six or seven hours of low tide to work with, we have none." The stranger at his shoulder shifted uncomfortably, tugging at the straps of his rubber waders. Beck gave him a winning smile, which he took no pains to return. "Joseph and his partner have been kind enough to provide us with the use of their boats. Transport to and from the cave, with a transfer to kayaks and dinghies once we're out to sea. It's quite dangerous to be out on the water in such weather," a muscle twitched in Joseph's jaw. "Which is why we are so very grateful for their assistance today." How much had Beck paid them for this? Clearly it was enough that they couldn't turn it down.

My stomach churned. This was a horrible time to remember that I hated boats.

Beck continued, unaware of the green pallor I'd taken on. He gestured then to the pair of strangers opposite me at the table, two identical blonde men, told apart only by the impressive scar on the brow of the one closest to Beck. They were perfectly coiffed, seemingly untouched by the rain. Their eyes were bright, smiles broad. I was reminded at once of every travel ad I'd ever seen for Sweden. "Again, we're thrilled to have Anders and Leon Grundstadt along for the journey," he said. I knew the names from his many rants, but had never been able to put faces to names. Cavers, divers, thrill-seekers; they were made of different stuff than I – that was for sure. I'd be sticking by them at all costs, no matter how in the way I was. "Their expertise will be invaluable," a twitch of a smile, and a self-satisfied laugh, "as will their equipment!"

I glanced around the table as the twins introduced themselves, one after the other like a practiced pantomime. It was impressive. And surreal. Meanwhile Glasses, so short and wiry that her feet barely touched the floor, cleared her throat as she rummaged in her overfull pockets, knocking loose an orange pill bottle, a crumpled tissue, and a dried dog treat before producing a Band-Aid, which she slid across the table.

She leaned down to retrieve her fallen bric-a-brac, temple thumping loudly on the edge of the table. The woman cursed, then guffawed, then leaned beneath the table again, seemingly completely unaware of the fact that Beck had stopped talking – again – and was watching her with open annoyance. I leaned in, pressing against the warped edge of the table, and found Beck's gaze, offering a conciliatory smile as Glasses emerged with her droppings in-hand. I looked back to our expert guides at once, relieved to see that, at the very least, Beard, Notebook, and Camera were all giving the appropriate attention to the presentation.

She turned to me then, smile broad, completely unaware of Beck's withering stare. "Another graduate student, I'm guessing?" she sniffed. "Senior?"

I nodded, keeping my gaze trained on the Grundstadts. They chatted among themselves; one of them polished a carabiner right there at the table. Seemed a little excessive, but whatever. Maybe Glasses needed to stick closer to them than I did.

She stuck a hand under my nose. Heat rose in my cheeks as the twins paused their chattering – and their polishing – clearly thrown off by her lack of attentiveness. "Hannah," she said. "Pleasure."

I took her hand and shook it shortly, glancing at her only once with a tight-lipped smile. "Caroline," I said.

Beard shot us a dirty look. He brought his finger to his lips, and the redness of my cheeks deepened. Hannah gave a scoff. She tugged off the top of the pillbox, and popped something small and white into her mouth with middle finger extended.

"What?" Hannah clipped, swallowing hard. She shoved the pills back into her pocket. "I'm a doctor, for Christ's sake. It's *ibuprofen*."

That was no ibuprofen I'd ever seen. And as a graduate student, I felt uniquely qualified where the subject of liberal ibuprofen was concerned. She didn't exactly *look* like a doctor either, though I guessed that it would be silly to assume she'd come all the way out here with a white coat and stethoscope. But I didn't care enough to question it; if our supposed medic wanted to pop pills at brunch, that was her prerogative. What else was the medical degree for if not that?

Across the table, Notebook raised a hand. Beck gestured to her, as encouraging and eager as if we were sat in a long lecture hall. "A question?" he prodded. "Yes?"

"I just want to make sure I've got your verbiage right," the woman said, propping the end of her pen between her generous lips. She held it there almost suggestively, the keen eyes behind her wide-rimmed glasses raking Beck up and down like she was working dutifully at imagining what he looked like in his underwear. I hated the twist of possessiveness that flared within me, and hated more that Beck seemed tickled pink by the very same idea.

"Which part?" he asked.

"Just – do you want to keep the bit about the equipment in? The Swedes; do you want to keep in the line about their equipment?" She said this so plainly, so bluntly; it seemed to take everyone at the table by surprise. The Grundstadts looked between one another like maybe they'd misheard, and even Beck seemed chagrined. Beneath the collar of his shirt, I could see telltale crimson beginning to spread.

I did my best to nudge Mallory under the table, but she looked up from her phone none the wiser. Again, Beard leaned over Notebook's shoulder, less careful in his snooping now that this faux pas seemed to make her fair game. I watched Beck consider her question, eyes darting from our guides to the woman – scribe, note-taker, whatever the hell – in a clear attempt to salvage the situation.

"Well, Dorothy, you could make a note about how grateful I am to have their expertise," he began, voice measured. His eyes flickered to me, and I shrugged one shoulder. "I appreciate your candor, and your determination to record this expedition appropriately, but if you could refrain—"

"Got it," Dorothy said, returning without another glance, or another word, to her notebook. Beck blinked, mouth hung open like a fish on a dock. Dorothy seemed unperturbed by the looming presence at her shoulder, nor by the fact that he seemed to be muttering under his breath as his beady eyes scanned the page. Beard seemed as unimpressed with this woman as I was. Maybe I could trust him, if he was this decent a judge of character. I nudged Mallory again, and this time she acquiesced; Beck had lost us all by now, as had our expert guides. Instead, the meeting had rerouted to hinge entirely on whatever the hell was in our note-taker's journal.

And then, as if to preserve the sheer discomfiture of the moment in amber, Camera lifted her equipment from the strap round her neck and snapped a photo of Beck. The flash went off, dazzlingly bright, and he blinked furiously.

Beard shot her a nasty look. "Sorry, Oliver," she said. "I mean *sir*." If I didn't know better, it looked like she wanted to salute him.

What a team. If we weren't taking said team into a long-lost cave in the middle of a storm, it would be one thing. A *funny* thing, even. But I wasn't amused. And by the looks of it, neither was Beck.

We broke for breakfast with the intention of collecting ourselves, making any last-minute preparations, and gathering at the docks in an hour. The fisherman left without a word, rubbing at the heavy, bruised circles beneath his eyes, as the group filed past me, introducing themselves with all the enthusiasm of the bartender and his favorite glass. Hannah, with her full-moon spectacles and loud personality, I already knew: a doctor from Orlando, recently back from leave. She'd rattled her bottle of "ibuprofen" at me on the way out, then hip-bumped the door to open it. I liked her.

Next was Iskra, the photographer; she seemed young, and stumbled over her own name like she was halfway to forgetting it. I couldn't blame her – this was a lot. She was pretty, with silken hair tied in a braid down her back and a flannel tied round her waist.

The strap of her camera hung heavily with pins that named no fewer than ten National Parks.

Beard followed shortly after, ramrod straight and utterly imposing. "Oliver Coramar," he stuck out a hand. It was easier to get a look at him this way, and I was glad I did. He wore faded camouflage cargo pants, thick-soled boots, and a thin t-shirt that spread taut over a broad chest. His lips sat in a hard line beneath the thickness of his beard as he waited for me to return the handshake.

"Nice to meet you . . ." a pause, a fumble, as I took his hand. "Officer?" I didn't know shit about the military aside from what I saw in movies. But I tried again, against my better judgment. "Colonel?"

It was small, but I caught it nevertheless. Oliver's lips twitched, his eyes darkening for only a moment. "Sergeant, formerly. Field grade."

I stared blankly. "Right. Formerly?"

"Honorable discharge."

"Oh." Whatever that meant. "Good to meet you, sir."

Notebook came last. She waved me off with no more than a name – Dorothy – and a declaration that she didn't have time for small talk. I watched her as she passed, dressed far too snappily for this place. Boots to the knee, hunter-green breeches, quilted vest; damn her, but she looked the part. Clearly rich. It felt suddenly all too clear that she'd written something derogatory about my sweater in her journal.

Half of the group meandered out into the street, muttering blithely about the selection at the diner down the street, while I made to collect my bag and find my way upstairs.

Mallory followed, taking hold of the other handle atop my suitcase and hoisting it onto her hip. "Let me help," she said. "Bet you're exhausted from such an early flight."

I nodded. In a perfect world, I would sleep away the rest of the day, forgotten about by Beck entirely. "Can't beat free airplane coffee, though," I mused, gladly accepting Mallory's help as we made for the narrow wooden stairs that led from the pub and up to the rooms Beck had rented above. The only other hotel in town had been closed down due to water damage; it was so close to the coast that the woman at the front desk had one morning come outside to find that the sea had swept away the valet stand, the hotel sign, and her bicycle in one fell swoop.

"Rough day yesterday, huh?"

I paused, turning to stare down at her from the step above. "What?" I immediately thought of my mother, of the deer on the side of the road. The pitying treatment I'd gotten after my mother had died was an insult, a guilty stain on a filthy conscience. I never spoke of her. She was no one's business. There was no plausible way for Mallory to know . . .

"You missed your flight," she said, adjusting her grip on the damp handle of my suitcase. "This fucking storm, right?"

I sagged, exhaling. "Yeah. As if airports weren't stressful enough already." The stairs creaked as we continued upward, banging the wheels of the suitcase on the corner as we made our way to my designated room. A number of buckets and piles of dish rags peppered the creaking wooden floor, for the rain had begun to seep through the less sturdy parts of the roof. A few streams dripped steadily, the fogged window at the end of the hall rattling beneath the pounding of the squall.

Mallory helped me hang my wet clothes in the small cabinet in the room, laying out my wool socks on the bathroom counter and attacking them with the weak hair dryer attached to the wall. I wrung the water from my hair into the shower, then did the same with my jacket. My boots squelched with rainwater, my socks dripping as I tossed them aside.

"I packed some extra socks if you want," Mallory said, chatting away cheerfully as I took stock of what had and hadn't been soaked through in my suitcase. "Beck's wife was at the airport, and she complimented my cat socks so *clearly* I'm a professional—"

Beck's wife. Fucking fantastic. With every day that passed, I was less and less secure in the beautiful lie he'd spun to get me into his bed. Separated, unhappy, distant, loveless; he was a veritable thesaurus of condemnations. "Divorce" was a Hail Mary that arose at opportune moments, and I was always inclined to believe him. But the woman kept appearing where I least expected her. Case in point, a loving airport send-off. Guilt roiled in my stomach. All at once, I felt dirty for being here. I had every right to be here, of course; I was his goddamn teaching assistant, after all. Anything that would look *this* good on a resume was a no-brainer.

But *fuck*. Did the beautiful and elusive Georgina Beck know that I was here? Did she pray to God that I drowned in the bay?

Luckily Mallory seemed not to notice my change in attitude. She chattered happily, as if she'd been saving up things to talk about since the last time we'd seen each other. I was happy for her company, and kicked myself semi-regularly for not seeking her out more. She was good-natured, talkative, and liked by most everyone. Mallory was a safe sort of person, a splash of vibrant color in every dull room. We couldn't be more different, she and I.

And yet one thing that we did share, which I was infinitely grateful for, was the good sense not to ask questions. She never shared anything about her family, and I never spoke of mine. One "family weekend" in our first year, she and I had both found convenient excuses to be elsewhere. While loving families swarmed the campus like locusts, Mallory and I found a sudden common interest in varsity golf – simply because they needed schmucks with nothing better to do to work the ticket table at a tournament in Bloomington.

The week after, she'd slipped a pair of earrings – pink golf tees, clearly homemade – into my backpack during a communications lecture. I'd turned to find her wearing a matching pair. That afternoon, I went to the mall to get my ears pierced.

I wasn't as good a friend to Mallory as I'd have liked to be. Maybe I could change that. Maybe I could start right now. I crossed to my bag while she dissected Georgina Beck's choice of shoes – "I mean, really? Kitten heels at the airport?" – and produced the brick-heavy collection of papers, notes, and photos I'd brought along. These were all the notes I'd kept and compiled about Beck's work, which I'd squirreled away for my own study. I had to keep up with him somehow; this was no corkboard with red string, but it was enough.

The spine of the old binder was cracked and flimsy. Mismatched and dog-eared corners poked from the binder on all sides, manilla envelopes and stapled stacks of research papers threatened to slide from the mass as I held it up like a gold trophy.

"Wanna see my notes?" I asked. "They're nowhere near as thorough as Beck's, but –" I shrugged. "I think it's pretty cool. And if you're planning a proposal, it's the least I can do to help. A fresh source, maybe. I know it's not the *most* relevant to your field of study, but . . ."

"No more 'buts'!" Her face split into a grin, and with a nod she plopped down on the rug beside me. "Everything is relevant." It was a bit of a stretch; Mallory was headed for museum curatorship and artifact preservation. She was a dual-major, where I could hardly handle one. Her encyclopedic knowledge of art history made her an asset in any anthropologist's study. It was her determination to do right by the field that I admired in particular.

"All right. But don't judge my sketches." I settled the binder between us, opening the paper-laden files with a creak of old plastic. A photograph here, a copy of Beck's notes there; all the world's understanding of the Leviathan, of her reclusive cult, of the strange monolith in the bay, lay before us now. I smoothed out a map of the world, marked with red pen where ley lines intersected with points of longitude and latitude and handed Mallory a folder labeled "*KNOWN SEA CULTS*," which she took gladly. One of my own essays slipped from the bunch, marked and graded by Beck himself. I'd written it at the beginning of the year, a study that posited a relationship between thermo-mineral springs, natural fault lines, and religious settlements. Multiple all-nighters had gone into it; disappointing Beck had never been an option.

I smoothed the paper over the rug. "Pretty proud of this one," I said. "See, water is a prevalent symbol in pretty much any faith; it's the basis of nearly any cultural system you could think of, because of how necessary it is. So it only makes sense that it would show up in spiritual texts. Water's always been used for ritual purposes, healing purposes. Like baptism, Wudu, bathing in the Ganges." I paused, glancing up at Mallory to see if she was starting to tire of the sound of my voice. But she wasn't. Her eyes had never wavered. I sat a little taller. "So, then, you think about ancient civilizations, and how they often thought of imperfect physical health. To offset that, it would make sense that the spiritual and the bodily interest in water – regardless of the source – would intersect. Cultic, religious, spiritual facilities all would be best served by water sources that the practitioners felt were significant somehow. Be it medically, like the way hot springs are supposed to be good for our muscles and such, or spiritually. I mean, and even thermal springs were considered gifts from the gods, right? Like Aquae Patavinae." Another pause, another deep breath. And still, Malloy hadn't moved. "So, then, what about the sea? The Greeks and Romans in coastal towns lived and died by it. So many cultic traditions thought of the sea as a source of spiritual rebirth, salvation, trial and judgement – the possibilities are as endless as, well, the *sea*, I guess!" I tapped the paper again, color swelling in my cheeks. "So that's where Beck's research came in. It's hard to put a label on just what he thinks this cult has been worshiping all this time, but . . ." I shrugged. "I guess we'll find out."

Mallory blinked, then hunched over the paper to scan the first page. "Caro, this is fucking *awesome*."

"Yeah, I think so, too," I said. "Beck's research is pretty much in line with my own. This cult seems to be all about the idea that water is purifying, and that whatever *thing* they worship – angel, or creature, or divine entity – is the arbiter of that. But it's weird. All of the text he's found on it is in *Enochian*."

Mallory raised a brow. "Isn't that kind of . . ."

"Weird and mired in skepticism?" I chuckled. "Yeah. And what's more, the Enochian is really poorly rendered in all his sources, too. Like someone's writing it in a British accent or something. That's where the connection to the biblical Leviathan comes in."

"And that's what he's brought us all out here for?" Mallory asked. There was no derision in her voice. It was a welcome change. "The not-quite-Enochian that aligns with your work on aquatic cults?"

I flushed, fiddled with a loose strand of hair that curled around my ear as I looked back down at my marked-up paper. "I think his research has legs. Anyway, I thought about trying to get this thing published, in a journal or something, but Beck wanted me to hang onto it."

The open, curious expression on Mallory's face twisted, wilting in on itself like a rusted lattice. "Why?"

I shrugged, the uneven tip of my fingernail tracing the indentation left behind in the paper by Beck's heavy-handed marking. "He thought it was a decent case for his own research, I think. Into the Leviathan, the cult, all that. And fair enough, too. Our combined efforts got us here, after all. He made a copy and kept it with his own notes." My chest puffed, swelled, the pride still lingering. "It's a damn good paper, if I do say so myself."

Mallory's expression soured further still, pink lips twisting into a scowl that had no place on her pleasant features. "Well, *obviously* it's a good paper," she said, chewing each and every consonant and spitting them out with great purpose, petulant, and clearly aggravated. I wasn't sure what I'd said wrong.

I blanched at her tone, leaning back from the messy assemblage of papers between us. "And that's . . . bad?" I ventured.

She huffed, rolling her eyes. "*Yes.* Well – no, technically. But yes."

"You lost me."

"It's a good paper for *you.*" Mallory thrust a manicured finger between us, straight and accusatory. "Not Beck. You should do what you want with it."

I blinked. "I mean, I have no real issue sitting on it. Not if it's going to help him with his own research. No one takes him seriously, y'know, and it's bullshit." I was talking fast, I realized; talking without taking a breath as I rattled off the defense of Beck that simmered, omnipresent, at the back of my throat. "He values my research. My opinions. Could even be that we'll collaborate on something, get me a co-contributor credit on the whole shebang when it's all said and done. He values me, Mal. Seriously." He'd said so himself. Time and time again. He was actually one of the first people to ever tell me as much in no uncertain terms. Everybody needed someone to believe in them; for Beck and I, it went both ways.

The same couldn't be said for Georgina Beck, as far as I knew. She wanted no part of this. But *me?* I believed in him wholeheartedly. And he gave me the same in return. It wasn't just sex, though that was a nice bonus. It was support. Love, even.

Mallory's eyes narrowed, her pink lips puckering like she'd sucked on something sour. Her gaze was withering, like she could see right through the flush of my skin to the bones beneath. The way she looked at me – I couldn't help but wonder, all at once, if she knew about my – *our* – extracurriculars. I doubted she'd judge; it didn't seem to be in Mallory's chemical makeup to judge anything beyond superficialities like questionable airport fashion choices and show tunes at karaoke bars. I could tell her right now; I could tell her everything. Maybe then she'd understand why I needed so badly to prove myself.

And then she spoke, two load-bearing syllables that chipped at my already weak will. "*Uh huh.*"

I shifted, casting my gaze down to the notes assembled between us. Clearing my throat, I thumbed through the damning essay before placing it among the painstaking notes I'd assembled during my years under Beck's wing. "It means something," I said. "All of it. This is huge, groundbreaking shit. And he's the expert, so I might as well do what he—"

"*Lame.* Expert schmexpert." She yanked the paper from my grasp, lips pursed. "I think you should publish it anyway." Her eyes drifted from the inked pages to the assemblage of maps, and notes, and printed articles between us. "No offense, but I think it's bullshit."

"What is?"

"That he'd want you to sit on all this research, that he wants to use you as a repository for good ideas. I know he respects your work or whatever, but *I* think you're perfectly capable of publishing on your own."

I shrugged, picking at a loose bit of skin beneath my thumb nail. "But Beck's research—"

Mallory waved my paper in the air between us. "But *your* research. You're smart as hell, Caro. You're *so* concerned with what Beck thinks, but have you considered that he wouldn't have schlepped you all the way out here if *he* didn't think your brain was worth picking?"

"I mean . . . I *guess*."

Before I could stop her, she rolled my paper into a narrow tube and lifted it high, bringing it down like an executioner's ax atop my head. "You stop that. I'm gonna start charging you a dollar every time you underplay your own work. Got your wallet handy?"

I snorted. "Sure, but I hope you're prepared to settle for five bucks and a 7/11 Slurpee punch card."

The serious expression that twisted her features alchemized, softened like unfurling petals, the welcome warmth of her laugh filling the room like midsummer sun. "It'll have to do, I suppose."

A shadow passed across the space between the door and the warped wooden floor, followed by a short-patterned rapping that I knew all too well. A signal Beck and I had. Four short taps followed by two long; it was how I announced myself during his office hours, just in case anyone else was around to see me. And there it was, four and two; the toes of Beck's shoes tapped, and thus the spell was broken for me.

"Speak of the Devil, and he shall appear," Mallory droned, returning my paper to the stack and giving it an affectionate pat. She hoisted herself up, both hands flat on the faded bedspread, and groaned as her knees cracked. A laugh bubbled from me as I collected my notes, essays, and maps, and she returned it in kind.

"Thanks, Mallory," I said, following her up. At the door, Beck's shadow stilled. I could tell that he was listening. Impatiently, probably. He would just have to wait. It would be a first for him.

She gathered her things, and I followed as she went, eddying in the dark bathroom doorway. The room smelled of wet socks and old hair dryer cables. If ever there was proof of our friendship, it was this. "For what?" she mused, head cocked. Her eyes fell upon me as she paused at the door, a sparkle of knowing in her eye.

"For the socks," I said.

Mallory smiled. *My friend.* I'd make this count. "Sure thing, Caro."

Beck knocked again, and Mallory was quick to answer. The door flew wide with a creak of old hinges and a groaning of condensation-warped wood; maybe she'd wanted to surprise him. Maybe it even worked.

"Oh hey, Professor Beck," she said, leaning against the doorframe. As small as she was in stature, it was clear that she did her best to block his view inside. Girl code was sacred. No boys allowed. "Just helping Caro unpack."

"That's good of you, Mallory," he said, his voice an echo in the wooden coffin of the hallway. He was almost inaudible over the roar of rain on the roof. "Could I have a word with her alone? I need to debrief her on what she missed yesterday."

Mallory shifted. I peered out of the bathroom in time for her to turn and seek my approval. Beck spotted me at once over the top of her head and gave a wave. No hiding from him.

But Mallory didn't move. Not until I gave her a small smile, a smaller shrug. She'd have stood there for years if I asked, that much was clear.

She left us, disappearing in a flash of color down the hall. Beck slipped inside, shutting the door quietly. He lingered in the doorway, watching as I replaced the hair dryer and collected the socks that Mallory had set out on the counter. I'd had no time to collect my notes, the papers and maps that scattered at the foot of the bed, and could feel the very moment where his attention left me and fell upon the mess.

"I'm glad you finally made it," he said. There was an edge to his voice, as if I had somehow knocked a few points off a grade that I didn't know I'd be receiving. It made me uncomfortable, antsy; just for something to do, I moved to my wet suitcase. But then, as I went, the agitation dissipated. Beck's lips tugged up at the corners, and he sighed almost dreamily. "It hasn't been the same without you. Feels like I've been walking around with a missing limb."

My chest swelled, heat blooming in my cheeks. He *needed* me. That was something.

"Oh, yeah, sure," I rolled my eyes, casting him a conspiratorial look. "However did you manage?" I matched his raised brow, his sideways smile. Outside the rain angled with a gust of wind, lashing angrily against the window. The gray light shifted, twisted with the thickening bloat of clouds, and the shadows beneath Beck's eyes lengthened.

"I'm serious," he said. I couldn't help but notice as he glanced once more to the mess of papers at the foot of the bed. Not like he was making a real secret of it; everything in this room was fair game. "Don't downplay your importance here." A pause. "With me. *To* me."

My eyes fell again to the suitcase, cheeks hot. All this time with Beck, and I was still shit at taking compliments. And so I busied myself, rifling through what was salvageable. I produced a pair of dry thermals, jeans, and a flannel from within. Just twenty-four hours before, I had googled "what to wear in a cave" and so I considered myself something of an expert.

"I need to change," I said, glancing up at him at last. "I got soaked on the way here." Served me right for skimping on the cost of a raincoat.

Beck didn't budge. He made no secret of watching me as I stood away from the suitcase, clutching my dry clothes like a knight and her shield. "You missed quite a lot last night," he said, leaning against the dresser as I conceded and began to strip. His fingers tapped an impatient rhythm on his forearm, wedding band flashing in the low light of the bedroom. "We've got a good group here. Professionals."

"I can see that," I said, turning from him as I unclipped the bent clasp of my bra and discarded it in favor of the more comfortable alternative of a sports bra. "The Swedes sure do have stage presence."

He huffed a laugh, running his fingers through his mussed hair. "A small price to pay for all the goddamn equipment they brought with them." The floor creaked as he drew closer, and I shivered at the feeling of his hands on my bare skin. His lips found the curve of my shoulder, breath ghosting hot and fast over my collarbone. Practiced fingers traced the knobbed length of my spine. "No one understands this like you do," he muttered, voice low. "No one knows what this means to me but you. You understand that, yes?"

"Of course," I nodded, holding tight to the half-unbuttoned flannel crumpled in my grasp. "Of course I understand. I know how hard you've worked for this."

"And you've seen it all, Caroline. Ridicule. Hardship. This is the culmination of my entire professional life. The work—" a deep breath, as if he might be sick. I wouldn't blame him. He leaned heavily against me, pressed flush to my back like I was the only thing holding him up. I liked the idea. "The work has all amounted to this. All of it. The importance of this day *cannot* be understated."

I would have hardly called a tenure position and a two-story in Hyde Park hardship, but what did I know? However, there was no denying the former. Professor Edward Beck was a name used as a punchline. The man who believed myth, who had built a career on fantastical nonsense. I wondered what the skeptics thought of him now. No doubt he lay awake at night wondering the same thing.

Beck gripped my freckled shoulders, turning me round and barring me to his front with a strong arm at the small of my back. He was warm and solid against the bareness of my back, my stomach. It was as if he could press the cold from me, smooth the gooseflesh that rose to meet the cold with nothing more than a touch. His fingers slipped down the length of my arms, falling to the band of damp denim at my waist.

"You're beautiful," he murmured, bending again to kiss the slope of my neck as he hooked a finger beneath the clasp of my jeans. Beautiful felt like a lousy way to describe me given the present circumstances, but beggars couldn't be choosers. "I need you by my side, Caro. Always." His voice was low, ripe with a saccharine headiness that I understood like reflex. As if on command, the hum at the back of his throat pooled heat at the pit of my stomach, and another shiver danced the length of me.

I couldn't help but touch him. The flannel lay forgotten at my feet; I hadn't even realized that I'd dropped it. I lifted my hands, one to grip his collar and the other to trace lithe fingers along the sharp angles of his face. He leaned into my touch, his head heavy in my hand, and sighed. The heat of his breath ghosted over my wrist, ruffling the hair at my brow. Blood roared in my ears, hot and red and fervent enough to chase the gray away. How easy, how quickly I lit at the wick beneath his touch.

His mouth was on mine, honey-sweet and insistent. A small, petulant sound slipped from me, and the rumble in his chest answered in return. "Beck—"

"They won't miss us," he said, the words muffled against my mouth. "The Swedes will keep them busy."

It didn't feel like the most appropriate time to be thinking of undressing my professor – and it was clear that he was thinking much the same – but the thrill of it all was too much. The nervous energy, the anticipation, the wild power of the unknown, of validation after so very long had to go *somewhere*. And I was weak for him. Of course I was.

A trill of fevered laughter tumbled from me as I rose onto my toes, raking my fingers through the mess of greying curls at the nape of his neck. "Whatever would the Leviathan say if she saw us now?"

Beck's grip tightened at the small of my back, and before I could say another word I was lifted and deposited easily onto the faded bedspread. He settled over me, elbows framing my head as he tugged again at the band of my jeans with one hand and smoothed my hair with the other. "Well," he rumbled, lips curling higher still as he settled between my parting thighs, "We'll just have to ask her, won't we?"

Sharp pain lanced through the heady haze as the silver band on his ring finger snagged in a rain-damp curl, pulling my hair hard enough to tear a tuft of mousy brown from my head. Beck cursed, startling. I jerked away, the hairs floating freely from where they caught on the glinting – and damning – wedding ring. My eyes watered as I reached up to prod at the tender patch just above my temple.

The words slipped from me before I could quell them. "Guessing you'll want to leave that behind. Would hate for you to lose it while we're out there."

Beck stilled. He stared down at me as if I'd struck him. For a long moment, we merely looked at each other, the ring glinting in the gray light. And then he stood, adjusting himself through his pants and turning from the bed. Gingerly, I slid to the edge of the bed and tucked my arms over my bare middle. My first instinct was to apologize, but I bit my tongue.

He moved, and I followed. Gaze sharp, I found his profile in the warped mirror over the armoire. He opened his mouth, then closed it again, as if he struggled to reconcile what would be best to say.

"Right you are," he said. I stared down at a whorl in the wooden floor, a singular watchful eye. The boards creaked again as Beck retreated to the doorway, leaving me to collect my shirt. He paused, and then, "You know that separations take time, Caroline."

I gave a noncommittal nod. "Of course. Just an observation. Rings are expensive." It wasn't my fault that he and his wife weren't as separated as I'd been led to believe. I could tell myself again and again that I was a victim, that I was blameless. But that would be a lie.

A sharp pang of regret cramped in my abdomen. Being stuck in a cave off the coast with no budget for a faster flight home was a wonderful time to bring up relationship woes, of course. Relationship, or lack thereof – what did it say about me that the only people on Earth who cared if I lived or died were Mallory and the married professor I'd been fucking for an entire academic year? I'd turned down classmates in favor of slipping off to Beck's office after-hours, abandoning parties and mixers in the hope that he might finally take the ring off for good, like he'd promised.

And he *had* promised.

I turned in time to see Beck disappear into the hall, the door to my room swinging shut behind him. Fleeing at the first mention of his wife – of the supposed separation that dragged, and dragged, and kicked its feet in the dirt – was not new behavior. But, even as I stood alone in a drafty hotel room with nothing but the sound of the rain to accompany me, I knew that it wouldn't matter in the end.

I filled my pack with extra socks and a pair of long johns. My notes lay abandoned on my bedside table at the inn where they'd be safe from the elements. I'd be back for them. And then . . . something. Maybe I would do, finally, *something*.

While the crew set about assembling their equipment on the dock, I helped quietly and dedicated their names to memory. Oliver, his beard dripping rain water; Iskra, who flinched every time the algae slapping against the dock threatened to splash up onto her camera; Hannah, who huddled beneath an umbrella and scrubbed mist from her glasses; and Dorothy, who acted like she might die if she looked up from her notebook for more than a second. She was an author, Mallory had told me.

"What's that author doing here?" I mused. I'd never heard of her.

Mallory shrugged. She slipped the aforementioned pair of socks – impossibly neon, like an emergency flare – into my bag, and gave my shoulder a little pat. "Beck's in his main character era," she said. "I'd read this book, honestly. And I'd watch the HBO miniseries, too. As much as I hate to admit it, Oscar Isaac *is* Beck."

What a horrible insult to Oscar Isaac.

Ellis ran a long checklist with Beck. "Gonna need those permits," he said. "Wanna give them a once-over before we cast off."

"Of course." Beck rifled through his bag for a stack of papers, each identical save the signatures at the bottom from what I could see. I hadn't signed any forms, any waivers. I'd never even heard that we *needed* permits.

Ellis thumbed through the stack, and I caught a glimpse of what was meant to be my own signature. I hadn't signed a damn thing. "Looks like that's everybody," the fisherman mumbled. "All checks out." He sounded disappointed, like he'd been hoping for any reason to tie the boat to the dock and head back inside for a warm cup of coffee.

"Of course it checks out," Beck said. His gaze slid to mine, and I quickly looked away. I knew better than to ask questions. He foisted his leather-bound notebook onto me as we began to pile onto the pair of fishing boats awaiting us in the harbor. He said nothing to me, and offered no help as I clambered onto the boat. Instead, Oliver held out a hand and hoisted me up as the boat tipped and bobbed on the rough waters at the pier. Maybe he'd decided to take pity on me for my earlier flub.

"Good material for a thesis, huh?" he huffed. I scuttled aside as he reached over the rail to help the spectacled woman, Iskra, onto the boat behind me. "What're you doing yours on?"

"I, uh—" the backs of my knees knocked against the crates of equipment he had stacked on the starboard side, on which Hannah now perched, and I wheeled my arms to catch myself. My face flooded with heat as I scuttled sidelong, wondering idly if anyone would notice, or care, if I simply leapt off edge and into the surf. "I have no idea."

I had googled "graduate thesis topics" not twenty-four hours prior. Oliver didn't need to know that.

He smiled at me with unmistakable pity as he made his way to the front of the boat. It wasn't condescending, or mocking in any way. At least not that I could tell. Hannah absentmindedly adjusted the pin on her jacket – "Live, Laugh, Lorazepam" – and curled her lips into the sort of simpering smile that, in Beck, usually meant a lecture was coming. The surf looked more and more welcoming by the second. "You have time," she said, making no secret of the fact that she'd been listening. "And hey," she gestured broadly to the rain, the boat, and the crashing surf. "No time like the present to get inspired."

"Are *you* feeling inspired?"

It was only then that I noticed the green pallor of Hannah's complexion. Her glasses were wet with ocean spray, and every time she attempted to wipe it away, the sea undid all her work. As the fishermen clomped about, tossing ropes and rolling tarps, Hannah seemed just as eager to shrink as I was. She was just better at hiding it.

"I'm feeling inspired to find the nearest patch of solid ground available," Hannah said. "If that's a rock formation in the middle of the bay, so be it."

"I'm sure it'll be—" a muttered apology, a flush of red, as I was brusquely instructed to move out of the way, "*great.*"

Hannah appraised me for a moment, perching at the edge of one of the many crates of equipment as we started through the harbor. "You nervous?"

"Terminally."

Again, a moment of silence passed. We shielded our eyes against the spray as the boats picked up speed. I tugged up the collar of my jacket.

"Here's a joke," Hannah began. My heart sank. I would have been perfectly happy with uncomfortable silence. But it was good-natured, an earnest attempt at connection. At least, it seemed that way. Maybe she just thought I was dumb.

"All right," I said. "Hit me."

Hannah cleared her throat, adjusting on her perch. "So the doctor says to the patient 'I'm afraid you have chlamydia, gonorrhea, and onomatopoeia.' The patient, flabbergasted, asks him, 'Hell, what's onomatopoeia?' And the doctor looks at his patient and says, 'Well, it's exactly what it sounds like!'"

She slapped her hands on her knees just as our boat slammed into a wake at the mouth of the harbor. Hannah nearly toppled from her seat, lurching sideways and grabbing onto the photographer, who snapped a flash of a photograph directly in her face, and purely by accident.

My laugh, a honking guffaw that I'd rather no one *ever* heard, was mercifully swallowed by the sound of the waves, the rain, and the boat's roaring engine. The bay was deafening, effectively killing all chance of further conversation. So that was that.

The boats forged through the surf, arrowing away from the coast one after the other. The fishermen, Joseph and Ellis, said very little to the lot of us as we made for the stone monolith. The Grundstadts – one on each boat – debriefed us as we went, hollering over the rain and clinging to the slick railings as the waves tossed us this way and that. My stomach churned.

"It is imperative that you do exactly as we tell you," said Anders. "Even the smallest shift in the direction of the rain, and the cavern could flood in minutes." *Oh, great.* Through the mist, I thought I saw Iskra gag. "When we go aground, we will assess the safest possible route in and out. Such a sudden appearance of this thing is . . . is . . ." he smacked his lips, like he struggled to find the right words. "It is unpredictable. Mapped cave systems are hazardous on their own – from loose rock and open shafts, to narrow dead-end passages – and so you must *listen*. And follow."

Listen and follow. I could do that. At the back, if possible.

Anders held up a finger, only to jolt and reach for the nearest railing as the boat rocked over a wake. "Remember the statistics!" he hollered, accent thick, "and you will not become one! Now, a reminder about oxygen deprivation and hallucinatory panic—"

I turned away from Anders and watched the coast as it grew smaller and smaller beneath the oppressive deluge. Maybe it was naive of me to only half-listen, but I couldn't imagine us going any farther into this cave than necessary. Certainly not far enough for oxygen-deprived psychosis. I fixed my gaze on a singular spot on the coast, took a deep breath, and settled with myself all at once that I would maintain *boundaries* here. If ever there was a time to do it, it would be now.

But then, all at once, the sea quieted. I'd been so tense, perched atop a box of survey equipment, that I almost slid to the floor. Suddenly, as if the boat had slipped inside a bottle, the roiling waves smoothed and the rain slowed to a drizzle. Anders gasped, turning to meet his twin's gaze in the other boat. The monolith loomed over us, a protruding stone limb that stretched from the water, unmoved by the surf.

Just beyond the stern, like a somber curtain, the rain continued to fall. I held out a hand behind the boat and rain pelted the tips of my fingers. A divide, as if something imperceptible hung over our heads; Mallory squeezed water from the length of her ponytail, and Iskra rose to take a flurry of photographs. She was impossibly eager, mentioning over and over again how utterly lucky she felt to be here, filling in for a friend who'd fallen ill. Hannah produced a phone from her pocket and held it aloft. Dorothy scribbled furiously in her notebook. In the other boat, Beck shot to his feet. His lips, bright red and visibly trembling from the cold, spread into a wild smile. His eyes found me, and at once it seemed that all was forgiven.

What is this? I mouthed.

He shook his head, pointing up to the monolith. His lips took shape. *Her*, he mouthed. *She's in there.*

My ears popped, the sound of my own voice suddenly impossibly loud without the rain. "What is this?" I turned to Oliver first. I craned my neck, peering uselessly up at the slate sky. Nothing hung over us that could obstruct the rain to this degree – it had simply stopped.

Oliver shook his head, rising to stand alongside me. I watched as he held a hand in the air – "no breeze"– and then stooped to hang his hand over the side of the boat. "There has to be a sand bank somewhere round here," he said. "Current's just plain stopped."

"Can sand banks do that?" I mused. And then, again, I held my hand out to where the rain pelted mercilessly into the bay, just beyond the boat. "Or this?"

Again, I glanced to Beck. His eyes were on the monolith, and the single break in its towering surface.

The fishermen outfitted us with life vests and helmets. We strapped our headlamps to our fronts, and tucked plastic goggles in our pockets.

I turned my eyes upward, craning my neck to appraise the narrow column of stone that obscured the sun above us. It was too small to be considered an island, too narrow and craggy to support any kind of wildlife. No moss grew atop the quartzite protrusions, no birds' nests or tide pools. It was perfectly clean, like it had been pulled from the crust of the Earth itself. Unblemished, so dark that it was nearly obsidian in color, and impossibly high. From far away, it had looked like a stray piece of an oil rig, if I was being optimistic. Or skeptical. But there was always something about stone that felt old. And this felt *old.* Older than Seal Harbor. Older than the sodden ground we'd walked to get here. And yet it felt purposeful. Like it had been designed somehow. *Made* to be here, like this.

A single opening had been carved from the face of the stone, a sliver of opaque darkness that led further into the rock face. I had underestimated it, had attributed its grandiose descriptions to overstatement and media hysteria. But it was just as wild, as uncanny, as out of place as Beck had made it out to be. Out of place, and yet exactly where it was meant to be.

Yes – this was purposeful. Beck had said time and time again that the cult showed itself only when it wanted to. As did the elusive Leviathan. That something so purposefully carved, so free from the bric-a-brac that one would expect on a *natural* rock formation, could appear here, in a biblical deluge that seemed to dare not touch it – it had to be on purpose. Otherwise, how the hell else was I going to reconcile this with my own skeptical brain?

I'd have to write this down. Cross-reference. The rain – or lack thereof – was new. Beck hadn't prepared me for this. But maybe there was something we'd missed. Something, anything, that could explain why, all at once, we were completely insulated.

The boats drew closer to the mouth of the cave, unperturbed by the torrent beyond the invisible barrier in the sea. It was much easier, here, to transfer the experts' belongings to the inflatable dinghy, and the rest of us to shared kayaks. My hands trembled as I lowered into the boat I was to share with Mallory, knees knocking as the vibrant orange polyethylene bobbed beneath me.

"Jesus Christ," I muttered, flushing violently red as Ellis stooped to tighten the clasp on my life vest. I felt like a child at a water park. It was humbling – I couldn't even tie a vest right. Mallory took it in her stride, as she did all things. Her legs jutted on either side of my narrow frame, the toes of her vibrant yellow boots tapping blithely on the kayak's hollow inside.

"Figure he's got nothing to do with it," Ellis muttered, his hard gaze meeting mine for but a moment. "Be smart in there."

A push with the heel of his rubber boot, and Ellis sent us surging after the others. Beck had already begun to forge ahead, leaving no time for Oliver to steady himself on the dinghy they shared. A litany of curses and half-hearted condemnations floated across the calm water, and a chorus of nervous laughter followed. No one but Beck seemed to be able to turn away from the strange divide in the sky, the wall that separated us from the storm that battered the coast. Our boats bobbed like a school of orange fish, in absolute silence. He watched the rain as it battered the surface of the water just beyond us, looking only inward as if he'd forgotten the fishermen altogether.

"We'll be back in six hours," Ellis called. "Like we agreed on. Not a minute past."

Beck said nothing. I gave him a thin-lipped smile and a short nod, if only to let him know that *someone* was listening, and that *someone* would be counting the seconds.

And then, with no ceremony, they were gone. They turned the boats quickly, sending us cresting toward the monolith on their wake. I watched them as long as I could, marking the exact moment that they passed through the invisible perimeter, the curtain of rain and gale that snaked, unyielding, around the rocky megalith. The boats were battered, the sound of the rain atop the roof over the console something like gunfire. Ellis and Joseph were swallowed by the rain, leaving us in the cool quiet of the storm's improbable eye.

I could hear no sea birds. Only the lapping of gentle waves and settling wake against the vertical rock, and the rain just beyond, marked our presence here. Once more, I craned my neck toward the coast. But the fishermen were gone. And we were alone.

We followed the dinghy single-file into the impossibly dark opening in the cliff face. It was no more than a sea stack the size of a high-rise, a cragged finger stretching up from the gray surf. The stone walls towered over us, vertical juts of unbroken limestone and quartzite. The air was cold – much colder than it had been in the bay.

I'd never felt so impossibly small, so insignificant. Maybe this was why people liked churches so much, why so much stock was put into them. Something monumental, something undeniable; my skepticism and moroseness alchemized into absolute and undeniable awe. Fear. Wonderment. They all tasted the same, all at once.

And there, cut and painted just as clearly as Beck said they'd be, were the runes, meticulously carved into short phrases neatly arranged in the grooves of the rock. Identical to the ones in Beck's notebook, ones that he had copied over and over and over until he and I both could have written them out blind. Something like Enochian, if you squinted; a few words stood out, while others seemed to be nothing more than cobbled-together gibberish, like a child learning cursive. The "angelic script," the "celestial speech." The theology faculty had declined to contribute to Beck's research. Not close *enough* to Enochian, apparently.

It was one thing to study all of it, to take notes and write papers from the removed and unaffected safety of the university. There was distance in it, in the purely academic. But now, as my fingers twitched, itched and keened to reach out and touch that which had existed only on paper – I'd never felt so present. I felt almost light-headed with the *realness* of it.

How real, how tangible – and how far from home. From all I'd left behind. If only my mother could see me now.

I stretched to read the runes in full. *Wormwood*, said one. I remembered it from class. One semester, and I couldn't get the stuff out of my head. The phrase below it – again, familiar characters, but twisted nearly beyond recognition – was either *lamp* or *consumption*; there was no telling which. Beyond that, the rest of the runes were incomprehensible in the low light. In a perfect world, we'd come back here with industrial lamps and spotlights. Beck could ascribe meaning to them easily, but I wasn't getting paid enough for translation duty.

Come to think of it, I wasn't getting paid at all.

The first fisherman to investigate this strange island that rose from the sea had fled at the sight of them with nothing more than a snapped photo on an iPhone camera. It had been enough for Beck. Enough for me.

I recognized the symbols from a table in an old textbook. We'd been forced to memorize them all for the purpose of being able to translate, but instead the entire class had only memorized words that seemed relevant, theologically sound – God, sin, mighty, wrath, righteousness, seal, so on and so forth. We could cobble together a few holy proclamations on demand, and that seemed to be enough for our professor. But Beck had been resolute. I was to understand it, to know it, if I was to be of any use to him. And so I studied. I learned. I printed the table, and I made my notes. And I understood as best I could.

Here they were now, tall as cathedral windows. The kayak swayed as I leaned back to take them in. They were real. *This* was real. And maybe Beck was right.

I understood implicitly that Enochian was not something that the everyday scholar talked about at water coolers or at coffee socials; texts "revealed" to occultists in the sixteenth century through scrying rituals and divine visions weren't exactly considered above-board. It was a secret study, and one that Beck undertook like he himself had been passed down the knowledge from John Dee and his cabinet, his esoteric rites under Queen Elizabeth something that the divine conclave of Cincinnati, Ohio, was destined to do somehow. To think – an antiquarian, an alchemist, an occultist, a *scholar* despite it all; if only he'd known, back in the court of Elizabeth I, that his work would come alive here, now, in this place. He'd been painted as a deluded madman, a dreamer who believed the stars over the material, much like Beck. I could only imagine how the comparison would bolster him. Beck, in fact, had been the only member of the faculty to teach Dee's works and theories. Not a madman, who dabbled in alchemy and spoke with the divine, but a genius.

A modern John Dee, Beck would be called. I could see it now.

No matter how silly it had felt at first, I couldn't deny the magnetism of the idea. *Angels.* Something unprovable, but something widely believed in; who was I to argue with a bunch of angels if they decided they wanted to transmit the entirety of a language to John Dee – or, hell, to Beck – based on vibes alone?

But here they were, the perfectly preserved letters given to John Dee by the angels. Geometrically sound, carved with the utmost care; it had been difficult to make them out in the photo taken by the fisherman and plastered all over every media outlet and internet forum, but it had been enough. This was, perhaps, the first time that the Enochian script had ever been seen outside the work of esoteric shut-ins and occult scientists. This was something tangible, and impossible.

The letters stood tall, so high that no human hand could have made them.

I bobbed beneath a purposefully struck symbol, a careful curve with a strike across its base. I squinted, propped my hands on my hips. The others seemed similarly taken, though it gave me strange pleasure to know that only Beck and I understood the full significance. A chorus of fervent murmuring and pitched questioning filled the cavern, the cacophony bouncing higher and higher to the imperceptible heights above our heads. Iskra snapped photographs, chewing on her lip; Dorothy hunched over her notebook; Hannah and Mallory both stared open-mouthed, the latter shaking her head in disbelief. Only Oliver seemed keen on pressing forward.

And only Beck shone with the triumph of a man whose whole solitary career had been validated. Only Beck – outside myself, of course – seemed to understand the magnitude of our situation. The importance.

Beck's study had taken many shapes. The mundane, the divine, the weird; from Ecclesiastical Latin, to Aramaic, and now this. I would have preferred the Ecclesiastical Latin. At least *that* made some sense, and was legible without the cost of a sore neck.

A shiver danced the length of my spine. The air felt different here beneath the towering script. Colder. Thinner, maybe. This was a place between places, a moment between moments. Immortal, disincarnate; the others moved on either side of me, poking and prodding at the rock, but all I could see was the care with which the letter just above my head had been carved. Meticulous, and untouched by the elements; I could almost hear Beck now, bemoaning the fact that there hadn't been enough room in his backpack for his copy of the *Monas Hieroglyphica*.

I could joke all I wanted. And I would, because how else was I supposed to parse out the fact that I was looking up at a script said to have been given to its translator through seraphic visions? And I was – there was no doubt about it. This wasn't bullshit. This wasn't something the rest of the faculty would laugh about later. This was, in and of itself, the very heart of the ancient *something* that Beck had worked so hard to find.

I leaned back further still, spine groaning from the effort. The letters stretched high, etched carefully beneath an illustration. Above the runes curled the scaled body of something much taller than the impossible geometry of the runes, and drawn in thicker scrawl. By the light of the water, reflected weakly onto the face of the rock, I could have sworn it moved.

The *Leviathan*. That which Beck had so desperately believed to be real, obscured, as if meant to remain a secret. Hidden, as if it wasn't for my eyes to see. No one knew what it looked like, really – even Beck. But this . . . this felt right.

One by one, we flattened onto our backs in our kayaks, the rock so low overhead that I could smell the salt and limestone. The gentle lapping of the water carried us inside, and Mallory and I clutched our paddles to our chests as we lay back. My heart thrummed wildly, the feeling a choke at the back of my throat. I squeezed my eyes shut tight and narrowed my focus on the belabored heave of my breathing. My teeth chattered, and spots danced behind my eyes; I could feel the closeness on all sides, and as the water billowed and receded beneath us the tip of my nose brushed the rough rock that hung over our heads.

But then the rock lifted from above, and the claustrophobic passage opened into a high cavern, where the seawater lapped onto a bank made of stone, rock, and shells. The dinghy made landfall, and then the kayaks, one by one.

I wandered toward the far end of the cavern, fumbling as I replaced my helmet with the head lamps that the Grundstadts had provided for us. They were talking loudly now, gesturing broadly as they described how such a place, such a pocket of air and land, could be created inside a monolithic rock formation.

Oliver waved Iskra away as she attempted to photograph him. "Come on now," he said. "Sure you've got better things to document." Iskra flushed, muttered something inaudible, then hurried away to get another picture of the cave entrance. Once she'd gone, Oliver enlisted Hannah in taking stock of our first aid supplies. Dorothy, who sat cross-legged in the dinghy, notebook in hand, offered no help as the Grundstadts erected work lamps on extendable stands, powered up a generator, and unfolded a table that was quickly overfull with ropes, wetsuits, rappelling gear, thermal blankets, and a number of highly technical-looking gadgets that I had no business touching. Personally, I had no memory of signing up to *rappel* down anything. I was perfectly fine with sketching the paintings on the walls and counting the shells on the cavern floor.

"Dorothy," Oliver called. "Could you give 'em a hand over there?" He nodded to our guides, who still inconceivably looked as if they'd peeled themselves out of a magazine ad for hair gel. I was grateful that there was *someone* assertive around here.

Dorothy, however, seemed to think otherwise. "I think they've got it handled. Don't you?" She gestured vaguely to the equipment table with her uncapped pen. "But if it makes you feel better, I will *absolutely* add a stock list to my transcription."

Oliver said nothing, leveling a blank – and utterly unimpressed – look in Dorothy's direction. Hannah snorted. This, too, seemed not to impress him.

"Oh, good," Dorothy droned. Not once had she looked up. And not once had anyone else said a thing. "No objections."

Beck appeared before me like a specter. I jumped, so enthralled with the drama playing out between the others that I hadn't even seen him coming. His eyes were wild, his lips pulled into a hyena's grin. "If you would, Caroline?" he held out his hands, waiting expectantly as I fished in the smallest pocket of my pack for the little black journal that I had been in charge of keeping safe and dry. He snatched it from me without any thanks, gesturing for Mallory and I to follow. We did as we were told, skidding down the slope of rocks and shells to where the cold ocean water lapped gently. He had somehow, somewhere, acquired a pair of waders that were two sizes too large. I wondered idly if they'd belonged to one of the fishermen, if they sat on their boat wondering what had become of their pants.

"See there . . ." He stepped into the water, sinking in the loose footing. "The runes on the walls. They perfectly match those in my research. If my decoding is correct – and I know it is – then it should read something to the effect of . . ." he thumbed through the first few pages of his notes. "'*Self* . . .' and then here it reads '*profound offering*'," he said. Iskra appeared at his shoulder as an over-quick explanation of the symbol-to-letter translations spilled from him, and she snapped a photograph of the newly translated runes. He'd started with an Enochian dictionary, which hadn't been fact-checked or updated since the late 1500s. None of the runes had matched exactly, but it was close enough.

A profound offering of the darkest self, or something adjacent. Whatever the hell that meant.

Beck demanded that she get a photo of him beneath the text, posing like a fisherman with a prize-winning catch. Mallory held Iskra steady as her spindly legs were thrown to and fro by the current. Oliver appeared at her side with an industrial flashlight and turned it up to illuminate the wall. The serpentine creature above the text came into full view at last, and I followed its twisting body with my gaze as far as the beam of the flashlight would allow.

Something hot and quick, a sharp exhalation, warmed the back of my neck and fluttered at the flyaway hairs. A long sigh, the familiar smell of ginger and rose . . .

I spun, headlamp skewed sideways. A flash of movement passed into the shadows beyond the survey lights, slipping through a crack in the wall wide enough for only a single body to fit at a time. No one seemed to have noticed it; they all went about their prescribed duties in relative silence.

But I'd seen it.

"What are you looking at?" Mallory's voice was loud in my ear, echoing throughout the chamber as if she had called to me from out at sea. She studied my face, then followed my puzzled gaze to the darkness beyond base camp. "Caro?"

Absently, my hand flew to the back of my neck. "Was there someone standing behind me just now?"

Mallory's manicured brow quirked. "Nope."

I tightened my headlamp and slipped from Beck's side. He didn't notice; he was far too busy explaining the decoding he'd done in order to determine what exactly the writing on the wall said. Dorothy and Iskra were a willing audience, recording anything and everything. Mallory followed as I skirted past Hannah, who counted packs of antiseptic. At the edge of the water, Anders and Leon were hard at work erecting an anchor for the flag-marked guide line that we would use if we descended further into the cave – which, no doubt, Beck would call for any moment. There was no way he would be satisfied with this. He would need *more.*

Water dripped from the ceiling as we slipped from the group, feeling our way along the wall as we cast the light of our headlamps down to the stone floor. "Something—" I huffed, gritting my teeth as something oblong and insectile crunched beneath my boot. "There's something over this way, I think." I couldn't tell Mallory that I thought I'd *seen* something, *someone*.

This wasn't the first time I'd imagined someone who wasn't really there. Ghosts lingered in my periphery more often than not. And not the shapeless black masses that the witchy girls in my cohort liked to theorize about, but rather *tangible* faces. Familiar ones. Specific, as if they hung around me on purpose. It was always the same voice, the same smell. I threw myself into the blind work of Beck's obsessive study if not to busy myself with a pale shade of *purpose*, but to drown that which I knew I'd see if I left myself alone for too long.

Mallory followed in silence, from skepticism or blind acceptance, I didn't know which. Ultimately, it didn't matter. I was simply glad that another living, breathing, tangible body was so close to mine. Mallory was warm. The stone, slick beneath my hand, was not. It changed beneath my touch, texture turning from the smooth face of a limestone slab to the protrusions, rounded edges, and vertical dips of something purposefully carved. Beneath my boots, the watery rock shifted downward. I adjusted the lens of my headlamp and turned my head, casting light across the wall.

An arch, half-absorbed; it jutted from the wall like a head peering from behind a curtain, as if the wall had solidified halfway through its passing. As if it had been left there, and slowly digested. The stone was impossibly smooth. Time and weather had clearly worn away *something* here.

The opening in the rock face sat beneath the apex of the archway, an almost imperceptible sliver of dark space in the stone. I could feel air from within, a breeze that blew from the outside in. The loose hairs around my face, barely dried in the salt-damp sea air, fluttered gently.

"Hey, Professor Beck?" I called. It still felt strange calling him by his formal title, when *Edward* came to me so readily. The echo of his voice cut short, a lecture shunted at the knees. "I think I found something."

His voice was a boom. It felt good, for a moment, to know that he trusted me enough to come without question. "Everyone, follow!" he called, voice echoing to the highest vaulting point of the cavern. I couldn't help but look up, as if I might see the very matter of his voice disappear into the darkness over our heads. Even the light of my headlamp couldn't permeate it.

I stepped aside as Beck appraised the rock and the archway that had been partially absorbed into the wall. He stuck his head into the narrow opening, and without a glance he thrust his journal into my hands again.

"Do . . . do you want me to write this down?" I asked.

He nodded, the light atop his helmet rattling, and shifted the rope that had been affixed to the harness on his person. "Of course I do, Caroline," he said, breathless. "This is an incredible discovery. A shame that any markings that might have given us a clue as to what this archway signified have all been worn away by time."

As he began to think aloud, I flipped to an open page and produced a pen from the breast pocket of my coat. To my dismay, he wedged himself into the open space, stripping off his safety gear and leaving it in a puddle by the wall. Oliver opened his mouth to object, and I cast him an apologetic look; there was no telling Beck what to do. He was paying them all to be here, after all.

"This is a *gate*," he called, voice muffled as he slipped – much thinner now – into the narrow opening. "Curious that the wall seems to have absorbed it like a living thing." He pressed his palms flat on the rock and gave a shove, as if expecting it to give way. "I imagine that once upon a time, one could come and go freely beneath this arch. But much like the growth and expansion of coral," – a great huff, and a splashing of feet in shallow water – "the structure has changed."

I could just barely see him through the narrow corridor. And he was alone, by the looks of it; no dark passenger lurked at his shoulder, blowing hot air into his ear. The smell of rose and ginger had gone, leaving nothing but the dank wetness of the stone and the salt of the sea.

"What do you see?" I called, pen hovering over my half-wrought notes. If I didn't record everything precisely the way they were meant to be – and in a way that could be replicated and waved in the face of everyone who called his research a waste of time – he would be disappointed in me.

His boots shuffled on the stone floor. He gave a huff of a laugh, the sound swallowed as he turned from the passage, and then another more triumphant, "Ha ha!" His footsteps stretched in echo as he moved further from the passage and into the adjacent cavern.

"Does he expect us to *follow*?" Iskra hissed, turning to Hannah as if the only person present with a medical degree was the de facto leader in Beck's absence. I was inclined to agree. The *author* certainly couldn't be trusted to set a bone or staunch a wound. By the looks of her – frenetic and twitchy, like a yappy dog that would bite at any provocation – she couldn't be trusted with a box of tissues. "I don't—" Iskra gulped. "I don't do well with confined spaces."

"You're in a *cave*," Dorothy countered, shifting the crotch of her rappelling harness. "What did you expect?"

I could barely hear Beck. How far into the next cavern had he gone while we all dragged our boots? It didn't feel right, leaving him alone in there. The Grundstadts had told us to stick together, at least two people at a time. What if he had fallen?

While Dorothy and Iskra bickered – ironic, given that they were likely the ones Beck wanted nearby the most, in order to preserve (and embellish) his great discovery – I stepped away from the archway and flagged down the Grundstadts. Someone had to follow him, and it looked like it was going to have to be me. Fantastic. "Hey!" my voice echoed. "Beck went further in. I need—"

The water began to recede. The sea, the gently lapping waves that had carried us so gladly into the cavern one by one, crept slowly from the rocky bank, spilling fish bones and mollusk shells down the steep incline. Open-mouthed, I watched as the waterline slipped away, like a stopper had been pulled from somewhere on the ocean floor. The brackish foam slipped away from the walls, the meticulous runes.

There, on the floor of the inlet, bones scattered amid the rocks and shells. A human tibia rolled down the steep hill into the empty space left behind by the receding water. A skull peered up from between a pair of jutting quartzite boulders. And from behind the orbital bone, the fragmented arrow of a mandible.

The ground rumbled beneath me, rattling the rocks and shells between my boots. My gaze snapped to the Grundstadts, who stood the closest to the mouth of the cave – and to the receding water. They hadn't noticed; the pair of them bent over the table that held all of our supplies, and they worked hard at fixing descender clips to thickly woven ropes.

A polished carabiner slipped from Leon's grasp and skittered down the steep incline. He huffed something that sounded vaguely profane in Swedish, and set off after it as Anders shook his head disparagingly.

The stone beneath my feet rumbled again. A boom like a gunshot cracked through the still air, swallowing the sounds of fickle bickering at my back.

Rock plummeted from the dark above, collapsing into the inlet. Leon disappeared beneath a sheet of limestone. The sound of it was deafening. Bile rushed into my throat. My ears rang, and my head spun. I froze, mouth hung wide. A scream lodged with a choke in my throat as again, the rock all around us rumbled and cracked.

It didn't compute. I didn't – couldn't – understand. Leon had just been right there. He'd been *right there.*

Mallory screamed, flattening her back against the wall. The others skittered away from our makeshift camp, scrambling to squeeze into the narrow passage after Beck.

A heavy slab of limestone arrowed down from the ceiling and bisected Anders at the thighs. Fast – too fast. He howled, blood splattering the rock as the sound of crunching bone was swallowed by the cracking and groaning of crumbling stone overhead. Leon had been quick; too quick for me to parse out. But this was tangible. This smelled of rust and salt water. There was no time to think. I tossed Beck's journal to the ground and leapt for him.

An animal caught in a scope, a deer in a fluorescent beam; Anders's eyes were wild and wheeling. I cried out for him, but he seemed not to hear. He clawed at the floor of the cavern, bits of rock and shell jamming beneath his fingernails.

A pair of strong arms looped around my middle and threw me backward as Anders disappeared beneath another block of stone, arms still outstretched. His forearms jutted upward, like weeds growing through a crack in the pavement, as the bones shattered. For an impossibly long moment, his fingers continued to twitch.

The others clawed at each other, fighting to fit first into the hole in the wall. Oliver dragged me back against the wall as what remained of the Grundstadts – and our camp – disappeared beneath the collapse. "Go!" Oliver cried, voice no more than an echo beneath the wild rush of crumbling rock. "Fucking *go*!"

Dorothy had gone first, shoving Hannah to the ground. The medic was next, and then Iskra. Mallory called out for me, sobbing and slapping the wall with her bare hands.

"The notebook!" I cried, kicking and scrabbling in Oliver's grasp.

"Forget the fucking notebook!" Oliver barked.

I dove for Beck's little black book, wriggling from Oliver's grasp with a shove. It was his life's work, the conflux of all the knowledge too precious to speak aloud to anyone but me. Even his wife, to my knowledge, was disallowed from peeking.

I scrambled on all fours toward the leather book. Rock, bone, and broken shells scraped my palms and pricked my fingers. The moment I reached it, shaking fingers clasping over the worn spine, Oliver took me by the ankles and pulled me away. And in the very place where my head had once been, a slab of rock the size of a refrigerator plummeted from the collapsing ceiling, splintering the floor of the cavern beneath.

Oliver gave Mallory a shove once I was on my feet, and she squeezed into the narrow passage. She was sobbing, fat tears wetting the neck of her sweater. The thick knit slowed her, and she kicked her feet and clawed at the rock as she went.

I tucked the journal into the front of my jacket. Where the fuck was Beck?

"Come on, Mallory!" Iskra's voice. A pair of hands reached into the claustrophobic space and tugged at Mallory's arms. Oliver pushed me in next, not allowing Mallory enough time to pry herself free. Then he followed, pressing shoulder to shoulder. The closeness was impossible; I could feel my every breath doubled back twofold by the rock just inches from my nose. I pressed my palms against the stone and slid sidelong after Mallory. It rumbled beneath my touch as just outside the cavern continued to buckle in on itself.

I felt hot beneath the skin, stone on all sides, my lungs thick cotton and my limbs lead. With each breath I felt resistance, as if the passage had all at once decided to close around us. Oliver's shoulder pressed against mine, and his voice blared in my ear. I couldn't move, couldn't breathe; each belabored inhale felt heavier than the last. My legs knocked against Mallory's as my coat and hair snagged on sharp protrusions. Something dug into my calf – stone? *hands?* – and I cried out, the back of my head smacking against the rock.

"Move, Caroline! Move!"

Mallory spilled from the passage, scrambling on all fours from the narrow opening. She disappeared into the dark, the slick stone floor illuminated by the beam of a single headlamp. Somewhere beyond, beneath the rumbling of settling stone behind us, I heard her retch. My head swiveled, and the beam of my headlamp illuminated nothing but shifting rock just beyond Oliver's shoulder. Nothing remained of the cavern or of our only exit.

Hands found me, pulling me free of the claustrophobic rock. Oliver sank to the floor just outside as I fell into the arms of the body nearest, unseeing. He hunched, pressing his head between his knees.

It was Beck's face into which I looked now. He caught me as my knees sagged, an arm round my middle as he wiped warm redness from my brow.

Blood. Anders.

Leon had died quickly. Likely he hadn't even felt a thing. Anders had known. He had the time to see it coming.

"They're dead!" I howled, clinging to Beck with no sense of decorum. He held me up, searching my face. "They're dead, and we're *trapped*!"

"Caroline." His voice was even, his hand steady and firm on my brow, my cheek. "Caro, please. Slow down. Breathe."

"*Breathe?!*" I still felt the rock on all sides, pressing my spine rod-straight and leadening every billow of my lungs. "The entrance *collapsed*! That was our only way out!"

I buried my face in his shoulder, knuckles white in the bunched fabric of his sweater. "Not quite," he muttered. "Not quite."

"Wh—"

"The journal?"

"What?"

"My journal, Caroline," Beck said. His voice was impossibly even, and he held me still with enough effort to bruise. "Do you have it?"

Bile rose at the back of my throat. I placed my hands on his chest and shoved, wiping at my eyes with the dirtied backs of my hands. "You—you *fuck*." I reached into the front of my jacket and pulled it from within. Its cover was scuffed, the spine bent and pages damp. I threw it at him, and he hurried to catch it before it could fall into the dark beyond the beams of our headlamps. "Take your stupid journal," I spat. "You're *welcome*."

I sank to the damp floor beside Mallory, quietly tugging her hair away from her face as she retched onto the stone. Hannah dabbed frantically at the dark wetness at Iskra's hairline as the photographer babbled shrilly about a rock that she could have *sworn* was thrown from somewhere in the dark. The ringing in my ears was deafening, muddling Iskra's cries and the sound of Oliver's muttering as he scrambled to shine his headlamp into the narrow passage behind us.

I stared blindly at the back of Mallory's neck as she hunched on the cold stone beside me, her hair bunched in my hands. Sweat beaded her neck, her brow; she trembled, her teeth chattering. I could feel nothing – nothing at all. Numbness crept through me like frost, making heavy my limbs and blurring my vision.

Bones. Human bones, unmistakably. And I'd felt, just moments before the collapse – *something.*

My ears popped, and I flinched as pressure built and burst in the space of the same breath. To my surprise the others did the same, clapping their hands over their ears and shying from the open air as if they'd been struck. I cast about wildly, the beams of all our headlamps crisscrossing in the dark.

"It's just air pressure!" Beck called, though the heels of his own hands ground fiercely into his ears. "Can't you feel – don't *panic*!" But panic had already come and gone. Terror was as thick on the air as steam. Mallory began to cry again, her face painfully red. I clutched my skull, squeezing my eyes shut as I tried and failed to comb through my memory of Beck's notes, of what he had supposed this was meant to be. I wanted it to mean something, to signify *anything*.

I cracked an eye. Beck was *smiling*. It looked almost painful.

But he wasn't smiling at me. He was looking up. I looked up, too, into the dark. There was nothing. And yet, I could *feel* it. Awareness, prickling and acute, like eyes on the back of my neck. The pressure, the rising of the hairs at the back of my neck – it was there and gone in an instant.

Only then did he look down. He met my eye and nodded. As soon as it had started, the pain stopped. We were left with nothing but the deathly silence of the cavern. I tucked Mallory's hair over her shoulder, then struggled to my feet. My knees knocked beneath me as I stepped further into the cavern. The others didn't seem to notice me as I felt along the wall, marking every ridge and bump for any sign of a passage that we could squeeze through. I felt grooves, protrusions, as precise and measured as the runes in the entrance cavern. The flat stone floor stretched on for ever, far beyond where my light touched. I craned my neck up, appraising the wall. To my surprise, the grooves and notches in the stone were not random, not created by some wayward sea creature chasing prey – they looked purposeful. Carved, as if by hand.

I crossed to Oliver, who sat alone, fiddling with the industrial flashlight he'd strapped to his belt, and looking as if he had abandoned all hope where the narrow passage was concerned. "Can I see that?" I snatched it from him before he could answer, and turned it to the wall. The beam was wide and fluorescent, blinding in the opaque darkness of the cavern. Hannah let out a yelp, skittering sidelong like a frightened animal. She clapped her hands over her mouth and slumped against the wall, muttering something imperceptible into her palms.

I had been right. Carved whorls lined the wall at head-height. Above, runes similar to those in the entrance sat neatly in a block of text. Beside it images shaped from the stone, sculpted meticulously, stretched on into the dark. I followed the scene with the flashlight, and the others slowly gathered at my side one by one.

The sequence depicted here followed a pattern I recognized from my anthropological studies. Humanoid figures; some assembled in what looked to be prayer, and some lying prone on elevated surfaces. They held their hands up to a great figure carved into the stone above. I lifted the beam of the flashlight, and a great serpent spread out before me. It was carved deep into the rock, deeper than the worshipers, and the humans, and the signs of a feast or a sacrifice – or maybe both – that littered the scene's empty spaces. I followed its winding body further down the wall with the light, along the unbroken stretch of floor. Some carvings looked fresher than others, as if the history depicted here had been revised and added to over the years.

There, just at the level of my eyes, a circular hole in the wall. An indentation, nearly imperceptible, surrounded on all sides by the uncanny humanoid figures, their hands outstretched toward the niche. The space within was dry, no wider than my torso and untouched by the dripping water over our heads. I took a step closer, rising onto my toes to reach for it.

My fingertips ghosted across the flat surface of the dry rock. I adjusted my headlamp. The edges of the cavity were scuffed, the lip of the bottommost curve crumbled and broken as if whatever lay within had been removed by force.

As I studied the indentation, I felt eyes on me. Every inch, watched; the faces painted and carved onto the wall hadn't moved, and yet their eyes felt positively *alive.* There were so many of them, here and further into the dark above my head.

Beck appeared at my shoulder. He moved quietly, suddenly; I jumped, and the flashlight beam wheeled wildly.

"Shine the light back up there, will you?" he asked, pointing to the stretch of dark wall just above us. I did as I was asked, illuminating the humanoid figures, and the head of the serpent, with a block of indiscernible text; Beck drew closer, thumbing through his notebook and muttering to himself. Beneath the text were hundreds of handprints, pressed onto the stone like signatures. I wondered with a faint disquiet what they had used for paint.

The others watched nervously, shuffling their feet and rubbing cold hands together. "Look—" he pointed a finger, the tip wrinkled and pale from the cold and damp, up at the figures on the wall. "They assemble around the Leviathan in worship. And further down," he moved his hand, and I followed with the flashlight, "they assemble in a sort of . . . *devotion* ritual. A trial, maybe. They give not only supplication, but physical goods. An exchange. The great old ones can't resist a deal. See?"

"*Great old ones?*" Dorothy's voice was a hiss. I heard Hannah make the affected noise that accompanied a theatrical shrug.

"And the text here," Beck returned to the block of runic lettering on the far left side of the wall. "This word, to my understanding, is '*story*' or something similar. '*First story*'. This implies, then, that there are more depictions like this deeper inside."

"*Deeper inside?*" Oliver's voice was a boom in the hollow cavern. "We're not going further inside."

I had to agree with the field officer.

Beck spun on a heel. "Don't you see?" His voice was shrill, his eyes wild. He thrust a finger over his shoulder. "The only way out is further in. The carvings prove it."

"The carvings don't prove shit," Oliver snorted. "They're just *pictures.* Our fucking *professional guides* just died, Edward, and you want to talk about—"

"They're accounts of past supplicants," Beck boomed. I looked between them both, the beam of the flashlight lingering on the serpent, the worshippers, and the prone bodies. What did *they* represent? Were they sleeping? "Treat it like an instruction manual. If this place was important enough to amass such an obvious breadth of recordings over time, then there'll be a logic to its layout. The Leviathan's worshipers couldn't just wander blindly." A pause. I could see him thinking, his brows twitching and lips twisting. "Anders and Leon knew better than anyone the risks of coming to a place like this. It was bound to happen this way to men who lived that dangerously eventually."

"How can you be so goddamn nonchalant?" Hannah's voice, now, raised to fever pitch. She emerged from the shadows, face pale. "This isn't a fucking *puzzle*, Edward. We're trapped, with no way out and no guides! I don't even know how to get this fucking harness off!"

Beck shook his head, wagging his finger at Hannah as if she were no more than a surly student. "You need to just trust me," he said. It was startling, this lack of empathy, lack of fear. He regarded us all like this was nothing more dangerous than the act of changing a tire on the side of a well-lit highway.

"I'm perfectly content to sit right here until the fishermen come back," Hannah said. "They'll see that the mouth of the cave collapsed, and they'll . . . they'll call the Navy or something. You'll see." She looked around at all of us, meeting our gazes individually. "We just have to wait."

Oliver spoke again. "Or we could look for another way out. Our supplies, our rations; most of them are under all that rock with the Grundstadts."

I flinched. Whenever I closed my eyes, I could still see Anders; his face, the terror upon it, and then the jut of his arms as the rest of his body was crushed beneath falling rock.

"I told you," Beck said. "The only way out is to go further in. I've studied this cult, this *theology*, my entire goddamn adult life. Trust me." No one did, but I wanted to. I could feel the disconnect in what my gut and my heart were telling me, and I wanted to listen to neither. That much was as evident as if we'd shouted it in his face. But the silence was enough. "We have to go further in. We'll find something in the texts preserved here to help—"

"Jesus *Christ*—"

"Listen!"

"Your woo-woo sea cult isn't going to have an instruction manual lying around, Edward!" Oliver hollered. "Sure, they came here and splashed each other with sacred seawater and had a grand ol' time – but we're here, we're real, and we're fucking *trapped*. Do you think they accounted for a group of dumb fucks who followed a professor from *Ohio* into—"

Beck moved fast, too quickly for my ill-adjusted eyes to follow. He was in Oliver's face before he could be stopped, a finger thrust beneath his nose. "You watch your goddamn mouth. I hired you to—"

"You hired me to keep this expedition safe, and that's exactly what I plan to do."

"Done a shit job of it." Hannah spoke again, voice weak. She gave a watery laugh, and in the dark beyond the headlamp beams I could hear her slide down the rock wall and to the floor of the cavern. "Just ask the Swedes."

Slumped against the wall nearest, her safety gear lopsided, Dorothy reached into the breast pocket of her jacket and produced a cigarette and a lighter. Her hands shook as she propped the cigarette between her lips and flicked the spark wheel once, twice. Iskra's visage curled into a frown, for she seemed to overestimate how hidden her face really was outside the concentrated beam of a headlamp or flashlight. Nevertheless, she lifted the camera from around her neck – which had miraculously survived the narrow passage – and snapped a picture.

A flame flickered to life, and Dorothy exhaled with visible relief. She lit her cigarette, inhaling deeply. But then her gaze narrowed on the flame, and she froze. Iskra snapped another photo.

Dorothy pushed from the wall as Beck and Oliver bickered by the carvings. Cigarette bobbing between her lips, she spoke. "Everybody shut the fuck up." She held the lighter aloft. Over her head, the flame danced and wavered, as if caught in a breeze.

A breeze?

The flame dipped and bowed. A current of air, almost imperceptible, from beyond the dark. Further in.

"See?" Beck hovered like a moth beneath the flame, hands outstretched in reverence. "Air, coming from further inside. Too long in this cavern, and our oxygen will begin to dwindle. Further *in* is the only way."

As much as I hated the idea of it, he was right. There was certainly no way that we were turning back. Even if we tried to squeeze through the narrow passage between this cavern and the one just outside, we'd meet nothing but crumbled and impassible stone.

I turned the beam of the flashlight up to the wall again, to the depictions of the Leviathan's worshipers that stretched the length of the cavern wall. For the second time, I could have sworn that movement rippled within the shadows above, at the junction between wall and ceiling. Movement, almost imperceptible, as if I was imagining it.

Again, the smell of ginger and rose; it blew in on the breeze as it curled around Dorothy's wrist with a flicker of firelight, and was gone again.

Caroline?

A voice, then. A hot breath at the nape of my neck.

Caroline, can you hear me?

I skittered forward, as if I'd been smacked on the ass. Mallory hiccupped, shying from me as I whirled in search of the voice's source. The beam of my headlamp blinded Iskra, and she cursed.

Caroline, are you there? Sweetie, are you listening?

"We should go," I blurted. I could feel the baby hairs at the back of my neck standing on end. "I can't stay in this fucking cave any more. We have to move, or I'm going to lose my shit." While the others looked at me like I was a rabid animal, prone to biting at any moment, Beck regarded me with all the reverence in the world. I wasn't losing my marbles, spun out like a loose thread undone by the sound of a voice I hadn't heard in years; I was an *ally*. I would, as I always did, do whatever the hell Edward Beck told me to do.

The cave played tricks. The salt water, the sea air; the oppressive darkness and the sheer horror of seeing a man die before my very eyes. I wasn't thinking clearly. None of us were.

Or maybe Beck was seeing clearer than ever before.

Loose rock shifted beyond the narrow passage in the archway. A shiver ran the length of us, terror as palpable as brine. And so we moved.

I had never believed in the Cult of the Leviathans. Not really. More than anything I believed in Beck, and his ability to make anything sound like gospel. The first talk he ever gave was attended by three people: me, his wife, and a surly theology undergraduate. I knew what I wanted to do with my life then as much as I did now, which said very little. But I'd been dodging calls from my therapist and my fosters, and my roommates were throwing a party. So I went, simply for the sake of having something to do.

Never had I met someone with such singular conviction. It didn't seem to bother him that the lecture hall was mostly empty, that the coffee and pastries he'd laid out had gone untouched. It didn't move him when his wife got up to take a call, or when the theology undergrad tried to argue that the Leviathan was a biblical beast that no one but Satan-loving demon-fuckers wanted to know about.

Leviathan. The Sin-Eater. Didn't exactly give the warm-fuzzies.

While Beck had pontificated about the sea-bound cult that had eluded historians for centuries, that left their mark in fossilized fish bones and scales pulled from the ocean's deepest trenches, my therapist left me a voicemail. I was doing what she'd wanted me to do, after all; I was out in the world, with *people*, and engaging in interests other than drinking, getting high, and watching *The Office* reruns.

While Beck showed slides on the projector screen of indentations in the sea floor, scales the size of church windows, and rock carvings with utterly nonsensical symbols – to the dismay of the undergrad – I knew that this was someone I needed to be near. I needed to inhale his conviction like incense. This was someone who truly believed in something, who knew precisely who he was. And he was so vibrantly, blindingly, himself. On purpose. For better or worse. He was unlike anything I'd ever seen.

I'd collected my things, hastening from the middle seat, and middle row, in which I'd stationed myself before Beck could make his way to me. It was strange, in the days that followed, to hear full-grown adults gossiping and snickering about Beck like they were middle schoolers making fun of the new kid's braces. They called him a fraud, a joke. But I had never been more impressed by anybody. I was directionless, a piece of discarded parchment that had been scribbled on and erased one too many times. But Edward Beck knew precisely who he was. He knew exactly what he wanted. And I would have given anything to be just like that.

Water dripped from the cavern's stone ceiling, pattering atop our helmets like rain on a rooftop. The slope of the floor and the angle of the roof began to twist, dipping as if the whole cavern had been picked up and tilted like a snow globe. Mallory slipped at my side, and her short, piercing scream ricocheted the length of the passage. She grabbed my arm, and I shot Oliver an apologetic glance as he looked disparagingly at us both. Everyone was rattled; the last thing we needed were sudden noises.

"This looks to be no more than a vestibule," Beck said, as if he stood behind a podium in a lecture hall. "It likely isn't even the biggest hall within the system."

Hall? He spoke of the cave like it was an antechamber in a gothic manor, a room in a house that was warm, and welcoming, and unlocked at every door. While he studied the wall, monologuing to anyone within earshot, I studied *him.*

His pack sagged. When we'd disembarked from the fishermen's boats, it had only contained his notes, his books, and the first aid equipment Hannah insisted we all keep on our person. It hung low, thudding heavily against the small of his back.

Odd – had his belongings gotten *that* waterlogged? Mine were soggy, and sloshing, and dripping down my ass. But his pack looked *heavy*.

Beck felt his way along the carvings in the wall until the ceiling grew so low that we all were forced to stoop. At the end of the cavern, the low ceiling and sloped walls converged on a single opening, maybe a foot tall, and two wide.

And above it, a final carving worn to nearly nothing by time and the elements. In the place where a full serpent's head might have been, a pair of hollow-set eyes peered down at us, its body stretching back toward the collapse.

"In we go," he said. Beck dropped onto his stomach and slid beneath the wall with no hesitation. The rest of us looked from person to person, open skepticism and blazing fear evident on every face.

Iskra shook her head. Her fingers trembled as she absently fiddled with the damp lens of her camera. "This is fucking insane," she said. "Why don't we wait? Why don't we just wait?"

No one seemed to have a proper answer for her. The current of air that had moved Dorothy's lighter was stronger here, and as I sank onto my belly I could feel it almost as strongly as if we stood at the bow of Ellis's boat once more.

"There has to be another way out," Oliver said. He tightened the straps of his pack over his shoulders, wiping a spray of salt from his set brow. "A current of air like this," he pointed to me, as if I was some kind of inflatable car lot balloon man, waving in a heavy gale, "means that there's an opening somewhere past this wall. And there's only so much space in this stack, right? You saw it from the outside. It's no wider than the Chrysler building. Walk any farther, and we'll hit the other side."

"Right," Hannah nodded, eager for any opportunity to assuage the clear panic that was beginning to settle over Iskra. "See? We're going to be fine." As I slid my head beneath the heavy wall, I could hear them all muttering to her like one might a startled animal. "I'm sure there's another cave just like the last one on the other side. Lots of pretty rock formations, and shells, and waves for you to take pictures of."

It was a nice thought. The sinking in my gut, like a rusted anchor, told me that it was also a terrible lie.

A light flickered to life ahead of me, vibrant red, and accompanied by the smell of charcoal and sulfur. The sound of a flare striking rock startled me, and I smacked my head against the low ceiling of the passage. The light shifted, the shadow of Beck's legs appearing and disappearing as the flare arced into the open air and disappeared.

I crawled on my stomach after Beck. He awaited me on the other side, taking me by the arm and hauling me onto my feet as the others followed. The flare had landed no more than fifty feet down, rolling across the stone floor and coming to a stop at the foot of what could only be described as a long stone table. The cavern opened up before me like a cathedral; the ceiling was so tall that even the light of the sputtering flare couldn't touch it. Stalactites and stalagmites encircled a long table flanked by limestone benches. I could hear the babble of running water, a narrow stream curving around the far side of the grotto. A niche had been carved into the column nearest, barely illuminated by the flare.

Beck put his hands on his hips. His chest billowed, and before I could stop him he let out a triumphant holler that echoed thunderously around the chamber. I flinched, hands instinctively flying to clap over my ears. Behind me, and at the level of my ankles, someone cursed.

"What the *hell*, Beck?" Hannah emerged from the narrow passage beneath the vestibule wall, futilely attempting to brush bracken and salt off her front. She went for Iskra at the first opportunity, checking her for bumps and scrapes as she shivered and twitched, clutching her camera tightly. "Dude – could you keep it down?"

Beck thrust a fist in the air. "What did I fucking tell you?" he boomed. In the light of the flare, his eyes were wild. He'd turned off his headlamp. The hard lines of his face, the hollow of his tired eyes, were all a startling crimson. "Look. At. That!" He gestured broadly, and Hannah looked on.

"What am I looking at?"

"Come," Beck gestured to us both. He didn't give a shit about Iskra, and didn't give a shit about the good doctor, clearly. "Come see." He took me by the arm, tugging me along with him as he hopped down onto the narrow outcropping below, and then the next. Surely there were safer ways to do this, but Beck was undeterred. "Name *one* ancient civilization that doesn't center the breaking of bread in their tenets," he said, paying no mind as I slipped in a splash of water that had pooled on one of the sheer steps leading down to the platform that housed the table and benches. "Name a single religious sect that does not include sharing in sustenance in its proceedings. Name one!"

I realized then that he was asking in earnest. "I—" I blanched. "I . . . can't?"

"You *can't.*" It was wild to me that he could *lecture* here. Now. Anders's blood was still in my lashes, and Beck had fully transformed into the professorial version of himself, albeit a touch more manic. Cast in nothing but glaring red and muddy shadow, we descended to the cavern's lowest point. Only then did he release me.

There was no denying that the space was magnificent. I had never given much stock to religion, and I had my reasons for it, but this . . . this was something else.

"A feast hall, on the bank of a naturally occurring stream . . ." he said, half to me and half to himself. "The first stage of a grand ceremony, where the Leviathan's supplicants wash, break bread and . . . and . . ." He muttered imperceptibly and disappeared at once into his notes.

I meandered away from him as the others followed suit. The sound of Iskra's camera was audible far across the space, beyond the stream. Somewhere further than the light of the flare could reach, the water rushed more fiercely. A waterfall, maybe. I'd always wanted to see one of those.

Shelf-like alcoves lined the walls on the other side of the stream. Low rocks had been flattened at the tops, like benches. I imagined this place to be something of a primordial dining hall, a place where Leviathan's undergrads came to eat ramen and sneak beer.

I looked back again to the table – and it was unmistakably a table, with long benches on either side – as Beck settled his pack atop it. From within, he produced a protein bar. Participating in local custom even in the direst times, it seemed.

Caroline?

"Fuck *off*."

The hiss of my voice snaked through the dark, no more than a whisper beneath the sputtering of the flare. But it had carried nevertheless.

"What was that?" On the other side of the water, from behind the waterlogged stone column, Mallory peeked her head out at me.

I blanched. "You didn't . . . say my name just now, did you?" I had to chance it. I knew the voice implicitly; I heard it in the quiet stillness of nighttime, whenever a lapse in my omnipresent music, or my white noise, or the babble of my roommates faded away. "I thought I heard someone say my name." The voice had not belonged to Mallory. This was fact. But I could hope to be proven wrong.

She shook her head. "Nope."

I turned away again, feeling along the wall. It curved away from the center of the chamber, into another sloping corridor untouched by the flare. Only one way out, it seemed. More carvings adorned these walls, and the columns and stalagmites that dotted the open space. Only Beck would know what they meant.

The flash of Iskra's camera blinded me. The light bloomed inside the cavern, catching me as I stood framed between two columns. I startled, shying against the wall. "Jesus Christ, Iskra!" I cried, throwing my hands up to shield my eyes.

I could hear above the babbling of water and shifting of stone a warbling apology. Her voice was shrill, words tumbling from her and spiraling up into the cacophony of the water, the footsteps, the lecturing. "I just – I needed something to do with my hands!" she said. "Won't happen again!" Her lip quivered as she tried and failed to offer me a chagrined smile, and she wiped at her brow.

Dammit. I immediately felt like a dickhead. I'd have to apologize when we were someplace safer.

Beyond the light of the flare, loose stone shifted beneath the weight of something heavy. Movement, shuffling, like the pattering of feet; it skittered away from the light. Almost imperceptible within the oppressive dark, I could have sworn that I saw movement. A flash of a bare ankle. The hem of a linen nightdress.

I whipped my head sidelong and counted. Beck, Oliver, Hannah, Iskra, Dorothy, Mallory. Everyone was accounted for. I fumbled for my headlamp. The narrow beam cut through the vibrant red of the flare, illuminating the curve in the wall and the passage beyond. A smattering of loose stone and a number of empty shells scattered across the otherwise empty stone floor.

"Hey!" Oliver called. He had spotted me, far from the others. Even in the dark, I could see the keen and disapproving glint of his eyes. This was a different Oliver from the one I'd met at the inn. *This* was who Beck had hired. "Don't go off on your own, Caro. Come back to the group."

He held up his hand to shield his eyes from the light of my headlamp as I turned to call back, "S-sorry. I just I thought I saw something." This, at the very least, seemed to catch Dorothy's attention. She abandoned her post by Iskra – much to the photographer's dismay – and hopped across the narrow stream to join me in my exploration of the far wall. Much to *my* dismay. But any novelized retelling of Beck's brains and bravery would need all the detail it could get.

Hannah paced at the far end of the platform as Beck implored the others to join him at the table. In my periphery, I could see her shrug off her pack and start to rifle through the first aid she'd brought. She was taking stock, counting bits and pieces. Her parched lips moved fast, too quickly for me to make out a word of what she so fervently said to herself. Brows drawn and expression hard, she looked like she'd bite the head off of anyone who interrupted her. She and Oliver were the only professionals here, clearly. The rest of us were merely the rabble they had to lead. Best, I figured, not to get in their way.

And so I moved, instead, to take Dorothy's place by Iskra. Like chess; one undesirable piece moves, and the others scatter. Mallory followed. This was the very first rule of sacred girlhood: it didn't matter that Iskra was a stranger. She was stricken, clearly, the sheen of sweat on her brow glistening in the vermillion light of the flare. I hopped over the narrow stream, loose pebbles scattering beneath my boot, and motioned to Mallory. It was a good enough excuse to get away from Dorothy, who didn't even look as I arrowed away from her.

"Hey—" I pulled Iskra aside, and Mallory angled her body so that the others couldn't see the slowly worsening tremble of Iskra's lower lip. "It's okay, I swear. Just scared me shitless for a second. But, I mean, we're all scared shitless."

Mallory nodded. "*Totally.*"

Iskra took a deep, rattling breath. "I just – I *hate* close spaces. The dark. *Caves.*"

A rueful smile tugged at the corners of my lips as a cruel spot of malice deep inside me wanted to laugh at the sheer stupidity of it. "Well, you picked a bad job then, huh?" I ventured. "How'd you get stuck with this?"

Behind us, Beck called out as he shifted a boulder – strangely symmetrical, and smooth on all sides – to reveal a cubby in the floor by the furthest stone column. He motioned to Oliver, claiming that he'd found *tools* of some sort, pieces of carved and molded stone that had been squirreled away not unintentionally. His voice startled Iskra, and her camera jumped on the strap around her neck. Oliver cursed, turning on his heel to implore Beck to keep his voice down.

"This wasn't even supposed to be *my* gig," Iskra hissed, as if saying it aloud might make the cave swallow her up where she stood. "I thought it would be *fine*, but—" She shook her head.

"I understand," I said. I did, more than she understood. It was easy to swallow fear and self-doubt for the sake of decorum, and for the sake of just getting through the damn day, but in the heart of the horror that plagues us, there's no wishing it away. Iskra shook violently, her teeth chattering.

Mallory chanced a hand on Iskra's shoulder. "Just think about Dorothy's light, okay? Air currents mean there's an exit."

"I know," she nodded. "I just . . . I haven't had the best experience with caves. When I was little, my sister and I – I—" She clamped her mouth shut and shook her head. I didn't pry.

Instead, I shrugged off my pack, full of Hannah's mandatory stock of first aid equipment and what little climbing gear I'd cared to squirrel away. I tugged off my jacket and slipped it over Iskra's shoulders. It hung over her back, her camera pack and climbing gear jutting out like a turtle's shell.

"You need to stay warm," I said. "It'll help."

A smile tugged at Iskra's pinched features. She seemed comforted by the warmth, her shoulders sagging. Iskra wiped at the dampness in her eyes with the heel of her hand, and motioned for Mallory and I to stand closer to one another.

"Might as well do my job," she said, voice thick. "Let me get a picture of you two. Not exactly the intended subject, but . . . maybe I'll keep a pic for myself."

I looped an arm around Mallory's shoulder, and hers fell to my waist. She held up a peace sign and puckered her lips, and I held up a thumb. Dripping water slicked our hair to our heads, and we shivered, but we said "cheese!" and Iskra snapped a picture.

We dispersed as she hunched over her camera, at the edge of one of the two stone benches flanking the long table. Beck's gaze was hard on the three of us, and he cleared his throat to snag our attention.

"I would thank the three of you to keep your eye on the prize, all right?" he clipped. Beck's arms were laden with the stone tools that Hannah had unearthed. Flint, by the looks of it. He laid them out on the table, and tossed me his journal. A pen clattered across the table, and Beck shifted so that the flare could light my work. "This isn't social hour. We are professionals at work. Now, if you would, make a record of these."

If Mallory and I were professionals, then we'd surely emerge from the cave to see pigs in flight. But we didn't argue. Instead, we muttered half-hearted apologies and sat down at the table as instructed. I appraised the tools: an oblong instrument that sat somewhere between an arrowhead and a carving knife; a stone flake with divots and scrapes from use; a hammerstone stained a color that I couldn't make out in the light of the flare. It was all textbook, exactly the sort of thing that Beck would have used as an exam question.

Caroline?

I dropped the arrowhead with a clatter. The voice was an echo; no more immediacy, but rather the distance of someone calling, desperately from another room. A familiar voice. A voice that I never wanted to hear again. A voice that I couldn't *stop* hearing no matter how hard I tried.

Caro, are you out there?

I could hear it as clearly as if Dorothy had called to me from the far wall. I turned round and searched the dark. At the far end of the table, where she had retreated to examine the unlit brazier, Mallory looked up, too. She turned to look in the same direction, squinting and screwing up her nose.

At the foot of the table, where she chiseled away at a piece of rock on the floor with her ice ax, Hannah did the same. So did Dorothy, and Oliver. Only Beck seemed not to have noticed, intent on laying out each slate tool so that I might catalog them correctly.

"Not so barbaric and unimaginable after all," Beck said, like it was some kind of *gotcha*. "The act of sharing food is the oldest tradition in the world. That there's evidence of it here lends to the Cult's legitimacy."

"What did they eat?" I mused absently as I took up pen and paper, acting like I'd been paying close attention all along. "Virgins?"

"If that's the case, then you have nothing to worry about. Do you, Caroline?" Beck's voice was low, quiet, as if he intended only for me to hear. Voices carried in this cavern, but the rush of water beyond the grotto and the patter of footsteps on wet stone nearly swallowed his words. I looked up and met his gaze. Intensity burned behind his eyes, and the corners of his lips twitched.

So this *was* a kink thing. Fantastic.

I opened my mouth to speak again, but a scream from across the room shattered the thick stillness of the cavern. I jolted to my feet, the tops of my thighs scraping the underside of the stone table. Beck's tools, and his only pen, rolled across the tabletop and clattered to the floor as I whirled, casting about for the source of the sound.

Everyone was moving at once. Iskra fell to her knees, scrambling on all fours through the stream at the far end of the feast hall. Dorothy leapt out of her way, shying from her as if she'd begun to foam at the mouth. Oliver and Hannah leapt from the edge of the platform as Mallory and I struggled down the steep slope to the basin floor of the grotto. Iskra was crying, howling, tongue heavy as she tried and failed to form a word, any word . . .

And then I saw it. I skittered to a halt, slipping on the slick floor and landing hard on my backside. There, in the dark space beyond the flare – in the very place I had seen a ghost of my own mere moments before – stood a little girl. She looked just like Iskra, though in miniature. Her black hair was cropped to the chin, almond eyes wide. But her skin, unlike Iskra's tawny glow, was gray and bloated. The girl stood impossibly still; the darkness moved around her, like a shadow refracted through brackish water.

She was soaking wet. Water gurgled from the corners of her lips, her pink unicorn t-shirt was dripping, and she missed a shoe, a single jelly sandal hanging half-off her heel. The girl opened her mouth, sodden chest billowing. Water spilled over her tongue. Even from where I'd fallen, I could hear the pop and gurgle of wetness in her lungs. Iskra shuddered to a halt. The specter's clouded eyes turned down to appraise her, where she had stopped on all fours.

Not a specter – not really. Not if we all could see it. Not if we all could *hear* it.

"You . . ." the girl began, water burbling over her tongue. She lifted a single bloated finger, and pointed at Iskra. "You aren't supposed to be here."

She made no noise as she turned, darting back into the dark. Iskra cried out again, sobbing wildly, manically, as she scrambled to her feet and careened from the light. My jacket slipped from over her shoulders, over the heavy sag of her pack – and she was gone.

A chorus of voices followed, calling out to Iskra as she hurtled into the dark. I followed without thinking, scraping my hands on the stone as I hauled myself up. Iskra's voice echoed as she descended into the passage. "*Priya!*" she called. "*Priya, come back!*" I fumbled with my headlamp as I went, shoulder catching on a hard jut of rock as I sprinted after her. Oliver called out to her, and then to me, but his voice was swallowed, his warnings against splitting up lost to the hysteria. Mallory followed close behind, the light atop her hardhat sputtering.

Thunderous footsteps followed as we descended from the grotto, the floor tilting and splitting. It was rougher here; I slipped, and my ankle turned, but I kept running, calling after Iskra, who was far beyond the reach of my headlight.

We scattered. I followed the sound of Iskra's voice as best I could, calling out to her as I careened from wall to wall, slamming into columns and tumbling down low drops in the rocky floor. I'd left my safety equipment behind, I realized; my backpack lay useless at the foot of the ceremonial table.

The sound of running water grew closer as I kept pace with Iskra, following the stream that cut through the feast hall as it trickled down the center of the corridor. I couldn't see her, couldn't catch her, no matter how hard I pushed. Her voice sounded as if it came from all directions, the echo disorienting. I felt along the wall. The floor dipped beneath me, and I stumbled down, down, losing my footing and tumbling until I came to a splashing stop in the basin of a waterlogged cavern.

The water was freezing, droplets of glacial mist dappling my face as I hauled myself up. It soaked through my jeans, filled my shoes. If only I had my jacket – if only *Iskra* had my jacket.

I cupped my frigid hands around my mouth, flinching against the feeling of the cold on my cheeks, and shouted, "Iskra! Iskra, come back!" I clambered from the water and looked up. The beam of my headlamp followed the impossibly tall body of the roaring waterfall up, up, over a stone lip and into a crevice in the wall far above. Up to the feast hall. Up to the others.

"*My sister!*" Iskra's voice was an echo, everywhere and nowhere. "*Oh God – it's my sister!*"

A pebble pinged off the hard top of my helmet and clattered across the stone floor. I yelped as a second fell, and then a third. Scooting across the stone, I squinted up to the dark ceiling of the cavern, so far over my head that the beam of my headlamp would barely touch it.

But there was movement within the shadow. It was unmistakable. Only faintly touched by the light, the singular beam that arrowed through the oppressive dark of the cavern, something – *someone* – moved. Another piece of broken rock clattered across the floor at my feet, displacing what looked to be a shard of bone, broken and jagged, and pocked at the edges.

A flicker of red light, a flare, shone like a ghost-light from a passage on the opposite end of the cavern.

"Iskra?" How the hell had she gotten all the way over there? I'd thought there was only one way into this cavern – and out of the last one.

Something hard and solid slammed into me, knocking me sidelong. A hand clapped over my mouth, stifling my gasp as a strong arm barred around my midsection and hauled me away from the water. I struggled, kicking and wheeling my arms until a familiar voice hissed in my ear, breath hot on my skin.

"Be *still*, Caroline." Beck pulled me across the stone floor, tucking behind the wall of water that tumbled into the heart of the cavern. He pressed against the far wall and tugged me against his front, his legs wrapped around my midsection and holding me still. "Be *quiet*." His chest heaved beneath me as he reached up, hand slipping from my mouth, and switched off the light on my helmet.

I struggled against him, but he only held me tighter. "But *Iskra*—"

He slammed his hand over my mouth again, and I saw stars. "What did I say?" he hissed. "Shut your fucking mouth."

Indignant, I wanted to slam my elbow into the bruisable flesh of his abdomen. This was not the goddamn time for whatever stupid little fantasy he'd come here with. I opened my mouth – whether to scream or to bite, I wasn't sure. But before I could slip free of his grasp, the red light tumbled into the cavern, and Iskra along with it.

She landed on her stomach, mouth open as she sobbed into the brine at the base of the waterfall. Somewhere along the way, she'd lost her camera. I strained under Beck's grip, kicking my feet and reaching toward the heavy curtain of water, but he held fast, trapping me against his chest in the shadow of the stone overcropping. Iskra stumbled to her feet, sloshing from the water and onto the stone. I could only see so much; she left the flare discarded by the water, her open pack slipping from her shoulders and half-obscuring the vermillion blaze from view. Her shadow stretched across the uneven floor, reaching up the craggy wall.

Iskra tipped her head back, billowed her chest, and screamed. The name – *Priya* – rattled in my chest. She was sobbing, arms swinging limp at her sides as she called out over and over. I wondered if the others could hear her, if they were struggling in the dark to find their way here as well.

Iskra was bleeding. A dark swath of wetness, near black in the light of the flare, colored her brow. It dripped down her temples, over her cheek.

"Priya!" she called, voice ragged. "Please come back!" Rock and dirt rained down upon her face, clinging to her bloody flesh.

Beck's fingers dug painfully into my cheeks. He held so tight that I could barely breathe, let alone call out. His legs tightened around my midsection, and I could feel each shallow breath against my back.

There came a squelch and a pop from above, like a joint slipping from its socket. A shadow moved quickly from the corner. I could hear the scrabbling of digits on loose stone, and then the shifting of rock; on all fours, a shape darted from the shadow, skittering down the wall and arrowing out into the open air.

A retch, a scream choked; the scrambling of boots on stone and the splash of a body hitting water. The creature lunged for Iskra, wrapping its hands around her skull as it sunk its teeth into the flesh of her shoulder. Two bodies hit the water. Iskra choked, gurgling on blood as she thrashed, striking out at anything she could. The creature, the thing that might once have been Priya, threw its head back, and a spray of blood arced through the air.

From where I watched behind the curtain of rushing water, Iskra's face was imperceptible. Her frantic movements had slowed, the weak slapping of her hands against foreign flesh deafened beneath the waterfall.

And there, in the light of the flare, a single jelly sandal settled onto the stone.

Another shape emerged from the shadows, and then another. A third slipped from the passage down which I had fallen, and another still leapt from the very top of the waterfall. They converged on the pool of dark blood at the center of the cavern, descending on Iskra before she could muster the strength to cry out again. I couldn't look away. I willed away the sound of tearing flesh, the popping of bone and sinew from tight sockets, but it filled the cavern entirely. Even the roar of the waterfall couldn't dampen it. Animal keening filled the cavern, wordless and wild; the hunched humanoid creatures shrieked as they tore at Iskra's flesh, pushing at one another like children squabbling over a meal. Hairless, smooth in silhouette; they could have been human. But I knew, as an animal knows a predator, that they weren't.

I reached for the ice ax at my belt, trapped under my hip. Beck clocked the movement, and pressed the tip of his thumb hard into my jaw, hard enough to bruise. The pressure of his palm stifled my yelp – but even if it hadn't, the roar of the water and the tearing of flesh would hide us well enough.

A voice rang out from beyond the cavern, and the creatures froze. Their heads whipped sidelong. I could barely make it out over the rush of the water and the blood pounding in my ears. The creatures straightened, uncanny humanoid silhouettes stretching in the light of the flare.

Closest to us, the thing that had once been Priya, a *child*, rose on spindly legs. It moved toward the passage, its shape vacillating through the warped filter of the waterfall. It stood washed in the light of the flare, and when it moved the visage of the child had disappeared entirely. Instead, the distorted silhouette of its androgynous body stretched in the light. And then another face, and another, twisted and flickered onto its changing face, each with barely discernible silhouettes. And then, in no more than a flash of stretching features, a woman.

I would know her here, above, at the end of the world. My mother's crooked shoulders popped and rolled as the creature struggled to follow the voice above the sound of the waterfall. Her lips peeled away from teeth that dripped viscous black, and her arms stretched to twice their normal length. Iskra lay at her feet. My mother stepped onto her, a bare foot pressing hard into Iskra's stomach as if she wasn't there at all, as she craned her neck to listen.

The creature nearest gave a tug on Iskra's leg, and my mother spilled onto the stone with an inhuman shriek. And then my mother was gone, her visage wiped away. The creatures returned to Iskra, rumbling and keening as they popped her arm from its socket, an eye from her skull. They tugged at her, collecting pieces of her into their distended arms, until they were all satisfied. Once they had their fill, the largest of the bunch took hold of her ankle, straightened, and leapt into the dark without a sideways glance. What remained of Iskra's body thudded and slid over the stone and into the cold pool. The others followed, gnawing on their spoils.

We were alone. Iskra was gone. And for the first time in eight years, I had seen my mother's face.

Beck's fingers slipped from my mouth with all the gentleness in the world. The vice of his legs around my torso slackened, and he slumped against the wall with a hard exhale. The tips of my fingers were cold to the point of numbness, wrinkled and pale where they lay, limp, in the water beneath us.

My eyes remained fixed upon a point just beyond the waterfall: a patch of slickness colored black in the sputtering light of the flare, a puddle of something that had once been Iskra. I could still hear the voice over the sound of the waterfall: the pop of sinew and bone, like a splitting melon; the gargling of blood flooding a throat; the rip of flesh from flesh.

Beck shifted, and a picked-clean bone cracked over a smooth stone.

A horrible, braying yelp ripped from me as I came back to myself, pushing away from Beck and scrambling away from him on all fours. The waterfall misted my hair as I hunched, tucking my head between my knees and biting down on my tongue as I fought the urge to retch.

Beck's voice was low and even. "Now you see why I need you to do precisely what I tell you," he said.

I lifted my head, what little color remained flaring in my cheeks. With a gulp of cold air, I curled my fingers in the sodden fabric of my jeans. "You . . ." another deep breath, a shuddering exhale, "Is that *really* all you have to say right now?" Before I could catch myself, I sat upright and felt around the dark floor for a rock. With a cry, and a crack of my joints, I hurled it at him. The rock went wide, pinging against the rock wall and skittering off into the darkness beyond the flare's reach.

"It's for your *protection*, Caroline—"

"What the fuck was that?" My voice ricocheted higher, cracking in an ugly half-sob. My hands trembled, lips wet with tears that spilled hot and free over my cheeks. "Iskra! Iskra was just—" I whirled. "She was just right there. She . . . and then she—"

Beck reached for me, expression twisted with concern, and I shied away. "There's nothing we could have done."

"She's *dead!*"

He closed the gap between us, scrambling on his knees. His hands were hard on my arms, bruising the flesh beneath my sweater as he shook me painfully, harshly. He looked like he was only a moment away from slapping me. "Pull yourself together!" he hissed. "Dear God, Caroline, just listen to me."

"Get off!" I put my hands on his shoulders and gave him a shove. The effort sent me reeling, falling back until the cool condensation misting off the waterfall formed heavy rivulets on my brow. "Someone in *your* care just died, Beck! This is the third 'someone' actually, if you weren't keeping count—"

"I know, all right? I know." He wiped his palms on the front of his jacket, as if my hysteria had dirtied him somehow. "But *you* are alive, and that is all that matters to me right now."

I couldn't hear it, couldn't respond to it. Under different circumstances, I might have swooned at the heroism implied here, but it rang hollow. He had saved me, sure – but he *hadn't* saved Iskra. He hadn't even tried. "Who was that little girl? She was following a little girl, wasn't she? I saw it."

"So did I."

"What the fuck *was* that, Edward? Who were those *people*?" I didn't want to tell him precisely who I'd seen, who had flashed before my eyes like a grotesque phantom. But Beck was supposed to have all the answers. Surely he would have all the answers.

And yet he shook his head. Slowly, as if he could scarcely bring himself to admit it. "I don't think it's for us to understand," he said, voice measured. "I saw the girl, yes. And then I saw . . . what she became."

"You didn't see . . ." I began, biting the tip of my tongue. "You saw what they turned into? *Monsters?*" I baited him as best I could without showing my hand. There was no sound way to ask if Beck had seen the little girl that Iskra was following turn into my dead mother.

Beck shook his head. He opened his mouth to speak, furrowed his brow, and then closed it again. He reached into the front pocket of his coat and produced the journal, bending over it and rifling through its marked-up pages furiously.

Of course.

Carefully, I found my way to my feet with another rock clutched in my shaking hand. I wavered on my feet, the furious pounding of my heart making me lightheaded. With a grunt, I tossed it out from behind the water, listening as it bounced across the stone floor. I held my breath. Nothing came. The creatures had disappeared further into the cave system, with Iskra's body in tow – but that didn't mean that they were gone.

A glint of light caught my eye. Iskra's camera sat half-submerged in the water, the light of the flare reflecting off the broken lens. I crept out into the open cavern, leaving Beck to his journal. As soon as I lifted it from the water, curling my cold fingers around the neck strap, I felt terrible warmth squelch between my fingertips.

Nausea roiled in my stomach. My throat tightened. I shut my eyes as I hung the bloody camera around my neck. If we were lucky, Iskra would have gotten a shot or two of the creatures – or of the little girl. *Sister.* The word hung in the air like a scythe. I thought of her bloated skin, the dull, rotten color of her flesh, and the familiar haziness of her eyes. More corpse than girl; more specter than human.

And how quickly she had changed, shifted into something monstrous before my very eyes.

Would Beck watch *me* as I died? Would he write in his journal about how prettily I had spilled all across the stone?

Where the hell are we?

He emerged from behind the waterfall, lip trapped between his teeth. Without a care for his sodden socks, he sloshed through the water to stand at my shoulder.

"We need to gather all the others," I said. My voice was weak; I was in no position of authority, and had no grounds to tell anyone what to do. Surely Beck could see how hard I shook as I stooped and took up Iskra's flare. We'd all been given one. Iskra had used hers when it counted. "There's no telling where they are, how far they went; if those things found them—"

"It's a test." Beck cut me off. To my surprise, and my utter horror, the taut corners of his lips curled upward. His gaze snapped upward. Thrill shone there. Bloodthirst.

"*What?*" Maybe I hadn't heard him right. Maybe I was unconscious; it could very well be that he had knocked me over the head to keep me quiet as Iskra had been torn to pieces. But, then again, there was no imagining such a thing. I blinked, flare hanging limp at my side.

Beck tapped a page of his journal. "Look here," he said. I didn't move. "We're being *tested*, Caroline. In all my studies, it always came back to a Cloister of Trials—"

I scoffed, the sound ricocheting up the steep walls of the cavern. My knuckles had gone white around the neck of the flare. "Are you out of your fucking mind?" I spat. "We just saw a woman *die*, and you think that it was – what – some kind of *pop quiz*? Did . . . did she *fail*, Beck? Is that why I've got her blood on me?"

He shook his head, as if my words were nothing more than an annoyance, clouding his ability to focus. With a huff, he shifted his sagging pack atop his shoulders. "You don't understand, Caro—"

"No, I don't."

"This confirms everything I could only claim on the basis of a theory." He tapped the journal again, thrusting it toward me. I took a step back. "I always believed that it existed, that this was of paramount importance in their worship practices, but . . . but there was no proof of it. And this is why. It's a trial by ordeal. This is *it*."

My mind whirred. I felt dizzy, sick. "I don't believe you." I turned on a heel and started toward the wall, flare held aloft. The creatures had come from all directions; even if I'd fallen from a height impossible to reach now, I could find another way.

"You don't have to believe for it to be true!" Beck's voice was an echo. Iskra's blood had begun to cool at the back of my neck. His footsteps scuffed behind me as he followed, harried as he kept within the boundary of the red light. "If we can understand what's really happening here, we can—"

"Get the fuck out and never come back, yes," I clipped.

"Make the *best* of it. Make certain that no tragedy done here was done in vain."

I came to a stop. Anders, Leon. Iskra. They were merely collateral, unfortunate variables that didn't shake out in the solving of an impossible equation. I could taste bile at the back of my throat. Maybe I could give Beck the benefit of the doubt; maybe this was how he processed trauma, how he made sense of it all. Everyone dealt with shit in their own way. But I could hear no empathy in his voice, no sadness for the body we couldn't even bury.

My fingers were numb on the rim of my headlight. I fumbled for the switch as the flare sputtered and gasped at my side, fighting the deluge of cold water into which it had been plunged in Iskra's fall.

"We need to get everyone out," I repeated. "Find the other exit, call the Navy. People are *dead*, Beck." I turned to him, hoping beyond hope that I would see understanding written plainly across his face. To my relief, he seemed to wilt, brows drawing together and lips tugging down at the corners. But his eyes – they remained the same.

"We *cannot* call the Navy," he snapped.

"And why not?"

A long pause stretched between us, dissipating into the dark. "If – if we continue on, I believe that the exit will present itself to us," he said. I scoffed and turned from him again, dropping to my hands to begin the slippery ascent to the most accessible passage. "We don't *need* the Navy. This is what I was called to do, Caroline," Beck insisted, his voice growing louder. My toe slipped, and the heel of my hand scraped on the rock. I reached for a jut of protruding stone in the wall of the passage and hauled myself up. "We *will* see them through it. We just . . . We need to do it the right way."

I said nothing as I hauled myself up and into the passage, wasting no time in waiting for Beck as I pressed forward, holding the flare over my head. He had seen the girl. He had seen Iskra careening into the dark, chasing a specter. Did he imply, now, that it had been a test? What was she supposed to do? *Look away?*

I wondered what Beck had seen. What shape had it taken for him? A small part of me wanted to ask, to poke and prod without setting the beast of his ambition on a spiral. I didn't want to fuel this fire, didn't want him to believe that I, too, was part of some grand design. There was no design – there was only tragedy.

I opened my mouth to call out to the others, but quickly snapped it shut again. Beck and I weren't equipped to fight the things off. We had ice axes hooked to our belts, sure, but we weren't fighters. Hell, I had lost my membership card to the campus gym a week into my first semester. Maybe Oliver could fight. He seemed capable. But not the others. Not me.

And I couldn't shake the image of my mother from my mind. The sound of her voice, the familiar silhouette; she had haunted me only in dreams, in nightmares, until now. But there was no *losing* one's mother. Even dead, a mother was still a mother. She was part of you, whether you liked it or not.

If this was a test, it was a cruel one. Pull out the darkest and most diseased parts of us, and make them flesh. I wondered what the full inscription at the mouth of the cave had said. "*A profound offering of the darkest self.*" But what else? Instructions, maybe. A warning. Part of me wished to see what Beck's notes contained. Even the wildest nonsense carried *some* truth. Even if it wasn't a test, and the inscriptions in the collapsed cave weren't instructions, maybe they were a warning. Maybe I could learn from them, suss out just what it was that lived in here with us.

I didn't want to be tested. I knew with certainty what my dark passenger looked like. Her voice was everywhere, and her face had shown itself to me. Objectively, there was no way that my mother was here. I had been there at the very moment of her death – me, and me alone. But the moment had made me diseased. Ugly, beneath the surface. Were I to be tested, it would be my mother who I'd see here, who I would chase down the corridor to a watery end.

No – I wouldn't. I couldn't. Not again.

And what would Beck's test be? Would it be me? Would a dark double of my own face appear from the water to tear him limb from limb?

I hoped Mallory was safe. If anyone here were to survive this, I would want it to be her.

"*No.*" Such a foreign word to me. Caro was easy, Caro was agreeable; Caro never did anything contrary, and was simply born empty. My therapist talked over and over about boundaries, and I'd never really made an attempt. Now was as good a time as any to try. "No," I said again, voice louder in the narrow passage.

"What do you mean 'no'?" Beck came to a stop, the stamping halt of his footsteps echoing.

I turned on my heel, holding the flare like a sword at my side. In the red light, Beck looked inhuman. The shadows beneath his eyes were deep and endless, the hollow of his cheeks pronounced.

"*No* to this stupid 'rite'," I said. I inclined my chin and puffed my chest. "*No* to indulging in 'maybes' and 'what-ifs'. We need to deal in facts, in absolutes, or we're all dead as fuck."

Setting healthy boundaries requires self-awareness, my therapist said. *We need to be clear about our expectations of ourselves and others, and what we are and are not comfortable with.* I was uncomfortable with the idea of dying here because Beck was categorically convinced that an ancient civilization worshiped some stupid oversized sea snake. I had very few expectations of myself; my greatest defining feature was that I knew so very little about myself. I had been raised to be pliable, a canvas made for filling. But I knew this, and I knew it with startling and sudden clarity: it wouldn't be *me*, Caroline Anne

Destler, if I let anyone else die. It went against what I understood of myself, this fledgling *me*. It was a spark. I intended to follow it.

"Caroline—"

"S-so," I stuttered, face flushing. It was lucky that the flare hid the rush of color. "*No*, Edward. We get everyone out. We follow the air current that Dorothy found. And we come back later."

Beck took a step forward, and I took a step back. "What you fail to understand is that it's already been *done*, Caro," he said. "The trial has already begun, if my notes are anything to go by; and I've been right as rain so far. There *is* no stopping."

I scoffed, and the sound filled the passage like the cocking of a gun. "It's actually insane that you want to put your research above human lives."

He shook his head. "That's not what I'm saying at all, and I resent that you are willfully misinterpreting—"

"*Willfully misinterpreting?*"

"The *only* way to get out of this place is to carry on with the intention of completing the rite. It's not a goddamn scantron. You can't just tear it up halfway through."

The ground rumbled beneath us, loose rock clattering between the toes of my boots. I pressed my hand flat to the wall.

An idea struck me.

I tugged the ice ax from the loop in my belt, and turned to the wall. Propping the flare between my teeth, I took it in both hands and set to work drawing an arrow away from the waterfall, the cavern at our backs. Beneath, I carved my name. Beck's was omitted; a petty thing, maybe, but it made me feel better. If anyone were to stumble through here in search of the others, they would find this. And hopefully it would bring them back to us.

I carried on in marking the wall as we pressed forward in silence. Without the ropes and markers given to us by the Grundstadts, which sat, unused, in the bag I'd left behind, it would be difficult to make any sense of our position. This was better than nothing.

We said nothing else to one another as we pressed on, clambering up steep inclines and squeezing through narrow passages. There was no rhyme or reason to our trajectory; I recognized nothing as we moved from passage to passage, marking corners and intersections as we went. Not that it mattered much; it all looked the same, after a while. Harsh stalagmites arrowing up from the ground, columns of salt-slick limestone, holes in the stone floor with stagnant water so dark that it was black. We jumped the water, touched the stalagmites as if for good luck. I felt along the wall as we went, my legs heavy beneath me.

The tips of my fingers found roughness in the stone. I lifted the flare.

An arrow, carved sloppily into the stone and punctuated with a lopsided "*CARO*" cast shadow upon the broad wall. I lifted the flame higher. The tip of my ax was still dirty with limestone dust.

"I—" Eyes wide, I turned back to Beck. He had kept a steady pace with me, eyes down. I had been relieved that he'd said nothing, that he'd left well enough alone. But now his silence unsettled me. His lips were pursed in a hard line, his brow knit. "Didn't we just . . . We didn't turn around, did we?"

He shook his head, brow furrowed and lips drawn. Still, he said nothing.

"We must have. That's— that's okay. We should just keep going." I was talking to myself. Beck met my gaze and held it, but I could see in the thin line of his lips and the hard set of his jaw that he would say nothing to assuage the discordant note of fear in my voice. And so I turned round again, held the flare high, and quickened my steps.

We walked in silence for only a moment before another break in the floor – dark water, and a stalagmite. And then as I felt at the wall, my fingers found a hard line, the telling strike of an ax-tip, appeared on the wall at the height of my eyes. I stopped, and Beck did the same. An arrow. And my name.

I switched the flare to my other hand, willing the shadows to hide the tightness of my jaw, the quiver of my lip. Again, after a few moments of walking another mark – same as the last, and same as the first – in the wall appeared on our right. My name, and an arrow.

I didn't stop, speeding up further still. My heart pounded in my ears and my stomach ached. When was the last time I'd eaten?

There was a pattern here. My name on the wall, my wonky arrow. I should have counted the stalagmites, considered the number of steps between the breaks in the floor, the pools of obsidian water – or was it *one* pool? The same pool, over and over? Just as my name continued to appear over, and over, and over again – were we going in a circle? We had to be. Of course we had to be.

Beck's hand flew out, his fingers knotting in the damp fabric of my shirt. He pulled me back hard, hard enough to send me spilling onto my back and knocking him against the wall. The flare slipped from my grasp, and I flipped onto all fours and scrambled across the rock to retrieve it.

Beck merely watched, slumped against the wall with a hand pressed to his heart. He breathed heavily, nostrils flaring. I could read nothing in his face as I whirled on him, fist rigid at my side.

"What the *fuck*?" My voice was a boom. "If you think I'm gonna sit here and let you jerk me around—"

He pointed over my shoulder. I stared at him for a long moment, wondering what might happen if I lunged and bit his outstretched finger. But then I obliged, slowly turning to see what it was he had seen.

There, in the floor, was the same stretch of opaque water. Inky blackness, still as the surface of a mirror; we had hopped over it time and time again; it should have been muscle memory by now. But I was spiraling. I could feel it, each belabored breath more claustrophobic than the first.

"I will continue to save your life whether or not you like it, Caroline," he clipped, eyes hard. "Whether or not you believe me." A pause, a sigh, as his hand slipped from his heart. "And it is important to me, even now, that *you* believe me."

My mouth opened, then closed again. His expression was earnest, the shadows beneath his eyes warping and dancing in the light of the flare. It had always been thus: Beck and I trusted each other, believed each other, despite all the wildness and disarray of his work. He and I believed in every impossible thing; we believed in each other. A prickling of guilt tempted me, weakened me; I could feel it scratching at the indignation I'd built between us, a haphazard defense against the paradox of this place.

"Of course I believe you," I said, voice watery. "I'll always believe you. I—" *love you? need you? feel frightened of you?* "I just need to see it for myself. Theories and understanding, right?"

I left no time for him to rebut, to talk me off whatever ledge I was likely to throw myself off. Instead, I scrambled to my feet and leapt over the pool. My legs ached beneath me as I broke into a run, head throbbing and eyes wheeling. I knew that Beck would keep pace with me regardless.

To my right, an arrow. My name. Further ahead, a mark in the wall on the left. Further still, the unbroken pool of inky water. Again: arrow, mark, pool. And again.

At last, as I hunched with hands on my knees before the carved arrow, Beck spoke. "Have we reached the point where I remind you of the definition of insanity?" he asked. His voice was even, as if he had barely expended any energy in keeping pace. "We didn't turn around. We didn't get lost. We didn't make a wrong turn. Everywhere we look, Caroline, it's either a dead end . . . or this. The others came down this same passage to look for Iskra. Why do you think we haven't come across any of them?"

I sank to the floor. Loose stone shifted beneath me as I let the flare clatter from my grasp. There was no hiding the quivering of my lip or the wetness of my cheeks, no matter how much I wished to. Beck was the last person I'd ever want to see me cry. He was someone who meant something. He was someone to tell me who I was, and who I could be. And yet I couldn't stop it, couldn't staunch the tears as they flowed freely, sliding over my cheeks and down my neck to mingle with the cool slick of blood on the strap of Iskra's camera.

Beck slid closer to me. I could feel him hesitate for a long moment, and then a warm hand pressed to the shuddering space between my shoulder blades.

"Fear is good, Caroline," he said, his thumb drawing circles atop the damp fabric of my sweater. "Fear means that you're alive. If you weren't afraid, I'd be more concerned."

I wondered if he understood just what it was that I feared. There was darkness in all of us; it was what made us human. But I had fought to bury it, to let the past die in every way that mattered. My dark passenger was never meant to see the light of day. A legal name change, a set of adoption papers, and a shit-ton of therapy had *tried* to see to that, anyhow. And yet I had seen her, this dark passenger, with my own two eyes. If I was being tested, truly tested, as Beck believed, then I would see her again.

Nothing was more frightening than that. Nothing – no beasts, or darkness, or solitude. I was afraid of nothing more than my mother. And she was here. Somehow, even if she was nothing more than a specter half-remembered, she was here. And I was more afraid than I had ever been.

Idly, I lifted the camera from around my neck and turned it upright. The lens was cracked beyond repair, the flash shattered. I turned it over, and pressed the power button. The light of the screen was blinding, drowning the flare's red glow.

The first picture to load was of Mallory and I. Though no more than an hour and change had passed, it felt like a relic. I wiped my thumb over Mallory's face, cleaning away the grime and blood. My own face remained obscured; it was better that way. Even in the red light, I could tell that Anders's blood had dried between the freckles on my brow, on the bridge of my nose. My hair, ruddy brown, was a rat's nest. Mallory looked just fine. It was an outside-in sort of thing, I supposed. She was just *good* enough that it always poked through the cracks.

And there, in the background of the photo, a little girl peered out from the shadows. She didn't look inquisitive, puzzled in a way that a little girl should be. Her attention seemed focused over our heads, directly on the woman behind the camera. In the low light of the photo, it was hard to see the bloat of her gray skin or the dullness of her clouded eyes. Her lips were tugged downward, as if in disappointment.

You're not supposed to be here, she'd said.

If this had been a test, then there was no way for Iskra to pass. What was the answer? What was the question?

"I just want to go *home*," I said.

"We will." Beck pressed a kiss to my shoulder, and the tears surged.

I leaned into his touch instinctively, and he tucked a damp curl behind my ear. "*How?*"

He took a deep breath. "Are you ready to entertain my solution?" He said it in a way that a parent might ask a child if they'd finished pitching a fit. "There's no logical explanation for how we've passed the same landmarks three, four times. Right?"

"Right." My voice was watery. Pathetic.

"So we abandon logic. We abandon all pretense of what we think we understand of the way the world works." His hand slipped from my back, and reappeared beneath my knee with the black journal clutched firmly. He gave it a tap. "We follow the path prescribed for us by those who walked it first. Like the *true* anthropologist I know you are. There's magic here, and in the history. Let it happen."

I gave a weak half-laugh. Now was not the time to tell him that I had no intention of pursuing *anthropology* if we survived this. "Assistant anthropologist." The joke fizzled and splattered like mud. But Beck seemed to appreciate the effort, for he placed a hand on my back again and gave my spine a rub.

"Good girl," he said. "I've dedicated my whole life to this, Caroline. You can trust in me. And in my work. Have I ever led you astray?"

Well. Maybe not *me*, but his wife certainly lived somewhere in the territory of "astray".

I shook my head. Better to lie and get along than to peel off an old scab. "No, you haven't," I sniffled.

"Exactly. So we get up, we set our intention, and we see what shakes out. If we trust the research, there's no telling what will be revealed to us." He thumbed through the journal, the ink-heavy pages slapping wetly. "You and I are prepared. We know what's to come."

"Do we?"

"Yes." There was no doubt in him. Not for a second. Beck moved to sit across from me, towering and undeniable as he gripped my shoulders. He hunched, his eyes level with mine. "A profound offering of the darkest self, remember? What does that sound like to you?"

It sounded like insanity. Pure and fucking undiluted madness. But the arrow in the wall was madness. The sight of my mother was madness. What other option did I have but to follow where it led?

"Sounds like a test. Or a confession."

He nodded, giving my shoulders a squeeze. The flare spat sparks between us, but only I jumped. "There are no secrets down here, by the rules of this place. There's no disbelief. The Leviathan will keep us all suspended in amber until we relent. It's what she wants – what she's asked of her devotees for millennia. It's about absolute honesty." Another squeeze. "There's no true enlightenment without being broken down to your barest parts first. That's a given."

"Oh, good." I could muster little else. "So we'll all have our dirty laundry aired for the world to see? Is the Leviathan gonna show everyone a highlight reel of every time we've fucked in your office?" *No.* Certainly not. That was not my greatest shame. *Beck* was not my shadow.

But his lips quirked up at the corners nevertheless. If he knew I was lying, deflecting, it didn't show. And how could he know? "I appreciate your ability to find humor in these moments, Caro," he said, eyes softening. His head dipped toward mine, and I acquiesced, pressing my brow to his. "Hang on to that."

I sniffed. "This is insane."

"Of course it is," he said. "But that doesn't make it any less real."

A long moment of silence passed between us. I squeezed my eyes shut tight, scrunching my nose and puckering my lips. Maybe if I *clenched* hard enough, we'd pop out of this place and back onto the shore in a gust of wind and magic. Stranger things had already happened today.

But no. We were alone, with nothing but a flare to ward against the dark.

"*Fine.*"

"Fine . . . what?" His voice was goading, the edge of thrill unmistakable. Beck's hand remained at my shoulders, the thin veneer of comfort a direct contradiction with the unfamiliar edge in his voice. And as the decision crystallized in my mind, fear alchemizing to determination, the floor beneath our feet shuddered. A scraping of stone on stone, the keening of a beast.

I lifted my brow from his. "We do it your way."

The strap of Iskra's camera peeled off my neck like a bandage. Slick, squelching, the cold blood left behind a strip of congealing crimson. I held the camera lamely, shuffling my feet as Beck took the lead in the narrow cavern. What would I tell the others when we found them? How would I describe it to them?

It was a short journey. We rounded a sloped corner, ducked beneath a dip in the stone ceiling, and the grotto unfolded before us like a warm hearth.

"See?" Beck said. "All we had to do was give in."

The group's belongings scattered across the space; a dropped bag here, an abandoned notebook there. We'd dropped everything to pursue Iskra, arrowing out into the dark blindly. And what did I have to show for it?

Our footsteps echoed as we hopped the narrow stream in silence. Beck moved quickly, plopping his heavy bag down atop the table as I clambered up onto the dais. It landed with a thump.

"What's in your bag that's so heavy?" I asked. My voice cracked, raw and aching, as if it had been years since I'd last spoken. "That thing's gonna throw your back out."

"Supplies," Beck clipped. To my surprise, he looked unamused. The small smile I'd attempted, a marionette-string tug at the corner of my chapped lips, wilted. "The likes of which you would do well to keep on your person."

I sniffed, rubbing the bloody heel of my hand across my brow. "I don't know what to do now," I said. "Do we just . . . wait?"

Beck nodded. The sudden tension dissipated, as if it had never been. For a moment, he turned back to me. A hand outstretched, a swipe of clean fingers through the blood over my eye; he looked at me like he was proud of me, like maybe we were in this thing together after all. "For now. We need to wait for the others." And that was that. Easy, simple. He hunched over his notes, eyes darting across one page, and then the next. It sounded obvious, the way he said it; Mallory had just taken a wrong turn at the stalagmite, and needed to reroute. Hannah had simply ducked into the next room to take a call. He was back to his notes like this was nothing but a dark classroom, like what awaited us was a lecture hall and not . . . *that.* He'd said it himself: they all followed Iskra. All had gone down the same passage. But none had found her but us. I watched as he flattened an ink-riddled page full of familiar Enochian symbols with the practiced tips of his fingers, murmuring each phrase under his breath. His eyes darted up, past me, to the inscriptions on the columns lining the room. He looked off in the direction of the collapsed entrance, paying little mind as I fidgeted at his side.

"Are we not even a little concerned about the possibility that we could be attacked and *eaten* at any moment?" I ventured.

He lifted his eyes and held my gaze. Steady. Unyielding. "No," he said, unmistakable finality in his even tone. If it was supposed to be comforting, this surety, it almost certainly was not. "That's not how it works."

I set the flare on the table and wandered to my bag, which I'd left discarded at the edge of the platform. "Of course," I muttered, voice low. "Oh, yeah, that's how it works. Of *course.* 'Scuse me. Must have missed that section of the handbook. Was Iskra supposed to happen, then? Since you know." Beck didn't answer for a long moment. And then, infuriatingly, said, "It's not for us to understand. The grander design. We can be curious, sure. Question it if we must.

But saying that something was 'supposed' to happen feels reductive. There's more at work here than the black and white of a hypothesis and a conclusion."

A scoff cracked from me as I turned away. "That's sociopathic."

"It's anthropologically sound." His voice was hard. "I didn't want her to die, Caroline, if that's what you think. Obviously I didn't. I take no pleasure in her death. But accidents happen. Variables."

"*Variables.*"

I spilled the contents of my bag onto the floor: a first aid kit, the likes of which would likely do no more for me than patch a scrape, a baggie of protein bars and loose almonds, a thermal blanket tied with a Velcro strip, a length of rope in a waterproof bag, my phone, and Mallory's colorful socks. I looked down at my own. They hadn't been red when I left the hotel. With a gulp, I slipped off my boots and peeled the sodden socks off my feet.

As I took up my phone, a picture of the horses that lived in the pasture across the street from the co-op flashed onto the screen. The phone was nearly dead, stuttering and lagging. Futilely, I held it over my head, stretching high. No signal. Of course.

I paused, the wrinkled flesh of my thumb hovering over the clock. The time was wrong, by all accounts; the last time I'd checked my phone, before transferring from the fishermen's boats to the kayaks, it had been just before one o'clock. About a quarter till, if I remembered correctly. Objectively, there was no real way to tell how much time had passed between now and then, save the weariness in my bones and the telltale rumbling in my stomach. But time *had* passed.

1:18. About half an hour after we'd left Joseph and Ellis. It had taken half an hour to make landfall on the rocky shore of the cave, to poke around, to decode the runes on the wall and take stock of our now-lost caving equipment. Half an hour, and then the stone above our heads had buried the Grundstadts.

I gave the phone a shake and a slap against my damp thigh. For a long moment, I squinted down at the screen. I willed it to change, as if I could fry the water from my phone in a puff of steam and set it working again just by glaring at it hard enough. But the time remained the same. I watched the clock for well over a minute – and nothing.

"Can't unpack that now," I muttered under my breath. "Cannot fucking do that right now."

My head spun. There was too much to digest here. Beck seemed right at home, as if this were an exam that he'd been studying for his entire life. He scoured his notes, hunched over the table with his sodden curls hanging heavily over the page. By the vermillion light of the flare, he made his preparations.

I wondered what the trial might make of me; what the Leviathan would make of me, if it was real. If I was to be tested, like all the others, would I be found wanting? In such company, maybe the trial would skip me entirely. I was nothing noteworthy. There wasn't enough of me to test. For what of *me* was really *me?* What of the inscrutable "self" was really something stolen from someone else? The Leviathan couldn't fault me for what I'd had to do to survive. Could it?

If Beck was right, this was my choice. I would be presented with the truth of myself – the horrible, ugly reality of what I was and what I wasn't. Would I have to fight it? Apologize on my knees? Iskra hadn't been given a chance at all.

But she wasn't even supposed to *be* here. Did that mean that I was? Did that mean that my soul was already being weighed? Would I die when I was found wanting?

Once I was sure that my feet were dry enough, I tugged on Mallory's colorful socks: cats and rainbows, all colored red in the light of the flare. I wiggled my toes. Mallory needed to survive this place.

I let my eyes drift to the boundary between the flare's light and the passage beyond as I slipped on my boots. *You're not supposed to be here*, the girl had said. She'd stood right there, plain and real as any one of us. If Beck believed that we were all divinely called to be here, that we were the missing variables in the trial's incomprehensible equation, why had the creature told Iskra the opposite?

You're not supposed to be here.

Iskra had been filling in for a friend. I remembered her excitement, her gratitude. The camera wasn't even hers.

I watched the empty space at the edge of the grotto.

Was *I* supposed to be here? Was this the inscrutable, unobtainable *thing* that I had been without my entire life? Most people had purpose of some kind. Was this mine?

Movement flickered at the edge of my vision. I turned, expecting to see Mallory, or Hannah, or even that insufferable author.

Overlong fingers curled around the pocked surface of a limestone column, dirty fingernails grinding into the carved lettering of the inscrutable runes that lived there. Not dirt – *blood.* The fingernails were ragged, half-ripped from the broken skin beneath. The hem of a nightgown, linen with faded posies and daffodils, fluttered in the crimson light. A bare foot slid around the rounded edge of the column, then a leg. Hair hanging heavy with wetness dangled out from behind the column as an atrophied cheek, a half-rotted mouth, a bloodied chin drifted into view. Foam and bile bubbled at the corners of the specter's lips, which peeled away from filthy, broken teeth.

The aspect of my mother inhaled, wetness popping on her tongue and in her lungs. She was far – nearly all the way across the cavern – and yet I could hear the sound as if she stood over my shoulder. She inhaled, and I heard the rattling of hinges, the juddering of a jammed doorknob. Her mouth swung open, filth spilling down the front of her nightgown.

I wrenched my gaze back to the frozen phone in my hands. I watched the time, willed it desperately to change, to move, to give me *anything* to look at aside from the painfully familiar revenant. She was not an unfamiliar sight; I saw her whenever I closed my eyes, whenever I looked in the mirror for a moment too long. She was in every dark corner. And she was *here.*

With a flush of terror, I craned my neck to look back at Beck. I wouldn't know what to tell him if he saw her now; I was unmistakable in her likeness, even rotten, dead, and decaying far beyond her time.

This was a test. Nightmares made flesh; secrets made tangible. What was it about this very moment of her grave-deep decomposition that appealed? Was it the fact that, in this suspended moment, her face was still visible in mine?

But Beck hadn't looked up from his notes.

"Edward?" I called out to him, and I hated the sound of watery emotion in my voice. I shook, my teeth chattering.

He looked up at once, concern painted upon his face. And he looked to me – only to me. When I didn't speak, when I merely stared at him when I realized I had no idea what to say, he cast a glance around the room. I followed his eyes, tracked them as they traveled to the farthest boundary of the flare's light.

"Are you all right, darling?"

I could have wilted beneath the genuine concern. Even more so, beneath the relief that he couldn't see her, where she'd draped herself around the column with a hyena's smile. She was for me alone. My secrets were still my own.

"I'm fine," I lied. "I just—" I searched for something, anything to say. "I never thanked you for . . . for keeping me from doing something impulsive." It wouldn't have been an impulse to try to save Iskra. It would have been humane. It also would have been stupid, and fatal. "I think I would have ended up like Iskra, had you not—" I took a deep breath. It still felt cowardly, to have spent Iskra's last moments hiding behind the roaring waterfall. Better cowardly and alive, than brave and dead, I guessed.

A smile bloomed on Beck's face. His fingers pressed between the dog-eared pages of his journal. "You would have done the same for me."

I would have. I would have done it then, and I'd do it now. Foolish, undoubtedly. Once we left this place, he would go back to his wife, we would return to our pretending. But I couldn't help it. Love struck who it wished, without any say-so from those caught in its collateral.

"I would," I said.

"We'll keep each other safe," he said. It was a nice idea. I believed him wholeheartedly. "The two of us – we can best this thing together. I trust you more than anyone."

My gaze flickered sidelong. Even now, my mother watched. Did it kill her now, in this half-rotted state, to see me *happy* with someone who truly cared for me? We could leave this place together. He would leave his unhappy marriage, as he'd promised, and we would make our fortune telling the story of how we bested a *god*.

Whether or not the deity in question really existed was secondary. It was the story that mattered.

"Together," I echoed. "Absolutely."

What remained of my mother's thumbnail cracked on the stone. She dragged her hand down along the length of the column, as if she wanted nothing more than to pry it open and claw inside. I squeezed my eyes shut. She wasn't real. *Beck* was real. *I* was real.

I sat upright, and thought with some vindication of the method my therapist taught me for grounding myself in present moments. She had taken my admission of hallucinations, night terrors, and bouts of unexplainable anger in stride, and had given me a solution that came to her as easily as if she was explaining how to get to the nearest Piggly Wiggly.

"I look around to find five things I can see," she'd said. "Four things I can touch, three things I can hear, two things I can smell, and one thing I can taste. The last one's usually my gum, or a bit of errant toothpaste, but it works. It's called grounding."

I'd told her in no uncertain terms that I did *not* have time in my every day to sit around and count things. I was a graduate student with two jobs, after all. God, I barely had time to *eat*. But I had time now.

I counted. I could see my phone, Beck, the runes on the nearest column, an unlit brazier heavy with blackened stone, and the colorful pattern of Mallory's socks. Next, I touched the rough zipper of the waterproof bag that held the climbing rope, a tear in the knee of my jeans. I ran my finger along the ridge of the stone dais, and then the smooth plastic of the first aid kit I'd been given by the cavers.

I listened. All I could hear, at present, was the horrible thrumming of my own heart and the groaning of my empty stomach. Something told me that that wasn't what my therapist had meant. And so I listened, and listened.

And I heard . . . Mallory.

I shot to my feet, my phone clattering to the floor. Beck startled, nicking the tip of his finger on a loose leaf of paper.

"*Mallory!?*" My voice was ragged, and my head throbbed, but the boom of her name – it was everything.

"Caro!" Her name rang from beyond the dark, from the passage that Beck and I had emerged from. I scrambled down the slope, leapt over the narrow stream, and felt along the wall beyond the light of the flare.

She emerged from the dark, Hannah's arm slung over her shoulder. Hannah dragged her leg behind her, wincing every time she was forced to put weight on it. Sweat beaded Mallory's brow; it had all but wiped away her makeup, dark streaks of mascara trailing from her heavy lashes to the curve of her jaw. One hand was clinging to Hannah's waist, keeping her upright; her other reached out for me and I took hold of her with all the strength I could muster.

"I lost you when we all went running," Mallory huffed. I took to Hannah's other side, and she sagged gratefully against me. "It was so dark, I lost sight of you for no more than a *second*, and you were gone. Everyone was gone. Where are the others? Where's Iskra?"

I stared down at the dark floor, picking over holes in the stone as I helped Mallory guide Hannah to the table. There would be no easy way to describe it; I wasn't sure I had totally processed it myself. I wouldn't, not really, until I could see the sun again.

I couldn't say it. It had felt almost unreal when it was just Beck and I. But now that there were others here, now that her absence was more obvious than ever . . .

Before I could think otherwise, I stepped over Hannah's outstretched feet and wrapped my arms around Mallory's middle. She let out a small sound, a surprised "*oh!*" but didn't hesitate for even a second in pulling me close. In the corner of my periphery, I could see Beck pause, watching as Mallory squeezed me tight.

He spoke and the relief I felt at the sound of his voice, at the measured politics of his words, nearly turned my joints to water. "I think it's best if we wait for the others to find their way back," he said. "Better that we're all here when we . . . well, when we discuss what comes next."

Mallory pulled away, inclining her head to search my pinched visage. I shook my head. It was only then that her eyes fell to the dried swath of blood at my neck, to the telling swell of my eyes.

Hannah spoke before Mallory could. "Felt like I was going in circles the whole goddamn time," she said, leaning down and giving her swollen ankle a rub. "And then all of the sudden – *bam!* There's Mallory, and there's the sound of running water. We followed it back here. Lucky I found her when I did," Hannah nodded to Mallory, and she smiled sheepishly, rubbing her hand over the back of her neck as she skirted the platform toward her discarded pack. "Should have watched where I stepped. Where's my bag?"

"We had no sign of the others," Beck said, ignoring her request. "We've only just returned ourselves."

"So you two stuck together, then?" Hannah's gaze flitted between Beck and I. "I'd have wanted to stick together, too." I could hear the suggestion in her voice, and resented it. If she thought we'd taken the opportunity to *bang* while Iskra was being torn to pieces—

Anger rose like bile in the back of my throat. I had been the first to go after Iskra. I was more than just a goddamn toy that Beck carted around to sate his boredom. Beck trusted me with his work. He needed me – *want* had nothing to do with it.

I wondered if she'd still have jokes with *two* fucked ankles. We could certainly find out.

I spoke before I could stop myself. "Shame you couldn't watch where you were going. Are we going to have to pass you around? Take turns carrying your dead weight?"

Beck's eyes shot to me, wide with surprise. To my utter shock, his lips twitched and his brows ticked upward. He looked at me like I'd just shot fireworks out of my ears – amusement, and wonderment, and maybe a little pride. I could hear Mallory on the other side of the platform, tucked behind a column, barely audible over the pounding in my ears.

"Sheesh, kid," Hannah shifted, obvious chagrin on her face. By the light of the flare, she looked pinched, gaunt. The sheen of sweat on her brow was obvious, as were the hollow bruises beneath her eyes. "I'm just joshing."

"And I'm not a kid," I said. Though my hands shook at my sides, I inclined my chin. "Neither is Mallory."

She gaped, mouth flapping open and closed and open again like a fish. Angry tears prickled behind my eyes. The ground beneath my feet rumbled, and I felt along with it an unmistakable flush of satisfaction. Of *pleasure.*

The crimson light shifted, and a duo of silhouettes appeared, stretching long and looming up the rune-riddled wall.

Oh, thank fuck.

I was not the sort of person who could *do* conflict. In the moment, I did fine enough. But I did a great deal of crying in the shower – and rethinking every word I'd ever uttered – every time I'd so much as had to raise my voice. I was green, anemic; I fought like a child, simply because I didn't know any better, had never been *taught* any better.

But I was trying. Now was as good a time as any to *try.*

Oliver and Dorothy stumbled from the dark – from the single path in or out, I realized. Beck likely had expected this. He'd spoken of this place, and of the powers dictating it, like it was sentient. Maybe it was. Maybe it had simply waited to spit us all out in the same place when the dramatic timing felt right. I could respect it.

Hannah's gaze flitted from the others to me, mouth still hanging half-open, as I skittered away, grateful for any excuse to extricate myself from the conversation. I pressed the heel of my hand to my eye, coughing away the childish emotion that lodged in my throat. While Mallory rushed to greet them, I returned to where I had dumped my things and slowly began to collect them. The specter of my mother had disappeared with no ceremony. I was glad to see her go.

"Where's the photographer?" Dorothy's voice floated like a discordant note across the cavern to where I sat, hunched over my bag as I did my best to organize its contents. Anger flared within me. Sure, we all had only known each other for the better part of a day, but the least the bitch could do was learn *names.*

Luckily, once again, Beck spoke first. "That's . . . something we should discuss." I glanced over my shoulder to find his gaze on me, watching as I collected my things. His expression was inscrutable, the taut angle of his brow shadowing his eyes. But he watched me nevertheless, ready to leap across the space and save me from any other unfortunate and untimely death that I might throw myself at.

The others gathered. Hannah rose with some effort and slipped away from Oliver's outstretched arm, and I watched as she rifled through her bag and produced a bottle of pills from within. Her hands shook as she rattled a single pill out onto her palm, and swallowed it dry. She sagged visibly, glancing over her shoulder in a covert manner as the others gathered.

Mallory came to stand beside me, the ghost of a smile passing across her stricken features when her eyes fell upon the peek of color beneath the rolled hem of my jeans' legs. The socks endured.

No doubt they had all seen it coming. We were short one, after all. Not a word was spoken as Beck relayed Iskra's fate to the group. He did so clinically, like any affection he'd ever felt for Iskra had been washed away in the stream.

"I believe," he began, "that it is no mistake that our photographer was killed by the . . ." A pause. What to call them? I certainly didn't know. "The keepers of this place. We are intruding on sacred space, of course. Even if we *are* the latest crop to walk the path of our forebears, it stands to reason that intrusions are . . . to be met with skepticism."

He was doing an Olympic job of dancing around the truth of the matter. But there was no easy way to explain that Iskra had been torn to shreds, and that we had watched. My stomach turned at the thought, and I looked down at my hands. I didn't want to be an accomplice to this.

But Oliver spoke before Beck could continue. "Facts, Beck. Give us facts. I want to understand. Particularly, too, if I'm going to believe that some mythical cave-beasts crawled out of the stone to do it. Sounds like a shitty story made up to gloss over an entirely preventable tragedy."

Beck's eyes flared, and I felt the instinctive muscle-jerking urge to leap to his defense. Was the insinuation here that *Beck* had killed Iskra? Was it that she had fallen to her death and shattered like a doll on the rocks at the base of the waterfall? If Beck was dancing, Oliver was doing his darndest to step on his toes.

Hannah raised a single spindly finger, her glasses sliding lopsidedly down the bridge of her nose. "I'd like to see the body," she said. "Determine cause of death."

"You can't," Beck answered quickly, before anyone else could make demands.

Hannah and Oliver spoke in tandem:

"*I can't?*"

"She can't?"

Beck seemed undeterred. He shook his head, holding tight to his journal. "You cannot," he repeated. "Because whatever it was that Iskra pursued into that tunnel led her to others. She fell into a basin, a secondary cavern into which that stream feeds." He pointed across the cavern, and the sudden movement made me flinch. "And when she landed, she was descended upon by the very thing she thought she was in pursuit of. She was eaten. Torn to bits. So no, Doctor, you cannot see the body."

Only Mallory made any sound, a sharp intake of air punctuating the silence Beck had allowed for the news to settle over us all. She leaned over, putting her head between her knees. Hannah slapped her hands over her mouth, then wordlessly fumbled in her bag for her pills. She tore off her glasses, letting them clatter onto the table. Oliver didn't move, eyes hard on Beck's face. He sat ramrod straight – though I could see the muscles in his forearms flex as he balled his hands into fists under the table.

I felt like I was going to be sick. Again. And again, I wondered if I could have done anything to stop it.

At the far end of the table, even Dorothy paused in her note-taking. Her eyes lifted to study my face, then Beck's. She shook her head as she wrote, the sound of her pen dulled on the damp paper.

Oliver was the first to break the spell. "I mean – what the hell, Beck? It sounds to me like there are *people* here. Dangerous people.

Jesus Christ – cannibals, maybe. Psychopaths. Not some mythical creatures."

"Not quite."

Oliver scoffed. Beck's expression remained impassive. "Well whatever the hell they are, I'm sure they can die. If they show up again, we'll need to fight."

"That's not how this is going to work, unfortunately," Beck said.

"Like shit it's not. We have axes, flares, pocket knives. Hell, pick up a rock and get swinging. I am *not* dying down here."

Beck shook his head. "That's certainly not the intention, no. Iskra's death was – *is* – a tragedy that should be treated as such."

"Speak plain, *professor.*" He said it like it was something undercooked to be spit out. Disdain, judgment. I couldn't blame him, no matter how badly I wanted to kick at him until he respected Beck's authority here. No number of years toiling over the idea of the very place in which we stood now could account for tangible proof. Experience. A woman was dead; this, it seemed, was all Oliver understood.

And I was most often right. I was good at reading people. I could see Oliver for what he was: a pragmatist, a planner, and a thorough skeptic. Here, I could peg him as someone who'd spent some time in military service. The way he led us, appraised us, checked for exits like he was expecting an air strike at any second; it contrasted directly with what Beck required of us. Beck dealt in faith, while Oliver seemed only to buy facts.

Beck's eyes found mine. The explanation he had given me, after my years of following and believing in him, would do these people little good. He stood at the head of the table like a cult leader, guiding an unwilling congregation through a hymn that only he knew the tune to. All I could do was sing along and clap where appropriate.

"If my research is to be believed," he began, "which it *is*, if recent evidence is anything to judge by, then we find ourselves now in the Cult of the Leviathan's Cloister of Trials."

A long moment of silence passed. I wasn't sure what Beck had expected them to do or say.

He continued, "Whether or not we saw something, we all went after Iskra, yes? We were separated, and not of our own doing. This place is testing us, and will continue to do so. It only allowed us to return to this place once I had convinced Caroline," he gestured to me, and I wished nothing more than to melt into the stone, "of its legitimacy. Tell them."

I gulped. Their eyes were on me. What I had enjoyed thus far about being a research *assistant* was that no one expected me to talk. In fact, I was better neither seen nor heard. And yet here I was. "I—" I took a deep breath, meeting his eye. He nodded, the corners of his lips tugging up encouragingly. "I marked the wall as we were trying to find our way back, in the hope that if any of you came across it you would be able to follow our trail back here. But we . . . We kept passing the same markings, over and over again. We didn't take any turns, didn't double back."

"Because you didn't believe me," Beck offered. There was no blame in his voice. It was what it was. "But when you finally conceded . . . "

"Beck explained to me what this place is, according to his research. Sort of – I mean, he *tried* to, but I was freaking out." I wrung my hands. Mallory's gaze was warm on the side of my face, and encouraging. Even if she believed that every word I spoke was bullshit, she never let on. "When I managed to understand what it meant, where it sat in relation to the rest of his research, it . . . it dumped us out here. I swear I could feel the rock moving under my feet as I waffled about—"

Oliver held out a hand. "Dial this back for a second. You think that some higher power *allowed* you to find your way back to this particular cavern because what? You *believed*? Is this a fucking Christmas special?"

Beck's voice hardened. "If you're so inclined to reject things that are a mite difficult to wrap your mind around, then why did you come? Why did you accept the job?"

To everyone's visible surprise, Oliver laughed. "Because I thought we'd be reading cave paintings and taking goddamn *rock* samples! Not . . . not *this*! I understand that the only way to find a route out of here is to go further in. I'm not debating that; we have evidence enough, from that lighter, that there's *some* exit from this place. But there's no higher power—"

"You saw the little girl, didn't you?"

"Yes, but—"

"You heard her speak?"

"Dehydration can—"

"You sit at a table surrounded by ceremonial instruments that are basic to any elementary-level understanding of anthropological processes, and yet you remain determined to believe that there's *no* significance to this place?"

"This place was significant, sure," Oliver scoffed. "Maybe a thousand years ago, judging by the obsolete carvings on every fucking wall. But I am *not* staking our survival on theory and conjecture."

"Because facts and figures have done so well for your track record in the past, yes?" Beck's voice was a hiss, his eyes bulging.

Oliver's voice was quick, the crack of a whip. A muscle in his jaw twitched, and he rose halfway from his seat. "You watch your fucking mouth."

In every corner, on every wall, the shadows seemed to bloat. Even the flare, nestled at the base of the dais, flickered madly.

"The only way to be free of this place is to do what it wants, *Captain*," Beck said. He held his journal aloft, finger pressed between two pages that sagged heavily with an overabundance of ink. "There's no running from this. Running is the only way to fail. And we would hate to fail each other, wouldn't we?"

Oliver was on Beck before anyone could stop him. He leapt onto the table and crossed its length in two long strides. With a roar, Oliver ripped the journal from Beck's hands and lifted it overhead. He held his free hand out to Dorothy, who looked on, open-mouthed. "Gimme the fucking lighter," he said. "*Now.*"

Dorothy did as she was told, scrambling in her pockets with a wordless chirp. She held it out, and Oliver snatched it up.

My heart sank. "*Wait!*"

The journal was aflame before I could stop it. Beck leapt to his feet and clambered atop the table, reaching futilely for it like a child in a schoolyard. His eyes bulged, teeth bared. And then he swung, and his fist landed with a *thump* in Oliver's gut. Bodies descended on them from all sides; Dorothy and Mallory went to Beck, tugging at his jacket, his arms. Hannah crawled onto the table and tottered to her feet, so short that she could stand between them both and still allow the men a full view of each other.

Oliver went for Beck again. Heart in my throat, I lunged for him, leaping from the bench and slamming into Oliver's back. "Get off of him!" I cried. Oliver was unperturbed by my weight, tossing the burning journal to the side and turning his attention instead to Beck. I balled my fists in the collar of Oliver's jacket and pulled, the unyielding fabric straining against his throat.

Beck's voice was strangled. "The journal!" he cried. "Not my journal!"

I drove the heel of my boot into the back of Oliver's knee, and it buckled. He cried out, warbling and strangled, and he jerked his elbow backward. The crack rang through the cavern; I heard it before I felt it, before I went wheeling, tumbling, to the stone. Blood sprayed from my nose as my head snapped back. My eyes rolled, and I saw nothing but a starry dapple dancing, flickering, like a hundred watching eyes in the dark overhead.

I landed hard at the edge of the dais. My head spun as blood gushed into my mouth and down my front.

The rest of the room was still for a long moment. I rolled onto my side, clutching my face with one hand and my chest with the other. Breath wouldn't come; I gasped, choking on my own blood.

"*Caro!*" Mallory's voice broke the spell. She and Hannah were at my side at once. Dorothy released Beck's arm. Oliver stared down at me from atop the table, arms frozen as if he had expected to wheel around and throw a punch. I couldn't make out his expression; shadow danced across his visage, unlit by the crimson glow of the flare.

Assured hands pulled me upright. Through the ringing in my ears, I could hear Hannah asking me questions upon questions. Had

I hit my head? Could I breathe? Could I see? Mallory was crying, open-mouthed sobbing as if she'd just seen me shot in broad daylight. I could simultaneously feel nothing and too much; my face seared with hot pain, and the saline rust of my own blood choked my tongue.

Dizzily, I felt my face. My nose was, most certainly, not where it was supposed to be.

"*Fuck.*"

My head spun, and I sagged. Mallory caught me, materializing at my side and wrapping her arms around me. Hannah loomed over me. At her shoulder, for only a moment, I could have sworn that I saw another. Iskra – she was unmistakable. She lifted her camera and snapped a picture. And then she was gone.

I struggled to turn my head. Vaguely, I could hear Hannah protesting, saying something about setting my nose. I wanted no part of that. All I wanted was to see Beck, to see that he was all right.

Mallory, on the other hand, was concerned only for me. I could feel her fingers on my face, though my vision wasn't holding up its end of the bargain. "Hold still, Caro," she said, her breath hot on my face. "Oh, shit – stop moving or you're going to get blood in your mouth."

I found Beck on the opposite end of the platform, hunched over his journal. He curled the sleeve of his jacket over his hand and patted manically at the smoking pages. Not once did he look to me, to the spray of blood on the column, the bench, the table. He tended to his journal. And then, when he had finished, he slipped from the dais and into the shadow.

Oh.

A fresh wave of pain shook me, and I gagged, turning my head. I didn't want to puke in Hannah's lap, but she seemed prepared to allow it.

"It's okay," she said. "It's okay, Caro. Look at me, okay? You're gonna feel better when we set your nose. I don't have the appropriate tools with me, but I—" She was talking, talking, *talking*. Did she always talk so much?

"Uh—" I gulped a mouthful of blood. "'S okay. Where's Beck?" My voice was thick. I tried to shake my head, but movement felt impossible. I wanted to search for him again. Maybe he would come back. Maybe he just needed a moment.

I could have sworn I heard Mallory in echo, spitting Beck's name like a slur.

"Mallory?" My vision blurred. There were two of her. Both were vibrant red. "Hold her arms, okay? You don't have to look."

Mallory did as she was told. She repositioned me until I leaned against her front. Muttering apologies in my ear, she looped her arms through mine and held me steady. Hannah placed her fingers on either side of my nose, hesitating for a moment before meeting my gaze.

I spoke, and blood bubbled and popped onto Hannah's chin. "What are you—"

"Sorry, Caroline."

She flicked her wrists, a crunch of cartilage popping forcefully. My chest billowed and I was screaming, screaming, spraying blood on Hannah's face and bucking against Mallory's grip. Curses spilled from me as my vision swam, the starry canopy of eyes overhead blinking rapidly.

I sagged against Mallory, swallowing a wave of nausea.

"Fucking *bitch*," I groaned.

"Feel better?" Hannah grimaced.

Surprisingly, yes. I nodded slowly, wincing at the movement. Hannah disappeared from before me for just a moment, scrambling on all fours across the dais to where she'd left her bag. She produced a kit from within, one much more thorough-looking than what we had been given on our way in. Mallory petted my damp hair as Hannah returned, cutting a piece of gauze and a few strips of medical adhesive tape from a long roll.

"I don't have anything to pack this with aside from cotton balls and tampons," she said. "But that'll have to do for a little while. It's not realistic to ask you to keep it on while we're in here, but you need to at least wait for the bleeding to stop."

"You want me to stick tampons up my nose?"

Hannah chuckled, wiping her brow with the back of her hand before setting to work at taping my nose in place. "Unfortunately, I *am* asking you to stick tampons up there." She wiped the blood from my lips, my chin, my cheeks.

As my vision cleared, I could see Oliver pacing at the edge of the flare's light. He muttered to himself, gaze cutting back up to Hannah's makeshift surgery on the dais. Each time he found me, he wrung his hands and ran fingers through his hair. Even in the red glare, I could see that his face was stricken.

"Sorry I called you a bitch," I said, voice thick. Mallory laughed, and the sound rumbled beneath my back. She was still holding on tight, as if letting me go might send me spilling over the edge of the platform.

Hannah laughed, relief washing across her face in waves. "I've been called way worse," she said. "'*Bitch*' is a compliment at this point."

She worked quickly. Mallory insisted on remaining at my side, adjusting each time I did so that I could lean against her as much as I wished. "I'm a small talk kind of gal," Hannah said. "Even if patients find it annoying. Distracts them from the finer points of what I'm doing, like setting a nose or shoving a tampon in the wrong end."

"Okay," I grunted, voice thick. I sounded like an ogre.

Mallory came to the rescue. Clearly her people skills were better than mine. "Where are you from, Hannah?"

As for Hannah, she seemed relieved at the opportunity to fill the silence. This was as much for her as it was for any patient. "I'm from California," she said. "A Stanford graduate. Single. Cat person. *Huge* cat person." She paused to wipe a bit of blood off my top lip. "Believe it or not, emergency medicine is *not* my specialty. I'm a surgeon. Was, I guess. I am currently on *sabbatical*." The word came out of her like she considered it a slur. Like it was something shameful. Mallory and I couldn't blame her, and we told her as much; being trapped in a sea cave seemed preferable to working in the United States healthcare system. So kind and patient was Hannah that I did my best to swallow the discomfort as she pressed a tampon into each nostril, the strings hanging lamely over my top lip.

"Just for an hour or so," she said. "Long enough for the bleeding to stop. In an ideal world, we'd pack your nose for longer. But . . . this isn't an ideal world, is it?"

At this, Beck reemerged from the shadows. He looked harried, his hair askew and his sleeves rolled to the elbows. White-knuckled, he tossed his burnt journal onto the table and ascended the dais once more, with not a glance in my direction.

No – this was no ideal world.

This was made even more glaringly obvious by the fact that Dorothy had made her way to us, clambering onto the dais with a pinched expression and a notebook protruding from her breast pocket. She perched at the edge of the bench nearest, feet together and hands laid delicately on her thighs. As if she was gathering the courage to give a monologue, or pitch a book to the class.

"God, I hate blood," she said. Hannah rolled her eyes so hard that I wondered how she'd managed to keep them inside her skull. Dorothy continued, "Can't get enough of it in fiction, of course. It sells. But in real life? *Eugh.* Smells like rust."

I wasn't in any position to tell her what anything smelled like, given the matching tampon strings that tickled my lips.

My manners, too, had been dislodged in the scuffle. "Why are you here?" I asked, nose throbbing with every nasal syllable. Eyes narrowed, I glared up at her. "What are your qualifications?"

"My qualifications?"

Yes, bitch. "Yeah. I didn't know they gave out caving certificates at book camp."

Her lips curled into a sneer. She crossed one leg over the other. "Careful, Caroline," she said. "Any cheekier, and I'll have to kill you off in my next novel."

I scoffed, and pain shot through my skull like a rubber bullet. Mallory patted my shoulders, tutting. "What a weird fucking thing to say."

Dorothy shrugged. "A paycheck is a paycheck, all right? Edward wants to turn this into a vanity project, then that's on him. I'm just here to document it all in the best light possible."

"Not the most truthful light, but the *best* one. Right." I met Hannah's gaze as she leaned forth to dab at the blood on my chin. At the very least, I wasn't alone in my dislike. "Good for you, I guess. You could really make the big bucks." I knew that Beck was a bloated ego on two legs, deep down, but this was next level.

"Oh, I plan to," Dorothy sniffed, tucking a stray curl behind her ear. "Which is why I'm so utterly fascinated by your perspective. You saw Iskra die, didn't you?"

I blinked, incredulous. She'd said it so bluntly, so audaciously, with fingers itching to open her notebook. I stared up at her; even Hannah turned to shoot her a dirty look. Mallory made herself busy re-tying my hair into a braid. She seemed to hate confrontation even more than I did.

"Jesus."

"What?" Dorothy threw up her hands. "Not like we have room to beat around the bush."

I shifted, struggling to sit up higher on my own. My head spun, and Mallory muttered condemnations under her breath. I craned my neck to glare at Dorothy over Hannah's head. "Yeah, I saw Iskra die. Looking to do a little foreshadowing?"

The author's sneer curled higher. "Did Oliver knock your manners loose?"

"Seems like it."

"I can certainly just make it all up. Or you can tell me what you saw, and I can continue to do my job of documenting this little excursion to the best of my ability."

I blinked. Did she not understand the gravity of our situation? Iskra was the *third* dead. None of our phones worked. Something less than human lurked in the dark beyond this cavern, which Beck believed to be the agents of some old god who wished to test our mettle, simply because we'd wandered into the wrong cave at the wrong time. There was so much at work here that was unexplainable, otherworldly, far greater than any fiction – and she wanted to treat it like a *writing exercise*?

And so I gave her the truth. "It's like Beck said. Iskra was torn apart like a fucking carcass at a watering hole," I spat, blood and spittle bubbling between my teeth. As if I could protect her by doing so, I reached for her camera and shoved it into my bag. "She followed that little girl – that *thing* that took her sister's face – and she got torn apart by it. I'm sure you can pretty it up."

"What was the name Iskra kept saying? Penny? Prudence?"

"*Priya.*"

"Priya. Right." As predicted, Dorothy removed the journal from her pocket and the pen from behind her ear. "Look, kid, I understand that you can't really wrap your concussed head around the idea of a *job*, given the fact that you're riding Edward's coattails all the way to a graduate degree." I blanched. Even Hannah and Mallory froze. "But I'm going to continue to make a buck in the best way I know how, whether you like it or not. I didn't get hired to write a nursery rhyme. I'm here for the story."

I understood why Beck hadn't hired a journalist. Hell, a journalism *undergrad* would have been more appropriate. But Beck wanted the fame. He wanted the accolades. Dorothy had some kind of star power that he wanted. She was appealing to him, and that was undeniable. Put him in a bestseller while simultaneously publishing all of his research in the *Annual Review of Anthropology*, and he'd never be laughed at again.

Across the dais, Beck clapped once, twice, and the room stilled. Every face in the room turned up to him, and he boomed over us all like a preacher on a pulpit. Dorothy rose and slid away from the three of us, as if she'd be scolded for coming too close to Beck's favorite.

Maybe not his favorite any more. He hadn't even *checked* on me, though I'd bled in his defense.

"We would all benefit from some rest," he said. "I'll allow it." I could have sworn I heard Oliver mutter something sideways, his voice carrying across the cavern, but my head pounded too aggressively to confirm it. "But after we've sorted ourselves out . . ." a glance around the room. A challenge. "We carry on. And we do it correctly. *My way.*"

No one offered a rebuttal. Silence passed heavily between us all. And so, with a nod, Beck turned away from me once more.

Sleep brought me dreams of the sea. Waves lapped lazily over the checkerboard tile beneath my feet, salt clinging to my ankles. My hair whipped round my face as I watched the tide swirl, reaching for me not with the lecherous hands that I'd come to understand of the ocean – but with gentle ones. For one glorious moment, there was nothing but sun, and salt, and the rush of foam at my calves.

A heavy wave broke over the tile, pushing me back a step. The billow crashed against the tile with a sharp rap.

That wasn't right. I furrowed my brow, and lazily dropped my gaze to the receding water between my feet. Again, the waves broke upon the tile. And again, the familiar rush of water punctuated with the sound of a sharp thud. I lifted one foot, the dazzling light of early sunset glinting off the fresh paint on my toes, and stomped. The water splashed up the rolled legs of my jeans, as I'd expected, but the moment my feet made contact with the blue-and-white tile again the air was filled with the sound of tapping.

Tapping, tapping, over and over. The sound rattled me from my reverie, and for the first time I looked to my right, and then my left. The horizon remained the same, on all sides, but in my small pocket of the beach bits and pieces of domesticity littered the sand. I stood, still, on a square stretch of tile. To my right was a bathtub, overflowing with seawater and burbling foam. To my left, a chipped sink.

The waves crashed around my ankles again, and the rapping grew louder. I could *feel* the sound in my bones, could place it in the air just behind my ear. And beneath, the rattling of metal on metal. I took stock of my surroundings again: an unbroken coastline, a marigold sunset, a bathtub, a sink. With a tut, and a snap to my senses, I turned my back from the sea.

And there, in my periphery, stood a door. It protruded from the sand as if it had simply been placed there to be collected later. The doorknob jiggled, and it rattled on invisible hinges.

I hastened to the tub and reached within to search for the stopper. The foam on the rim of the tub was murky, the color of swamp water. It clung to my forearms as I rolled my sleeves to the elbow and felt around blindly. It was irresponsible to leave it running, after all. The tile was flooded, and the beach had been sullied.

My fingers hooked around a chain within the murky water. I gave a pull. All at once, footsteps rushed from the direction of the surf. A body hurtled to the door, weight thrown against the groaning wood. I gasped, leaping from the edge of the tub. The surf broke around my shoulders as I turned to find, throwing her body against the door over and over, rattling at the tile, coughing and spluttering foam down the front of her nightdress . . .

My mother.

She tugged at the door, but it was lodged too deeply in the sand. The water flooding the tile soaked the hem of her nightgown, a single posey drooping into the foam.

I knew the tile beneath me. I knew the tub, and the chipped sink. I knew the door; I could just make out the edges of height markings that had bled from the door frame and onto the wood of the door itself. And I knew my mother. Of course I did. I could never un-know her.

"Caroline!" she called, ruddy cheek pressed to the keyhole. "Caroline, please!"

I kicked my feet, pushing myself away from the tub, the sink, the specter. I clapped my hands over my ears, coldness and prickling salt bleeding into my ear canal. But I could still hear her. My mother tumbled to her knees. She pounded at the wood and clawed for the doorknob, her skin mottled and her hair falling in a wet curtain around her face.

"*Caroline!*" She pleaded, she begged, she bellowed until I could hear her lungs wring dry. Each inhale was ragged, a chore. Foam popped at the corners of her lips.

Again, the sea broke over my shoulders. The waves were aggressive, billowing in size. Water splashed over my head, whipping my cheeks. The bathtub continued to overflow, muddling the clean seawater with turbid spray.

"*Caro!*" My head snapped back, as if I'd been pushed. Searing pain arrowed up the length of my nose, splitting into the sinew of my skull. I squeezed my eyes shut. Again, my name echoed out to the sea. And again, I felt an invisible grip at my shoulders.

I fell backward, head cracking against the tile. A wave crashed atop me, and I was plunged into the brine. My mother disappeared, looming above as if at the lip of a pool – and then she was swallowed by the dark entirely. Seawater flooded my nose and again a lance of searing pain split my skull. There were hands on my shoulders, on my cheek, shaking me . . .

"Caro, get up!"

I woke to the feeling of water beneath my back and Mallory looming over me. She was shaking me, taking no pains to watch the way my head shook and the blood in my stoppered nostrils surged. "It's flooding!" I sat up, head spinning, and she disappeared from view. The dream gave way to the cavern, alight with activity, bodies moving and shadows stretching. And from a hole in the cavern wall, too high to reach and yet low enough to be illuminated by the dying light of Iskra's flare, water rushed. It spilled from the wall and splattered off the table's smooth surface. Already, the narrow stream on the opposite end of the cavern had disappeared, swallowed by the rising water level.

The roar was deafening. Across the dais, I could see Oliver's mouth moving as he surged against the current, struggling up the stone incline to the passage leading outside. His voice was nearly imperceptible, ". . . *dislodge rock!*" he called. Hannah was at his side then, tugging at his arm. I cast about wildly. Beck stood at the mouth of the passage, waving the flare wildly. He dripped at every inch with water, his bag clutched tightly to his side. It was clear that he would rather have drowned than leave without it, shying away whenever another body came close. Water rushed against his thighs, pushing him further into the dark corridor beyond.

I scrambled to my feet, sloshing off the dais as I tugged at the bloody strings dangling from my nose. Pain lanced through my skull as I ripped the makeshift padding free, tossing it aside. The water lashed at my calves, impossibly cold. I took up my sodden pack and slung it over my shoulders, fumbling to unclasp the helmet and headlamp from where it dangled off a carabiner.

I called out to Mallory, "*What the fuck happened?*" but my voice was swallowed, drowned beneath the deluge.

The water pushed us into the passage. We followed quickly behind the others, Beck at my rear, feeling the wall as the ritual cavern was flooded at our backs. Over the table, filling the space around the platform, scattering the stone tools that Beck had been so keen to code and file; seawater rushed in from all sides as the ground shook beneath us.

I struggled to clasp the straps of the headlamp beneath my chin, the heavy weight of the lamp tugging it down over my brow. My fingers trembled as I felt blindly for the light. The stone floor pitched downward, and we hopped from one jutting rock to the next as the water pounded over our shoulders. It filled the space below quickly, shoving us all into one another as we slipped and clambered from one patch of solid ground to the next. The tips of my fingers scraped the wet wall as I looked down to my feet, watching each unsteady step over the bloated ridge of my mottled nose.

I slammed into Mallory's back, the loose helmet sliding down over my eyes.

"Why did we stop?" I cried, rising onto my toes to peer over her shoulder. The others eddied in the narrow passage – had it gotten narrower, lower, darker since we'd last come through? – crying and yowling like wounded animals.

At the front of the pack, Oliver turned, illuminated by the light of my lamp and the glow of Beck's flare at my back. He called out, but I could hear nothing.

One by one, each member of the procession turned to parrot Oliver's message back to the next, and the next, and then to me.

"There's a drop," Mallory moaned, breathless. "There's nowhere else to go! It's just a fucking drop – and it's all water!"

I thought of the never-ending circle that Beck and I had been trapped in, forever following the markings I'd made in the walls. The ground had given way to a watery hole there, too, though it had been easy enough to leap over it and continue on our way. I craned my neck again, pressing my back to the stone as I slid past Mallory, then Dorothy, then Hannah. Beck scrambled to shine his flare back at the rushing water as it coursed through the passageway and sloshed heavily against the pool at Oliver's feet – and the low stone wall just on the other side. Oliver stooped, for the ceiling dipped dramatically.

It was a dead end. The water's surface rippled, only a breath of open air between the heavy rock and the surface of the pool. And the water itself was dark, impossibly deep. The walls of the pool, beneath the surface, were perfectly round and symmetrical, as if something colossal had passed through, slipping from below and snaking out into the corridor where we stood now.

I looked to Oliver. The water at our backs was higher now, crashing against the low wall and spraying my painfully swollen face with glacial water. It pushed and pulled at my thighs, ebbing and flowing from the stretch of unbroken air just beneath the low hang of the wall. The ground beneath us shifted, and I pitched sidelong. Oliver threw out his hands, catching me and holding me steady. He held my gaze, and I gave him a nod. All was forgiven.

"We have to go in!" Oliver shouted. "It's the only way!"

He was right. Damn it all, but he was right.

Oliver turned from Beck's flare and switched on the light of his own headlamp, removing it from his pack and fixing it atop his head. He descended into the pool, and before I could say another word to him, he disappeared beneath the wall.

And one by one, the others followed. I ushered Beck past Mallory and me, and he went gladly. I would bring up the rear, and she could follow him through. Mallory was all that mattered – Mallory was all I knew.

She hunched in the glow of my headlamp, and I reached for her. She was cursing, crying, wringing her hands. The water weighed down the thick fabric of her colorful sweater. She'd put on her climbing gloves backwards, and she was missing an earring.

"There's a pocket of air above the water!" I called, taking hold of Mallory's arm and bracing myself against the wall at my back. "Beck will go before you. Follow him, okay?" The water pounded mercilessly at my hips, and yet I couldn't bring myself to follow the others until I knew that Mallory had at least a *chance.*

"Will you be right behind me?" Tears and seawater slicked her cheeks, sputtering from her lips and spraying my face. I nodded, and she did the same.

Mallory disappeared beneath the water. I cast one glance back to the passage beyond, the light from my headlamp barely reaching the source of the deluge from the cavern above.

There, beyond the torrent, a shadow in a nightgown watched.

I plunged into the water, head spinning as the pressure crackled at the broken bone and cartilage of my nose. Eyes squeezed shut and cheeks inflated with a last gasp of air, I sank beneath the crashing wave and ducked under the low wall. I kicked my feet in the open water, propelling myself upward. There was no bottom to touch – only the wall a mere inch above my face, and the water that billowed at my back. The space between the surface and the rock grew smaller by the moment as the water from the flooding cavern surged, pushing me forward. I reached beneath the surface for Mallory; I could just barely see the light of the others' lamps and flares, pinpricks that bobbed and weaved beneath the waves.

I gasped for air as I lifted my face from the water, craning my neck and pressing my cheek to the rock above. The waves felt like hands, tugging me down and buffeting me forward all in one. Lecherous, needy, pulling at the heavy fabric of my clothing and ripping at the ice of my skin. Water lapped over my broken nose, my lips, my eyes. I kicked my feet fiercely, pushing myself as high as I could – but the watery passage had no room to give. Water spluttered from my lips, my throat, as I tried and failed to measure each belabored breath, moving forward with nothing but the space of my cheek above me.

The water surged again, a fresh wave from the cavern above. I turned my face upward, the tip of my nose scraping the rock ceiling. Glacial salt water flooded into my ears, rushed over my chin and lips. I pursed my lips as I kicked forward, head spinning as water ebbed into my nostrils. The lamp atop my helmet scraped on the rock, tugging at the strap under my chin. I choked, fumbling wildly with the clasp. I bobbed lower into the water, salt flooding my eyes as I struggled to loose it from my throat . The lamp and helmet fell free, sinking into the dark, and I propelled myself up again, willfully swallowing the rush of bile in my throat at the feeling of my broken nose crunching against the stone above.

I couldn't breathe. There was no light, no sound outside the roaring of water in my ears. I wheeled my arms wildly, thrashing forward. With each kick of my feet, I gasped for air, pressing my nose and mouth to the stone. The water lapped at my lashes, the corners of my eyes.

My hands found Mallory. She'd stopped moving – why had she stopped moving?

I could hear her fumbling, splashing in the dark as she pressed her lips to the ceiling, gasping, "*Stuck!*"

Shit. The darkness was oppressive; I couldn't even see the tip of my nose, or the walls closing in on either side of me.

I took a deep breath and plunged beneath the surface. Glacial water flooded around my broken nose, and as I exhaled sharply a flush of nausea choked in my throat. The ice ax hung heavily at my side, dragging from the tie affixed to my pack. I tugged it loose with one hand, feeling around in the dark with the other. I found

Mallory's hip, her thigh, her leg. I felt for the snag of fabric, a piece of her pack clinging to a jutting rock further down the wall to our right. The salt stung my eyes and my chest ached for air. Mallory kicked her feet, catching my elbow as I tugged at the strap, holding it taut. The water pressed against me as I brought the ax down on the rock once, twice, ineffectual beneath the battering of the waves. I turned the blade, then, to the strap, piercing the waterlogged fabric and tearing, pulling, until it broke. Beneath the water, I gave Mallory a shove – and she was free.

I kicked up again, lips barely breaking the surface as I hooked the ax on a belt-loop. I gasped for air, my lungs keening. Salt water flooded my mouth, my nostrils – but it was enough. The water surged, leaving nothing but the very tip of my plum-bruised nose to scrape the ceiling.

I held my breath. The water rose to meet the stone, and I was pulled beneath it. In the dark, I swam blindly; I could see no more of Beck's flare, or Oliver's headlamp. The top of my head rammed into the stone above as I bobbed, kicked, scraping the tips of my fingers on the walls on either side, no wider than a door frame.

A shaft of dim light cut the water ahead. I blinked heavily, chest groaning with the effort of holding a breath. My head scraped the stone as I surged forward, the tips of my fingers finding the thick fabric of Mallory's sweater for only a moment.

And then she disappeared, passing into the light and arrowing upward quickly, violently, as if pulled.

The stone above gave way, cool air at the top of my head. I threw my head back, pushing my face out from the murky water, and gasped. I was being touched, tugged, pulled from everywhere: fingers looped in the strap of my pack, a hand beneath my arm. A tight grip at the collar of my shirt jerked me up, pulling me, head and shoulders, from the water. A single hole in the stone, the light much brighter now; I couldn't focus, couldn't see for the water in my eyes and the blinding pain in my face and chest. My arms flailed wildly as I coughed, spraying water onto the faces that hovered above, the hands that pulled me upward. They hauled me onto a stone shore, up and over the lip of the opening. The ax pressed painfully into my hip as I rolled onto my stomach, spluttering water and blood onto the wet floor.

Flickering luminescence lit the cavern, casting strange, uncanny shadows across Mallory's face. She hunched over me, hitting my back over and over while I spat up icy brine. She was sobbing, apologizing over and over – she hadn't meant to get stuck, she'd been so afraid, it had been horribly dark. Her voice warbled over me, punctuated by the low murmur of the others. I craned my neck to look; all of them but Beck lay scattered across the stone, basking in the glow of the strange watery-blue luminescence emanating from iron braziers along the far walls. As I blinked away the water from my eyes, I could more clearly make out the lumps of rock within, glowing with dappled phosphorus that flickered like a flame.

I wasn't sure what startled me more – that the cavern was lit by anything at all, or that I remembered what *phosphorus* was.

Beck stood at the very center of the room, before a great slab of obsidian stone. Smooth at its surface and untouched by the looks of it; the monolith sat at the heart of the formation of braziers around the room, littered at its base with what looked to be worn books and journals. Tools, too, sat propped against the stone: pickaxes unusable from rust, and ropes long since frayed. And the walls, just beyond the blue glow of the stones, were, too, littered with books. Shelves upon shelves, half-swallowed by the stone walls much like the archway in the entrance cavern had been, as if over time the grotto had grown ravenous. Some of the books had fallen, pushed from their bracketed shelves by the effort of the stone's absorption. Some stuck half-out of the stone, pages drooping with condensation.

Where the hell are we?

On all fours, I took stock of myself. My face throbbed. I wondered if my nose had gone off-kilter again. Hannah would be pissed if she had to set it a second time. I felt dirty, like every inch of me had been *touched* without my consent. The glacial water clung to me like film. But I was all right. I was whole. And everyone had made it.

The water from which we had all emerged lapped gently against the hard edge of the hole in the floor. It rose and burbled as easily as a passing tide; there was no evidence of the deluge here. The cavern was impossibly quiet, the lapping of water on the stone subdued.

Libraries were, after all, meant to be quiet.

Perhaps that was what this was. I sat up slowly, sinking onto my heels and pushing the wet hair from my face. Up to the ceiling I looked, leaning back as far as I could go. Only darkness stretched above; the walls on all sides had no end, and the great monolith before Beck had no limit. The floor stretched on, and on, and on with no end. At our backs, the stone wall from beneath which we'd emerged stood proud. But beyond the light of the braziers . . . nothing. Blackness, empty and oppressive.

I rose, and Mallory followed. Past the others as they wrung out their jackets and fanned frantically at their equipment, I wandered into the light of the braziers. It was cold; I'd expected a basking warmth, like that of a fire. But no – there was nothing but cold air, stagnant and quiet.

Beck rounded to the far side of the monolith, paying no mind to me as I approached with Mallory in tow.

"What is this, Beck?" I called, voice small, swallowed, by the cavern. Nervously, and for something to *do* with my hands, I began to wring the water from my sleeves. I would have given anything for a dry change of clothes. And now I owed Mallory new socks. "What is this place?"

He said nothing for a long while. I stared at the smooth stone, as if I could observe him through it. And then, "I'm working on it."

I wandered to the base of the megalith and stooped to examine the books at its base. The warped pages were empty, the bindings worn and twisted from time, or maybe overuse. The tools that lay scattered amid the empty tomes were similar to ours, though they seemed far older – an oil lamp, a pickaxe, tinned soups and vegetables, and a pair of leather boots.

Beck's silence unsettled me. I was so used to him having all the answers, or at least pretending to. He appeared at the far corner of the monolith, sodden journal heavy in his hands. He'd settled his reading glasses atop the bridge of his nose; they were cracked and bent, and he pushed them higher as they slipped with regularity.

The others had begun to rise, eddying at the edge of the braziers' light like moths. The uncertainty on their faces was clear; Hannah and Oliver huddled close, exchanging furtive glances, while Dorothy stood alone, extending one hand over the cold light. Our fearless leader had told us that we needed to go further in, and the cave had left us no choice. There was no denying that it felt purposeful, though no one could accuse Beck of flooding the place for his own purposes.

But it gave credence to his theory. We were *supposed* to go further in. If we did what we were supposed to do, followed the path set for us by whoever had carved this place from the stone – and whatever it was that bid the stone itself to consume anything that lingered too long – maybe we could find our way out.

Oliver broke from Hannah and arrowed past the monolith, his sights set upon the darkness beyond the braziers. He stood at the outer edge of the light, hands on his hips, and stared into the dark as if willing something, *anything*, to appear from within.

Mallory gave the oil lamp at the base of the monolith a half-hearted kick with the toe of her boot, the metal handle rattling against the clouded amber glass. "Looks like someone else beat us here," she said, to no one in particular. "This is, what, a library?" Beck looked up from his journal, from the smeared ink that bled from one page to the next. It seemed futile, trying to decipher it now, but Beck persisted. He wandered to where Mallory stood, looking down at the old tools at her feet and then up to the highest visible point of the stone above.

Oliver turned to appraise the rest of us, spinning on his heel as he spoke at last. His voice boomed, filling the cavern with a sound that felt almost sacrilegious. Perhaps this really *was* a library.

But if that was the case, who was collecting these books? *Empty* books, no less.

"What now, Professor?" he called. "Is this all part of the grand design? Nearly drowning in a goddamn flash flood is a test, is it?"

Beck's brows knit together. He flipped to the next soaked page, and looked from the smeared ink to the monolith looming overhead. Sodden, ruined, burnt at the bottoms of half the pages; his notes, his work, were moot. There was nothing now but what lay before him, for even Dorothy's musings had surely been lost in the flood.

We had nothing to follow but what he knew himself, what he could recall from his years of study. For so long, Beck had followed his notes meticulously. They were gospel, religious texts of the highest order.

And now we had nothing.

I could *see* him thinking. I took a step closer, ducking my head like one might do in approaching a wild animal. His eyes darted from the ruined pages of his journal to the oil lamp, to the monolith, to Oliver, and then back again.

"Beck?" I reached for him. The vein in his brow bulged, the muscle popping in his jaw. "We can take a minute to think. Reassess." Water dripped from my sodden sleeves and onto the blank tomes between us. He needed to sit. When was the last time he'd eaten? It would do none of us any good if he passed out just because he was too absorbed in the work to—

His hand shot from his side, fingers closing roughly around my wrist. I yelped, and Mallory skittered backward, slipping on a loose piece of blank parchment. At the same time, he let his journal fall from his grasp, paying it no mind as it splattered wetly on the stone at his feet. The others leapt toward us, rushing from their various posts around the room with cries of alarm.

And then the sound of them was swallowed, shunted from the very air around us as Beck pressed my palm flat atop the stone of the monolith. He did the same, holding my hand parallel to his. I had no time to scream, to protest, to marvel at the sheer warmth of the stone.

My head snapped back, hair falling in slick, wet vines down my spine. My eyes rolled back, jaw wrenched wide, darkness clouding my vision. At my side, Beck jerked, then went rigid.

And then I saw nothing of the cavern, of the flood, of the bay beyond the skerry. There was only the monolith, and the dark on all sides. Bodies, naked and slick with black wetness, writhed in the light of a dozen fires, all lit at the stone's base. They melded into one another, like a great, singular body that split only in shadow. They smeared the moisture across the stone, and great runes flickered to life beneath their touch. I could hear screaming – not of fervor, of ecstasy, but of fear. In the air, encircling the monolith, barely recognizable shapes hung limp – not shapes, no. *Bodies.* Bodies hung, suspended in utter nothingness, heads bowed and limbs limp. Even in death, they faced the monolith, blood dripping from the tips of their bare toes to the stone below.

The image changed. I saw myself, alone; I stood before the monolith, my hand pressed to the stone. From my fingertips, bastardized Enochian runes danced like cracks along its surface. And then a stranger took my place, and another. A woman with buzzed hair stood over an abandoned journal, its pages ruined from moisture and flame. A pair of men kicked the oil lamp like a soccer ball, laughing as it shattered against the far wall. Each looked more foreign than the next, and each vanished in a flash – for only a moment – to give way to the dancing creatures, the writhing mass of bodies, and the forest of hanging bodies that trembled with every rumbling of the floor beneath the revelers' feet.

There came a whispering in my ear; it moved from one side to the other, muttering impossibly fast in a language I couldn't understand. Spots danced before my eyes, the monolith unfolding into a labyrinth of impossible geometry, ever-changing in the dark. The voice moved again, and I could hear something utterly enormous, a behemoth, sliding across stone. A body? A creature? I could hear Iskra's voice reflected within, and then a young girl's. I heard my mother, and then a thousand foreign voices that spoke in frequencies unheard of. I could feel a searing in my hand, somewhere far away. The rustling of pages, or maybe leaves; the whisper of a thousand voices, and the crackling of a bonfire; I could smell sea air, and the rust of drying blood.

I blinked, and it was gone. I was alone. Sand the color of iron shifted beneath my feet. I wavered, unsteady; one hand remained aloft, as if held there. I could feel no strain in my muscles, in my aching joints. Something gentle, something obliging, lifted my arm for me, holding it in place as I took stock of my surroundings.

An endless beach; a slate sky. The water that lapped gently at the sand was the color of nighttime. Fragments of stone buildings, of stained-glass monuments, vaulted ceilings crumbled and lying sidelong, statues and monuments littered the sand, disappearing into the water. Basalt columns scattered up stone walls, soaring cliff-faces that reached out to the water – but never quite touched. There was no end to the sand, or the surf, or the sky.

And there, just before the water, lay a long stretch of what smelled keenly, horribly, of rotting flesh. Pale, stretched beyond recognition; the edges were red with blood that had long since gone cold. It bubbled and roiled in the sand like molten lead, and from within the mass I could barely see a leg, an arm. There was movement from beneath. I startled, and began to step away – but my outstretched arm held firm.

A head? Shoulders?

The water rippled, and a great body moved within. Something smooth, roiling; gray light shone off scales the size of a market square. Beneath me, the ground shuddered so fiercely that I was knocked sidelong. Water rushed onto the shore as the cathedral wall nearest to me shuddered and crumbled beneath the tremor, sending thick blocks of stone scattering across the sand.

And then, from the water, the sea floor itself seemed to rise. Water and sand spilled from a squamous black hide, seaweed dangling from scales sharpened into pikes.

An eye opened, so high that as I craned my neck I couldn't see its topmost point. An *eye*, water spilling from its lower lid; a thin membrane shifted over a vertical pupil, a blaze of vibrant orange.

Pain seared through me as I was ripped from the monolith, tumbling back into reality as the flesh ripped from the tips of my fingers. My head spun, eyes wheeling; all I could see was the flesh, the eye, the fire. I flung my arms wildly, and my limp hand found a shoulder, and then a face. Arms wrapped around me, strong and unyielding. Someone was saying my name.

My eyes found Beck first. He stood, still, facing the monolith. Dorothy shook him by the shoulders, but he remained unseeing, his neck pulled impossibly far back, his mouth stretched wide and his eyes nothing but unbroken white, riddled with bulging crimson veins.

And beside him, inches from his spread fingers, five perfectly ovular patches of bleeding flesh. It was only then that I looked down at my hand, only for it to be yanked from my lap by Hannah. Her face was wet with tears, snot bubbling at her nose.

"God-fucking-dammit!" She was shrill, her voice simultaneously impossibly close, and terribly far away. Her hands shook as she produced a roll of wet bandage from her pack and set to work at my fingers. I felt disoriented, struggling to remember who, and where, and when –

I looked up. Nothing but unbroken air around the monolith; no bodies. No fire.

Beck slumped, and everybody in the room jolted. His hand slipped freely from the stone.

He was allowed to do so. It wasn't done showing me yet.

Dorothy cursed as she tried and failed to catch Beck. Mallory eddied over me, wringing her hands. It was only then that I realized that it was Oliver who held me tight and who had, presumably, ripped me from the monolith before my time.

Before my time?

The idea wasn't my own. I couldn't help but accept it anyway.

Light flooded the cavern, swallowing the weak glow of the stone in the braziers. Foreign lettering, runes like those in the cave entrance and in Beck's ruined notebook – like shutters thrown wide, they skittered up the length of the monolith, blazing with iridescence. I held my uninjured hand up, over my eyes. Oliver's breath was hot atop my head as he cursed, tensing at my back.

Beck struggled to his feet. It was a wonder he wasn't blinded, close to it as he was. He whirled, finding me in the light. As he moved toward me, visage ablaze with triumph, and wonder, and utter mania, bodies moved from all sides to block his path. They crowded around me as Hannah tied the bandages taut over my bloody fingers, eyes darting frantically from Beck, silhouetted by the violent light, to the monolith at his back.

No one seemed to notice that the small patches of flesh that had once been mine, my fingerprints, a wayward freckle or two, had disappeared from the stone. All that remained were five pinpricks of blood; wet, and shining, and illuminated like a Christmas bauble by the runes below.

"What the *fuck*, Edward?" Hannah cried, whirling to face Beck once my hands were well enough bandaged. "What the goddamn fuck was that?"

Beck opened his mouth, but Oliver spoke first. He tightened his grip on me, almost imperceptibly. It seemed as if he felt some duty to me, as he was the source of the ugly swell at the middle of my face. "Why did you do that to her?" Oliver bellowed. "Are you out of your mind?"

"*That's* why!" Beck thrust an unharmed finger toward the monolith. "Do you see that? *We* did that. It's a sign! Validation! This is a *library*, don't you see? The knowledge this place possesses—" He shook his head, pressing the heels of his hands to his brow. The runes shone impossibly bright. Just like in the entrance cavern, the runes were clearly the same Enochian script I'd encountered in various theological anthropology seminars over the years. But just like before, they were different. Changed, bent at divergent angles and rearranged to form a dialect that might as well have been a different text entirely.

But there, amid them all – familiar, from the outer cavern. *Wormwood*, in unmistakable lettering. And again, as before, the rest were indecipherable.

Wormwood. Like the angel? Bible camp was failing me spectacularly, but I hadn't the energy to try to redeem it.

I could only imagine what this brightness would attract here in the dark. Beck moved for me again, and I bit down on my tongue to keep from kicking out at him. "What did you see, Caroline?" he fell to his knees, reaching for me as if to take my face in his hands.

"What did she show you? What did you learn? She didn't want to let you leave the vision, it seems."

She?

I wouldn't even know where to begin, how to quantify in any words, in any language, that would make sense. Hell, I couldn't understand it myself.

And I felt *violated.* I felt dirty, and bare. My face ached, my head split, and my fingertips bled through the wet bandage. I could still feel Beck's grip on my wrist just as keenly as I could feel the wildness in his gaze as he'd pulled me to the monolith, the need to *use* that which was not his to use. I wasn't a tool in his fucking experiment. But he seemed to think otherwise.

Was I being tested? Was this trust? He looked down at me, salt-stained and electrified with terror, and I wondered what he saw. Someone to care for? Something to use?

"I don't know," I croaked. "I don't know what I saw."

"But you did *see* something. What was it? Was it her?" His voice was manic, and his fingers shook as he reached for me again. Fervor lived within each word, and yet there was something else – *fear?* "I wanted you to see it, too. I wanted you, more than anyone, to experience—"

Hannah held up a hand. Her eyes had moved beyond us, past the monolith. With her other hand, glistening crimson with my blood, she shielded her eyes.

It was only then that I realized that one of us was missing. One body, not crowded around me while Beck raved.

"Where is Dorothy?"

We called out to her, casting about for any glimpse of the watery waif who followed us like a shadow, chronicling our every word. For once, I wanted to see her, to catch a glimpse of her smeared lipstick and her gaudy cigarette case. Oliver helped me sit upright as the others diffused from Beck's orbit, cupping their hands over their eyes to combat the glare of the glowing runes.

A spot in the dark, the flicker of a waterlogged lighter appeared. It wavered, danced in a breeze that I couldn't feel from where I sat, illuminating Dorothy's ghostly visage. She looked past the darkness, eyes fixed immovably on something imperceptible, something beyond. The flame danced mere inches from her face. Smoke tickled the underside of her nose.

"There!" I thrust a bandaged finger in her direction. "Dorothy!"

And then, all at once, bodies appeared at Dorothy's shoulder, her side, above her head. Eyeless, bleach-white, bloated and dripping from every sodden inch; they bore no features save their mouths, stretched wide and dripping viscous black. They were everywhere, haloing Dorothy in bone-white by the light of the flame. Their heads angled toward her, stretching like distended shadows, mouths agape and oozing. The flame flickered, and she followed its trail as if hoping for a glimpse of sun, a hint of an easy breeze.

Her brows inclined, twitching up in surprise, as if she'd heard something. As if she'd been called.

I called out again, the relief in my voice souring, rotting, to absolute horror. "*Dorothy!*"

The lighter extinguished with no sound. And she was gone.

We were on our feet at once. I lurched into a run, careening past the monolith and stumbling over the abandoned tools, the books – the books, which now bore script in thick black text. The sight of it made me falter. Had I done that somehow? Had the monolith? Under different circumstances, I would have wanted to read every word, to parse out who else, or what else, had been lost here, but not now. Instead, I pressed on.

Mallory was on my heels, calling after Dorothy. Together, we hurtled into the dark; I cast a single glance over my shoulder for the others, who followed blindly.

All save Beck. He had stopped at the base of the monolith, his drooping pack half-open. He picked up his journal, then a book, and another. Anger flared in my stomach; he cared only for the work, for the mystery, for the indecipherable texts that would mean *nothing* if no one was alive to read them.

I could only think of Iskra, of the pop of her sinew and the tear of her flesh. Would they do the same to Dorothy? Was this her test?

The dark was all-consuming. I could *feel* the floor beneath me, the smooth stone, as I ran. But past the light of the phosphorus-lit rock, there was no direction. The walls, embedded with half-devoured structures and forgotten texts, were swallowed in black; the space above as inky and impermeable as ever. I held out my arms, feeling blindly for a wall, a corner, a body.

"Dorothy!"

No response. My head ached, the raw tips of my fingers throbbing. Could she even hear us? Was she already dead?

Hannah's voice, and then Oliver's, echoed at my back. "Dorothy, come *back*! Dorothy!"

A scream rang from within the dark, and I skittered to a halt. The others did the same. The sound had no direction, no source. I turned to the person nearest me, Mallory, and was shocked to find that I could see her clearly, even in the dark. I could see them all behind me too, perfectly illuminated as if beneath glaring spotlights. I couldn't see the floor, or the walls on all sides – but I could see Mallory as clear as day. We hung, suspended, in perfect darkness.

Another scream, but closer. And another, somewhere to our right. I whirled, aching eyes searching the dark.

"Dorothy?" Hannah's voice didn't carry, dying in the oppressive blackness as if we were domed beneath thick glass.

A pinprick of light flickered into view, too far to discern. I thrust a bloody finger out. "There!" I cried. "There's something!" Something, anything, any one material thing that might anchor us in the dark. If we could find our bearings, we could find Dorothy. And if we found Dorothy, we could get some answers. If she passed her test, maybe we could all do the same.

We started off again, hurtling through the dark toward the near-imperceptible prick of light in the velvet blackness around us. In chorus, we called out for our lost colleague, though the sound was swallowed by another scream, and then another.

And then a scream rang out, familiar and keening – and dissolved, all at once, into raucous laughter. A chorus of giggles and guffaws followed, and then a *whoop* and a clink of glass on glass.

The pinprick of light took shape: a single door, painted white, with a silver handle. Light flickered at the edges, and sound roared from behind. There came more laughter, and a trilling scream of utter delight. The door hung, suspended, in the dark. It had no frame, no hinges. I could see shadows moving in the light, the shuffling of feet just beyond.

Without a word from the others, I opened the door. It swung wide without a sound, spilling low, warm light across the pitch threshold. A hundred flickering pinpricks of golden light reflected off the smooth surface of the marble floor that stretched before us, giving way to a grand staircase that curved up and out of sight on one end, and a wrought-iron door almost ten feet high on the other. I could hear music from somewhere above, and chatter on all sides.

A group of three men appeared from beyond the door, bustling past us in a flurry of laughter and cajoling, tugging at pressed collars. They were dressed in tuxedos, with masks tied over the upper halves of their faces. They seemed not to notice us as we watched them pass, their polished dress shoes scuffing the marble floor. I could smell the booze from here; Fireball, if I was remembering correctly.

I stepped out into the foyer. At my back, Mallory gasped as if expecting me to fall through the floor. But I didn't. I gave the marble a short stamp to test it as I craned my neck, peering up at an ornate iron chandelier lit with a wild number of flickering electric candles. Then came the *clink* of glass in the other room, a gasp, a shatter – and an uproar of raucous applause.

I turned to look at the others. Beck had appeared among them. They all eddied in the doorway – but no darkness stretched at their backs. Instead of the endless dark of the library cavern, the others stood shoulder-to-shoulder inside a coat closet. They hadn't seemed to notice.

I opened my mouth to speak, to beckon them closer, but before I could make a sound a door one floor above our heads slammed open. A shrill, feminine voice filled the foyer, echoing off the gaudy marble floor like an alarm bell. I craned my neck high again, creeping closer to the heavy iron rail.

"*If you don't take a shot with me, you're a fucking pussy, Dorothy!*" A chorus of laughter followed, and a pair of shadows stretched across the portrait-laden wall. All women, posing like mannequins around an enormous blue-painted "ZTA", each letter the height of a city bus.

I whirled to face the others again. They were still in the closet. I wondered if, from where they stood, the space around them was nothing but darkness.

Dorothy! I mouthed.

Mallory was first to follow. I ascended onto the first step, holding onto the railing to keep myself steady. The shadows continued to move overhead, doors opening and slamming shut again as a stampede of footsteps came and went down the hall above.

I caught a glimpse of my own reflection in the glass of the nearest group photo hanging on the wall to my left. Grime coated every visible inch of my skin. My face was bloated, dark bruises blooming from the center point of my broken nose, arcing in dual crescents underneath my eyes. My hair hung in a halo of wet strands around my face, the diligent rubber band at the nape of my neck holding onto what little of a ponytail it could still manage.

I swiped the heel of my hand across my brow. It did nothing for me; in fact, it seemed to somehow thicken the spread of dirt, algae, and blood. Maybe it was a good thing that we were unseen.

Mallory and I crept higher, following the sounds of laughter and music to the next floor. A long hall stretched before us. Each colorfully decorated door was propped wide, and bodies moved in and out at lightning speed. A brunette in a strapless gown, arms laden with makeup and a ring light; a redhead with a handle of liquor in each hand – and then the source of the voice we'd heard call out. She appeared in the doorway nearest, curlers in her hair. She dabbed at her eyelashes, pressing the false plumes down into the drying glue, and called out again, "Where the fuck is my shot?"

"Coming, Emily!"

And from the end of the hall, from a room that seemed to be a shared bathroom, emerged Dorothy. Younger than the Dorothy I knew, and far different: she wore thick-rimmed glasses, her hair frizzy despite the heavy application of hairspray that struggled to keep a semblance of structure to the milkmaid braid that piled atop her head. She padded, barefoot, down the hall with a bottle of Fireball and a shot glass on each finger. This was nothing like the Dorothy I knew and loathed, despite my best intentions. This version of the woman I knew was meek, and clumsy, and pimply.

The girl nearest to us spotted her at once, giving a loud clap and a "*WOO!*" that was echoed by a number of other voices within the room at her back.

"You'll do one with us, Dorothy," the girl said. She towered over Dorothy, in stature and in presence. "Won't you?"

Young Dorothy gulped. She held out the bottle and glasses, but the girl didn't move to take them.

"Come take a shot." It wasn't a question. The girl turned on her heel and marched back into the bedroom. Young Dorothy followed eagerly, and so did I. Mallory lingered at the top of the stairs, gesturing wildly to the others.

A gaggle of girls lounged around the room, some taking selfies on digital cameras and others putting finishing touches on their makeup in the matching armoire mirrors. Dorothy was on their leader's heels, picking her way across the messy suite to the table laden with wine bottles and matching "*PANAMA BEACH 2009*" champagne flutes.

"You all look really nice," Dorothy ventured.

The girl nearest, a platinum blonde with extensions the length of my arm, sneered up at her. "'*Nice*'?" she simpered. "Really?"

Heat flooded Young Dorothy's cheeks as Emily cleared the table of glassware. "I don't have to be on that call with my agent until the afternoon tomorrow, so I wanna be *blackout*," she said, tossing her curled hair over her shoulders as she patted the tabletop. "Right here, little Dodo."

In the mirror, I saw a muscle in Young Dorothy's jaw twitch.

She obliged quietly as the others tittered among themselves about how *cool* it was that Emily had a literary agent, that she was *such* a cool writer. They mused about how she'd be the next Stephanie Meyer, that maybe she could write the next *Twilight*.

"My vampires don't sparkle," Emily snapped, teeth bared in a gleeful grin. "But they do fuck."

Uproarious laughter filled the room, and Dorothy looked from face to face as she joined apprehensively, as if they would disallow her from laughing. The less they seemed to care, the larger Dorothy's smile grew. She was happy to be here, among them. This made her one of them, surely, if she could laugh like this at their side.

"Carlisle Cullen fucks," said the blonde.

Emily guffawed. "*Where?*"

A cruel smile spread across the girl's face as her eyes snapped to Dorothy, who struggled to arrange the shot glasses in an aesthetically pleasing way around the bottle of Fireball. "Dodo knows, don't you?" Dorothy faltered, a glass slipping from her grip and rolling under the adjacent bed. "You have competition, Em. Vampire sucking and fucking fanfiction is an *art form.*"

I could feel the heat of her mortification from here. Mallory grimaced at my side. I hadn't even seen her appear; I turned, then, to find all the others watching from the hall. Something about this felt impossibly private, as if we betrayed the real Dorothy somehow by sticking around to watch.

"We should go," I said, pushing from the doorway and skirting past Beck to venture further down the hall. Mallory followed. Most of the others obliged, though Hannah lingered a moment longer, a disdainful look upon her face. "We need to find Dorothy. The real one."

"These are memories," Beck noted, following hot on my heel. "Her test has something to do with something that transpired on this night, surely. Her greatest secret; her darkest self."

I was surprised that what we'd just witnessed didn't qualify.

As we descended into the foyer once more, the winding stair rumbled beneath our feet. The portraits on the walls rattled, frames clacking against the wallpaper. I gripped the railing, the bloodied tips of my fingers aching beneath sodden bandages.

Above our heads, the wallpaper, almost too high to see clearly, drooped, peeling at the corner. As I looked up, watching the chandelier bob and dance beneath the tremors from down below, I watched the damask wilt. And there, beneath the fabric, glistening stone. All at once, I smelled seawater, and the rust of my own blood.

My stomach lurched. We needed to find Dorothy, to help her through whatever this wild shared hallucination was, whatever it meant. If this was to be a test, we couldn't allow her to blunder into it without help.

I couldn't help but wonder what this place's metric was for what was deserved, and what was to be given freely. Iskra had been given no rules. She seemed to have failed outright, pitching toward a spectacularly violent death with no warning and no explanation. Dorothy had been given a labyrinth.

You aren't supposed to be here. But Dorothy, somehow, *was*?

The rumbling beneath the house stopped. The curled wallpaper flapped lamely, as if beneath a breeze. My ears popped as pressure built painfully within them. I could smell the sea, the stone, the salt—

—and then a chorus of raucous laughter broke the silence, and the air was still once more. I stuck a finger in my ear and twisted. The others, scattered along the stairs like dolls flung from a toy box, looked to Beck.

He gave me a single nod. "Keep going," he said. "We keep going."

I did as I was told. We arrowed across the foyer, passing a sitting room lit by the dying embers in a stone hearth. Cubbies lined the wide corridor, each labeled with the name of its associated sister. Dorothy's was at the bottom, and far less decorated than the others. Emily's, of course, was at the very top.

And there, in the corner of a kitchen packed with sweaty bodies, stood Dorothy. *Our* Dorothy. She hadn't seemed to notice us, her gaze trained upon one of the boys at the center of the pack. He seemed to be the nucleus of the group, the gravitational force around which they all rotated. They looked to him before doing anything, if only briefly.

At my shoulder, Mallory let out a short, squeaking gasp. The others crammed into the doorway, struggling to see over one another.

"That's her husband, I think," whispered Mallory. She leaned in close, as if the boys would somehow gain sentience mid-whisper. "Right there in the middle. Younger than usual, of course, but like . . . that's *him*."

But she watched him now, from afar, with no affection. She watched as he guzzled Pinot Grigio from the bottle, cheese-greased fingers white-knuckled around its neck, close enough, *keenly* enough, for her gaze to bruise.

A flurry of bodies passed through us, a deluge of color bleeding into the wall of monotonous black. Emily led the pack, pushing through the crowd of masked boys and making for the object of Dorothy's attention. He kissed Emily sloppily, and the boys erupted into a chorus of jeers. And there was Dorothy, her younger self buffeted back and forth by passing bodies that didn't care to move around her. She stumbled on her towering heels, and fell into the wall of cubbies.

I slid closer, along the counter. The Dorothy we knew looked on silently, eyes flickering from her younger double and back again.

"Dorothy?" I hissed. "*Dorothy?*"

She didn't seem to hear me. If she did, she exerted great effort in pretending I didn't exist.

But then they were all moving, shouldering past Young Dorothy as if she were nothing at all. Except Emily – she saw her. Emily seemed to see everything, a keen predator with an eye for casual cruelty. She jeered down at Young Dorothy with a sickly falseness that turned my stomach. If it wasn't clear before, it certainly was now: Dorothy was made to be consumed. She was a bug to squash, to pick the legs off of for the amusement of her betters. It didn't matter how prettied and primped she made herself. She would always be less.

Young Dorothy followed Emily as she continued down the hall, much less graceful on her towering heels than the others. Our Dorothy pushed past us, and her body made contact. I fell back against the cubbies, scrambling to grapple her but failing. She slipped from our grip, storming after her younger self. We all followed in tandem, through the foyer to the great double doors outside of which a towering bus waited.

The moment we crossed the threshold, passing from the house and into the open air, the landscape changed. It was like blinking; there was no grand shift, no denouement, no bleeding from one scene into another. Rain struck us like bullets from above, glacial water harsh on our heads and shoulders. The threshold spilled us all out onto a grassy knoll, the water slick with rain and dew, and marked with muddy divots.

I cupped my hands over my eyes. Just barely, I could make out a steep drop over a dark edge, a cliff lit only by a single lantern swinging at the doorway of a tall, glass-walled building. Ferns and tropical trees stretched to its domed roof, humidity and condensation fogging its inside. Through the rain, I could make out the shape of a much larger building, a grand shape that loomed in the dark beyond my sight.

A body moved within, past the glass. The broad leaves of a fern rustled. A back pressed against the glass, and a pair of broad palms; I recognized Young Dorothy's dress even from here, her hair stuck to the glass.

I started down the hill, slipping in the muddy gouges that arrowed down the hillside.

Another body moved inside the greenhouse. Further in, a shadow slipping between the bowed trunks of tropical palms. There was no making it out, save a fogged silhouette.

And then another, slipping along the outside of the domed room. Dorothy – ours. She crept along the outside of the greenhouse with a spade in-hand. Even from here, from this far, I could see the whites of her eyes.

"Dorothy!" I called out, cupping my hands around my mouth. "Hey, Dorothy! Hang on! We're coming!"

I blinked, and we were elsewhere. Humidity flooded my nose, the drooping edge of a palm frond tickling my brow.

"*Wait!*" Young Dorothy's voice cut through the oppressive roar of the rain, and I started. Mallory slapped a hand over her mouth. "Logan, please—"

"Come on, Dodo. This is what you want, isn't it? *Me?*" The rustle of fabric, the knocking of overlarge high-heels against glass. Somewhere to my right, through the humid haze, a fern rustled with sudden movement.

I couldn't think of it now. A familiar fear settled like a poison at the pit of my stomach; it didn't matter to me that this wasn't real, that we were nestled deep inside the dream of a creature that could simply *blink* and pull us all far from here. I had to do something.

Beck took hold of my arm. My feet slid beneath me, mud slick on the soles of my boots as I tugged against his grip. "You can't interfere," he said. "That's not how this works."

I whirled on him, pulling hard against the vice of his fingers. "What the hell are you talking about?"

"This isn't real."

I gave another tug against Beck's grip. "Let *go*."

"I can't. This isn't your test."

Something vibrated near my foot. I could feel it rattling the concrete, shaking the thick sole of my boot. I cast about for its source, stretching as far as Beck's grip would allow to toe at a trampled palm frond.

A phone lay, cracked and buzzing, beside a plastic clutch. Its contents scattered: a broken tube of pink lip-gloss, a tampon, a ring of keys attached to a chained bauble in the shape of a book. On the phone's screen, a picture of a group of girls blazed brightly. The Zetas, with Emily at the very center. And there, in the bottommost corner, her face only half-visible, was Dorothy.

A text flashed across the screen as the call from "*Monica Roommate*" dropped: *Have you seen Emily?*

Beck made to tug me away again, and I dug in my heels. "Well, what the fuck are we supposed to *do*?" I demanded.

His lips pulled into a hard line. "We allow Dorothy to face what she's come here to face. And we wait." He'd allowed Iskra to do the same, and where had that gotten her? How could he be so calm, so easy in allowing this?

Emily burst from behind the nearest fern, iPhone with flash blazing held over her head. She was barefoot, leaping over fallen fronds and jutting roots. Wild, manic laughter rocketed from her, sweat beading on her brow. She passed by us, arrowing toward the sounds of activity just ahead.

Beck was startled just long enough to allow me an escape. I slipped free of his grip and hastened after Emily, breaking from the meticulously curated underbrush just in time to see Young Dorothy fall to the floor, her dress tugged down around her midsection and her heels scattered. Logan lurched from her, wiping Dorothy's lipstick from his mouth.

He was laughing. Emily was laughing. Dorothy screamed, her cheeks and neck mottled with hot, horrible crimson. Logan tugged up the zipper of his pants as Emily stooped, thrusting the phone in Dorothy's face.

"First you wanna steal my shit, and then my *boyfriend*?" Emily's voice was a screech, nothing of the utterly perfect and infallible queen of Zeta house that we'd seen previously. "What's next – you gonna fuck my agent, too?"

"*No!*" Dorothy howled, futilely clawing at the fabric of her bodice. She pulled it up, and it ripped again; a piece of tulle hung from the iron bones of the greenhouse, right where Logan had pressed her against the glass.

And there stood Dorothy – *our* Dorothy – outside the window. She watched with her brow and nose pressed harshly to the fogged pane, hands cupped around her eyes to shield from the rain. The blade of the rusty tool in her hand tapped against the glass, the sound barely audible above Emily's howling laughter.

"Did you really think that anyone would want *you*?" Emily spat, thrusting the phone's camera in Young Dorothy's face. "You need to learn your place." She seemed to think for a moment, to hesitate – and then she gave Dorothy a kick.

Dorothy looked up, past Emily. "Logan?"

He shook his head, running fingers through his hair. For a long moment, he opened his mouth and closed it again, as if struggling to reconcile with what would be required of him now. Emily jabbed an elbow into his side.

"Shouldn't steal, Dorothy," Logan said. His voice lacked conviction. It seemed to startle Emily as much as it startled me. Maybe he knew that this was not a fitting punishment for a stupid crime. What had she stolen? A paper? A pair of shoes?

Dorothy struggled to her knees, scuttling on all fours toward the door. Emily stamped down on the hem of her dress, and it tore further still.

I leapt forward and reached for Emily – but I fell through her, smacking uselessly into the glass wall.

Young Dorothy was on her feet, a long strip of tulle ripping off from beneath Emily's bare heel as she barreled toward the door and spilled, half-dressed, into the rain. She was running, sobbing open-mouthed, with mud splashing onto her calves, her thighs. Emily and Logan followed, led by the light of Emily's camera.

"*Admit it, Dorothy!*" Emily roared, her voice a boom despite the howling of the storm outside. "*Admit you want to be me!*"

Our Dorothy arrowed across the doorway, knuckles white around the neck of the trowel. She paid us no mind as she went, lips trembling and hair drooping across her brow; and she was gone before we could call out, before we could all battle through the greenhouse door and reach for her.

We hurtled out into the deluge. I could barely see, the rain wild and oppressive as it lashed against my cheeks, my aching nose. I cupped my hands around my mouth and called out, called for Dorothy over and over. The mud sloshed beneath us, slicking our thighs and splashing onto our hips. Pain lanced through my skull. I could feel blood in my nose, could smell the rust and salt.

The trio rose before us like pillars, haloed by the light of the moon as it peered through the storm clouds hanging, bloated, over the cliffside. Dorothy stood at its edge, hugging what remained of the ruined dress to her shivering torso. I could hear Emily yelling, her words indistinct. Logan stood a few paces away, arms crossed over his chest.

I drew closer and . . . No, the body at the edge of the cliff was not this memory's Dorothy at all, young, and slight, and blooming with tulle. It was *ours*, the fearful tremors of her younger self giving way to the blistering hate of the elder. Her waterlogged shoulders shook with every belabored breath, her teeth bared.

Emily spoke as if she didn't expect a response, though it was clear exactly to whom she spoke. She took a step closer, as if she expected Dorothy to move back. But she didn't. The younger Dorothy was gone. There was only *her*.

And there, over our heads, darkness bloomed like blood. It seeped into the clouds, obscuring what little moonlight had been visible through the deluge. In the dark, an eye flickered open – disoriented, and curious, like a waking baby. And then another. And another. Like a thousand winking lights, eyes poked from the dark and turned their multitudinous attentions down – to Dorothy.

"Admit you stole it all!" Emily roared. "Admit that you're *stalking* me, and that you tried to sleep with my boyfriend. *Say it!*"

In another life, Dorothy might have warbled, and cried, and scrambled at a dress that had long since been torn to tatters. Our Dorothy said nothing. Her chest billowed with every ragged breath, nostrils flaring. Her shoulders rose and fell, and her knuckles whitened around the neck of what I knew with utter certainty was a weapon.

Emily took a step forward. "I suspected it when you got that nomination for a story that sounded *eerily* like my own. I knew it for sure when I saw you wearing my goddamn *blouse*. I knew that if given an inch, you would take a fucking mile. After all we've done for you—"

Our Dorothy spoke at last, her voice a growl. "You never did a goddamn thing for me," she said. "But you will."

To my surprise, Emily seemed to hear this. This was a deviation from the memory, surely. Her expression dissolved, wild satisfaction replaced for a single moment with dark disdain. "Oh, what's this? Little Dodo found her voice?" She pressed a manicured finger to her chin. All at once, Emily found herself again. She held her phone higher. "Smile for the camera, bitch. Everyone is gonna see what a loser and a *fraud* you are."

Dorothy rushed her, colliding with Emily in a flurry of mud and hair; Emily shrieked, falling backward.

I blinked, and she was over the edge. Dorothy had fallen to all fours, peering over the drop at the body that dangled from a narrow ledge just below. Emily's phone sank into the mud by Dorothy's boot, the light of her camera swallowed. All at once, the rain stopped. I could hear them as clearly as if they spoke directly into my ear.

"Dorothy, please!" Emily cried. "It was just a joke!"

"I'm not laughing." Dorothy glanced once over her shoulder. "How about you, Logan? Are you laughing?"

He moved toward the pair, but Dorothy lifted the spade over her head, blade pointed down. She shook her head, tutting, and Logan skidded to a halt.

"You don't have to do this," he said. "You don't have to make this choice. You can fix it right now." The words sounded uncharacteristic, strangely sage for someone like Logan. I felt a hand at my shoulder, a squeeze: Beck. He gave me a short nod, a knowing half-smile tugging at the corners of his lips.

This was it. This was the test.

But what was wrong with me, now, in thinking that she had nothing to atone for? I could see the play performed before me now, acted out in shapes and shadows. Dorothy would let Emily fall. This was known. What transpired after was nothing but details and paraphernalia. Emily had humiliated her, abused her, and so she deserved whatever came to her.

Dorothy had nothing to atone for. If *this* was atonement, it was bullshit. If this was it, I would fail.

"You always wanted to be me," Emily hissed, spittle peppering the rock face. "You follow me, and you copy me, and you pick up the scraps that I leave behind because that's what you'll always be:

a fucking *pretender.* A rat, gobbling up what nobody else wants. Because you're what nobody wants. A nothing. A *fraud.* A—"

Dorothy brought the spade down hard atop Emily's straining fingers. Metal ground on bone; flesh tore and split beneath a dull and rusted point. The fingers of Emily's left hand split from the whole, sinew and muscle clinging to flesh by strings. Dorothy struck again, severing the violin-string tendons and denting the spade at its tip.

The eyes that hung in the sky above remained trained upon Dorothy's back, blazing in their unflinching watch. Every so often one would blink. None flinched from the sound of metal on stone, or the ragged cry of the girl on the rock. They simply watched, turned from Dorothy's audience as if we weren't here at all.

And then Emily fell. Her fingers slipped from the ledge, her detached digits still propped on the stone. And she was gone.

Logan rushed to the edge, hands on his brow. He doubled, retching charcuterie and Fireball into the mud as Dorothy stumbled to her feet. She dropped the trowel, then kicked it over the edge for good measure.

"What did you *do*?" Logan cried. He fell to his knees, leaning as far over the edge as his stomach would allow.

Dorothy stooped, retrieving Emily's phone from the mud. She turned as she tucked it into her pocket, searching the dark scuff of earth. "*Ah.*" She lowered once more, fingers plunging into the mud. From the muck she scooped a delicate golden chain, its glint barely visible beneath the filth. Dorothy held it up. She examined it, as if for imperfections.

And then she pulled its perfect twin, the very same gilded chain, from beneath the collar of her shirt.

"I'll be keeping these," she said, tucking it into the same pocket as the muddy phone. "Come help me push the fingers over the edge, Logan. Find a stick."

He looked up at her as if she'd started speaking in Latin. "*What?*"

Dorothy paused. "Or . . . do you want me to tell them it was you? I'm not sorry." All at once, the Dorothy I knew and the one we had seen in her memory were one and the same. They always had been. The dark truth of herself just needed a little coaxing.

Logan shook his head lamely, like a dog working water from its ears.

"That's what I thought," said Dorothy. "So if you want to keep this between us, you're going to have to do exactly what I say." A pause. "And that starts with finding a stick."

They set to work. There was nothing to do but watch and wait while Dorothy and Logan pushed all that was left of Emily over the edge of the narrow outcropping beneath the ledge.

You don't have to make this choice, he'd said. *You can fix it right now.*

What would have changed if she had helped Emily up? Would the world right itself, or would this girl – this forgotten girl, replaced in every way by the woman before us now – still be lost to Dorothy's ambition?

The ground beneath our feet trembled. The mud sloshed, the dew-drenched grass danced. Mallory reached for me, and I reached back, clinging to her damp arms as we slid in the muck.

The multitudes turned to us all, each eye flickering and whirling until the attention of the universe, *this* universe, was upon us. Logan seemed not to notice; he moved about as instructed, his cheeks wet with tears and his nose bubbling with blubbering snot. Dorothy, however, froze with the rest of us.

All at once, the eyes hanging like a thousand bloated moons flickered closed. The earth bowed beneath us, mud turning viscous. I sank with a jolt, in to my calves. Logan was gone; I looked up, past Dorothy, to nothing but empty space.

A hand, massive and distended, and dripping mud and black, viscid muck reached from beneath the ledge, fingers digging into the flattened grass at its edge – and *pulling.* The earth tremored and Dorothy screamed, leaping away as a second hand shot high into the air, the top of a head following. Oliver reached for Dorothy as she hurtled away from the edge, reaching for us with arms outstretched. All pretense was gone; before us now stood the frightened teenager, the outcast, the fraud.

A face rose from beyond the ledge as arms stretched, clawing at the earth and scrabbling up, up, higher until a head, and shoulders, and torso flopped into the mud with a squelch and a crack of bones and twigs. The face fractured, fragmented, whirred with impossible speed as it changed from one visage to the next. It cycled from one to the other – Dorothy, and then Emily, and then Dorothy again, with Emily's eyes – its skin drooping at every joint, melting and stretching to reveal the muddy bones beneath.

The creature reached for Dorothy, mud and seawater spilling from its toothless gums. We pulled her away, slipping and stumbling over one another.

Bone cracked and mud popped as its chest ballooned, jaw stretching wide, wide enough for the muddy tip of its chin to swing and swipe across the grass beneath. It screamed, muck and blood flying like spittle from its maw.

Dorothy slipped, and Oliver went down with her.

"Get up!" Hannah cried, tugging at Dorothy's sleeves as she scrambled back, kicking her heels into the mud.

An oil-slick of mud fell from the creature's cheek like a slab of rotted flesh. Dorothy's, by the look of it; the same pattern of freckles rendered in two, flesh splitting and giving way to a rune which was carved into the fully visible marrow of the creature's mandible.

It dragged its body closer, broken legs and tilted pelvis sliding uselessly through the mud. I could hear its bones shifting, groaning as it curled up and over the ledge, reaching for Dorothy with misshapen fingers.

The creature opened its mouth and screamed, loose jowls and tattered cheeks shuddering beneath the rush of acrid aid. In tandem, just as I reached her, Dorothy's mouth shot wide, jaw wrenched at a horrible angle as a cry ripped from her chest. The cry was an echo, a single note sustained between Dorothy and the creature that loomed over us all.

It tossed its head high, spine writhing, broken legs flopping uselessly in the mud at its tail. Dorothy's spine arched, seemingly not of her own volition. Hannah skittered away, shrieking. Dorothy twisted, head snapping back and jaw stretching in a mirror of the creature's grotesque war cry. The creature shuddered, overlong fingers and bloated joints digging deeper into the mud.

And then it flipped onto its back, arching at the middle like a child in a fit of petulance. It shook its head, and Dorothy did the same. It stretched its arms to the sky, and Dorothy's elbows stretched, popped, fingers trembling as she reached, and reached – the creature howled, and a shoulder popped from its joint.

Mallory screamed. She lunged for Dorothy, but Beck was faster. He grabbed Mallory around the middle, barring his arms beneath her ribs, and hauled her away.

Oliver scrambled in his pack, at his belt; he ripped his ax from its holster and bolted toward the creature, a cry of terror on his tongue. The mud beneath him liquefied. He sank to the knees, the inertia doubling him at the waist. He flopped uselessly to the ground, ax slipping from his grasp and sinking into the muck.

I stumbled back, the pop of suction as I tugged my feet from the mud swallowed beneath the sound of Dorothy's screams and the creature's keening. It flung out an arm, and Dorothy did the same. It bucked its hips, broken legs sagging uselessly as the crack of Dorothy's hips struck through the starless sky like thunder.

The face changed once more. Less Emily, and more Dorothy. Eyes bulged, tongue lolled from a jaw stretched too wide; Dorothy's jaw cracked, falling slack, and her screams deepened to a moan, a cry for help that none of us could answer.

Legs twisted; a kneecap popped sideways; an arm flung across a billowing chest. Dorothy crumpled, every angle crooked. Every move the creature made, every thrash and twist, reflected twofold in Dorothy's breakable form.

A crack shook the very soil beneath our feet. Dorothy's eyes bulged, broken jaw hanging limp. An expression of shock passed across her features as her ragged cries choked, gasping, in her throat. Her legs stopped their thrashing, hips and bowed back suspended above the mud.

There was no reaching her. The harder I struggled – the harder we *all* struggled – the further in we went. Mallory broke free of Beck's grasp and began to sink at once, splattering face-first into the ooze.

Dorothy's eyes rolled, landing on me, closest to her. Her pupils were bloated against whites riddled with blown swaths of telling red. I froze beneath her gaze, clawing fingers descending into the dregs. Her jaw shuddered, tongue flopping against the roof of her mouth as if she wished to speak, to cry out, to do *anything* at all.

The creature sagged. Its face drooped, as if its convincing mask had begun to fit poorly. Too loose at the edges, sagging and dissolving. Dorothy, however, remained unchanged. She was rigid, trembling; if she had been able to reach for me, I knew she would have.

Beneath us, the ground gave a tremor. As one, we all sank further into the mud. Another lurch, and I could have sworn that I felt hands at my ankles, rough roots and whorls of underground wood hooking round my feet and prying into my shoes to pull me further down.

"Dorothy!" I moaned, scrabbling at the mud. "I—" I couldn't think. She was not the first person I'd watched die. I hadn't known what to say then, and I certainly didn't know now. But I did know, with the utmost certainty, that Dorothy was already dead. "I'm sorry!"

A single sound, a croaking and wordless grunt, shook from Dorothy's broken mouth. And then, as if it had been a goodbye after all, the grip at my ankles tugged me down. The mud rose to my chest, and I threw my arms over my head, reaching for the open air above. I could hear the laughter of Dorothy's sorority sisters, the pounding of music, the hollering of the fraternity brothers. I felt it all, every moment of Dorothy's greatest darkness played back for me in blazing color as we were all pulled further into the mud. It was cold and heavy against my chest, pressing the breath from me in a horrified gasp. My arms pressed over my head, I craned my neck to look for Mallory, for Beck.

And I found him. He stood with his face upturned, lips pulled into a blithe grin. Beck didn't struggle against the pull of the mud as we were swallowed, sucked into the mud. No fear colored his expression. Only the joy of something untenable, finally understood.

The mud rose to my chin. I took a deep breath, lungs aching, as I was pulled under. All at once, it felt like water, like nothing. Cold mud poured into my ears, my nose. The weight upon my chest should have been oppressive, crushing; but I was buffeted downward easily, dreamily – and then my feet found open air.

I was falling, reaching for the mud above as we fell, deposited, into the dark. Water rippled beneath us, almost arcing up to meet us as we flailed, tumbled, and splashed into the saline surf. The cold was shocking; I blew out all the air I'd been holding, and my head spun as I thrashed, feeling wildly at stone, and fabric, and flesh.

And then my head broke the surface. The others fought their way up, gasping for air.

Dorothy was gone. The monolith rose before us, runes dead and dark. Water from the narrow pool at the mouth of the grotto sloshed over the shallow stone ledge, sending a fresh wave of salt rushing over Beck's journal, the books, and the abandoned tools.

All was quiet. And we were alone.

I looked up again, half-expecting Dorothy to fall down atop us, a little delayed in her descent. We had been plucked so unceremoniously from that place and dumped back here, like a holding room that would churn us about until it decided to spit another one of us into the thick of our worst fears.

It had all happened so quickly; I felt disoriented, displaced. There was no time to understand, to process. But then again, it wasn't for me. For us. The magic at work here, the horror, had been for Dorothy alone. Which of us would it select next?

Beck was on his feet at once and at my side even faster. He held out a hand, and I took it with visible uncertainty. He moved about the space like he had been delayed in his study by no more than a missed bus, or a misplaced file. He seemed to care very little that there was a hole in our ranks. Dorothy's absence was nothing. It was science. It was expected. And it was proof that he had been right.

Nothing about this felt random. The test had been real.

I didn't want to be next.

"How is she just *gone*?" Mallory's voice was a wail, high and keening and filling the cavern to its very top. "What—what *was* that?"

It was almost comforting to know that this wasn't some kind of shared delusion. There was mud in my shoes, and in Hannah's hair. I cast about at every shadow, and Oliver walked the perimeter like a prey animal anticipating an ambush. There was nothing about this that we could quantify, that we could explain away.

It seemed, however, that Beck was willing to try.

"It's curious," he said. His voice was level, as if he discussed nothing more pressing than a curious lecture. "We all inhabited the same liminal space, the same hallucination that—"

"No fucking way that was a *hallucination*," Oliver spat. He turned from the dark perimeter, sodden shoes squelching with every inch. "No hallucination is that real. And if it was just our imagination, then where the fuck is Dorothy, huh? Where's she gone?"

"Those are the rules!" Beck boomed. He seemed not to care about Dorothy's brutal fate. This had always been about his research. "This is the way it *works*, Sergeant." His lips twisted, and his brow twitched. Something knowing, something ugly, flashed across his features. "Atone or die."

Mallory crawled to me on all fours. I met her halfway, rising onto my knees and shuffling to meet her with arms outstretched. Her lower lip trembled violently, an omnipresent stream of tears wetting her cheeks. Mallory's brows were caked with mud, her jacket heavy with displaced grass and bits of soil.

"Caro," she moaned. "I don't want to die."

I clutched her arms, touched her face. There was nothing that I could say here to make it better. Beck, the only one of us who could offer any direction, had disappeared behind the monolith, tracing the dormant runes with the tip of his finger.

I tucked Mallory's muddy hair behind her ears, wiped at the salt on her brow. "You won't die here," I said. "Not as long as we stick together." It was a horrible kind of promise to make, simply because it would be so easy to break. How could I promise something so wildly out of my control?

"We'll stay together no matter what?" she pleaded.

I nodded. A fat well of tears rolled down her cheeks. I scooted closer to her, on my knees, and she hunched, face pressed into my thighs. Mallory was gentle. Mallory was kind. This was no place for someone like her. If this was all purposeful, what had she done to deserve a test like Dorothy's? What sin had she committed to earn *that*? I couldn't fathom it. I knew what *I* had done, and had come to terms with it long ago. But nothing in my mind could reconcile the idea that Mallory deserved punishment of any kind.

And even if Dorothy had done wrong – was there not a hint of *rightness* in her actions?

I could hear nothing but her cries. The crunch of bone and the sickly stretch of sinew rang like a bell in my ears. My stomach turned, and my head swam; I couldn't afford to collapse, to be sick, to lose my nerve, and yet I felt stretched thin. Like I, too, could tear at any moment.

Hannah was crying, wailing and sobbing, ugly and open-mouthed. She shook, on all fours. Nearby, Oliver paced, and paced, gaze distant. He could have been anywhere else.

"I have dreams, Caro!" Mallory cried. "I have things I want to do, things I want to . . . to *make up* for! I've done wrong in my life, but *God*!"

I held tight to her hands, lacing her fingers with mine. I gave her a tug, encouraging her to sit upright, to look into my eyes. "You're a good person, Mallory," I said. "I know that. Everyone here knows that."

In my periphery, Beck paused, listening. I wanted to swat him away. Mallory's pain – *all* our pain – wasn't for him to dissect and study like an artifact.

"But Caro—" Mallory moaned. "I've done bad things!"

"We all have," I shook my head, tightening my grip on her hands. "It's not something to die for. Okay? I'm going to find us a way out of here."

"But Dorothy—"

"What happened to Dorothy was . . ." Was *what*? A tragedy? Sure. An accident? Almost certainly not. Even now, I felt as if we were being watched. Marked. Monitored. The name *Leviathan* flashed across my consciousness like a neon sign at the end of a dark alleyway. No, this was no accident. This was a grand design. And I wanted no part of it.

"What happened to Dorothy," I said, struggling to school my voice into level evenness, "was a fucking tragedy, okay? We – we were all there. We saw. I won't let it happen to you." And I wouldn't. My grip on life and death was tenuous at best. Incidental. But I could try for Mallory.

I felt my refusal like conviction, like a sturdy rod pressed into the hollow, anemic spaces between my bones. If this was the divinity that Beck so desperately sought – if this was divinity at *all* – I didn't want it. Was this horror what he had expected? Had he hoped for it?

No. I wouldn't be a part of it. First Iskra, and now Dorothy; I wouldn't, couldn't allow it to happen to Mallory. To me.

I could only imagine the shape that my darkness would take. My sins, my guilt, laid bare – I would become a monster. And I knew, with certainty, that I couldn't best it. How was I supposed to, when I had refused to acknowledge its rot for so many years?

No. If not for myself, I would refuse for Mallory. She deserved none of this. She was good, and kind, and full of potential that I lacked. I could be lost to the mud and the salt for ever, and the world would go on unperturbed. Not Mallory.

And then she spoke again, and I felt the rod go slack like a cut fishing line. The room spun, a dizzying blow to the head, as her words settled in the air between us. "I only came here for you," she said.

I blinked into the dark, eyes finding the muddy splatter across her brow. Bits of pebble and salt clung to her hairline. Any urges I might have had to smooth them away dissipated, my fingers numb where they curled over hers. I could hardly feel my lips move as I answered, "*What?*"

Mallory rubbed the heel of her hand under her nose, sniffing wetly as she gave a shrug. "When I heard about all this," she gestured vaguely, to the oppressive dark and the bloody strike of the red flare, "about Beck's wild speculations coming true, and then that you were coming with—" A watery half-smile, a shrug. The movement crackled at the salt that dried in the slope of her neck. "I'm only here because of you."

It felt accusatory, blame that fell over me like rainfall. But she hadn't meant it that way, of course. Mallory wasn't capable of that kind of thing. It was earnest, this confession. A declaration of intent at the bitter, dark end. I wanted to shake her, to demand her reasons, but of course I knew them already. She believed in me. She'd said as much before, back at the inn. And she'd said as much in a million other ways, at a million other opportunities. I was just too stupid to hear them.

Until now.

Maybe I could make Beck see reason. I had to try, for her. I rose, Mallory's hands slipping from my wrinkled, salt-slick fingers. "I'll be back," I said. "Don't go anywhere."

Not like she had many options.

He stood by the monolith, picking over books heavy with indecipherable text and tracing the dormant runes with the tip of his finger mere inches from the warm stone.

"Beck?" My voice was painfully small. I lacked the conviction that I wished I had, that I knew would be necessary in shaking him from this delusional death trap. He seemed not to hear me. So I spoke again. "Edward?"

He was on me at once, arms outstretched and cold hands cupping my face. I gasped, but the sharp breath was cut short, caught in my chest as he kissed me, *hard*, with no regard for who watched. My eyes flew wide as I stumbled back a step, bending at the waist from the sheer effort of the kiss. I gripped his biceps, solely for the sake of keeping upright – but it seemed to drive him, to embolden him. A hand slipped to the curve of my lower spine and lingered there.

I yelped, the sound swallowed. Pain sliced like a knife through my skull. He cared little for my broken nose, or the bruises beneath my eyes. My head spun, stomach lurching.

His breath was hot on my face. He pulled back, and the mania reflected in his eyes made him near unrecognizable. I opened my mouth to speak – but to say what, I didn't know. To reprimand him? To beg for our lives? To demand another kiss, another bold and unashamed display of affection? There were no rules here. We weren't ourselves, so far from home and so close to the precipice of the unknown.

But that was the problem.

Beck's words came quickly, swallowing mine. "How happy I am, Caroline, that you are here. How *relieved*."

"I—"

"We're in it now. The thick of it." His fingers knotted in the sodden fabric of my sweater. "It's exactly what I surmised it might be. This . . . this liminal space. We are neither here nor there. The world is unreal in every sense. We sit, suspended, in the membranous heart of the in between."

I blinked. "You—someone just *died*, Edward. We all saw the same thing."

His grip was unwavering at my back. Beck nodded, the tip of his nose brushing mine. I could feel eyes on us, but he continued to act as if we were entirely alone. "I know," he said. "I had hoped Dorothy might understand, as we do. She had every opportunity to take the olive branch given to her. It would have been easy—"

"*Easy?*"

"The Leviathan doesn't test her acolytes with riddles and paradoxes, Caro. She wants us to succeed. She tailors each trial to us *specifically.* She doesn't give us more than we can handle. It's the manifestation of the darkest self – the darkest shadow. Whatever form that takes, we must defeat it. A shame that Dorothy couldn't—"

I strained, tugging away from him, but the hand on my cheek rose to cup the back of my head. He held me too close. His body was hot, trembling with fervor. At the far end of the room, Oliver rose from where he'd hunched, wringing out his socks and scraping the mud from his boots. His eyes were hard on Beck's back, gaze flickering every so often to my face for a sign that he should intervene. Beck's grip was hard enough to bruise – anyone could see that.

Even still, there lived inside me a horrible flush of satisfaction at being wanted. Openly, no less. Valued. He was glad to have me. He *loved* me. He wouldn't let me die here.

But he would allow it of the others.

"Beck . . ." I gripped his shoulders and gave a push. "We need to find a way out of here. It's gone too far."

"*Too far?*" He scoffed. "I don't think it's gone far enough!"

All eyes were on us now. I squirmed beneath his grip again. "This isn't worth dying for, okay? This—"

"But you see it now, don't you? You were there. I was *right.* It's impossible to deny it now."

"I— sure, Beck, but I don't think *belief* is—"

"Belief is everything, all right? For the first goddamn time, there is irrefutable proof that belief in me, in my *work,* is not misplaced. I will not allow it to be squandered."

"People are dead, Beck! Injured! Hell, look at *me*!" I thrust a bandaged hand before his eyes. He didn't flinch. "If you care so much about me, then hear me when I say—"

"Do you think that we would even be *allowed* out now?" Beck hissed. His eyes were hot, keen, and appraising on my face, as if the blood under my nose and the bruises ringing my eyes were somehow trophies of his utter triumph. "We're in it now, Caroline. The only way out is through. To fight it is to ensure failure."

I didn't believe that. I couldn't.

And so therein lay the paradox: to be loved and accepted, to be cherished for once, or to survive? It was a question that had plagued me since childhood. I could be loved, or I could be safe. There was no having both.

Who do you want to be, Caroline? he'd asked me once. *What do you want to become?*

I don't know, I'd said. *But I want to find out.*

I had been made in the image of something fillable. Something empty. I was made to be told what I was, who I was, what I was meant to be. I was an accessory to a grander design, one that was never my own.

But this – here, now – could be my own. I could choose now.

"I don't want anyone else to be hurt," I said.

"Neither do I." It sounded like a lie. It sounded like all the times he'd whispered sweet nothings, promising endlessly that he was mine, and I was his. I was a fool then. I wouldn't be one now.

"Good," I said. "Good. So we're in agreement. We find a way out."

His brows furrowed, lips twitching at the corners. "*Out* is *through.*"

"*Out* is *out.*"

Beck's hands fell from me, hanging lamely at his sides. I felt rudderless. Cold. It was suddenly apparent that he had kissed me in front of everyone, a married man and his favorite student. Though it felt as if the rules of the world didn't apply here, once I was free of his orbit, it didn't feel like that was the case. I wanted so desperately for him to approve of me. To love me. If only I could make him see.

"I don't know why you're doing this to me," Beck said, voice low. A familiar line, a blow to the chest; I was the villain, no matter where I turned. There lived a coldness there that I understood implicitly. My mother had known its candor well. "This *place*, Caroline. Can you not feel it?"

I *could.* That was the worst part. I felt the magnitude of this place like I'd felt nothing before.

But to be loved by Beck was to be tested. To be tested was to be chosen. He tested me again and again, and I endured it simply because I wanted, needed for *someone* to choose me. Just once. My fingertips ached. I wanted nothing more than to dig them into my chest cavity and give him my heart as proof. *Here!* I'd say. *Feel this!*

"I'm sorry," I said. It was a knee-jerk, a well-placed thumb pushing into an old bruise. "I don't— I'm just afraid."

His expression softened. "Fear is good. Fear is understandable. It means that you understand the gravity of our situation, of the work we're doing here. The Leviathan will see that, too. She'll take it into account."

We were no acolytes, no slaves to a god of the sea the likes of which I'd never seen. We were just *people.* None of us had chosen this.

But I was helpless. We were trapped, and we weren't alone. What options did I have?

"Compromise, please?" I wrung my hands, unable to temper the trembling of my digits. "We need to rest. And then we need to move. We can't just sit here and wait for the ceiling to fall down on our heads."

Beck considered. He craned his neck, looking up to the point where the stone monolith disappeared into the darkness. "Fine," he said. "It can't hurt to explore. We'll rest, for now."

I sagged, relief flooding my aching bones. It was time, at least, to formulate a plan. If we kept moving, maybe we could find something. *Anything.* Dorothy's lighter had picked up a trail, after all. The steady flow of air had to come from somewhere.

Mallory and I retreated to the far wall, settling against a half-absorbed bookshelf. She shrugged off her jacket, draping one arm over my shoulders and the other over hers. We pressed together, huddling under the jutting shelf; the jacket barely covered us both, but the warmth of her body was enough.

"Sorry I ruined your socks," I muttered, stretching out my legs on the stone before us. I would say anything, anything at all, to drown what lived in the silence. In each stretch, I could hear Dorothy. Iskra. My mother. They lurked, waiting for any opportunity to bleed horror into my ears and mire what little sanity I maintained. And so I spoke to Mallory. Only Mallory. "I owe you."

A laugh bubbled from her, a watery and shrill thing; it was a welcome sound, and one that I would have taken over the silence of the cavern any day. She rubbed the heel of her hand over her eye, and moved closer to me. "You saved my life," she said. I wanted to protest, to shrug off our frantic escape from the flooded passage, but it would do neither of us any good. "I think we're even. There'll be more funky socks in the future."

"Yeah. For sure."

"Caro."

"Mallory."

A pause. She stared intently at a scuff in the stone, like something big, something heavy, had been moved past the spot where we sat. "I'm glad you're here," she said. Her smile, seemingly infallible and unflapping, warmed me again. "Maybe the next time we want to hang out we just . . . get margaritas."

"Of all the people in the world to be stuck with—"

"You're number one," Mallory said, her shoulder bumping mine. "Pedro Pascal is number two."

I snorted, the sound echoing throughout the cavern. "High praise."

"*Right?*"

"For what it's worth," I began. I wasn't good at this kind of thing, but for Mallory I could certainly try. "You're the one person I'd want to be stuck with, too. You're pretty damn cool."

She inclined her chin, a satisfied smile curling on her lips. "You think?"

"Fuck yeah."

"*Fuck yeah.*"

It was strange, this idea of being needed, of being liked, with no pretense. She didn't seem to want anything from me. There was no trick, no upper hand poised with claws. Mallory had no motives. She was my friend, and that was all.

No—

"You're my best friend," I said. I ventured to reach for her, to squeeze her fingers, and she squeezed back. It felt somewhat silly to say now. Here. But it needed to be said. It was a first for me.

Her lips curled up. "Is this news to you? The whole 'best friends' thing?" She gestured between us, and I felt my cheeks flush. "You're wearing my *socks*, for Christ's sake. That's love."

I wanted to tell her everything. I wanted to come clean, to bare the darkest parts of my soul to the one person who I was beginning to think might stay despite it. There was no part of me that believed that Mallory belonged in a place like this, though I certainly did. Maybe if she knew, if she understood, maybe then I could lighten the load.

Once we left this place, I could try. And we *would* leave this place.

I leaned against the wall and Mallory followed, huddling further still under the narrow stretch of her jacket. My gaze turned upward, to the dark above our heads. I could only wonder at how high the cavern went, how far above the rock stretched. This place was impossible, in every sense; it had looked so meager from the outside, like we might venture half a mile into the dark and have to turn right around. But here we were. The place was limitless, endless. Maybe Beck was right. Maybe we truly had slipped through a crack and *stuck* there.

For a moment, I could have sworn that the opaque blackness above our heads trembled. It moved, slid along the stone, as if it were a singular body. I rubbed my knuckles over my eyes. Mallory gave my arm a gentle pat, almost absentmindedly; she might have thought that I was crying, that the fear had gotten the best of me.

But the darkness moved again. It seemed to curl, a snake finding its own tail, and then it stopped. None of the others seemed to see it. Maybe I was imagining things.

I closed my eyes. Dorothy swam behind my eyelids, contorted and frantic as her double writhed in the mud. The *thing* here had torn her to bits. And I'd felt it, in every turn of the wind, in every rumble of the earth. It had been . . . *satisfied.* Satiated.

No. I wouldn't let it happen to Mallory. If my life was worth anything, then let it be this. Mallory deserved to be saved.

The dark stirred once more. It listened. It understood. And then it was gone.

I didn't sleep. Mallory's head fell onto my shoulder shortly after the others settled in their various corners. I was glad that she could rest, but I wasn't so lucky.

I watched the dark above our heads, searching for any hint of movement within.

Who's up there?

Nothing.

Who's watching?

Maybe I was losing my mind. There was no telling how much time had passed since we'd parted from the fishermen, but clearly it was enough for me to start talking to shadows and attempting telepathy with ghosts. Some things were better left unsaid. I could be *crazy* in the comfort of my own head.

For a long while, I hadn't been sure of whether or not I truly believed in Beck's research. It all seemed so fantastical: an ancient cult of sea-bound recluses who dedicated their lives to the service of the Leviathan. Hell, centuries passed and no one had even thought to record what the Leviathan *looked* like. There were enough mentions of the beast in various mythologies and religious texts, but Beck's study of the patterns therein, and the connections that bound each iteration of the creature, were conjecture.

He'd received some acclaim after finding a trove of Phoenician artifacts and texts that didn't quite match the current literature in the field, and didn't jive with the academic understanding of the material. The symbols carved into the bases of the artifacts were written in no context the scholars could recognize: the original Chinese serpent-gods Fu Xi and Nu Wa, with their human heads and animal bodies; Annunaki Nin-Khursag and her husband Enki of the Sumerian mythos, and Enki's connection to the serpent in Genesis; the cosmic serpent Ananta, as told by the Hindus. None of it matched; the text was scrawled in foreign symbols, in form and vernacular that matched no one's understanding. Beck slaved endlessly, exchanging fervent emails with Norse scholars and the American University in Cairo, demanding all their texts on the snake goddess Wadjet.

It was fanaticism, plain and simple. He made rubbings of the symbols inscribed on each artifact, taping the rudimentary alphabet up onto whiteboards in his office. Beck slept on the sofa, missed meals, agonized over and over, until he cracked the code. Or so he thought. Academia was never quick to throw in with the mystic and the unseen. Beck was asking of them the impossible: to double their suspension of disbelief, and divest it from fiction.

When the school denied him a travel stipend – no one in Cincinnati wanted to spend a *dime* on two flights, a train, a car rental, and a local guide in rural Norway, to Beck's dismay – Beck had known that he was alone in his study. And so he did it alone, and did it well – until I walked into his most detested undergraduate lecture. After me, everything changed.

I had seen enough manmade horrors that I struggled to comprehend the mystical. I didn't believe in God; what kind of God would allow the things I'd seen? It was certainly a lot to ask of me, to suggest that I believe in a deity that had no worshipers to speak of, who had no temples or idols. All that existed of the Leviathan was what lived in Beck's work. There was no denying that the code in the text was real. The symbols he'd spent years formulating into an alphabet were tangible enough, whether he'd made them up or not. This was popular opinion; he'd simply lost the plot, and was doing his best to gaslight the world into thinking that an unknowable inhabitant of the unexplored depths was anything godly.

But what I'd seen here was real. Monsters or acolytes, it didn't matter – they were real. And they were dangerous.

Again, the dark shifted overhead. I could feel eyes on me. I looked around at my colleagues, all huddled in their various corners as they struggled to cling to any warmth their tired bodies might afford them. None looked to me, nor to Mallory's head on my shoulder.

I looked up. I considered. And then I stuck my middle finger high into the air.

Caroline?

My mother's voice. It came from above; I could pinpoint its exact location, as if her body hung just past the light of the ever-lit braziers.

Caroline, come here.

The voice was closer. I looked up again, but nothing had changed.

"Go fuck yourself," I hissed. "You aren't real."

Why are you doing this to me?

A familiar condemnation. I shouldn't be responding, indulging in the fantasy of whatever power followed us, lurked in every corner. We were being tested, of course, but I couldn't fail if I simply didn't participate.

And yet it was my mother's voice I heard. It was my rawest wound, a bleeding bruise. There was no ignoring her.

From above, I heard a long inhale. Ragged. Wet. I squeezed my eyes shut and stuck my fingers in my ears.

But I could still hear her. *Don't make me do it, Caroline*, she said. Briny air gave way to an acrid breeze, a breath upon my face. I let my head fall back against the cool stone and bit down hard on the inside of my cheek.

I gritted my teeth. "Not real," I hissed. "Not. Real."

You need me more than I need you, she said. It sounded like her voice was moving, circling me like a predator over a carcass. *You have no one without me.*

"Fuck off."

I'll do it, Caroline. Because you made me do it.

"Fuck *off*—"

"Who are you talking to?" Oliver's voice was close and sudden. I startled, enough to wake Mallory and send her slipping from my shoulder and into my lap. My eyes flew wide. At once, I craned my neck to look into the darkness above, but there was nothing there.

Heat flooded my cheeks. "What do you want?"

Oliver blinked. The words had come out more bitterly than I intended. "I just wanted to make sure you two are all right," he said. "Given the circumstances, at least."

Mallory yawned. I shrugged. "We'll be all right when we're out of here." I felt like a guard dog, like a yapping mongrel with no teeth. Instinctively, I wanted to put myself between Mallory and Oliver, though he was likely the safest of the bunch.

Oliver opened his mouth to speak, but a third voice rang out from across the chamber, silencing us both. Hannah, shrill and immediate, had shot to her feet. She overturned her bag, spilling its contents onto the floor, and cried out, "Where the hell is it? Who took it?"

Oliver whirled, shying from the gunshot of Hannah's keening voice. Beck drew closer, as if he intended to watch her like an animal in a glass exhibit case.

"Where is what, Hannah?" Beck prodded.

"My . . . my—" Her eyes wheeled. There was no color in her cheeks, and the sheen of sweat on her brow was out of place in the cold. "My *medicine!*"

I thought of the bottle of pills she'd produced at the slightest inconvenience, rattling them around like they might stave off the ghosts. She fell to her knees and dug through her belongings, tossing aside her first aid kit, her rope bag, a baggie of batteries. It burst, batteries scattering across the stone floor. Oliver moved wordlessly, arrowing away from where Mallory and I huddled to chase after a battery that rolled toward the monolith.

"Who *took* them?" Hannah cried. Her eyes flew up, wide and frantic, to lock upon Beck's sagging pack. She thrust out a finger, a damning accusation. "Empty out your bag."

To my surprise, Beck took a step away. He slipped the bag from one shoulder and swung it round to cradle against his chest. "I will not," he said. It was a petulant refusal, his voice curt. I wondered for a moment if I had fallen asleep and if this was all a stupid dream.

"Fucking *empty it*!"

"Hannah, you need to calm down." Oliver approached her with his palms splayed, retrieved batteries propped between water-wrinkled fingers. He spoke to her, drew nearer, like he expected her to start foaming at the mouth. Maybe she would.

"*Calm down?*" In her defense, that is categorically the worst thing that a man could say to a woman. But I'd allow it, just this once. "You want me to calm down when I've been stolen from?" A bottle of water arrowed past Oliver's head, bursting on the stone behind him. Hannah's breathing was ragged, her eyes unfocused.

She lunged stiltedly for Beck, half-hobbling as she lurched, clawed hands reaching for his bag. I shot to my feet. Mallory screamed as Hannah tore at Beck's pack, the effort knocking him sidelong. He fell past the monolith, tumbling to the stone and losing his grip on the bag.

"*Edward!*" I went to him without a second thought, with no regard for the fact that he hadn't done the same for me.

He didn't seem to notice me. "Get it away from her!" he boomed, wincing and groaning as he struggled upright. I didn't listen, falling to my knees at his side.

"Edward—"

"The *bag*!"

It was too late. Hannah unzipped Beck's pack, which had long since been far heavier than the rest of ours, and turned it over. Out onto the stone spilled the supplies we'd been given by the Grundstadts, a wrapped condom (*awesome*) and . . . something else entirely.

A heavy discus the size of my head thudded to the floor. The sound echoed throughout the cavern, dissipating into the dark on all sides. Each one of us froze, transfixed, as it rolled at the edges, then settled. A pattern faced skyward, gnarled ridges jutting in a spiral. Lettering, runes the likes of which we all knew by now, ran alongside the outer ridge of the spiral, converging at the centermost point.

For a long moment, we all merely watched it as if waiting for it to float into the air and batter Hannah over the head. Beck was the first to move, scrambling ungracefully onto all fours and making for the disc.

"Give me that," he snapped, snatching it off the ground and shambling to his feet. "How dare you touch another person's – another *professional's*—"

"What is that?" Mallory piped up, lingering at the outskirts of the conflict. She looked bleary, like she hadn't quite decided to wake from her too-short nap just yet. "What is that thing?"

All eyes were on Beck. He hugged the circular object to his chest. "I found it," he began, his voice short, waspish. "In the vestibule off the entrance cavern."

"You *found* it?" Oliver sounded out each syllable, like they were new to him entirely. He started toward Beck, skirting around Hannah who had resumed the search for her pill bottle. "Let me have a look—"

"*No.*"

"Wait—" I held up a hand. "You said you found it off the entrance cavern. Is that where you went when it collapsed?"

He nodded. "Lucky for me that I was absent, it seems."

"Lucky," I echoed. I knew precisely what I wanted to say, what I *thought*, but I couldn't bring myself to do it. This was all too convenient, the timing too specific. There had been no signs, to my untrained eye, that the cave would collapse on us, that it would kill the Swedes where they stood. But Beck had disappeared – and only moments after, the world had gone to shit. He knew too much of this place, had been too calculated in his every move, for it to be a coincidence.

Oliver seemed to think the same. For once, I was grateful for his skepticism, and for his open dislike of Beck. "Interesting timing, isn't it?" he mused. Oliver paid no mind to Hannah, who had begun tossing Beck's things about at his feet in search of her pills. "You slipped away just in time. Almost like you caused the collapse by swiping it. You know more about this place than anyone. I have a hard time believing that you would just dislodge a goddamn artifact from the wall without knowing what it's for. What it would do."

Beck spluttered, face reddening. "I thought it was a map!" he cried. "I only wanted to get a better look—"

"Don't bullshit a bullshitter, Edward," Oliver hissed. "You've been prancing around like this is a goddamn museum field trip, rattling off '*fun facts*' that in no way pertain to the more pressing issue of getting the hell out of here unscathed. You've had an answer for everything, and yet you want us, now, to believe that you simply plucked this thing from the wall because you were *curious*? And what's it a map of, huh?" Oliver stooped, swiping Beck's flashlight from his discarded things. He switched it on, pointing it down at the seal, which Beck refused to let go of. It seemed too heavy, too slick with water and algae, to hold; he struggled with it, fingers straining. "Turn it around," Oliver commanded. "Come on. Let's see this map."

To my surprise, Beck snapped back immediately. His voice was childish, spittle flying from between reddened, pursed lips. "*No!* I will not. I don't have to answer to—"

Oliver's open hand made contact with Beck's cheek, the acute smack reverberating around the cavern as Beck spilled sideways. The circular stone slipped from his grasp, and Oliver scrambled for it. In the low light, I could see its patterning, spirals, cut and bisected at seemingly random intervals. Each cut was marked with a symbol reminiscent of the Enochian-adjacent runes in the entrance cavern and on the monolith, but they were too small to make sense of from where I watched.

Mallory rushed to the stone, turning it so that its patterned side faced up. I eddied in between, gaze darting from their hunched backs to where Beck slumped on the wet stone. His eyes were wild. They found me, and I flinched; there was no affection there. Only desperation.

"Stop them, Caroline!" he cried, thrusting a scraped finger at Oliver's back. "Don't let them destroy it!"

I opened my mouth, then closed it again. Mere hours ago, I might have done whatever he told me to do. Hours ago, I would have trusted him with my life. But now . . .

Oliver scoffed, and the sound reverberated around the cavern like another slap. "This isn't a map at all. It's just more nonsense!"

"What does it say?" Mallory's voice came next, pitched and trembling. "Is it like what's in the journal? Maybe we can translate."

"No!" Beck scrambled onto his knees, and I stumbled back a step. "I swear, I needed it to—"

Oliver whirled. "So you *did* take it for a reason!"

Beck shook his head, rubbing his scraped and dirtied hands on the front of his sodden jacket. "The spiral is key. The spiral, the serpent, it's the most easily recognizable symbol of the Leviathan that we have. I figured it was a map, not a goddamn *start* button. What I mean is—"

"Did this set off the collapse?" There it was. A bold accusation. "Did you do it on purpose?" Bolder still. Mallory let out a little gasp, skittering away from the circular seal as if it might shock her.

Beck blinked. "If I want to pick up a pine-cone for study, am I killing the whole forest?"

"You said it yourself," Oliver continued, looming over Beck like an executioner. "There's no such thing as chance here. It's science, right? Cause and effect."

Beck's lips twisted into a manic smile. From where he'd settled on his knees, he thrust a finger up into Oliver's looming face. "So you believe, then? You want to blame me, to imply that I took the damnable thing and started the trials on purpose. In doing so, you suggest that you agree that there *is* divine purpose here, that it *is* part of a test that we are, at this very moment, *failing* by wasting time—"

I found my voice at last. "People are dead, Edward," I said. "Finding out the cause of that isn't a waste."

Oliver met my gaze and held it. I could see open relief in his expression, as if he'd expected me to jump to Beck's aid regardless. I still didn't fully believe that Beck would ever get someone killed on purpose – he was a professor from Ohio, for God's sake – but it was clear that he knew more than he was letting on. He'd gone to great lengths to keep us all from knowing what he hauled around this place. Why?

Beck threw up his hands. "You think that by picking up a rock, I killed the Swedes?"

"It's not that—" I began, but Oliver held up a hand.

"Yes," he said. "I think that's precisely what happened. Sure, you didn't mean for them to die. Wrong place, wrong time. But the second you disappeared into that antechamber, we were all thrown into the pits. You said it yourself, Beck. No chance. No coincidence."

"I don't mean for *any* of you to die!" Beck cried. "Of course I don't!"

"No, maybe not," said Oliver. "But you're more than happy to allow whatever's been following us, watching us, to do the job for you." He paused, considering. "What happens if we destroy it? Just break the damn thing in half. You say it's a map in one breath, but then in the next you implore us all to trust this place, the Leviathan, whatever you want to fucking call it. Fate, or divine design – *whatever.* We don't need a map, do we? So why don't we just—"

He made a move for the discus, which sat untouched just feet from Hannah. The blue light of the phosphorescent rock flickered strangely across the runes, the single ridge that spiraled to a point at its center. A small part of me wanted to look closer. Another part, a much larger nag, wanted to smash it to pieces simply to absolve Beck of this guilt, this blame.

I wanted Beck to be right, to be a hero. But guilt was sour and heavy on the air, like a fresh spray of blood.

Beck scrambled to his feet before Oliver could reach it. He bent at the waist and leapt for Oliver, slamming his shoulder into his side and pitching him sidelong.

The ground rumbled beneath my feet. No one seemed to notice it, too fixed on Beck as he threw Oliver to the ground.

"You will *not*!" Beck cried. "We need it to carry on. *I* need it to complete the work I came here to do. You will not soil it like this!"

No denial, no rebuttal. But no acceptance either. I didn't know what to believe. I didn't want to know. I just wanted to *leave*. We could hash out blame and circumstance on the outside.

"Get the fuck off me!" Oliver's voice was a broken woodwind, the rough rock floor jutting into his back as he fell, and rolled, and struggled against Beck. Beck leapt away, scuttling on all fours toward the stone disc. To my surprise, Mallory was faster. She vaulted over Hannah and hauled it up, though it was clearly too heavy to move far.

The heavy edge dragged gratingly across the stone as Beck reached for her. "Give that here, Mallory," he barked. "*Now.*"

"Tell us what it does!" Mallory's voice was shrill, her body hunched and crooked as she tried and failed to gather the disc into her arms. Oliver was on Beck at once as he advanced, hauling him back by the arm. "Tell us why it's important enough to lie about!"

On the floor, Hannah let out a shriek. I startled, and Mallory yelped. She'd found the prescription pill bottle that I'd seen her tending to so meticulously back on shore – and had found it empty. The men paid her no mind as she turned it over in her palm, futilely shaking the empty plastic, and then lobbed the container into the dark.

The floor shuddered again, and a shifting of dust and broken rock skittered down the flat side of the monolith. I turned my face up to see, again, near-imperceptible movement within the dark. A shadow within a shadow, a single body; it shifted, sliding through the dark like a watcher. No one else seemed to feel it, to hear it.

"Hey guys?" I ventured, voice swallowed by the sounds of Beck and Oliver struggling against one another, Mallory's wretched tears, and Hannah's manic muttering.

Caroline.

The voice was at my shoulder, as clear as the scuffle itself. I whirled, knowing beyond a doubt that I would find my mother there.

Just within the shadow, not more than a step beyond the phosphorescent light's boundary, a door stood upright on the stone. No wall, no frame, and unmolested by the grime that seemed to cover every surface of this place. The sterling handle rattled, like a hand on the other side was struggling against a lock.

Why are you doing this to me, Caroline?

The door lurched, a heavy thump on wood. I jolted. The handle continued to rattle, jiggling and twisting in the dark. Again, the door shuddered with unseen weight as, behind me, the disc slipped from Mallory's grasp.

"Why are you doing this to me, Mallory?" Beck's voice was a howl, a familiar tone that plucked at a deep cord that had long since gathered dust. I returned to the group to find Hannah feeling at the floor with open palms, muttering to herself; Oliver held Beck by the arms as he knelt in what remained of his first aid supplies, and Mallory shook violently as she stood firm between him and the damnable artifact.

"Just tell us what it is, Professor Beck!" Mallory moaned, voice muffled by the firm clasp of her hands over her face. "Just tell us what it is, and why you took it, and it'll all be fine!"

"The seal is *mine*!" he cried. "It's for *me* to know; this is *my* work! *My* legacy! Give me the fucking seal, Mallory!"

The floor shook as the braziers winked out one by one. Too quick to stop, too quick to discern any sort of pattern; the last flickered and sputtered at Oliver's hip before fizzling in a spray of acrid smoke. The grotto was cast into darkness before I could scream.

But there was movement everywhere. And through it all, through the shuffling of feet, the screams, the bodies hitting bodies, I could still hear the rattling of a doorknob and the thud of a force throwing itself against a locked bathroom door.

I fell to the floor, feeling around the discarded contents of Beck and Hannah's bags. It would be useless to try to reach my own. A long, foreign moan rattled from above, wet and popping like a throat overfull with insidious liquid – a familiar sound, a cry I heard in every passing silence. I cowered from the sound as somewhere to my right Hannah cried out.

A body crunched heavily against the monolith, and it blazed to life, light dancing through the incomprehensible geometry and flooding the cavern with color. I scrambled for a flashlight, an ice ax, a first aid kit. While I hooked the ax over my belt, I stuffed what I could into my pockets. We needed to *move.* Beck may have trusted the benevolence of this beast, this place, but I did not.

And then I looked up.

A thousand faceless forms swam above, knotting and undulating and twisting like their joints were liquid. A head broke free here, a hand there. Many of the faces were entirely eyeless, leaving only stretched-wide maws to gnash and drool and gargle sea foam as they slithered through the dark, bloating the shadows above like a distended womb. Some bore hints of what might have once been eyes, a nose, a defined cheekbone; unblemished flesh stretched over eye sockets, webbed beneath nostrils, pulling any distinguishing features into the mass of bleached skin.

They moved as one, a misshapen body that slid through the bulging dark like the body of a serpent. Where was its head? Its tail?

And which craning neck was the source of my mother's voice? They all angled at once, like a dog waiting for a command. My mother was someplace within. I leapt for Mallory as she appeared around the broad side of the monolith. "Come on!" I cried. Beck arrowed past me, his shoulder clipping mine and sending me reeling sideways. Hannah screamed, the sheer force of it enough to slip her glasses from the sweat-salted bridge of her nose. Oliver scrambled for the nearest weapon, an ax, and held it above his head.

Mallory leapt against the wall, slipping in a patch of standing water. Beck paid the rest of us no mind, leaping for the stone discus and shoving it into his bag. With wild eyes, he hugged the pack to his chest, gaze snapping to the lit monolith.

His lips moved, but I could hear no sound. I could read them easily; he spoke with such animated fervor that it would be impossible to misunderstand him. *Who touched it? What did you see?*

And then his eyes turned upward, and his wild visage split into a smile. The shape within the shadow turned downward as he pulled the lip of the bag down over the seal's runed edge. Looking, maybe. Seeing. Thinking.

It was as if it could smell our chaos, could taste the strife the disc had created on the air like a spray of acrid blood. Maybe it had been drawn here. Each time we fought, whether we came to blows or not, the creature came running. Was it our long-suffering proctor, watching the Leviathan's pupils squabbling in the schoolyard? Did it disapprove? Or did it like the taste?

I took Mallory by the wrist. "Find an exit," I commanded, pulling her close. The sounds overhead grew louder, a cacophony of groans, and whispers, and the sliding of flesh across stone. Beneath our feet, the stone trembled.

"The others!" Mallory's voice was a moan, and her resistance was weak. "We have to stick together!"

Fuck the others. "They'll catch up," I insisted, holding tight to Mallory with one hand and feeling along the wall with the other. By the light of the monolith, I felt the half-swallowed ridge of a bookshelf, a tome crushed by the hungry stone. My fingers grazed rough granite, a trickle of water from somewhere above, a patch of algae. I didn't want to go further into the dark beyond the monolith, the swallowing blackness that had no end. We'd lost Dorothy within it; there was no telling where this place would deposit us if we went into it again.

And so I felt along the wall in the direction of the hole in the floor, toward the quietly lapping pool through which we'd all emerged. The others cast jagged shadows across the wall, the cobalt runes stretching them until they melted into the dark above. They obscured my vision, darting back and forth – though one stood still in the very center of the room. I knew it was Beck implicitly.

A piece of rock shifted beneath my touch. I gasped, scrabbling for it with no care for the pain in my bandaged fingers. Mallory followed wordlessly. A sliver of space ran between two drowned bookshelves, as if the rock had shifted and half-collapsed over a narrow passageway long ago. I hadn't noticed it before – maybe it hadn't *been* there before. It was impossible to tell. The rock filled the crevasse in bits and pieces, jammed too tight to pry out by hand.

The metal of the ax was cool in my hand. It almost felt too light to do the trick, but it was all I had. I instructed Mallory to stand back, and she did as she was told. And with a steeling breath, I lifted my arm high and brought it down onto the loose rock. The impact shuddered through me like an electrical shock, rattling my teeth and vibrating in my nose's broken cartilage. But it did the trick – a bit of stone broke from the wedge between the shelves, and it loosened.

"Again!" Mallory cried. "Do it again!"

I swung the ax, hacking at the loose rock and prying it from the collapse. Overhead, the great body continued to move, passing further into the light. It curved, a stretch without end, its shadow joining the others on the wall.

Enough rock had come loose that I could fit my arm into the opening. I slammed into the wall, reaching my bandaged fingers for any hard edge I could find. I dug, and I dug, but the opening wouldn't grow. Big enough for an arm maybe, a leg. The passage stood at Beck's height, as if once upon a time it had been carved specifically for bodies to come and go. But it was closed now.

I held out a hand to Mallory. "Lighter?" I demanded. Mallory seemed to startle; clearly she hadn't thought she'd been seen picking it up. But she acquiesced, producing it from her jacket's breast pocket.

One try, two. The lighter flickered to life, the single flame dancing atop my curled fingers. I held it into the narrow space. The flame bowed, as if beneath a light breeze. This was a way out, if I could make an opening in the rock. Our way through. Or *past.* Anywhere but here.

Beck hadn't moved. As the bloated shadow curled and twisted overhead, bodies breaking free and returning again to the mass, he hugged the stone to his chest. With a free hand, he patted at his pockets as if searching for his journal. His brows furrowed – no luck. There would be no recording this. And even if he were to find the space to do so, what would he say? What would he call this thing that hovered above us now?

It had come to us before in pieces, descending upon Iskra in a pack. What had changed?

And then a familiar face broke from the whole. Smooth at the edges, as if every jutting bone and bump had been smoothed. Hair thin and watery like seaweed hung from a half-bare scalp. Dorothy peeled from the mass by what once had been her hips, arms distended and stretched. Her joints were bruised and loose, as if they'd been put back together after breaking. The upper half of her swung clumsily from the body, eyes cloudy white, her jaw hanging open too wide, too loose. The body dipped, and she swung like a scythe over Beck's head, arms outstretched.

I was running before I knew myself, wrapping both hands around his bicep and pulling hard.

And then it spoke. In a million voices and in none in particular. Dorothy. My mother. In a language I couldn't comprehend, its voice filled the cavern, my skull, the spaces between my bones. It hissed, each unknowable syllable languishing at the curve of my ear and rattling behind my eyes.

Dorothy's mouth peeled wide. Wider than it should, than it could in life.

"I have the seal!" Beck boomed. "I took it! And I will carry it to the heart of the spiral, as your acolytes are called to do!"

It was in my head. I could feel it. It felt hungry, hungry, *hungry.* Ravenous, it plucked at the dark thread of guilt entwined with my spinal cord, the shameful thing that held me aloft. Beck shuddered.

Had he felt it, too? There was darkness in all of us. Did it hunger for our shame, just as it thirsted for our chaos?

It made no sense. My head was full of thoughts that weren't my own, and when I blinked I saw the monolith, the runes, the split of Iskra's skull on the rock. The tips of my fingers ached. And still, Beck didn't budge.

I felt . . . *trepidation.* Anticipation. Like a kid on Christmas Eve, hovering over a present they so desperately wished to tear open. The emotion was keen, natural, as if I'd conjured it up myself. Eager, hungry; if I felt it, did Beck feel it, too? Did the others?

It felt wrong to turn my back to it, like some animal instinct I actively disobeyed. But I did it anyway. *For Beck.* I slipped around to his front, taking him by the shoulders and shaking him.

"Edward, please!" I cried. "We have to go!"

Caroline, baby? Why are you doing this to me?

My mother's voice was somewhere above, further into the mass of flesh. I couldn't look for her. I wouldn't. And so I shook Beck again.

Still, nothing. I took a deep breath, reeled my arm back, and slapped him. His head snapped sidelong, but still he clung to the seal. I wanted to kick him between the legs, to bite him. Were I stronger, I could simply toss him over my shoulder and run.

"Caro, come on!" Mallory's voice was impossibly far away. I looked for her in the dark, a spot of silk in a forest of sea-blue wool. Had the cavern grown longer?

Only she waited for me. Oliver and Hannah crowded the passage I'd chiseled open without any regard for the rest of us. Oliver went first. He pushed the doctor aside without a care, shoving his arms into the narrow passage with a grunt of effort. Hannah offered me no more than a glance. Even in the strange light, I could tell that she was impossibly pale and slick with a sheen of sweat. The shadows beneath her eyes were sunken, black. I felt sick just looking at her.

But I couldn't think to worry for her – not when the uneven face of the rock wall began to move at her back. The stone gave way for Oliver with a rumbling of granite and a raining of loose pebbles. Where I'd hacked futilely at the narrow slit in the wall, Oliver slipped into the stone like it had taken him no effort at all to push the opening wider. Like it was a jammed door, or an obstructing bookcase. The floor beneath my feet shuddered, the keening of stone over stone like a popping joint; Mallory slapped her hands over her ears and Beck, transfixed, seemed not to notice.

The way opened for Oliver without hesitation. Like this place *wanted* him to escape. Like it wanted him . . . somewhere else. It was like Dorothy all over again. An opening presented itself to her, too. A door in a sorority house, an opening in the wall; it was all the same, to the very same end.

I understood. Or, at least, I thought I did. Would a test await us on the other side? Would we die if we didn't follow? If we didn't spectate?

The burbling of guttural voices was nearly lost beneath the shifting of the rock, the sounds of effort as Oliver wriggled into the passage which now was just wide enough to accommodate him. I watched, dumbstruck, as the wall moved beneath his touch, and then stopped altogether as he disappeared into the dark.

"Oliver, wait—"

And for a moment, the formless beast over Beck's head gave pause. There was no counting its eyes, no tracking its attention. But it seemed, for just a moment, that it watched Oliver go.

"Wait!" Hannah called, grappling for him as he disappeared into the wall. She slipped in after him, a much easier fit than our broad-shouldered guide. I couldn't think to question the easy shifting of the rock, the quick accommodation for Oliver, and not the rest of us. All I could see, all I could hear, was Beck.

"*Just run!*" Mallory's voice again; if ever I needed evidence that she didn't give a shit about Beck, here it was. But I cared. It would have been easier if I didn't, but fuck. I cared.

"He won't budge! It's – it's *talking* to him!"

"What?" Could she not hear it? It was so loud. How could she not? "Come on!"

A body squelched, popped, and fell from the mass. It hit the stone with a wet *splat* of bare flesh on wet rock. And then another. Dorothy sagged, her fingertips so close to the top of my head that I could almost feel her tugging at my flyaways.

I acted without thinking. Onto my toes I rose, fingers knotting in Beck's hair. I kissed his too-still lips, pressing my mouth to his hard enough to bruise. He inhaled deeply, a gasp of surprise, as if he hadn't even known that I was there. Beck's body, rigid as it had been, slackened as another disfigured shape squelched from the amalgam overhead and splattered in a mass of limbs onto the floor. It scattered the antiquated tools, fumbling over them on untested feet.

Beck's eyes found mine. "It was called to us," he said, breathless. "It smelled us."

I didn't want to know – didn't *need* to know. I took him by the arm again. Wiping at my mouth with the back of my hand, I shook him. "We have to *go*!"

He acquiesced, blinking as if through sleep. I pulled him toward where Mallory waited, away from the monolith and what remained of our belongings. Thick masses of bleached flesh hit the stone, and what once had been hands, and arms, and wriggling toes reaching for us as we moved.

"It won't hurt us!" Beck insisted, struggling to zip the seal into his bag as I pushed him toward the narrow passage. "It only wants to observe!"

Like it had *observed* Iskra? Like it had merely watched as Dorothy had been twisted and stretched like putty?

Another fell, and then another. The first had found its feet, wavering unsteadily on spindly, milky limbs. It looked liquid, dripping from every joint, like a tendon fresh-pulled from the muscle.

And it was looking right at us. Eyeless, sure. But I could feel its attention just as keenly as I'd heard its voice.

"Just *move*!"

I pushed Beck into the Oliver-sized passage, and then Mallory. The others had been swallowed whole by the darkness ahead, but I had no time or space to think of them. My spine straight, stomach sucked in and breath held, I slipped into the crevice in the wall. Outside, in the glow of the monolith, the bloated dark dripped viscera onto the stone. The wilted bodies stumbled toward us, shambling and sloshing, blotting out the light.

And then there was nothing but the dark.

Stone pressed on all sides. It rumbled almost imperceptibly, vibrating the space beneath my sternum and tickling behind my eyes. Mallory's fingers found mine as we shuffled sideways, disappearing into the wall as the formless beasts crowded the passage. I sucked in breath as the wall angled, sloped, accommodating for years and years of settling sediment. The passage was barely big enough, just as wide as Oliver's shoulders – just as wide as he'd made it. An impossible thought, that he'd somehow changed the anatomy of this place with nothing more than brute force; the idea rang wrong in my head, like an equation that didn't shake out.

I looked up at the low ceiling. Just like the width of the passage, the height was set to Oliver's specifications as well. Just over six feet; just tall enough that he wouldn't have to stoop. This place had bent and warped reality to allow Dorothy inside – was it doing the same for Oliver? Or was he having one of those moments where adrenaline gave him super-powered strength, like a mother lifting a car off a baby? Didn't matter, ultimately; wouldn't matter, as long as we got out of this place without being pancaked.

A shriek, a curse; Hannah's voice rang from up ahead. "Oliver, wait!"

The floor shuddered beneath us, reverberations shaking every inch of the stone that pressed us from all sides. I could feel my own hot breath on my face. I squeezed my eyes shut and shuffled sideways, the tips of my fingers tangled with Mallory's.

And then the walls began to move. Bits of pebble and dust ricocheted off the tops of our heads as the passage began to narrow, stone scraping over stone. Solid rock rutted against the tips of my boots, the jut of my chest. Up ahead, barely lit by what remained of the monolith's light, I could see the stone ceiling scraping the top of Beck's head. Any tighter against my chest, my spine, the backs of my legs, and I would burst. No longer wide enough to accommodate Oliver, no longer tall enough to allow him a little breathing room, the gully squeezed us, pressed us between great sheets of granite as the great body of the cavern settled back into place. An inhale for Oliver, an exhale for the rest of us. It was as if whatever watched us all now didn't care if we popped like zits before we had the chance to be tested. What mattered – and what was abundantly clear – was that Oliver had gotten through.

And he had, for all I could tell. I couldn't hear his voice, couldn't see his head above the others.

A bone-white hand pressed into the space behind us. An arm, a chest; I heard bone crackle and spread into the passage. It was impossibly slow, languid, as if it cared little whether or not it caught us. Its jaw hung limp as if broken, brushing uselessly against its shoulder.

I tightened my grip on Mallory's fingers as the stone at our backs shuddered again, rumbling with an imperceptible note of sound from deep within. A crack, like a wayward shot from a gun, split the rock over our heads, raining stone into the narrow space between *us* and *it*. Dust coated my shoulders, rock littering my hair.

Another crack, another flurry of sound. It was closer now, and as the ground rumbled beneath us I heard a great *boom* from far ahead.

And then a voice said "*Turn back!*". Hannah, invisible and muffled, the sound of her fear nearly swallowed by the thunder beneath our feet. Beck shuddered to a halt, then Mallory. Oliver's voice was followed by a chorus of condemnations, the voices of our allies muffled and frantic above the shuffling of flesh and fabric on jagged stone. I heard fabric tear; Mallory cried out as a piece of jutting stone by her calf sliced her jeans.

"Go back!" Hannah was closer now. Mallory's shoulder slammed into mine as Beck fell sideways. Elbows scraping painfully on the stone, I scrambled for the lighter in my pocket, flicking it to life in time to see Hannah scrambling at the close press of the wall, which seemed to grow narrower and narrower by the moment. Her fingertips were bloody, the nail of her middle finger cracked and crimson.

"We *can't* turn back!" I cried, shuffling and stumbling as Mallory pushed into me, a domino spilled from a long line of others. Again, a *boom* shook the floor beneath us and a fresh rain of heavy rock fell before the mouth of the passage, obscuring our pursuer entirely.

Another crack split the air, clearer and cleaner than the last. Beck clapped his hands over his ears, elbow catching the back of Hannah's head.

It sounded like . . . *gunfire*? A single shot, fired into open air. I lived in Kentucky; I knew well enough what an errant gunshot sounded like.

"Fucking *move*, soldier!" The sudden crack of Oliver's voice was far away, an echo swallowed by a roaring boom beneath our feet, rattling my bones and knocking my knees. Something up ahead jostled Hannah, who fell into Beck, then Mallory, then me. I slid back toward the crumbling rock, pebble and dust raining onto my head.

Soldier? Who did he think he was talking to?

I could hear Oliver more clearly now, and as I lifted the lighter to the ceiling above I could see a sliver of light over Hannah's head. An opening in the quickly narrowing passage; a way out. And Oliver's face, wild and manic as he tried to shove his way back into an opening that wouldn't budge a second time.

"Let me back *in*!" he bellowed. "*Go back!*"

Vaguely, I could hear Hannah pleading with him, begging for Oliver to pull her out of the crack in the wall rather than pushing her further in. She screamed as he shoved an arm inside, pressing her more tightly against the rock, and she pushed against Beck in turn. The rock rumbled again, and I turned my feet outward like some second-rate ballerina.

"Somebody has to fucking move!" Beck hollered. "Oliver, get out of the goddamn way!"

My ears popped, and all sound deadened. I could feel vibrations beneath my feet, at my thighs, above my head. But I could hear none of it. I prodded uselessly at the top of my head as Mallory pushed me sideways again, lighter wavering over my head. Was there a blunt force wound that I hadn't accounted for?

Hannah gave another push. She was panicking, and the sensation was quickly spreading like mold. Oliver blocked her way, *our* way; we were going to be crushed. My shoulder rammed against the rock. I cried out as it popped painfully, the weight of the group pushing, pushing, *crushing.*

I couldn't breathe, couldn't think. Each ragged inhale was met on all sides by rock, and flesh, and jutting bone. The narrow passage seemed to shrink with every heartbeat as the rock over our heads shifted. At my waist, the smooth head of the ice ax pressed up and into my ribs. I could hear nothing but my own breath, reverberating like a dying gasp over and over inside my skull.

The rock at my left shifted, a spindly trio of fingers prying through the rubble. Oliver would crush us, force us into the arms of the creatures that pursued us all before we could reach him unless we moved. Or more likely, we would be trapped here, crushed into pulp and bone for Leviathan's warped failures to pick through. This would be our tomb if we didn't free ourselves. *Now.*

And then, from above, a whistle, a spark, and another boom – impossibly loud, and impossibly close. It shook my eyes in my skull, rattled my teeth. I'd never heard anything so painfully loud, so violent that the ringing in my skull drowned my own thoughts.

My lips moved, and I could feel myself speak – but I heard no sound from my lips. "Mallory, move!" She didn't respond. Had she been deafened, too? I reached across myself to prod at her shoulder, the lighter's weak flame wavering over us. Mallory's head whipped to me, eyes frantic. I pointed to my mouth, then tried again: *Push.*

She nodded, and pushed back against Beck. He understood, shifting his bag until the heavy weight of his pack hung against his front and using it to push back against Hannah. We fought against her as one, though outside the passage Oliver dug in his heels.

What was he so afraid of? What lay behind us was sure to be *much* worse than anything ahead.

But the ground rumbled again, a *boom* reverberating through the stone. My teeth rattled. Within the wall at my back, I could have sworn I heard the crackling of stone and dust, like shrapnel.

Another crack resounded, much closer than the first. This time, it was unmistakable: a gunshot. Oliver thrashed against the wall of our bodies, and an errant elbow knocked Dorothy's lighter from my grasp. There was only darkness now; darkness, and the feeling of eyes on my back as I pushed against Mallory again.

As if in answer, light arrowed overhead. I screamed, though I could hear myself make no sound, and looked up.

Open air hung above us, though the dust and smoke that permeated it was so thick that there was no way to see how high it stretched. Another rumbling boom – this time, accompanied by a flash of white-hot light somewhere within the haze – shook the walls on both sides, and bits of pebbled rock and dirt tumbled onto my brow. I inhaled, and the smoke choked me; I coughed, and spluttered, and at my side Mallory did the same. She slid her arm along her front, jutting outstretched fingers up into the open air.

A muffled bang resounded from somewhere in the rock at our fronts, and something small and furiously fast whizzed past Mallory's hand. She gasped, choking on the smoke and dust as she yanked her hand back to her chest. I met her wild-eyed gaze as she looked down to me – and I had no explanation to give.

And there was light, coming from somewhere above. It was enough, in brief flashes, that I could see the others – but only just.

Keep going! I mouthed.

Ahead, Beck gave Hannah a shove. Another flash of light, another peal of metallic thunder; she and Oliver fell out of my field of vision, past the walls on either side and into the pitiless dark. The sudden absence of Oliver's body sent us pitching, tumbling forward, scraping through the rock as it shuddered and cracked all around us.

We spilled, one by one, into an open trench as the opening in the wall slammed shut behind us. Muddy rock rose on all sides, a trio of passages lined with bags of sand and broken bits of wood stretching out before us. I slumped into the soil, chest heaving and arms trembling as I gasped for air. I clutched at my chest, feeling at the scrapes and the tears in the fabric of my jacket.

Something heavy and metallic arrowed past us, slamming into the wall over my head and sending a spray of mud and rock raining down on us all. Mallory was thrown back into the mud, and Beck leapt to cover my head with his bag and the damning contents within. He hunched over me as light burst from the point of impact, flame licking from the hole in the wall and reaching outward.

All at once, my ears gave a *pop*, and sound returned in full. I could hear yelling, a chorus of indistinguishable voices, from somewhere up ahead.

"My *ears*!" Mallory cried. "What the fuck!"

My head spun. I dug the heels of my hands into my ears.

It was only at this that Oliver seemed to stir, breaking into horrible, wretched sobs as he curled in on himself in the mud. He pressed his hands over his ears as I peered out from beneath the sodden fabric of Beck's bag.

I pushed Beck away, sloshing through the mud to reach him. "Oliver?" I touched his back with only the very tips of my fingers, but it was enough – he gave a howl and swiped blindly, clawing and pushing at the open air.

I understood.

Soldier. We were in a fucking war zone, a battle well in motion. The walls of the trench were packed with ruddy sand, the barbed wire that jutted up into the open air coated with dust and snagged here and there with loose bits of cloth. There was no sun, no moon – only opaque, unbroken sky, and an endless ricochet of smoke and metal. Dust filled my nose, and russet mud sloshed into my shoes.

He had to get us out of here. Only he could. Just as Dorothy, alone, could interact with that world – *her* world – only Oliver could find the end of this one. It was his trial, after all. And he would have to pass.

"Oliver, listen to me." This illusion was less concrete than Dorothy's had been; I could still smell the seawater, could still see the telling jut of stone through the cracks in the wood that buffeted the trench's walls. If I stuck my hand into the mud far enough, surely I would find stone there as well. "*Oliver!*"

Mine was not the only voice that called his name. A multitude spilled from me, a chorus that used my tongue. I startled, clutching at my throat. Oliver tucked in on himself tighter than before, pressing his head between his knees.

"Oliver, please!" Mallory was at his side, and still the strange and unfamiliar chorus rang from her chapped lips as it had done from mine. Oliver shied away, but Mallory seemed not to understand why. "Please, get up!"

He shook his head, hair dipping into the muck. "This isn't real! I got out!"

I opened my mouth to speak, but Hannah's scream cut me off at the tongue. My head flew up, away from Oliver as he rocked back and forth on his knees. Hannah was pointing, the tip of her pale finger shaking.

"We have to fucking *go*!" she cried. For a third time, her voice was one of many, as if a Greek chorus waited in the wings to buffet along each word we said. Oliver shuddered with each syllable, as if he'd been shot. "Look!"

A pale, featureless head and shoulders tugged itself free of the crack in the wall from which we'd all fallen. Distended arms, too long and spindly to be human, clawed at the mud on either side of the opening. Drool and blood slicked from between its teeth, over its lolling tongue, as another barrage of metal and fire rained overhead, arcing over the trench and lighting up the space beyond my vision.

This was Oliver's test. There was no telling what his transgressions were, nor why his guilt had manifested here, in this way, but we were in the belly of it. And we were not alone. The body squelched and plopped from the narrow passage, then languidly set about reassembling its liquid limbs into something solid. Tangible. *Dangerous.*

More yelling, a chorus of wordless cries, came from within the fog at the end of the trench that stretched to our left.

I dropped into the mud and took Oliver by the shoulders. I shook him, digging my fingers into his bicep hard enough to bruise. Maybe *that* would snap him back to reality. "Oliver, tell me what you did!" I demanded. "Tell me what you did, and we can all get through this together!"

And then, as the ground rumbled beneath us, the trio of gangways, each leading into a different stretch of smoke and gunpowder, began to move. Serpentine, they shifted, tangling among one another and arrowing away again with a squelch of mud, a grinding of stone, and a crackling of breaking and rearranging wooden beams.

As if we'd had any semblance of direction before. This time, the sound of hollering voices and the harsh punctuation of gunfire came from the right.

"No," he moaned. "No, I had to do it."

Another boom, another spray of russet sand and mud. Through the deafening din, I could have sworn I heard other voices. Strangers, wordless as they sounded off to one another. How many bodies were in this trench? And what had Oliver done to all of them?

"Do what, Oliver?"

Another bleached body slicked from the passageway, legs crackling back in line with an overlong spine as it stretched through the mud.

I reached for Oliver again. "Get *up*, Sergeant!" I barked. "We aren't leaving anyone here!"

His gaze flew up to meet mine, the sodden tips of his hair flinging mud and sweat across my front. I startled, slipping backward in the mud. His lips trembled as his eyes searched my face. Behind him, Hannah let out another blubbering cry, finger still outstretched.

I could feel our pursuers reassembling, drawing closer with every passing heartbeat. What would they do if they caught us?

Oliver spoke at last. "What the fuck did you say?" To my surprise, it was not solely recognition that painted his face in bold, stark colors. It was blind, senseless horror. It was *shame.*

Another explosion rocked the trench, sending splintered wood and bits of curled metal flying into the air around us. "You got us this far," I said, grappling for Oliver's hands. He seemed unwilling to hold my gaze, no matter how hard I tried. "This is your test, okay? Whether you believe it or not. You can't just tap out on us."

"Where is my squadron now?"

I opened my mouth to speak again, but before I could a trio of bodies appeared from within the dust as if summoned. Dressed in mud-splattered army fatigues, their faces cast in permanent shadow, they hurtled toward us.

"Sir!" one yelled. "Don't leave us!"

Oliver's head whipped sidelong in time to see a flash of light at their backs, deep within the smoke. Understanding and horror beyond reason stretched his features wide, taut over his skull. He shook violently, watching as the explosion lit them in a violent vignette, blinding us all. And then, with a sickening pop of flesh and a shower of blood, each of the men was shot through, a bullet catching every one between the shoulder blades and ripping out again through their ribs. They arched like dancers, arms flung wide, and then they fell, face down in the mud.

And then, as if called, our faceless pursuers stopped. All at once, they were nothing but bodies in the trench. Watchers. Silent harbingers of whatever decision would fall upon Oliver at the end of this. And Oliver didn't even seem to notice them, to register them whatsoever. When he looked at them, did he see soldiers?

No, maybe not. Now, all he could seem to see were the three all-too-human bodies in the mud. "Please!" Oliver wailed, his voice the only lighthouse in a sea of muddled echoes and choruses without source. He clapped his hands over his ears, shaking his head like a wet dog. "No, no, no – not again! I did what I had to do!"

"Oliver, come on!" I howled. I pulled at his arms, his collar. But he was all muscle, a solid fixture that refused to be moved. "You can fix it!"

Through the smoke and mud, Hannah and Mallory called out in echo. They said his name, over and over. They clasped their hands, begged him to make it all stop. And he could – right now, only he could.

And Beck just watched. Waited.

Oliver was on his feet. The sudden movement startled me, and I reeled backward, falling against the wall of the trench. His eyes were wild, bulging as they darted from face to face. He lingered on the trio in the mud. One body had begun to move, peeling himself from the muck with a squelch and a spray of blood. He didn't notice me; none of the soldiers seemed to have seen anything but Oliver before they were gunned down.

"Sergeant!" The body – I could see him as he steadied himself, clutching the blooming bullet wound below his sternum – stumbled and fell against the wall. He reached for Oliver, hands slick with mud and viscera. "Please help. Help me. What do we do?" I could just barely make out a name badge. Something bright and whizzing arced overhead, and I squinted through the mud that splattered the soldier's front. This wasn't some random, illusory creature. This was someone Oliver had known.

And by the look on Oliver's face, twisted and pale as the Leviathan's creatures, the soldier was a ghost.

"Private—" Oliver took a step back, hands outstretched. "Stay away."

The soldier blinked rapidly, a bubble of bloody spit popping between his lips as he lurched forward again. Behind him, still down in the mud, the others lay unmoving. Gunfire split the sky again, an arcing beam of something burning illuminating the trench in stark light for but a moment.

"Sergeant Dawes." The soldier took another step. All at once, he looked no older than me. His eyes were wide, and wet, and horribly afraid. And yet he still looked at Oliver, at his sergeant, like he hung the moon. Like he'd save them. "I don't want to die."

I hadn't interfered with Dorothy's, hadn't saved her, but I could try now. I could help. And Oliver could make this right. My eyes snapped back to Beck, who hadn't moved from where he had rooted in the mud. He was expressionless, surely waiting for the other shoe to drop.

Again, I reached for him. "Oliver, you have to—" *Atone or die. Repent. Apologize. Do fucking anything.* The words died on my tongue as Oliver wheeled and shoved me into the mud. The soldier tracked his movements, paying no mind to me as I splayed onto my back.

"No!" Oliver roared. "I'm not gonna fucking die here! I survived this hell once, and I'll do it again!" The soldier flinched, and then his expression fell. It was like a Halloween mask slipping off, an act going dead. The open, supplicating wound closed. The sadness slipped away into the mud. This was a deviation. This was his choice.

"Sergeant," the soldier deadpanned. "Look at us." Behind him, the others had begun to stir. One rolled heavily onto his back, and through the mud and tattered camouflage I could see the place where his chest had been blown open. A great, sucking wound, spilling desert mud into the chest wall. The other hauled himself to his knees and leaned against the wall of the trench. He spit, and great congealed fists of blood spilled from his mouth. And when he turned away from Oliver, I could see into his skull.

I closed my eyes, snapping my jaw shut as I swallowed down bile. Oliver was failing. But it wasn't over.

"I *am* looking," Oliver hissed. "I see myself surviving. War is about *survival.*" He thrust a finger into the open air in time with another boom, another rain of shrapnel.

And then – without a word, without a glance at the rest of us – he turned on his heel and ran.

Fuck.

"Jesus Christ, Oliver!" Hannah howled, smacking her brow with the heels of her hands. "Jesus Christ!"

I leapt to my feet. I took Beck by the arms and hauled him up, shaking him from the curious way in which he watched Oliver's retreat. "Edward, look at me!" I barked, voice nearly swallowed by the boom of an explosion and the sharp peppering of bullets and shrapnel into the wood somewhere within the smoke. "I'm going after Oliver."

Before he could speak, the ground trembled beneath us again. Once more, with a shuddering of mud and a creaking of boards and stone, the path of the trench curved, changed before our eyes. The ground beneath our feet bucked, rising in an arc as the shape of the trench rearranged, and Beck was thrown away. Mallory screamed, reaching for me. The crack in the wall widened, and the bodies that had followed us surged two abreast. Another explosion rocked us, lighting the open air above our heads in shades of vermillion and ochre.

And there, the bloated amalgam hung. Without beginning, and without end, it skittered through the dark, darting this way and that. Pieces of the whole still followed Oliver through the trench, no doubt. Watching, waiting, as he was tested. Had he already failed? Was there no coming back from this?

Bodies slicked like rainwater from the mass, dropping in bone-white splatters into the trench. One landed no more than ten feet ahead of me, and another at my back. They paid me no mind, taking shape and shambling after Oliver without a sound. They were coming from all sides now, spilling through the crack in the trench wall and splattering into the mud from above. The body of Leviathan's great beast came apart before my very eyes, slicking past failures – *Dorothy among them* – into the mud. Sending them, with a singular goal in mind, into the fray.

No, no, no. The choice had been made. His sentence was passed – he had failed, no doubt, and they were going to tear him apart. The Leviathan, omnipotent as she was, had made her decision, sending her flock to pass her judgment.

I could help him. Maybe if Dorothy had had someone to urge her along, to help her solve the riddle of her trial – maybe she could have made it right. It wouldn't have changed anything, in the grand scheme of things. My understanding of the Leviathan wasn't that she could reverse time. But Dorothy could have been absolved. She could have healed the broken thing, the dark thing, that had brought her here. And she would still be alive.

It didn't matter what Oliver had done. Not now. We needed him. So maybe, desperately, I could give him a second chance. He could make the choice, here and now, not to desert me. Us.

The shadows bent to the left, and so I followed. The wood lining the walls of the trench in intermittent bursts groaned, cracked; the illusion was not holding up under the strain of the changing landscape. Unhooking the ax from my belt, I readied myself to run. I had to follow Oliver. I had to find him, to see to it that he passed his trial one way or another. We couldn't lose him. We *needed* him, rules be damned. If the Leviathan wanted him dead so badly, she could swallow him herself. Digging my heels into the mud, knuckles white around the neck of the ax, I broke into a run. I craned my neck, watching the massive body overhead as it twisted. Whatever way it turned, I would follow. In a wave, limb over limb, the faceless creatures pursued, blowing past the others to scramble over one another. They surged after me, a billowing mass of tattered fatigues and ghastly flesh.

I called out to Oliver, hoping beyond hope that he could hear. Again, a chorus of unfamiliar voices spilled from my throat, obscuring my own. He'd seemed so afraid, so aflush with recognition at the sound of the voices – clearly they were ones he knew all too well.

Had he heard them in a place like this? Had he looked at us all and seen only ghosts?

The beasts surged over stacks of sandbags, careening against the splintering wooden slats on the walls and digging deep enough in the mud to touch the stone beneath. Beneath me, the floor shuddered. My pursuers scrambled over one another, bloating in a wave of thrashing limbs and undulating bodies. I called out to Oliver again as I skidded around a slope in the trench floor, tumbling over a broken beam and nearly splaying. Through the gun smoke and dust I could see very little – but I couldn't stop now. I was breaking the *rules*, after all.

An explosion shook the walls on both sides, much closer than before. Light flared just overhead, dirt and ash pelting the top of my head.

There, illuminated by the blast, stood Oliver. He moved erratically, hunched over an immobile figure in the mud. Over and over, he raised his ax over his head and brought it down again. I called out to him as he tossed the ax aside and made for the sloped trench wall, scrambling up the splintered wood and slamming a fist into the mud as he tumbled down again.

"Oliver, run!" My voice was swallowed by the churning of limbs over muck and wood at my back, and yet he seemed to hear me as clear as day. But when he turned to me, half-crouched as if to flee, it wasn't relief that colored his features.

He stumbled away, lurching for where he'd abandoned his ax. "Get the fuck back!"

It was only as I skidded closer, close enough to see the vein-riddled whites of his eyes, that I realized he meant *me*. Oliver's eyes darted from me to the mass of bodies struggling to push through the narrow curve of the trench to reach us, clawing and swatting at its own bloated form and roiling through the mud, to me – and it was at the sight of *me* that he trembled, a keening, ripping cry shuddering from him.

"The others are somewhere out there," I said. "I wasn't going to leave you—"

He swung the ax blindly, and I lurched away, slipping in the mud and landing hard on my backside. Steam puffed from his nostrils and open mouth as he stepped back, holding the ax aloft like a sword. "Stay away!" he boomed. At my back, the sound of splintering wood and splashing mud cut the air, only to be swallowed by another explosion and a barrage of debris and shrapnel. I flung myself onto my side, covering my head with my arms.

"Oliver, please!" I cried, voice lost to the mud. "It's me!"

It was no use. His eyes wheeled, animal and wild. The Oliver before me now wasn't the Oliver who'd encouraged me on the boat, or who'd welcomed me at the pub. This Oliver was lost, somewhere in the war in his mind.

At my back, one body stretched from the mass. Like a piece of putty ripped from the whole, it squelched into the mud and started toward us on all fours. I scrambled for the ax on my belt.

"I'm not sorry for what I've done," Oliver boomed, voice trembling and thick with tears. I looked up at him from where I lay in the mud. "I see you in my sleep every fuckin' night, and I'm still not sorry." He pounded at his chest with a closed fist. "I *lived*! I *survived*! And I'm not sorry for doing what I had to do for it!"

I blinked up at him, struggling and failing to understand. It was only then that he seemed to notice my pursuers, oil and sludge slicking off the whole and scrambling through the mud for us both.

He lunged for me, taking me by the arm and hauling me up. I could have – should have – fought back; should have swung my ax, kicked at his knees, spat in his face. I wanted to shake him, to slap him, to rouse him from whatever nightmare colored his vision. He needed to understand; *we* were here. *We* needed him. Whatever plagued him did not. No matter how real it seemed now, we could see him through it. Before I could speak, he kicked down hard on the back of my knee and struck between my shoulders. Pain lanced through my leg as I went flying, spilling uselessly toward the mass of bleached bodies.

"Sorry, soldier," Oliver said, voice stretching as he backed away from me. "I have to live."

I hauled myself onto all fours, scrambling to the nearest stack of sandbags as the first of the bleached bodies overtook me. Loose joints crackled and stretched beneath faded army fatigues as it splashed through the mud. Another lurched over the top of the partition, a distended hand slamming down atop my head and using me as leverage to pull up and over. I cried out as Oliver turned on his heel and ran.

I swung blindly. The tip of my ax found flesh, squelching into the soft belly of the humanoid monster nearest. It screeched as its flimsy disguise tore, black blood spilling from the wound.

"*Oliver!*" I shoved the bleeding body aside, sparing it no more than a glance as it writhed in the mud and clutched at its split abdomen. "Oliver, help!" I struggled up, only to be pushed down again, the next bone-white beast unseeing and uncaring as its counterpart bled into the muck. Another, and then another; each time I tried to stand, I was pushed down again, a barrage of feet and hands pushing me further and further into the mud. They ground me down, stepping over me like I was nothing more than a piece of debris. It was Oliver they wanted – not me.

He had left me. Deserted me, and all the others. A hand pressed down between my shoulders, a knee at the back of my head. They were heavy, sloshing, like a sponge that had taken on too much water. I could barely lift my head to gasp for air. I struggled to grip the ax, to find a space between bodies to act – I needed to get up. Still, uselessly, I thought of Oliver. He was afraid – but hell, weren't we all?

I rolled onto my back in the space between footsteps and swung into the space above, across one bare belly and another bulging knee. A creature with only a few strands of oily hair protruding from its bleached scalp fell sidelong, howling as the tip of my ax embedded between its ribs. Its jaw swung, loose and heavy with mismatched teeth jutting, as it crumpled. The body was enough; the others leapt over it and curved around it, crushing it into the mud. It gave me enough space, enough time, to scramble behind the stack of sandbags, hunching down with my hands over my head. My nose bled freely again, spilling crimson down my front.

They pursued Oliver without a second thought for me. I wondered if they even saw me at all. Or maybe they just didn't care; I wasn't being tested. Oliver was.

And I wasn't failing. Oliver was.

Maybe I could still help him. Fix him. That was what I was made for, wasn't it? To fix broken things at the detriment of my own mismatched parts?

I peered over the wall of muddy sandbags. As the last of Oliver's pursuers disappeared into the smoke, I craned my neck to look for him. Then I looked back the way we'd come. No sound save the boom of explosives and the arrhythmic pattering of bullets and shrapnel came from either end of the trench. There was no telling which way it had shifted, if the very earth beneath our feet had changed course, looped Oliver back around to be spilled out at my feet and punished before my eyes.

A small, dark part of me wondered if I might enjoy it, if it might bring me some vindication. He'd thrown me to the wolves, after all.

The trio I'd managed to fight off were nothing but bodies in the mud now, spilling black blood and burbling foam into the viscous murk. They could be killed – they could be stopped. Faceless, they roiled in the muck, squelching as limbs congealed and distorted, leaving something half-digested in their wake. Here, in the brief stillness, I could see that they *did* look dissimilar, as if the constitution of their bones hadn't yet been clean washed away. The curve of a cheekbone here, the ghost of a tattoo on a calf there; up close, it was clear that they had once been people. I wondered if Dorothy was among them now. Maybe she herself – or what was left of her – would catch up to Oliver first.

I rose, mud-sodden legs shaking. My knuckles were white on the neck of the ax, and with each explosion overhead, pain lanced through my skull. I wiped at the blood streaming from my nose, swiping it away from my lips. There was nothing I could do but move.

I inhaled, chest aching. "Oliver!" My voice was my own, no others echoed from within. Maybe he was too far to hear. Maybe he was already dead.

I started off into the smoke again, body aching and head spinning. My legs felt leaden, and there was mud in my ears. Bullets soared overhead and explosions rattled the boards along the walls, but I no longer feared them. This wasn't for me. I wouldn't be harmed – not purposefully, anyway. The Leviathan seemed to have no issue with collateral.

Again, I called out to Oliver. I broke into a jog, slipping and sliding in the mud. With my free hand, I felt along the wall of the trench, fingertips dancing over bullet holes and slick splashes of warmth. In a way, I understood Oliver. If this was what haunted him, I would be just the same. *Afraid.*

A voice rang from ahead. Wordless, the sounds of exertion broke the silence, drifting to me through the smoke between explosions and hailing gunfire. I cupped my free hand around my mouth and yelled again, his name dying in the open air.

Caroline!

I could have sworn I heard my own name then, as if imagined. From far behind, my name was no more than a whisper. A man's voice – maybe Beck's? For a moment I slowed; it could be an illusion, a lure meant to lead me away from Oliver and his intended punishment. Or it could be real, and he could be looking for me.

Caro!

Again, and closer. Beck's voice a second time; I could hear the concern within, the stricken desperation. Such a tone was usually only reserved for a lost notebook or a misplaced scrap of a hastily-written breakthrough. Never me.

But I couldn't turn back. I had to find Oliver. Even if he had thrown me to the wolves, he still deserved a chance.

Or maybe that had been his chance. Maybe his fate was already decided.

I turned away from Beck's voice, loping forward on aching legs once again. The ax was heavy in my grip, my wrist trembling from the effort of holding it aloft.

"Oliver!" I cried. "I'm here! I'm not abandoning you!" It was likely more mercy than he deserved. But if we didn't show one another mercy here, show some grace, then what did we have? We'd all be like Dorothy. Like Iskra. We all had someone to mourn us.

Most of us.

I emerged from the smoke in time to meet Oliver's eye only once. He stood with his back to a flat stone wall, swiping uselessly at the creatures that eddied around him like an encroaching tide. I called out again, and he looked up to me for no more than a moment.

Fire arced through the air, a flaming mass of metal and twisted shrapnel, and landed with a boom in the center of the gaggle. Bodies flew as I was thrown wide, skidding on my back in the mud. My head spun, the wind knocked from me. Burning bits of splintered wood and warped shrapnel littered the floor between Oliver and I; he had been flung forward, and as he struggled onto all fours I tried and failed to call out to him again.

And again, I heard my voice from somewhere behind. Through the ringing in my ears, the crackling of fire, the gurgling of faceless creatures that scrambled to tug strips of hot metal from their bellies, I heard Beck.

He'd come for me, as I'd come for Oliver. That had to count for something.

Oliver screamed, a ragged cry that shot through the din like a bullet. All around him, the bleached bodies had begun to sink into the mud, tucking into the grime head-first and slipping beneath like it was nothing more than water. The muck billowed like a lung, the sound of shifting stone audible above the sounds of warfare overhead.

I struggled to my knees. Oliver's hands were in the mud, planted firmly. He leaned back, squeezing his eyes tight as his shoulders strained – but he was stuck. Teeth grit, sweat beading his brow, he groaned as he threw his weight back to no avail. The mud rolled like an ocean swell, and it lapped at his elbows, his biceps. I scrambled to him as his body gave a great jerk, and he was pulled by his arms further into the mud.

"It's okay!" I cried. "I'm going to get you out!" I tossed the ax aside and scrambled to him, positioning myself at his back and wrapping my arms around his waist.

Oliver was crying, fat tears rolling in heavy streaks through the mud and soot on his cheeks. He opened his mouth as if to speak, but the ground shuddered again and he was pulled deeper. His face pressed to the mud, neck craned and back arched to keep his mouth and nose free. I strained, kicking at the earth as I tried and failed to pull him out.

An odd sensation tickled behind my ear. A voice. *Can't run now*, it said. *Nowhere to run.*

"Come *on*!" I wailed, throwing my weight back. Oliver howled, and with a pop I heard his shoulders dislocate. Nausea rolled through me, an acidic flush of bile at the back of my throat. I fell away from Oliver, splashing back into the mud with a squelch.

The ground shuddered again, and his head disappeared. He kicked his legs, hips bucking and back arching. I could see his belly shuddering, his chest seizing; he couldn't breathe, couldn't move.

I flung myself toward the ax, hacking uselessly at the roiling mud. Again, the ground rumbled as Oliver was pulled further in.

I lifted the ax again and again and again, bringing it down futilely in the ruddy muck. With every breath, he was pulled further and further, mud and rotten oily blood splattering onto his hips, his thighs, his calves. He'd stopped kicking. Struggling. But I didn't – couldn't. I slashed at the mud as it curled around his knees and gave one last tug.

And then it stopped. Oliver's feet jutted from the earth, surrounded by burning refuse and a sea of oil and mud. The bodies beneath the grime settled, flattening. With a crack of thunder from far overhead, brackish water began to fall on my head. The first hint of the sea since we'd been spat out here, in a desert far away. It wasn't a comfort – it was a sign that the world, this world designed just for Oliver, was ending. The deluge of seawater washed away the oil and the mud. It doused the fires and cleared the smoke. Oliver's pursuers were gone, leaving nothing more than a torn bit of camouflage fabric here, a tuft of seaweed hair there.

They were gone. And he had failed.

7

I let the ax slip from my grasp, the oily blood cooling on my clothes as the ocean spray soaked me from above. Beck and the others rounded the corner at my back, vaulting displaced sandbags and slipping in the dissipating mud as they ran to me.

Mallory and Beck were at my side at once. Beck smoothed the sodden hair from my brow, and Mallory wiped at the spray of black blood on my cheek, my lips, my chin.

They spoke in tandem. Beck's voice was low, heady with curiosity and open fervor. "Tell me what happened." His eyes darted from my face to the feet that protruded from the rock like headstones.

Mallory looked only at me. "What happened, Caro?" she pleaded. "Are you hurt?"

The difference was palpable. One was academic, calculating. I was a case study, and Oliver a byproduct. The other was the very picture of concern. Empathy. How ridiculous it felt, to be preened over while Oliver's legs protruded from the mud and stone.

I turned to look at Hannah, who was caked from head to toe in mud and trembling violently. "Are you okay?" I asked, my voice a warble. She nodded. "Good."

Hannah pointed over my head, wordless. I followed the stretch of her pale, wavering finger to the slab of stone that had blocked Oliver's path. Where once had been nothing but unbroken rock now stood a narrow metal door, rusted and pockmarked with the evidence of bullets and shrapnel. The handle hung loose on blackened screws, like the door had been slammed open and closed against the adjacent wall one too many times. And the door itself looked as though it had merely been propped there, an afterthought of a set piece left behind to round out the fantasy in which Oliver was meant to die.

Beck went to it first, abandoning all watery attempts at concern for my wellbeing. He looked it up and down, like it might jump off the wall and flatten him. And then, with a studious *hmph*, he wrapped his fingers around the handle.

Mallory hooked her arms beneath mine and hauled me up. I obliged blindly. What else was I supposed to do? There would be no pulling Oliver from the stone, like a mythical sword wielded by a king. I had tried to save him.

But I hadn't tried hard *enough*.

My voice tumbled from me, heavy and thick on a tongue that didn't want to form coherent words. "If only he hadn't run," I said, leaning on Mallory as she led me toward the door. "Maybe he would have passed."

That was what this was. Surely. The creature came when called, the ringing tone of our chaos and discord a dinner bell. It came when we fought, when we suffered. It shuffled us from place to place, setting us down in the presence of the manifestation of our darkest self, one after another. There was no use in denying it now, in trying to explain it away as a trick of the phosphorescent light, or of dehydration.

Beck was right. The Leviathan was real. And she would strip us bare one by one until someone – anyone – conquered themselves. Complete honesty. That was what she required of us.

The door in the rock opened with a creak. Only a narrow threshold of stone lay on the other side, sloping down into the darkness of an unlit cavern. I could hear running water, could smell the brine of the sea. Beck held out his hand and asked that someone reach into his pack and find a flare, which none of us seemed inclined to do. The fabric still sagged heavily, bloated with the evidence of Beck's subterfuge.

I didn't believe that the removal of the seal from the vestibule at the mouth of the cave, and the subsequent collapse, was any kind of coincidence. I also didn't fully understand what it was necessary for. If it was a map, it wasn't a very clear one. Maybe it was something purely symbolic, like a token carried by the god's chosen champion to the end of the trial. No one else wanted to touch it either, to carry on as if he hadn't started all of this, be it by accident or not. He was the reason that our expedition had a body count, not the Leviathan. *He* started this.

Finally, after a moment of pregnant silence, Mallory obliged. She muttered to herself something about cursed objects, about how Dungeons & Dragons should have taught us all better. No one could find it in themselves to laugh. Pushing past Hannah, who was pale and slick with sweat, she reached into Beck's bag and produced the only flare he had left. Beck lit it without a word and tossed it through the door. It arced through the open air, illuminating a wide cavern with a low overhang, beneath which a steady trickle of water spilled. It ran through the heart of the cavern and over a sharp ledge like an artery, darting past towering stalagmites and great limestone columns. The flare illuminated the way down: a drop high enough to require rappelling gear.

We set to work quietly, gathering what we'd managed to salvage from our things. My bag still carried a harness and a rope, with a carabiner clip and descender attached. I didn't know how to use it; none of us did. But we made do. We wrapped our sleeves over our bare palms, for lack of the gloves lost to the rubble with the Grundstadts, and made our way down the steep drop into the cavern below.

By the time I reached the bottom, the door above our heads had disappeared. The rope, which we'd affixed to the low wall of sandbags nearest the door, jutted from the wall. It had been swallowed by the stone, leaving nothing salvageable but the clip.

So we were out of rope. We had little food, save the jerky and nuts we could scrounge from our bags. And we had nowhere to go. Dorothy's lighter had been abandoned to the narrow passage in the wall, trampled as we'd been pursued by the Leviathan's bastardized imitation of Oliver's squadron. Though the cavern opened up in a multitude of directions, all of which looked to be a much easier journey than the descent, we had no direction.

Beck plopped his bag down beneath the stone overhang, regarding us all as we picked our way across the stream and into the center of the cavern. We eddied there like corralled cattle waiting for instruction, or maybe condemnation. "We'll rest here," Beck said. "Eat, if we can." His gaze flickered to Hannah, who'd slumped against a column, her head between her knees. I could see her trembling, wiping at her brow with the heels of her hands. "It's important that we do our best here, all right?"

Do our best? I wanted to scream.

"What are we going to do, Professor Beck?" Mallory ventured. I wanted to tug her away, to shove her behind me so that Beck and his curiosity couldn't wheedle her any more than he'd already done. "I want to go home!"

"You will," he said. "You've seen now what this place requires of you. You're a bright girl, Mallory. When the time comes, I know you'll see it through."

She looked to me, like I might have something to say that might shake him from this. But there was no fighting it. There was only going through. I had failed Oliver. And Iskra, and Dorothy. But I wouldn't fail Mallory.

Mallory spoke before I could, voice reedy. "But we can't just wait around. Some of us need serious medical attention." It was good that she'd opened this door. Someone had to vouch for Hannah when she clearly couldn't do so for herself.

We all looked to her. There was no helping it. She trembled, poured sweat like bullets. The evidence of her last spell of dry-heaving and vomiting bile was dry at the corners of her lips. She had devolved so quickly, ankle swollen to the size of a baseball, it was a wonder she could walk at all. Her condition was familiar to me, painfully so. And Mallory was right – she needed help more than any of us.

Beck extended a hand. "Maybe this is her test. See?" We didn't want to look, didn't want to see. There was nothing divine in Hannah's suffering. She had done it to herself. It plucked at something foul, something too familiar, in the pit of my stomach. "She gets clean, and she passes. She detoxes, and she passes."

I shook my head. "How long will that take? She's suffering, Beck."

"*Hey.*" Hannah's voice was a croak. "Stop talking about me like I'm dead."

"Come on, Hannah. Be serious about this."

"I had it under control—"

"Clearly not!"

"Listen!" Beck clapped his hands, the smack reverberating through the cavern like a gunshot. I looked up into the dark above our heads, where the light of the flare barely touched, and almost expected to see a bloated, serpentine body looking back, something tactile moving along the ceiling, drawn by the sounds of our squabbling. But there was nothing, and we were alone. Maybe the Leviathan was digesting. Maybe she still wanted to savor the sweetness of Oliver's failure. "What happened to Oliver, to Dorothy, was a tragedy," Beck said. "But it was avoidable, on both counts. If they'd only listened—"

Hannah shook her head, wiping the back of a sweat-damp hand across her brow. "They were all good people," she said, voice trembling. "We're *all* good people."

I wasn't sure I believed it.

An unworthy acolyte, a voice said. Half my own, half a stranger's, tapping like a finger on a frosted windowpane at the back of my skull. *Unfit.*

Maybe it was Beck's influence. Long days and nights spent in his office, helping him unscramble runes and map cave systems made the Leviathan feel utterly real. Or maybe I was just making her up, scrambling for something tangible to pin the blame on. If I could convince myself that there was a god in my ear, maybe I could make some sense of this mess.

Better her than my mother. A preferable haunt.

I settled beneath the hanging rope, pressed against the wall with my backpack tucked behind me and Mallory at my side. I waited with her until she fell asleep, then rose again and made my way to the furthest reach of the narrow stream. Dipping my hands into the frigid water, I set to work scrubbing the blood from beneath my nails. I rubbed the mud and soot from between my fingers, up my wrist, beneath the sleeves of my jacket. With a shuddering gasp, I splashed water onto my bruised face, muddy rivulets trailing from my hair and across my brow. With a tender fingertip, I wiped the blood from beneath my nose, and scrubbed it from my upper lip.

I pulled my phone from my back pocket. The screen was irreparable, cracked beyond the point of use. In the corner, the battery flashed madly. And there, beneath the cracks, the time: *1:18*. Same as before.

"Caroline."

I startled at Beck's voice, low and even at my shoulder. I hadn't even heard him approach. With a short gasp, I slipped on the slick stone at the edge of the stream, and his hand shot out to catch me by the arm before I fell in.

"Come to quiz me?" I clipped, shrugging free of his grasp and turning my attention back to the dried blood on my face. "I don't have my notes."

Beck sat beside me, dipping his fingers into the glacial stream. "You think poorly of me now," he said. It wasn't a question.

I gave a shrug, then a huff. "I don't know what to think."

At my side, Beck lifted his hands into the red light of the flare. It glinted mockingly off his wedding ring, which seemed to have miraculously avoided all the grime that now coated every inch of me. How poetic.

But then he slipped it from his finger and tossed it into the stream. I froze, watching as the sterling band tumbled across the stone, buffeted by the steady flow of water, and then disappeared from view.

I looked at him then – really looked – for the first time since we'd arrived. Beck had always been handsome, composed to a fault. He'd been unflappable for all the years I'd known him, undeterred despite the constant mockeries and harassments thrown at him from all sides. He was the lunatic who believed in stories. But that was what we all were in the end, wasn't it? Stories?

What story would we tell Oliver's family? Dorothy's? Iskra's?

Mine? What would Beck tell the world if it was *my* body he left behind?

"For what it's worth," Beck said, "I'm happy that you're here. With me, specifically." A pause, as his eyes lingered on the place where the ring had disappeared. "You believed in me, in this. I trust you more than anyone. And now here we are."

"Here we are," I echoed. It should have made me happy, the bareness of his finger. The affection in his voice. But it didn't. Strangely enough, it made me feel like I needed to dunk my head in the cold water.

"This is the beginning of something," Beck said. "I thought that my journey with this . . . this *knowledge*, this *deity*, this *place* began long ago, but I was wrong. Think of it, Caroline! I've considered it time and time again, and I think I understand in full. An *angel*, don't you see? Wormwood, just like the runes spelled out. And in Enochian, no less. *The* angelic script."

I wanted to say something, to posit that the vernacular, and the physical letters themselves, were like a poor translation, like someone making up Enochian on the fly. But I kept my mouth shut.

And so Beck continued, "An angel, the likes of which religious texts have never touched. It's only just started. A new beginning, a rebirth, just like the Leviathan teaches her acolytes."

I watched as his eyes passed across the flat stone above us. It didn't seem likely that an angel could inhabit a place like this. I didn't really believe in angels necessarily, but if this *was* one, then it wasn't doing a great job of marketing itself as such. A single name pulled from the depths of the Bible meant very little. Wormwood was nothing more than a footnote in Revelation, some third or fourth angel that turned the world's water bitter and hallucinogenic. I could see Beck's mind working, brows twitching together in the way they always did when he battled with something insurmountable.

"To repent, to make amends for our sins . . ." He shook his head. "I never understood the idea. Ash Wednesday, for example. Easter.

It felt nebulous when it came from God. The Bible. It never felt tangible to me."

"You were religious?"

He settled onto the stone and tugged off his boots and socks, splaying his feet in the water. A shiver ran the length of him, and he chuckled. "Once upon a time," he said. "We all look for meaning. Sometimes we get desperate and hope that someone else will figure it out for us."

"Oh." I shivered, and my eyes fell away. It was a wonder he'd ever felt that way, felt that keen ache that I'd lived with my entire life. I had always assumed that Beck always knew. He'd always known precisely who he was, what he wanted. It was why I had been drawn to him so fiercely.

"I never understood the Bible's idea of divine punishment. It made little sense to me; what kind of God was this that allowed atrocities to occur without a single chance given to those who followed him? It all seemed so random. So much . . . asking for forgiveness. That didn't feel right to me."

Again, I said nothing.

"God wants us to repent, to atone for our sins, and to continue to do so over and over and over. But how do we do it? Through prayer? Talking to a wall, when there's no guarantee that he'll answer? No – I didn't want that. And *sin* . . . this darkness, this blackness that's spilled into us. God believes it's inherent, predestined. We'll always have it, and so we'll always repent. We smudge ash on our heads to represent death, and sin, and all that bullshit, but . . . it doesn't *mean* anything. And what's the reward? Some . . . intangible happily ever after?"

He looked to me as if I'd have an answer. I shrugged. "My grandma used to say that faith was its own reward," I offered. "And the search for it is what gives life meaning. Or maybe the other way around. It gives us meaning when we don't know what we're searching for."

"Maybe so. But restoration, rebirth, eternal life; there's no guarantee of it."

I heard the implication plainly. God may not have the answers, but this place – this Leviathan – maybe she did.

"And you think that you can find all that here?"

Beck shrugged. "Who knows? What I do think is that I prefer a god who gives real chances. God wouldn't allow Oliver," he gestured up at the rope, which hung limp against the rock, "to face the blackest parts of himself. God wouldn't allow him to make it right in a real, tangible way. Sure, Oliver's acceptance of his sins, his guilt, of the fact that he abandoned his squadron to die out there in that trench," he took a deep breath, and for a moment I tasted ash, "it wouldn't bring them all back. But it would absolve him in a way that prayer never could. No number of church Sundays can wipe out a stain like that. But this . . . facing it all like this? It can. Dante and the Inferno; walking through Hell so you can better understand it. Slaying your own dragon, and all that. She's the greatest plagiarist, the Leviathan. Dante is in the Labyrinth instead, with the minotaur, carrying string through until the ugly truth at the very center."

"But is it worth dying for?" I countered.

Beck studied me for a long moment. "I believe that the Leviathan sees you. *You*, truly. No pretense. God sees what you want him to see. Leviathan shows you yourself. Your chaos. And there is so much chaos in the world. It's only fair that we get a chance to make sense of it ourselves, rather than talking to the sky in the hopes that it'll be solved with magic."

A long moment of silence passed again, which I filled by scrubbing the last of the blood and muck from beneath my fingernails. Beck took my hand, the feeling of skin on skin strangely startling. I simultaneously chafed and melted at the idea of being touched. He was something tangible. He was glad to have me here. *Me* – not for anything that I could do for him, but for me.

Beck curled my fingers over his, then lifted my hand to his lips. He kissed my knuckles, one at a time. The flesh of his ring finger was indented, like the very shape of him had gotten used to the squeeze of the ring. The skin there was paler than the rest, and unmarred with mud and salt.

"I want to understand," I said. "But I'm scared. I don't want to die."

"And you won't," Beck answered, his lips moving against the back of my hand. His eyes rose to meet mine. Shameful that even now, my stomach lurched with keening desire. "You just have to trust me."

I considered, watching as his lips traced every inch of my battered hand, before asking, "What are you trying to fix by coming here? What are you hoping to face? Clearly you came with something in mind."

His lips twitched, and for a moment his grip tightened over mine. "I could ask the same of you."

I scoffed. As a shiver danced the length of my spine, I wiped the cold water onto my jeans. "Who says I want to be absolved? Who says I have anything to be sorry for?"

But I knew precisely how I would be tested. It would end in the same way all my nightmares did – at the end of a hall, with bathwater spilling beneath a locked door.

"You don't have to be sorry. You just have to be honest. Regret isn't useful. It doesn't make you stronger. Honesty does. A full and complete acceptance of who you are . . . that's what the Leviathan asks of us."

"And what do we get in return? If we survive this – will we be changed?" Would I have purpose? Would I be happy?

He paused. I could see the gears turning behind his eyes. "I hope so," he said. "I want you there until the very end."

"You know I only came here for you."

And Mallory had come for me. Where did that leave us?

"I know," he said, grip tightening over my hand. "You have been so very good to me, Caroline. You and your unflappable belief. I want you to live, to find purpose through this place. Forgive yourself. Let go of everything, everyone. What happened between you and your mother—"

I jerked my hand away, lurching from him, my boots splashing in the water. "What the fuck did you just say?" I never spoke of my mother, nor my father. Beck knew that they were both out of the picture, cut so decisively out of my life that he knew not to speak of them. Any time parents were involved in any classroom ceremony, any departmental accolades, he didn't even *mention* them. He knew not to. He didn't know *why*, of course, no one did. But the sympathy on his face, the pitying, simpering curl of his lips . . .

He knew.

Even in the red light of the flare, I could see Beck's face flush with heat. "You don't need to be ashamed," he said, reaching for me like I was a startled animal. "We all – all of us – have demons. Your secrets were always safe with me. That's why I chose—"

"*Chose?*" My head spun.

"Of course I chose you," Beck countered, voice firm. "I wouldn't let someone I don't trust – someone I don't *know* implicitly – into this, the culmination of my life's work. This is the most important thing I've ever done, or will ever do. Of course I chose you."

"*No*," I held up a finger, soiled bandage sliding down to my knuckle. "My mother— You . . . you knew all along?" What did it mean if he'd chosen me solely for this? Was I his most shining example of sin and guilt personified? Was he going to fix me, or make an example of me?

Beck pursed his lips and nodded solemnly. Again, he held out a hand. The affection on his face, the blistering ferocity, chafed with the words that hung heavy in the air between us. He might as well have been asking for my hand in marriage, judging by how his eyes brimmed with affection. "I know what you did, Caroline. And I love you regardless. There are no secrets here."

My head spun. I wanted to curse. I wanted to puke. I wanted to claw at the stone and pelt him with the pieces I could pry free. To be loved by Beck was to be tested. Every word, every gesture, was something to be marked and measured. And to be tested was to be chosen. He would test me so he could love me, and love me so he could use me. *Love?* I heard the word as if I'd never heard it before. He loved me like a person loved any broken thing – to be fixed, and to be used for a new purpose.

I tasted bile and salt water at the back of my throat. The familiar warmth of his affection, the balm of his approval, soured. I was unclean. I was burning.

Love? What the fuck did he mean by *love*? What a horrible, false time to hear it.

I got to my feet. "I need to go for a walk."

"Where?" The question was measured, calm. But beneath . . . a threat? A promise? I couldn't tell. I could make a song of every syllable, a threat from every breath. I understood nothing; that much was clear.

I turned away, then back again, hands curling into fists at my sides. "Do you . . . do you know what's coming for the rest of them, too? Did you study us like you did your notes?"

Something inside me creaked wide, spilling in coldness and bile, like an old window in an older house, the panes cracked and muddied and the frame dented. To be used in this way was not new, but it stung like it was fresh, a clean slice of glass.

Beck nodded, and I felt a scream clawing at the ridge of my jaw. "I do this because I care, Caroline. I want us to survive. To succeed. It's all for nothing if we fail."

I laughed, a horrible warbling thing. "Yeah, because if we fail we're fucking *dead*!" The last word echoed through the cavern like a death rattle. Mallory stirred in the corner. "I thought we were partners, Beck. Not test subjects."

He rose at this, and I took a trembling step back. "Of course you're my goddamn partner, Caroline! All the others – we all need each other here."

In the corner, Hannah shifted. It appeared that she hadn't really been sleeping at all, though she tried. With sweat heavy on her brow, lips pale and vaguely green, she appraised us.

Was this why he had chosen me to be his partner in the first place? Had he fucked me for the anthropological hell of it all? Was my love for him a variable to be cited and measured? Maybe I was overreacting. Maybe he'd stumbled upon her obituary by accident, and had simply put together the pieces. Maybe it was obvious; my father pretended I didn't exist, that he'd never had a daughter at all. Her funeral had been closed-casket. And the family home had taken over two years to sell, after three drops in asking price.

"How much do you know?" My voice was a pitched warble, something childish and fearful that didn't belong to me. Or maybe it did. In the corner, Hannah sat up straighter, a fly attracted to the rotten smell of my guilt, maybe. It was enough to drown out hers.

Beck sighed and shoved his hands into his pockets. "Enough," he said. "But I don't fault you for it. In fact, I admire your resilience. There's nothing wrong with being a survivor, Caroline."

"A *survivor.*" It felt fake, like an ill-fitting costume he'd forced me to wear. There was nothing brave about me. I couldn't even face my own mother as she died. And it had been my fault. My doing.

"Yes," Beck nodded. Clearly he could sense the horror and disbelief written plainly on my face. "And I trust you because of it. I wouldn't do this with just anyone."

"So you know what our tests will be, then?" I challenged him, though I shook as I struggled to incline my chin. "You know what I'll see out there? What it'll show me? What about Hannah? Mallory?"

He said nothing. His silence stoked the anger and disgust in the pit of my belly, and I backed away from him again, the heel of my boot splashing into the stream. Beck watched me, brows furrowed and lips pursed. He acted like this had been obvious, like we'd all been required to whisper our dirty secrets into his ear before boarding the boat in Seal Harbor.

And now here we were, in the thick of them all. Any moment now, I'd turn around and find my mother there. I could already hear her clearly enough. She whispered all the same condemnations in my ear, the wheedling narcissisms that kept me threadbare. My mother never hit me, sure. But she left a bruise all the same.

I took another step away, glacial water splashing beneath my boot. My fingers clenched and unclenched at my sides, the scald of where his lips had touched my skin enough to make me itch for the ax that I'd left with my things.

"The ring is gone, Caro!" Beck reached for me, but I held fast. "Just like you wanted. It's lost to this place for ever. It's just you and me. After this, everything will be different."

It was what I had wanted, what he had promised me long ago. Silly as it was now, here in some mythical cloister of trials, the idea of a promise fulfilled tugged at my weary heartstrings.

But now I saw just how silly, how stupid, how terrible and wrong I had been. My mother had always been right, it seemed. I was the villain. I was the creaking floorboard. And I was nothing. Nothing at all.

I spun on my heel, kicking up water as I went. "I need to get some sleep," I said. "It's been a long day. *Days.* Who fucking knows?"

"Caroline, I'd like to explain—" I could hear him following, a puppy chasing a toy.

But I held up a hand, fingertips trembling. "*Nope.* No need. I understand."

"Caro, you know that I love—"

"No thanks, Professor Beck," I clipped. "I'm good."

At this, he didn't follow. I didn't want to look back at him, because I knew that if I saw him wilt like a dying flower at the formal title, I would fold. How dare he throw around the idea of *love* like something disposable? Now more than ever, now that I knew how little I understood of it, his use of the word felt particularly cruel.

My mother said she loved me, demanded that I hear it from her even when she was at the bottom of the barrel. But what she'd done to me, what she'd made of me, wasn't love. It was only *use.* She loved me the way a carpenter loves a tool. And Beck . . . he loved me the same. It was clear now.

Maybe I would come to my senses once we surfaced, breaching from this place and into the fresh air. I was hearing things, seeing things. My mind spiraled and curled in on itself like an animal fending off a pursuer with spikes and fangs, ready to bite the first hand that came closest.

I crossed to Mallory, who'd shifted onto her other side. She curled against the wall, hair splayed in damp tendrils over her back. Beck had asked me once what I wanted my life to be. How sad it was that I still didn't have an answer for him.

But I did know this – my life was not his to use. It wasn't anyone's. I would see this through, fulfill my promise. We would all leave this place, if we helped one another, and Beck would receive all the accolades and attention that he so desired. Maybe he'd find another plucky grad student to make his protégé and forget about me altogether. And I would leave – for good. I would do something wild, something frivolous and impulsive, for *me*. And then I would start my fucking life.

I would bring Mallory. I wanted her there regardless.

She mumbled in her sleep as I lay beside her. I settled onto the rock, reluctant to let myself sleep but knowing full well that I'd need it if I were to survive this place. Beck promised that he would keep me safe – but for how long? What would he do if he decided that I was no longer useful to him?

His priority would be, and always had been, his work. The research. This place. It was his greatest love, the only true devotion he had ever known. And he would always choose it.

Fuck love, I thought. *I choose survival.*

When I woke, the flare had gone out. Mallory snored quietly. I rolled onto my side, pulling the ruined phone from my pocket, and lit up the screen again. And again, the time had yet to change. Perpetually at 1:18, the battery indicator in the corner flashing angrily as a droplet of water ran the length of a crack in the screen; the light was blinding, even at the lowest setting.

I opened up my photographs and scrolled past the pictures of horses in fields along my commute, cows who never seemed to want to come close enough to pet, birds on campus, pages of notes, screenshots of recipes I'd never make. I scrolled to the very last photograph and the pad of my thumb sliced painfully over a break in the screen.

I cursed, sticking my bleeding thumb between my lips and sucking on the spill of salt that bloomed there. A thin line of crimson stretched across my mother's face, obscuring most of the only photograph I still had of her. I hadn't been able to delete it, no matter how I tried. All the others had been lost to the fires of my overfull phone storage. But this *one* . . . it was good.

She was happy. Smiling. The wide stretch of her plum-painted lips didn't seem forced, or false. She looped her arm over my shoulder with all the love and honesty that a mother should have for their child. My hair stuck up in all directions, the paint I'd put on at the beginning of the local production of *Alice in Wonderland* smearing into an indiscernible gunk on my face. I clutched a bouquet of pink roses, the flash reflecting in my eyes and hers.

There was no ill will here. That night, there had been no arguments, no blame. We'd gone to dinner at Red Lobster – the fanciest place I could imagine at the time – and I'd been allowed dessert and all.

My therapist had told me to delete the picture. Family didn't matter, she said, unless it was who you chose. Just because she's your mother, she'd said, doesn't mean you owe her anything. Boundaries, boundaries, boundaries. But it was a glimpse into an alternate world, this photo. It was proof that there had always been a possibility. She could have been a good mother. She could have loved me for me, and loved me true. I couldn't let it go, the idea. Maybe in another life.

Just not in this one.

"It's okay to not be okay," my therapist said. "And it's never too late to learn who you are after so many years of someone else deciding it for you."

A week after the photo had been taken, after the roses had started to wilt, and the rot of normalcy had begun to creep back in, my mother threatened to kill herself for the first time. This wasn't a story one could lead with when swapping family photos with a partner. I believed her wholeheartedly the first time, and every time after – save one. She dangled the threat over our heads like fishing lure, and my father and I had scrambled to bite. It had been over nothing; even now, I couldn't remember what had done it. Maybe it was because it had happened so many times after. She'd only ever tried it once. And that was enough.

She was lonely, and unfulfilled, and hateful, and sad – and I was there to fix it. I sat and prodded at the colorful bands on my braces as she soliloquized, bemoaning the state of the world and the disappointment of her life. Then she told me in great detail why, how, and where she would do it. And it was up to me to stop it.

It was always up to me. I was the tightrope on which she walked, after all. One wayward wind, and she would spill right over. It would be all my fault.

Why are you doing this to me? she'd ask. And I'd have no answer for her. I hadn't done anything at all, not on purpose. I would never. I loved her more than anyone, simply because I'd been made to do it. And yet it was always my fault. I was a terrible, rotten, defective thing. And it was my fault.

But this picture . . . she looked so blazingly alive, so full of possibility. I could look at this photo and imagine a whole life around her. A fiction.

Caroline.

But I heard her voice now, in the dark. And I knew the truth.

Caroline?

I heard her, clear as day. And another voice, too, echoed like an afterthought – Mallory's. Was I asleep? Dreaming? I craned my neck to find the patch of stone she'd occupied empty, barely illuminated by the light of my dying phone.

"Mallory?" I turned my phone outward, the watery light swallowed by the dark, and sat up. My voice was a croak; I sounded like I'd slept for years, though the heaviness of my eyes told me that it had only been an hour or so. Only the sound of trickling water over stone cut the silence of the dark cavern.

And then, from far within one of the pitch-black corridors that webbed off from the cavern in which we slept, a light flickered on. It moved, shifting back and forth across the rock like a pendulum. Warm and luminescent, it shone unbroken from within the dark.

"*Mallory!*" I hissed. The light looked nothing like the flashlights we'd been given, or the vibrant red flares. Where had she gotten hold of it? No answer came from within, or without. It sounded like the others were still asleep. I rose, slipping my hand beneath my makeshift pillow to retrieve the ax. I hooked it onto my belt loop and held my phone aloft. It was as good as I was going to get. The light was nothing compared to the headlamps we'd left behind, but I felt safer armed with it.

I started toward the light, picking over bits of loose stone and hopping the stream that continued to flow unfettered. The warm spot continued to move, rhythmic in its endless back-and-forth.

Caro, where are you?

This was Mallory, without a doubt. Her voice, and the light, in one. I called out again, ratcheting my voice higher. I didn't want to wake the others, but my friend was more important than any measly sleep they might be able to eke out in this place. Neither of them stirred, to my great relief, though I couldn't help the prickle of annoyance in the pit of my stomach that no one else was alert enough to hear someone who needed help. No one moved as I descended into the passage, following the swinging light toward the sound of Mallory's voice. It was stupid to go off alone. She should have woken me.

The passage curved to the left, the floor dipping beneath me. I could hear the running water from the cavern, the spill of cold water over a sharp edge.

"Mallory?" My voice echoed much louder than I'd anticipated; likely, beyond the weak stretch of my phone's light, the passage opened into another cavern. But the light ahead of me continued to swing, a single point fixed in space.

The toe of my boot knocked into something solid, and it skittered across the stone. I jumped, the phone slipping from my hand and clattering to the floor. In the beam of the flashlight, the shadow of a human skull stretched up the adjacent wall. Ringing around the orbital bone, the skull was marred with jagged markings. Shallow divots had been gouged into the bone, spidering out from the socket. The scratches looked frantic and random rather than any kind of religious markings; I could recognize none of Beck's runes within, or any other symbols that could constitute letters. No, this had been done haphazardly. And judging by the jagged cuts and nicks in the bone, it looked like it had been done against their will.

I reached for my phone, holding it close to the ground as I stepped around the skull to find a spine, a tibia, and then an overturned lantern similar to the ones we'd come across in the library grotto.

I reached out and touched the metal. It was still warm, as if the light inside had only just gone out.

Caroline! Please!

I leapt back as my mother's voice rang out from the direction of the light ahead. I shot upright, head spinning. There was no hint of Mallory's voice within, no chorus of voices like I'd heard before. I was hallucinating, clearly. Maybe I was still asleep.

My phone went dark. A low curse slipped from me as I turned it over in my palm, the rough edges of the broken glass sharp against my skin. I could see nothing behind me, and nothing ahead save the light. It continued to move rhythmically, swinging in an unbroken arc. If I turned back, I could feel my way—

"Caro!" I heard Mallory's voice now, without a doubt. It wasn't in my head, or in a dream; it wasn't my mother, and it wasn't the dark passenger that followed us all in our descent into watery purgatory. It was Mallory, and she echoed through the darkness like a beacon. The light had to be hers, resilient and shining as she picked her way through the dark.

"Mallory! Hang on!" I started toward the light, tucking my phone in my pocket and feeling my way with both hands pressed flat on the stone wall.

The floor of the passage sloped up. I fell forward, clambering up the incline on my hands. With each step, the light grew warmer, clearer. I could see the shine on the wet floor, the cuts and bruises on my fingers as I climbed.

And then the floor leveled, and the source of the glow revealed itself to me. The light fixture hung from a single golden chain, a cable running its length. The chain disappeared into the stone wall, and the power cord besides. Not a phone, not a flare, but a single pendant light, with a clear glass shade covering a warm bulb; it swung, as if someone too tall for the passage ceiling had bumped it in passing. It shone brightly, swinging lazily.

It was only in this light that I realized that I was alone. I'd expected to find Mallory here, excitedly pointing up at her find. But there was nothing; just the light, and the dark beyond its reach. I stepped closer until I was directly beneath the swinging bulb. It was free of dust and grime, seemingly untouched by this place.

Something about the crack at the curved bottom of the bulb's covering was familiar. Something familiar too in the way the light swung, casting shadows. I looked behind, then forward. Was I hallucinating? Was I dreaming?

"Caro?"

I paused. Mallory's voice had shifted. She'd moved. My head whipped to the side; she'd almost sounded as if she'd come from inside the stone.

And then, just ahead, "Caroline, why aren't you coming?"

A dream, then. A bad one.

I stepped out from beneath the bulb. Just beyond the light's warm reach, there was movement. Skittering, like bare digits on the stone something moved, a flash of white.

"Mallory?" Not Mallory. I knew it as I said it.

She came into the light on all fours, wet hair swinging like algae from a pale scalp. *Not Mallory.* Her nightgown was soaked through, clinging to skeletal ribs and jutting arms. As she reached from within the dark, darting across the stone, the light went out. The passage was plunged into darkness, and I turned on my heel and hurtled forward blindly.

"Wake up," I hissed, my own voice impossibly small in my own head. "Wake up, Caroline."

A hand clamped around my ankle like a shackle and pulled my foot out from under me. I landed hard, biting down on my tongue. Blood bloomed in my mouth.

I ripped the ax from my belt and kicked at the hand on my ankle. My boot met something solid. Its grip loosened, and I flipped onto my back, swinging wildly overhead. The ax sang through the air, lodging in the adjacent wall. Cold fingers curled around my other ankle and gave me a tug. I shot upright, head swimming and pitching nauseatingly as I swung again, the tip of the ax narrowly missing my own leg.

I felt a tug on my arm, then my thigh. I swung. Hot breath ghosted across my face and I swiped at it with my free hand. Fingers slipped beneath the leg of my jeans, into the neck of my sweater.

Curious, almost. Prodding. But I swung again, the ax clanging off stone and splitting it into crumbling pieces on all sides. I could hear creaking overhead, like the groaning hull of a massive ship, but I could see nothing.

I swung, and swung, leaping to my feet and falling sidelong into the stone wall. I could have sworn I heard my name, though it was nearly impossible to make out anything above the ragged pull of my own breath in my ears and the rush of blood with every belabored heartbeat.

With a ragged cry, I staggered to my feet. A trio of fingers swiped across my cheek, another tugged at my hair. I could smell salt water and algae, the familiar musk of ginger and rose. My name came from everywhere, in whispers that I couldn't make out. And my mother's voice— her voice—

A hand clamped down hard on my shoulder. I pivoted and swung, teeth gritted as blood burbled and spat from between them. This time, the tip of the ax found something solid. I heard a wet pop and a gurgle. Something heavy tugged at the end of the ax, and I struggled to hold it steady. The body in the dark before me wavered, and the hand slipped from my shoulder. I felt hot wetness on my front.

And then a voice. "Caroline? Please, Caroline, say something!" I could hear the shuffling of feet on wet rock. Beck . . . Beck's voice.

Then – "Caro! Where are you?"– Mallory.

The light flickered on again. Ever in perpetual movement, the single bulb blinked to life once more, sending warm light spilling across the broad stone on either side. It was almost blinding, a shock that made me want to skitter behind a rock and cower in the dark – but there was something blocking it. Something stood between me and the swinging bulb, between me and the others as they ascended the slope and came into view.

Hannah's bloodshot eyes were wide, her mouth open in a look of surprise. The tip of the ax protruded from her throat, the blade embedded deep in the meat of her neck. Blood spilled from her open mouth, and with each horrid attempt at breath it splattered onto my front. Her knees buckled beneath her and she fell, the weight of her body pulling me down. I gave a tug on the handle of the ax. It gave a squelch, but didn't budge.

She held my gaze as she fell, lips closing and opening like a fish on a dry dock. I looked on wordlessly as her weight tugged me down, down, until I stood over her on the flat rock like the killer in a horrible final act. Hannah tried to speak, a gurgling cough, and blood sprayed across my face. Her fingers grappled at my sleeves, my sagging sweater.

And then, with all the strength I could muster, I pulled the ax from her neck. The sounds of my effort, the splatter and tear of blood, and sinew, and muscle; I could no longer hear the others in their approach, though I could feel their eyes on me.

I knew I shouldn't have removed the ax from the moment I did it; blood spilled from the wound freely, a torrent on the stone beneath Hannah's body. Her back arched as she felt at her neck, eyes sliding, unfocused, to the space above my head. The ax hung limply from my trembling hand.

At last, I looked up. Beck was already on us, falling onto Hannah and pressing his hands over the gushing wound in an attempt to stop the bleeding. I let the ax slip from my grasp. It fell to the stone with a clang, and as I looked down at it I saw the blade slick with crimson, and thick with clods of torn muscle and tendon.

And there, at the mouth of the corridor, stood Mallory. She was alive and well, her hair mussed from a few hours of half-sleep and a flare gripped tightly in her white-knuckled fist. Her eyes were on Hannah, the whites visible even from here.

Beck was screaming, bellowing, his voice breaking at every syllable. "What the fuck did you do?" he howled. "What did you do?"

Blood ballooned at Hannah's lips. Hot redness spilled from her neck, surging with each gurgling half-breath. Beck clapped his hands over her neck, squeezing hard. He called out to Mallory, demanding a bandage, a tourniquet, a spare shirt – anything to staunch the bleeding.

And as Mallory rifled through her bag, the darkness between each swing of the pendulum overhead shuddered. As before, eyes blinked open sleepily, like stars dotting a canvas of endless night. They nestled deep within the dark, shying from the bulb. I felt the buzz of their attention peel from me like wet nylon from salt-dappled skin; it was no longer me that held their curiosity. And no longer *me* that they wished to test.

Pop quiz. How long does it take a human being to bleed out?

Hannah's skin looked yellow, sickly, beneath the slick sheen of her blood. Sweat beaded in thick droplets on her brow, and as she gaped blindly at the ceiling, I could see that her lips were pale and chapped. I stumbled back a step, shaking my head. The discarded ax clattered beneath my shuffling heel. I had nothing.

"I thought—" I could hear my voice, as if from far away. "I was looking for Mallory. Someone grabbed me. It was dark. I was— I was just looking for Mallory."

As if it was an excuse. The name seemed to echo, to refract. She was *right there*, so plainly alive and untouched. What would have happened if *she* had come up behind me? Hannah had just been trying to help. Even if she was sick, and struggling, she'd tried. They all had; they'd all come looking for me. What would have happened if Mallory had reached me first? Would she bleed dry just as fast?

Beneath Beck's grasp, Hannah's body gave a shuddering lurch, her eyes whirring beneath pale lids. I could hear his voice, a low babble beneath the gurgle of blood from Hannah's lips. "An artery—" he said, warbling and shaking and trembling at every edge. "Fucking minutes—"

I met Mallory's gaze over their backs. It was difficult to make out, for she'd stepped just beyond the boundary of the swinging light, but it looked like she was crying. She wasn't looking at me. No one was; the eyes overhead, in the dark that suddenly seemed to stretch for a mile overhead, seemed not even to know that I was there.

"Beck?" My voice was small. He didn't stir; either he hadn't heard it, or he didn't want to. I wasn't even sure what I would tell him.

Would I apologize again, as if he could pass the message along to Hannah? Would I tell him that we were being watched?

Beck cursed, and his shoulders shook. From where I stood, there was no making out the clutch of his hands around Hannah's neck, but I could hear the squelching of blood and the splash of wetness on cold stone.

And then Beck fell away, scrambling from Hannah's body until his back thumped into Mallory's stock-still legs.

Hannah's body.

She was still. The lurching of her chest, the shuddering of her limbs, had ceased. I could hear no more belabored breaths, no pop and gurgle of blood blooming in her throat and over her pale tongue.

Mallory whirled round, bent at the waist, and vomited bile and foam onto the stone. It splashed into the generous puddle of blood that had begun to trickle down the sloped rock and toward the dark cavern behind. Beck hung his head between his knees, squeezing his eyes shut and flinching as Mallory retched again. Over our heads, the starry constellation of mismatched eyes blinked and whirred. Startled by the sound, maybe; disgusted by the open display of humanity, maybe. And then their attention returned to the body.

Hannah was dead. I had killed her. Light refracted off the tacky pin on the lapel of her jacket. It hung from the wet fabric, text obscured by the splatter of her blood and an ugly chunk of torn flesh. My knees buckled, and I dropped to the floor. The pool of her blood was expanding, blooming, reaching for me like the fingers that had tugged and prodded at me in the dark moments before.

One would think that if you'd seen a dead body once, you'd seen it a million times. A body so known to you should prepare you even more readily for the body of a stranger. But Hannah or Mama – the horror was just the same.

There was too much blood on my hands. Why was there so much blood on my hands? I hadn't paid attention in biology. How much blood did a human body hold? And how could it all so easily come out at the neck?

"I didn't *mean* to." My voice was small. Had I not felt the pain of it in my throat, I'd have believed that I'd never spoken at all. No one seemed to hear. No one seemed to care.

Overhead, the eyes blinked shut. Like dying stars, one by one, they darkened. And then we were alone.

ε

Beck was on me before I could move.

He shook me, hands on my shoulders hard enough to bruise, and my head lolled uselessly. I could vaguely hear Mallory crying above the ringing in my ears. It was this that shook me from my reverie, from the fantasy I'd conjured of Hannah hurtling through the dark in the clutches of the shades of Dorothy and Iskra that dangled like boils from the great body that shepherded us.

Flesh slid over stone, the sound slick and invasive, and Beck stopped. His mouth hung half-open; I hadn't even heard him speaking. Three heads snapped to search for the sound, the great groan of a body tugged over rock and blood. All at once, the corridor seemed impossibly long. If I blinked, the rock walls swam before my eyes and rearranged into a pattern of floral wallpaper; a trick of the light, a spot of blood in my lashes. The floor beneath my feet was nothing but stone, and yet in my periphery I could have sworn I saw the lip of a rug curled beneath Hannah's limp arm.

I blinked, and blinked, searching the stretching hall; it arrowed out on both sides, endless. The bulb overhead danced on its chain, as if something enormous had landed hard just above us. The light unfurled like refraction through water – Hannah's body was suddenly impossibly far away, the deluge of her blood a splatter long enough to wrap once, twice round the library we'd been forced from so unceremoniously.

A hand stretched from within the dark. Distended fingers, crackling at the joints and crowned with jagged, unclean fingernails, scraped across the stone. An overlong wrist followed, and an elbow that bent back at the joint. A second hand, and then a third, stretching at the knuckles as they reached for Hannah and wrapped around her legs, her arms, the bloodied mess of her neck. The shadows bloated and billowed, a diseased lung filling with air before a scream.

We could only watch. We knew this beast by now; we knew what it needed. The hands tugged at Hannah, as if checking to see if she was well and truly dead. Curious fingers pressed into every place where they might discover a pulse, digging filthy nails into the flesh when they found nothing. And then they took her, leaving nothing but a thick swath of blood in her wake. Beck was shaking me again. His voice came to me as if through deep water. "You don't understand!" he said, digging his fingers into the flesh of my shoulder like he was the beast itself, tenderizing every piece of me for his own consumption. "You don't understand what you've done!"

I had killed someone. I had killed Hannah. What more was there to understand?

Overhead, the light slowed in its swaying. The swimming half-imagined spots of carpet, and wallpaper, and burning bulb-dust settled, dissipating. And then the scene was gone, as quickly as it had come. No bulb on a chain, no floral wallpaper. Maybe it had never been there at all. Maybe I was losing my mind. There was only the light that shook in Mallory's grasp, a waterlogged phone flashlight. And the blood on the stone.

Beck turned me round by the shoulders and pushed me from the pool of blood that was all that remained of our medic. He pushed me past Mallory, who had still said nothing at all. She slipped behind us, and I craned my neck to glance at her – numb, as if watching myself from afar – as she stooped to retrieve my weapon.

No longer a tool. A weapon.

I spoke then, my voice unfamiliar and unwieldy on my tongue. "Hannah . . ." I began. "I didn't— I didn't see her."

"I know," Beck muttered. "I know."

But did he? Did he understand? Or did he tell me what I needed to hear because I had *killed* somebody? Did he do so because he knew that it was not my first kill? Every heartbeat was the thumping of a closed fist on a locked door. Could he hear it, too?

At my back, Mallory lit another flare.

"There's only two more," she said. "Except—" I heard her jaw snap shut, teeth on teeth. She bit down on something.

"Except Hannah's," Beck finished. "Whatever's left in Hannah's bag."

My knees sagged. Beck cursed, taking me beneath the arms. "Hannah—" I echoed, voice breaking. "Wait – we have to go back for Hannah." I pushed against Beck, but it was futile. I was weak, and the blood on my hands was too slick. My stomach rolled and dropped and pitched; the floor was moving, and I was tumbling along with it.

Beck shook his head. "It's too late, all right? She's gone."

It occurred to me faintly that he didn't sound afraid. He didn't sound sad. He sounded *agitated.* Annoyed. Like I'd turned in a paper late, or had failed to show at a lecture. I could feel his fingers shaking.

I craned my neck again, searching for Mallory. Beck moved a hand from beneath my arm, grabbing me by the jaw and shoving my face front. I reeled from the shock of it, blinking away the sting. "Stop fucking around, Caroline," he hissed. "I'm making this right."

"I swear I was only looking for Mallory," I moaned, my voice a pitiful, watery ricochet in the body of the adjacent cavern. He shoved me along, and my feet slipped into dips in the stone floor. I could see the light of a dying flare up ahead, likely one they'd left behind when they'd come for me. I reached for Mallory again, and again Beck's insistent fingers found the soft flesh of my bicep.

"I'm here." Mallory's voice was small, but it was there – it was real. And it was alive. "I'm right here, Caro."

Why were they talking to me like I had lost my mind? They spoke to me like a dying animal, one that lay prostrate on a table awaiting a lethal injection. I spun between remorse and indignation, wild and dizzying. I had been attacked – did they not understand? We were never alone here. It was Hannah's own damn fault for . . . for—

Beck shoved me into the open cavern, and I spilled onto all fours. I hung my head, trembling as he plucked the flare from Mallory's grasp and marched to the far wall. She fell at my side, hooking loose hair behind my ears.

"I thought you were gone," I said. I had no strength to force myself louder. I was confused. I was sick. Suddenly I wished I'd listened closer to the Grundstadts. "I woke up and I thought you were gone. I didn't— I didn't see you."

"It's okay," Mallory said. "It's okay." Each rattling breath sounded like a crashing wave. All I could hear was the sea; all I could see was the dark.

"I just wanted—" I inhaled deeply, and I could taste blood and salt on my tongue. "I just want you to get out of this place."

"Caro . . . Her hands went to my shoulders. She gave me a tug, imploring me to sit upright, and I shook her off. "I know you didn't mean to. I know you'd never kill anybody on purpose."

I shook my head, a dog with water in its ears. What she failed to understand was that I *would.* I had. And I would do it again if pushed.

The pounding of ever-weakening fists on a locked door; the splash of bare feet past an overflowing tub; the gurgling of foam over a swollen tongue; a name – over and over and over. Why are you doing this to me? Why have you done this to me?

If I told Mallory about my mother, would she hate me for ever? Would I be the villain in her story, too? I could be that if she needed. I could be anything.

Beck appeared above me again in a ring of blinding vermillion. "Up," he commanded. "Get up."

I did as I was told. Mallory's hands fluttered about me like butterflies without a perch. She didn't want to touch me, not with so much of Hannah's blood on me. I rose, knees shaking and teeth chattering. Each clash of teeth on teeth was flesh on wood, rattling hinges, an echo down a hallway.

Beck forced me to the far wall, to the patch of stone where Mallory and I had slept fitfully. He kicked aside my belongings, and hers, and when I opened my mouth to protest, nothing but a watery groan shambled from my cracked lips.

"I don't want to have to do this, Caroline," he said, turning back to me as I shuffled lamely to a halt. "I need you to say, out loud, that you won't fight back."

I opened my mouth, then closed it again. His shadow stretched the length of the wall, obscuring what remained of the rope that dangled from the space above. At my side, Mallory looked between us both, eyes wide. The cavern had gone silent. Even the sound of running water, the gentle tinkling of the stream that spilled into the dark beyond our camp, had stopped.

I would do whatever he asked of me. I could make it right if I did exactly what he said. I was sure of it. Beck was a problem-solver. I was a problem. It would be simple math.

Tell me what to do, I thought. I pleaded, raging against the inside of my skull. *Tell me what I am.* I wasn't a killer. I wasn't a saint. So what was I?

The Leviathan could tell me. She could tell me anything. But I loved Beck – and so I would let him decide first.

He held out a hand. "Give me your arm," he said. I did so at once. "Good. Don't make this more difficult than it needs to be."

"What are you doing?" Mallory stepped forward as Beck gave me a tug. I tumbled numbly over my own feet, but Beck was undeterred. He tugged me against the wall and turned me round so that I faced the open cavern. "Professor Beck, you're *hurting* her."

Beck wrenched my arm high. He *was* hurting me. The realization dawned on me late, like a delayed signal. I gasped, my shoulder cracking and my ears popping, as if the advent of *pain* had pulled me through the ether and back into my own skin. I could feel everything, all at once.

"You fucked us, Caroline," he said. My stomach fell into my shoes. "You fucked us all. And so you and I are going to make it right."

He reached for the stretch of rope that dangled above my head, hanging limp from where it had been absorbed into the wall. "I'm sorry," I said, voice small. Something small and animal at the back of my mind told me to fight back. But I couldn't. "I didn't mean to—"

"There's no precedent for this, you see." He spoke clinically, as if he merely recited a lesson plan. "Cheating Leviathan out of an acolyte like this. There's no text, no instruction, for what's to be done if one kills another. She's been cheated out of a test, and I don't . . . I don't know."

This didn't compute. Beck knew everything. Beck had the answers.

"I can make it up to you—"

"To *me*?" His voice was hard. "To *her*. We have to make it up to *her*." Beck reached for the rope with his other hand, tugging it down to meet my wrist. "You cheated her out of an offering, Caroline. I need to let her judge you for it, dole punishment as she sees fit. And I need to carry on." He tugged the rope around my wrist. I hissed, pain lancing through my shoulder as he stretched me higher.

At this, I finally shook myself awake. "Punishment?" I demanded. It occurred to me absently that Mallory had spoken, too, her voice swallowed by the ringing in my ears and the pounding of my heart. She'd protested, and she stood two paces from us now, fists balled at her sides.

"I don't know what to do with you," he muttered, looping the rope around my wrist once, twice. I tugged against him, and a knee flew up to catch me beneath the ribs. I crumpled at the middle, the wind knocked from me. "I don't want to be punished for what you did. I have to finish . . . I have to finish the work. I need to reassess, to . . . to—"

Mallory flew at him, fists raised. But he heard her coming as she swung, her breathing ragged and her footsteps slapping and wet on the cave floor. He turned and gave her a shove with his free hand, still holding my wrist with the other. She tumbled to the floor, landing hard in a tepid puddle. I tugged against the loose tie, and Beck whirled to shove a knee into my gut again. He pressed me into the wall, teeth bared, and set to work tying the rope taut at my wrist, my arm hauled over my head.

I jerked like an animal in a snare, paying no mind to the fragile hollowness of my bird-bones. He was going to leave me. He was going to hurt me . . . he was going to hurt *Mallory*.

"Beck, *please*," I moaned. With a grunt, I kicked at him. But he dodged my foot easily. "This is insane! You can't just leave me here!"

"It's not for ever," he said, voice quick. Low. As if he only had himself to convince. "You'll be tested here, of course. All you have to do is pass."

And at once, his face changed. The open, convivial man who'd so spun me into a willing web of manipulations and sweet nothings collapsed in on himself, a facade crumbling before my very eyes. He didn't care for me, not now. Perhaps not ever. I was merely a task to be completed. An unruly variable in a deadly hypothesis. I felt like I'd had water tossed over my head, sea salt and brine flooding my eyes and washing the lovelorn idiocy away.

I felt stupid for allowing myself to be pulled along like a child waiting to be punished. Stupid, naive, and wrong. I'd believed myself something worthy of protection, that he would do it implicitly. He had promised as much. He had promised many things that I'd taken blindly. But now the cut of wet rope into the flesh of my wrist was enough – I was nothing to be loved, or used, or tested. I was meat.

"But you won't come back for me!" I knew he wouldn't, even if he insisted otherwise. This place was ever-changing, a living body that evolved with every heartbeat. Turn my back for too long, and the very cavern in which we stood would be no more. "You can't leave me!"

"Pass your test and we'll come back for you. We can't have you jeopardizing—"

"*We?*" Mallory's voice was high, shrill. She scrambled to her feet, the back of her jeans wet from the fall. "As if I'm going to let you *tie her up* and leave her here! You're fucking insane!"

"Stop struggling, Caroline," Beck hissed, tying the rope in a knot round my wrist. He paid Mallory no mind. "This is only temporary."

"Like hell it is!" I kicked at his shins, but he dug his knee deeper into my stomach. Mallory leapt at him, wrapping her arms around his neck and her legs around his middle. She hauled backward, and Beck stumbled. He wheeled backward, clawing at Mallory's forearms.

She craned her neck, tucking her elbow beneath his jaw and squeezing. "Get *off*!"

Beck turned, teeth clenched, and threw himself back against the wall. Mallory hit it first, head cracking against the stone. The sound reverberated sickeningly. I cried out, sagging beneath the rope as it dug into the raw flesh of my wrist. My thumb cracked and my knuckles ached.

"Mallory!"

Her arms went limp over his shoulders, legs unhooking from around his middle. She slumped like a marionette, strings cut, as Beck rubbed his throat, gasping for the air she'd wrenched from him. He returned to me with brow set, rolling his sleeves to the elbows.

"If you've learned anything at all from me, Caroline, then we'll see each other again soon."

"You're *insane*!"

"You know what you have to do. You know what this place will require of you." He looked me over as I pulled at the rope, checking the constitution of the knot at my wrist. "We've studied. Prepared. If the work has been for anything, let it be for this."

I kicked out again, swinging at him with my free arm. "You're insane! Fuck the test—"

His flattened palm made contact with my cheek before I could brace myself, the sting reverberating like a false note through the sore swell of my face. I could smell blood. "Don't say that, all right?"

he hissed. There was desperation in his voice, no matter how subtle. "Don't say that. You *will* survive this if you remember the work. The work is everything. The *work* is how we persist."

"The work'll mean fuck all if we're *dead*!"

"I don't plan on dying. Survival, Caroline, is why we're here. Survival is how we're *rewarded*. You won't be touched by the specter that follows us; it's merely here to shepherd us, and to collect the refuse that—"

"*Refuse?*" I gaped, eyes flickering from Beck to Mallory, and back again. She hadn't moved, lying crumpled and still on the floor. I gave a tug at the tie around my wrist, reaching up with my other hand to pick at the knot with my jagged nails. He'd tied it too tight; there would be no loosening it on my own. Beck watched me do it. He knew. "They're *people*, Edward. People who trusted you! And you led them here!"

As if to double-check his work, he reached over my head and gave the rope a tug. It held fast, rooted at the point where it disappeared into the stone wall. "You all know what you signed up for."

A horrible laugh bubbled from me, pitched and manic. "No we sure as fuck didn't!"

Beck paused. His eyes remained level with the knot over my head, brow furrowed. He pressed his lips into a hard line, then sighed. "You would have come anyway." At this, his gaze flickered to mine. "Of course you would have. You would have done whatever I asked."

I gaped, but said nothing.

He stepped away from me, and I kicked out again. "I won't leave Mallory," Beck said. "She'll be easy enough to carry. No need for interruptions. I do want you to succeed, you know."

He was really doing it, leaving me here, tied and bloody like chum in rough water, to be picked apart by this *thing*, this aspect of the Leviathan that followed us, monitored us, took our bodies and our faces as penance for our failures. I wondered if the Leviathan herself watched us now, watched as I dangled from the overextension of my elbow, up on the balls of my feet as I strained against the tie that I had so stupidly allowed myself to be quartered into.

If I passed, would the beast come herself to cut me loose? Would she apologize for the inconvenience and send me on my way? Or would I simply have to wait for Beck to return whenever he'd found what he came here for?

"You're insane," I spat. My voice was anemic, lacking all the conviction he might have required of me. "This is all fucking insane."

Beck's lips twitched at the corners. "Discovery, Caroline. Innovation. The world wasn't made without sacrifice."

"So I'm a sacrifice? Is that it, then?" Once more, I looked to Mallory. She still hadn't moved, a crimson patch blooming at the back of her skull.

He shook his head. "Your pain *is* the sacrifice. It always has been, for all of them. The test is how you use it. What you make of it. Dorothy failed because she refused the chance to save a life that she took years ago. Oliver did the same; his crime was inaction, an abandonment that led to the death of his squadron. And in that way *we* were to be their replacements. You saw how easily he threw you to the wolves. But Hannah . . . Hannah might have passed, you know." A sigh, a shrug. "But you robbed her of that. You robbed her of any chance she might have had to face her darkest self, to cast it away in service of the Leviathan's favor. And I can't afford to jeopardize my work if she comes to collect."

I spat on the stone between us, blood and saliva and sea foam. "Fuck your work."

A pause. His eyes flickered to where my spit wet the floor, as if curious to study it. As if it might lend him some insight to the theoretical and purely academic concept of betrayal. "You're angry. It's understandable. But the best work is done at the point of breaking. Diamonds and pressure, and all that. Pass the test, Caroline. Think critically about what the Leviathan asks of you. Her tests are for your benefit, after all. You can leave this place cleansed. *We* can – together."

Beck gave me no time to answer, nor to plead for Mallory's life in any way that could have mattered. He turned to scoop up his bag, which lay heavy and discarded by his makeshift bedding. The seal within sagged, straining at the straps over his shoulders. Then, he returned to Mallory. He stooped and took her into his arms, cradling her against his chest like a bride.

"Edward, *please*!" I moaned. "I-I love you! You can't do this!"

It felt like a lie. Wrongness, acrid and thick like bile. I didn't love him. I needed to. Desperately. But I didn't. It was a sudden break, the shattering of a fragile bone. But it was broken all the same. Devotion without cause was sickly. Anemic. It meant nothing.

"I believe in you, Caroline," he said, gaze raking Mallory's unconscious face. He seemed unmoved by every word that left my mouth, like I'd spat out gibberish. "I always have. Don't prove me wrong."

He turned away without another word, leaving me to flop heavily at the end of the line. I jimmied my fingers round the wet fibers, hooking them at the base of the knot, and *pulled* – but the rope was lodged in the rock, absorbed by it. It would be no use, and as easy as pulling the whole wall down around me. I turned and braced my feet against the rock, the rope digging painfully into my wrist. At my back, Beck stooped and took up the flare from the center of the room. It had begun to sputter out, slowly darkening with each passing moment. He would run out of flares soon, and then we would be in the dark.

I strained against the rope, the tips of my fingers numbing as the blood stoppered in my wrist. "*Edward!*" My shadow stretched and distended on the wall as he shifted the flare into the crook of his neck, holding Mallory with both hands. My feet slipped on the rock and I fell, swinging on the pendulum of rope and smacking with a horrible crunch into the wall.

Beck's shadow paused its stretching across the stone. I wanted him to say something, anything, as I scrambled to right myself. But as I slumped against the wall, dangling by the leash over my head, he disappeared from view.

"Make it right, Caroline." His voice was an echo, a ghost from within the dark. It stretched, twisted, refracted; a fragment of shadow, no more than a crumbling of stone. "Release yourself. It'll be all right in the end."

The last flicker of vermillion light passed from the cavern and into the next, following weakly as Beck carried Mallory and their packs further in.

I strained, pain searing my wrist and shoulder. My own fate didn't matter; the Leviathan could pick me apart bone by bone if that was to be my lot. But not Mallory.

My chest billowed, her name spilling from me like a foghorn in search of a lighthouse. What I felt for her now, this animal response, this torrid horror that ripped my throat raw, I understood implicitly. I'd told Beck that I loved him, and he'd said the same. But *this* was love – the fear of loss, and the fear of losing. I loved Mallory. *This*, at least, didn't feel like a lie.

I had loved my mother, too, in my way. And she'd loved me in hers. Look where that had gotten us.

I was stripped to my barest bones. No one remained to tell me who I was. What could I possibly be, alone? In the dark?

The cavern was black as pitch. I felt with my foot for my pack. The rope hung close enough to where Mallory and I had made a makeshift camp that if I could just *reach* it, I could find something useful within. My shoulder strained and popped. Not dislocated – but close. The tip of my boot found something soft in the dark, hard shapes beneath the pliable texture moving as I gave a gentle nudge.

Yes! I pressed the toe of my boot into the fabric and tugged, scraping it bit by bit across the rock. In the pitch dark, I could hear the contents of the bag moving as I tugged it to me, over the corner of the crinkling thermal blanket Mallory had used as a makeshift bed. Bits of rock rolled beneath my foot as I tugged it closer, stooping with a groan and a stretch of my shoulder as it came within distance.

There was no telling if the pack was mine or Mallory's; they were largely indistinguishable. I lifted one foot, propping it flat against the wall so that I could use my knee as a makeshift table. Twisting my wrist in its too-tight tie, I struggled to feel through the bag with one hand. I felt at the smooth edges of a first aid kit and a water bottle. I took out the latter and greedily unscrewed the lid with my teeth, gulping down the entire thing in one go. How long had it been since I'd had water? My head hurt and my mouth was dry, and it was only as I drank that I realized the pains in my stomach were from hunger.

I tossed the bottle aside. The Leviathan would have to forgive me a bit of litter. I felt in the nearly-empty bag – Mallory's, judging by the circular tube at the bottom of the bag which very much felt like lip gloss – and produced the last of her flares. If Beck had *my* bag, then they'd be shit out of luck; I'd used all of mine already. Small mercies.

The flare blazed to life, and for a moment I was blinded. I held it overhead, rising onto my toes to give my straining shoulder some rest. The cavern was once more flooded red, the light sputtering and spitting sparks onto my shoulders and the thermal blanket at my feet.

It was there in the vermillion cast that I realized I was not alone. A flash of movement at the far end of the cavern caught my eye, somewhere beyond the thin vein of arctic water that gurgled and flowed uninhibited. I stretched the flare higher, the flickering light dancing over the unmistakable bow of a moving shadow.

A deer emerged from the dark, stepping gingerly into the red light with its head low and nostrils flaring. It ducked beneath the steady drip of water from overhead, striding with purpose to the edge of the stream. The deer nosed at the cold water with a splash and a shake of its head. It hadn't seen me, by the looks of it. Unperturbed, unbothered – it could very well have been anywhere else.

A deer was just a deer. There would be no telling them apart in the wild. But I knew this one. It was mine.

When you see a creature die, you learn it in a way that feels implicit. Like nature. Like a tree knows a root, like soil knows rain; the deer took stock of the stream, the cave, the dark that stretched like limbs on all sides, and I knew it without question.

The deer looked up, its gaze level. It saw me, at long last. And it was unafraid.

My fingers wavered around the thin neck of the flare, shoulder sagging as it leapt the stream and made for me. The deer's russet fur was damp, slick and beading with salt. She had no antlers, and the spots on her rump were just as faded as they'd been when I'd found her on the side of the road. But she bore no evidence of her final moments, no blood on her muzzle, no gravel or mud ground into her haunches.

I let the flare slip from my grasp, paying it no mind as it clattered and rolled to lodge in a juncture between two jutting stones. Fingers trembling, I stretched out my hand. I strained against the rope, the tips of my bound digits numb and my shoulder aching. Palm outstretched, I reached for her. My toes slipped on the stone, and I scrambled to stay upright, but the deer was undeterred.

She held my gaze in the way a friend might. Gentle, and unrepentant, the deer approached me evenly, with no shock and awe. She didn't startle as my boots scuffed the rock, nor as I groaned beneath the pain in my shoulder. The deer approached me, and all at once I could feel the heat of her breath on my palm.

This was no illusion. The press of her muzzle into my fingertips was real. So were the tears on my cheeks, as sudden as they were surprising. I had held this creature while she died, had sat in the rain with her blood on my jeans, and yet here she stood.

"Did you come back for me?" I muttered. The words came from nowhere, and they meant very little.

The deer didn't shy away at the ragged warble of my voice. She merely drew closer, allowing me to slacken my pull on the rope as I ran my hand along the broad slope of her cheek, the ridge of her brow bone. Her warmth was a blessing, a balm, and she was real. Gloriously so. She was real, and I was not alone.

A voice rang from within, and from without. It sounded like it had come from my own head, from a space above me, from across the cavern. At the heart of the darkened space, the vein of frigid water surged, spilling in a foam-riddled wave over the stone bank.

"How long have you been here, Caroline?"

I tugged my hand from the deer, and she looked up at me blithely. She was unbothered, unmoved by the sudden jerk. I blinked at her, watching as the light of the flare refracted in her eyes. Of course the deer hadn't spoken – and yet she regarded me with such a keen awareness that I couldn't be sure of it.

"I—" A gulp, a flex of numb fingers. "I don't know."

The voice began again, the deer's mouth unmoving. "Time moves strangely in the dark. But here you are, fixed in it."

The deer looked over her shoulder, ears perking. Her nostrils flared, steam spilling out with a sharp exhale. For the second time, movement stirred within the shadows beyond the light of the flare. A consciousness, an undeniable presence. I felt it in the way I felt the deer before me now.

"Beck?" I called. But I knew, at once, that it was not Beck who had come for me. I looked up into the dark above, waiting at any moment to see Dorothy, or Oliver, or Hannah dangling from the ever-evolving mass of bodies at this place's behest.

But there was nothing.

"Not Beck," the voice said. Its presence narrowed, as if deciding exactly where it should land. It tapered to a singular point, the sliver of dark from which the deer had emerged. She turned, hooves scraping against the stone, and watched the space as I did.

"Then who?" My voice echoed, an arrow into open air. I dared to ask where the others hadn't. But, then again, had the others heard her voice? Did they hear the woman in the dark?

I hadn't needed to ask. There could only be one here. I didn't believe in God. But I did believe in the thing that lived here. I believed whether I wanted to or not.

I could see a silhouette now, at the edge of the light. With gritted teeth, I stretched and gave the flare a kick, dislodging it from where it sat propped between two rocks. It clattered across the floor, rolling to a stop at the edge of the stream. And yet, despite the shift of the light, the shadows beyond it remained in place. A shroud, maybe. A curtain. I wanted nothing more than to peek behind.

"Tell me about the deer," the voice said.

"Tell me who you are first."

An angel, maybe. Or something more. Maybe it really was nothing more than my imagination. Dehydration, hunger . . . desperation.

A low rumble shook the cavern, like the sea floor itself had shifted at the question. "You know who I am, Caroline."

I gulped. Of course I did. I knew it like I knew myself. But seeing was believing. "Come into the light."

"I don't think I will. Not yet."

"Why not?" I strained against the rope, and numbness spread to my wrist. "What do you want?"

A pause. The body within the shadows was unmoving. "What do *you* want?"

I gaped. "I want to get the fuck out of here, for one."

Another rumble. The deer's ears swiveled. "And then what?"

I opened my mouth, then closed it again. More than anything, I wanted the creature to come into the light. "Why have you been speaking to me?" It felt strange to admit aloud, this idea that the voice I'd been hearing in my head and the one before me now were the same. Under different circumstances, I would have thought that I was losing my mind. But there were no rules here. Anything was possible. Everything was real.

"Because I like you, Caroline. And I want you to succeed."

I couldn't help the laugh that bubbled from me. "I bet you say that to *all* your human sacrifices."

"*Sacrifice?*" All at once, the room shifted. The rope at my wrist went slack as I was pitched sideways. The floor tipped, and the deer fell along with me, scrambling on slick hooves and braying into the cold air as we were spilled into the dark. The blanket, flare, and pack fell through the open air, the rope flying loose overhead as it severed with a crackling rip of wet fibers.

I landed hard, crashing not into rock but plush carpet. The deer kicked and bellowed, righting herself only to fall sidelong into a floral-patterned wall and a narrow table. My head spun as I sat upright, the painful pins and needles in my shoulder and arm weighing me down to the earth. I reached for the deer with my good arm, fingertips swiping at her damp haunch.

A single light hung overhead, warm and unabated. Music rang tinnily from the radio on the table, the framed picture and landline telephone on either side knocked prone by the deer as she scrambled to right herself.

And at the end of the hall, which stretched and loomed like a spine, a single wooden door. The handle rattled and the hinges shook. I lurched, slapping my hands over my ears.

I knew precisely where I was. I knew the nature of my test.

I was home, at long last. And my mother was dying.

The doe turned from the door at the end of the hall and came to stand over me, nostrils flaring. She looked down to one end, and then the other. I did the same, stomach falling as I realized that both ends of the arrow-straight hall were identical. A door. A handle. And a keyhole.

Despite the press of my hands to my ears, I could still hear the voice. The uncanny voice, both familiar and foreign; it was an amalgamation of every voice I'd ever heard. Everyone I'd ever loved and everyone I'd ever let down.

"You took something from me, Caroline," the voice said. "Why is that?" In every syllable I could hear the rush of sea foam, the spilling of an errant wave over wet rock. The Leviathan spoke, and the sea answered. Every time. It spoke in a million voices: Dorothy's, Oliver's, Iskra's. My mother's. Look too close, and I might see a thousand faces within the wallpaper.

I shook my head. When I spoke, my voice was too loud. I turned my attention to the deer, to the rapid billowing of her sides as she stepped over me, searching for an exit. "I didn't mean to!" I cried. "I didn't want to kill anybody!"

"*Hmmm . . .*" Again, the floor rumbled. The picture frame, the radio, the corded landline all rattled atop the table. The deer startled, skittering further down the hall. "I don't think that's quite true. You swung the ax after all."

"I didn't know that it was Hannah!"

"Who were you hoping to find at the end of that blade? Your mother?"

"No!" Yes. Yes, and assuredly so. I could still hear her, echoing like a faulty radio in my mind. I had killed her once. The Leviathan knew it.

"Tell me what you're hoping to find here."

I didn't know what she meant. Here, lost in the cave beneath the sea? Here, in the hall I'd seen every night in every nightmare for years and years? Here, in the darkest heart of my guilt? Beneath the eye of a judging god that I had only just begun to believe in? What I wanted didn't feel relevant; I hadn't come here to ask for anything. I hadn't come here to worship. That was all Beck – I was merely collateral.

But I did want. Everyone wants.

I was speaking before I knew myself, before I could feel my tongue as it lashed against my teeth. "I want to be free. I want to have a fucking *choice*."

The voice shifted. All at once, it sounded as if it spoke to me from behind the door at the end of the hall. "And yet here you are. Again."

The door gave a lurch, a fist making contact with the wood on the other side.

"Caroline, open the door!"

I felt the deer's hot breath on the back of my neck, wet muzzle nudging the slope of my shoulder.

Someone on the other side of the door was coughing. Spluttering. Choking, banging on the door and rattling at the handle. All of the sudden, my hand was leaden with cold weight. I looked down at the key in my grasp.

An eye appeared at the keyhole, barely visible from where I slumped so far down the corridor. "Open the fucking door, Caroline!" My mother's voice was loud enough to deafen, a wet pop after every syllable. Even from where I sat, I could see the redness of her eyes; bloodshot, and wide, and afraid.

As I shambled to my feet, I turned to the other end of the hall to see the very same. An eye, a finger poking through the keyhole – and then nothing. My mother fell from the door, and I heard her land on the flooded tile with a splash. She coughed, and wetness sloshed into the running water.

The deer nudged my hand. I took a step forward.

And then it was gone.

The bodiless voice spoke again. "Why did you stay with the deer?" it mused. "An animal on the side of the road, with no more than moments to oblivion. Why?"

I took another step, and my foot squelched into the wetness of the carpet. I looked down; water spilled beneath the door and out into the hall. *No, no, no.* I turned on my heel, tucking the key into my pocket, and went to the wall. Rope dangling from my wrist, I felt at the wallpaper, tossed aside the narrow table. The framed photo upturned. My parents smiled out at me. I turned it over again.

"Why, Caroline?" The voice sounded as if it were right over my shoulder, though the hall was cold and empty at my back. "You have no qualms with the cycle of life and death. In fact, you welcome it readily. Prematurely, even."

I whirled, taking up the corded landline and hurling it in the direction of the Leviathan's voice. It sailed through the open air and clattered against the opposite wall. "That's not true, and you fucking know it," I hissed.

"Then why?"

"Because the deer didn't deserve to die."

"And your mother did?"

"*Yes.*" I spat it out with vitriol, with conviction. I felt sick. I felt powerful.

The floor shuddered beneath me. "Good," the voice said, moving further down the hall. "Now we're getting somewhere."

My mother's voice rang from behind the door again. This time, it only came from one; the door at the opposite end of the hall had gone quiet. "Caroline, why are you doing this to me?" my mother cried, voice thick. "Help me!"

I cast about for the deer, gripping my hair as I jammed my palms over my ears. The door closest rattled and shuddered beneath the force of my mother's pounding fists. I knew this night well enough to know that it wouldn't last for ever. She would weaken. Eventually. And then she would go quiet. Only then would I call for help.

No – I couldn't do this. I didn't care how this place, how the Leviathan, wished to test me. This wasn't my destiny to fulfill. This was *Beck's*. I only wanted to be free.

I turned on my heel and made for the opposite door. I could feel eyes on me as I hurried forth and flung it wide – only to find the same hall stretching out before me.

I crossed the threshold. Wet carpet sagged beneath my feet. At my back, the door swung closed and at once fists railed against the wood. I lurched away, tripping on the rope fixed to my wrist.

"Caroline, please! I-I had an accident!" A gurgle, a retch, a curse. I heard the heaviness of a body sliding down the door frame.

The voice, once more, nestled inside my head. I was alone now, with nothing but a door between me and my most persistent burden. I almost missed the presence of the Leviathan there in the hall. For I knew, beyond a shadow of a doubt, that it was the Leviathan. An angel. Something more. Beck had been right.

She always did make a great show of it, didn't she? the voice said. *How were you to know that this time she meant it?*

I arrowed down the hall, making for the opposite door. Again, I threw it wide only to find myself back where I'd started. If the others' tests were any indication, I knew what I'd need to do to survive. To open the door, to face my mother; to save her, even. It was startling, the fervency, the conviction, with which I knew that she did not deserve to be saved.

You knew, didn't you? You knew that this time was different. Not a bluff. Not a play for control. This was real.

"No!" I barked. "I won't do this!" Again, I hurried down the hall only to open the door into the very same stretch of carpet and floral wallpaper. Again. And again. At every turn, my mother threw herself against the door, weakening with each pass. She was crying, sobbing, retching wetly into the spilling bathwater.

But each time, the hall grew shorter. I didn't notice it at first, until it was unavoidable. I was being squashed, pushed closer and closer to my mother as her lungs filled with sea foam and her nose bled anew. The gaudy florals swam and danced on either side, the tinny music on the radio interspersed with static that dipped and crescendoed each time I made for another door. Another, another, and another. The single light overhead danced on its chain. The carpet sagged beneath my feet. And the hallway carried on.

The loop never ended; I broke into a jog, shouldering through one door and then another, each step a squelch of wet carpet. Again, and again my mother railed at the door, cursing and pleading and coughing and spluttering – and each time, her eye found me in the keyhole. Every so often, I thought that I could see, as she shifted, a glimpse of the bathroom behind her. Proof, maybe, that this loop had an end that did not involve me facing her directly. But then it was gone.

My legs were tired. The hallway was shorter now, two doors facing one another across a stretch of carpet that was no longer than a yardstick.

A pop of bile and spit, the gasp of a mouth pressed to wood: "Just open the fucking door, all right? Open it!"

Her fingers scrabbled at the keyhole; I heard her seizing, thrashing, choking on spit as she blindly kicked away an empty pill bottle. This time, I was too close to avoid her gaze. She found me through the narrow passage, and her bloodshot eyes widened.

"Open the door, Caroline," my mother pleaded. "Please, baby. The key . . . you have the key, don't you? You locked the door?"

I did. And I had. I hadn't removed it from my pocket, and yet the key weighed heavily in my palm. I gulped, and I could taste brine on my tongue. It would be easy to unlock the door, to hobble to the phone and call an ambulance while she choked and spluttered on her own spit in the middle of the hallway. I would tell them that it wasn't her fault, that she'd only mistakenly taken her medication four times the normal amount. I would lie to them, tell them that this was the first time that this had happened; I would tell them that we were happy, that I loved her and that she loved me. And we would be happy. My mother would be alive. And I would continue to live in fear of the day that she *did* die.

It was my fault. I had chosen to allow it.

Try again.

It wasn't my fault. She had taken the pills. How small could a person become until they were nothing at all? I didn't want to find out.

That's it.

I had chosen to remain outside. I had chosen to leave the door locked. I had sat in the hall, with my hands over my ears, as my mother choked, bled from the nose, convulsed and seized and popped blood vessels in her eyes.

She'd told me she'd do it, too. She'd looked me in the eye and told me with the utmost clarity that when she killed herself, in every way that mattered, it would be my fault.

"You make me want to kill myself," she'd said. "You make me want to die."

What a horrible thing for a little girl to hear.

But all I had ever done was mold myself for her. I took a thousand shapes to hide in her shadow, to prop her and prod her where I was needed. What was I meant to do when presented with the chance to be free? I had lived in fear for so long, dangling at the leash of every threat, every ill-begotten promise.

Who would blame me if I allowed the promise to fulfill itself?

No one.

My father blamed me.

I blamed me.

No one who matters. I don't blame you, Caroline. My therapist's voice. Familiar at first, and then . . . changed, but no less recognizable. *Be not afraid.*

I pressed my back to the wall and slid down to the carpet, the damp back of my jeans and the hem of my coat soaking in the overflowing bathwater. Dorothy and Oliver had been tasked with righting their wrongs. Hannah might have done the same. Hannah, who I had robbed of a chance. Would she have atoned? Or would she have failed just like all the others?

I knew at once that I would fail, too. I jumped as my mother hit the door again, her sobs weakening, slowing. I wouldn't open the door. I wouldn't atone.

And why not? The voice in my head, the voice of the Leviathan, was my own.

I could feel the presence draw nearer. A caress, like the deer's hot breath on the salt-dappled stretch of my neck. I pressed my hands tighter over my ears and squeezed my eyes shut. Letting my mother die was the first real decision I had ever made. And it had set me free.

Until Beck. And then I was shackled once more. But it had been a choice. And it had been mine.

"Caroline." My mother's voice was wet, thick, and heavy on the other side of the door. No matter how hard I pressed my hands to my ears, no matter how desperately I tried to numb her in every waking moment of my pitiful, blank existence, I could still hear her. "You can open the door," she said. There was an awareness to her voice that she hadn't possessed before. Much like with Dorothy, the illusion turned inward. This was the test. This was the heart of the labyrinth, just as Beck's seal had promised. "Open the door, and you'll be forgiven."

For what? For letting her die? For relishing in it in the secrecy of my own mind?

"I don't want to," I said. I felt the Leviathan's numberless eyes narrow on me; this was the heart of my darkest self. I didn't want to free her. I didn't want her to live. I didn't want to be shackled by someone who would whittle away at me for their own use until there was nothing left. And then when the threadbare remains were all used up, I would be told that I wasn't enough. I would be the villain, the abandoner. It would happen with my mother. It would happen with Beck.

"I love you, baby," my mother said. "You know that."

But she didn't. She loved the idea of me. She loved what she could use me for. I didn't miss her. I wouldn't. If it meant failing here and now, if it meant being swallowed by the Leviathan and left to sink into the wet carpet and endless stone for ever – so be it. I would be free regardless.

And so I let my hands fall away from my ears. My gaze fixed on a single flower in the gaudy wallpaper-pattern – a begonia, faded and curling at the corner – and I listened to my mother. She was dying, as she had done over and over in all my dreams. I heard the wet slosh of a nightgown drenched in water and sick. I heard nails scrabbling at wood. I knew what I would see when the door opened, when the paramedics finally arrived and declared her dead on arrival. I would see what I always saw, what populated the dark space between every blink, between sleep and waking.

They would open the door long after she'd stopped struggling. They'd turn off the faucet and pick up the pill bottle. My father would rattle off all the times she'd pulled this stunt before, and point a damning finger at the little girl in the hallway. *She* was the condemning variable. *She* had killed her mother.

So be it.

If I were to die for it, then so be it. I wouldn't lie, wouldn't make myself small, to accommodate my mother even in death. I wasn't sorry. And if I had to listen to her die every day for the rest of my life to be *free*, so be it.

My mother went quiet.

Tell me again about the deer, the Leviathan said.

I let my head fall back against the wall as the low gurgle of the overflowing tub carried on beyond the door. "No one deserves to be alone at the end," I said. "The deer was innocent, and it was a selfish and heartless person who left her to die alone. No one should suffer on their own."

Bit hypocritical, don't you think?

I shrugged, though there was no telling if the Leviathan could even see it. She was in my head, for all I knew. "Maybe." I looked to the door, which shook no more. "I'm not sorry. I have nothing to atone for."

On the table, the radio flickered to life. The voice that was both foreign and familiar rang from within. *Is this your final answer?*

"I'm absolving myself of this," I said. "I'm sorry I killed Hannah. But I'm not sorry that my mother is dead." I didn't kill her. Not really. She did that herself.

Static crackled over the radio for a long moment. And then: *Do you want to be free?*

"I do."

Good.

All at once, the floor dropped from beneath me. The carpet disappeared and the wall dissolved. The rope flung overhead and I fell and fell, landing with a splash in a pool of icy water. The red light of my abandoned flare burned brightly, a sprig of cut rope protruding from the wall where I had been tied just before.

And again, a body moved silently within the darkness beyond. A shadow within a shadow, it stretched up the length of the wall. There, within, blinked hundreds of watchful eyes.

And beneath them, framed by the swinging pendulum of a single light, the deer nosed at a patch of algae on the stone. The eyes watched as the doe meandered mindlessly around the damp stretch of verdant green, pawing with a delicate hoof at a hardened patch of sea salt.

I wanted to go to her, but refrained. Even if I was dreaming her, imagining her, conjuring her simply for something to cling to, her peace deserved to be undisturbed.

And so I turned my gaze upward, to the thousand watchful eyes that bloomed off the body of my watcher like a generous plumage of black feathers. "Are you going to let me live?" I questioned, my voice a watery echo in the towering cavern.

The silhouette sharpened within its shadowy shroud. "The one who started you on this path, who took the seal and summoned the flood, will be surprised to see you," the Leviathan said. "But I surmised that it would be you in the end."

"End?" This was no end. This wasn't over – Mallory was still out there, trapped with Beck in the machinations of his obsession.

"You and the other possess the same delicious desperation that I do so strive for in my chosen. Devotion without a certain level of desperation is wasted. Your greenness makes you keen; his obsession makes him fervent. Equally valuable qualities in an Icon."

I blinked. I suddenly felt as if the creature was speaking gibberish. "Icon?"

"That's the aim of all this, you see." The body moved, stretched, serpentine in nature. Suddenly every shaft of blackened wall seemed to move, like I sat beneath the great belly of a serpent. "Human intellect is like peacock feathers; nothingness, flashiness, an elaborate mating ritual. The peacock lives in the dirt, pecking insects out of the muck, consoling itself with its great beauty. I have come to think of human consciousness as a burden, a weight. Without help, humans light the match every time. In my service, as my chosen, you unburden yourself. With me, you can be free. I will never tell you who you are. I will simply allow you to discover it for yourself. I've done it since the dawn of the first day. That is what the other has come here to do."

Beck – he'd never relinquished his true aim here. Study, and the thrill of knowledge, sure. But there was always more.

"Oliver was right, then," I thought aloud, and the Leviathan listened willingly. "When Beck took the seal from the vestibule in the entrance . . . "

"The game began." Humor rumbled in every syllable. But this wasn't a game – not really. This was life and death. This was religion.

I shifted, lifting myself from the water and onto the nearest patch of semi-dry stone. I didn't know where to look; the eyes or the shadow, or the slithering body above. "Let me see what you truly look like," I said. "I want to see who I'm talking to. I'm owed that, if I passed your trial."

"No."

"*No?*" I scoffed. "Why not? What are you?"

No answer. For a long moment, there was only silence. And then: "An angel."

I felt delirious, like I had hit my head somewhere along the way and was dangling from the end of the rope that now hung from my wrist like a cheap bracelet. But there was no illusion in this; my heart felt too alive, too fervent, for this to be a dream. I could still feel the roughness of the wet carpet beneath my hand, could hear the rattling of a stalwart hinge beneath an ever-weakening hand. It was as real as the shrapnel, the mud, the greenhouse. This place was everywhere, and nowhere. Everything was real, and nothing.

The deer looked up at me then, and steam blew from her flared nostrils.

I spoke again. "What would you have me do next?"

Finally the voice returned, shaking the cavern with its might. It was a wonder Beck hadn't come running at the sound of it. Perhaps it was something only I could hear. "I would have you decide that for yourself," the Leviathan said. "Isn't that what you want? To choose?"

I pressed the heel of my hand to my brow, wincing as the salt on my forehead stung at the damaged skin of my wrist. "I feel like I'm going insane," I hissed. "I don't *feel* like I have a choice. I'm still here, aren't I?" I peered into the dark. "You're going to test Mallory, aren't you?"

"I am. But you are my favorite."

"Why?"

"Your tears become the sea, Caroline Destler. Nothing is a place of possibility. And you are nothing."

I struggled to my feet. My head spun, and I pitched sidelong. The deer exhaled sharply, watching as I stumbled on the length of rope hanging from my wrist. I felt of two minds, both warring with one another beneath the pounding slope of my skull: on the one hand, I needed to find Mallory. I needed to save her from this place, from the instrument of the Leviathan's divine will that so readily consumed those who failed her tests. There was no room for disbelief here. There were monsters in the dark, and they would have no mercy.

But then, at the same time, I felt powerful. I had been forgiven, and had forgiven myself in equal measure. This wasn't about a test, or a trial, or some long-forgotten cloister that housed an angel from a forgotten time. This was about forgiveness. And I had done it beautifully.

So why did I feel more afraid than ever?

I paused. "Will Beck be tested?"

"Like the rest." The voice moved with me as I stumbled across the cavern, making for the discarded bag and crumpled thermal blanket. Beck could be tested all he liked. He had started this after all – the very purpose for our coming had confirmed it verbatim. Oliver had been right. I shouldn't have doubted him. Beck started this on purpose so that he could walk the path of all the Leviathan's others. He had started this with every intention of finishing alone, the rest of us nothing more than shiny trinkets to be gifted as collateral. And so alone he would be.

I took a deep breath, emboldened, and said, "I want you to spare Mallory."

I could feel the Leviathan considering. She seemed to shrink, to pass higher into the shadows that hung above the cavern as I collected what meager supplies remained. I had limited time to find my friend.

I straightened, calling out into the dark. "Well?"

"Those who come here are not afraid to die, because when they do they become something else. Something greater. Like Alexandria. The story of the fire is greater than the fire itself. What sort of angel would I be if my cloister sat empty? This is the value of a human soul. Even *one* is worth the multitude."

I thought of Dorothy, Iskra, Oliver. I thought of the hundred featureless faces I'd seen stretching from the body of the beast that hunted us, each gasping for air and struggling to reach for the only flicker of life this place had seen in a hundred years, maybe more.

This was the Leviathan's flock. This was the assemblage of her worship. This was what would become of Mallory and Beck if they failed.

But what would become of me, since I'd passed?

"That's not an answer," I said.

The floor trembled beneath me. At my back, the wall shifted, what remained of the rope swallowed in the stone. The room was changing, the vein of water cutting through the floor diverting and arrowing off toward another ledge, another passage, another room entirely. As it had done so many times before, the cloister was evolving. This was no longer my test.

I blinked into the dark. "Let me see you." This thing that believed itself to be an angel spoke in riddles, in contradictions. It was no wonder Beck had spent so many years studying rites and runes, she made so little sense. I toed a dangerous line. Carefully, as if the floor might drop out from beneath me at any moment, I took a step toward where I imagined the Leviathan stood.

"You will," she said. Her voice was warm. Welcoming. I had passed her test, after all. I was one of hers. "At the heart of the cloister, and the end of all things. It is a gift, you know. Worthy is the Lamb who is slain, and the Icon who is chosen, to receive power, and wealth, and wisdom, and might, and honor, and glory, and, blessing—"

Be not afraid.

It echoed in my mind, over and over. I felt her voice skitter beneath my skin like electricity. Like locusts. An angel, yes. But not one of this world.

And then it dawned on me. With startling, terrible clarity, I turned my gaze up to the multitude of eyes once more. "*Icon*," I said, rolling the word like a sour candy on my tongue. The voice from above and within and without echoed on after I spoke, as if the Leviathan would continue to list blessings and accolades that I might receive until the end of time. "Singular."

No response. Beck had spoken idly of devotees, of followers, of acolytes brave enough to release themselves of all their burdens in the Leviathan's cloister. But an *Icon* – it had never occurred to me that there could be only one.

One by one, the eyes blinked closed. The deer turned and slipped into the shadows beyond the light of the flare. The floor beneath me tipped, and I was sliding, falling, pitching toward an arch in the adjacent wall that curved and rose to meet me. The shadows curled around me, bleach-white limbs scrambling through the dark on all sides.

All that remained were Mallory and Beck.

I heard the rush of water before I saw it. Frigid sea and bubbling foam rushed from all sides, curling up and over me like fingers. Salt flooded my broken nose, and as I struggled, craning my neck for the open air I only felt myself being pulled further down, down, tugged by every inch of skin until all was water. Salt. Sea.

It pressed between my lips, pried open my clenched teeth, rough digits reaching over my tongue and filling my throat. Salt burned into my eyes, and for a moment I couldn't breathe, couldn't see—

A hand, cold as ice, smoothed my hair over my brow. Almost loving. Almost tender.

I was pitched unceremoniously into the dark, a plaything flung into a box. I landed hard, crumpling. My nearly-empty pack slipped from my grasp and skidded across the stone, slamming hard into a salt-slick stalagmite.

Come to me, said the voice. It sounded like my own. There was no hint of my mother within. Only my own consciousness played back to me, a broken record in a dark room. *Come find me now.*

I righted myself. My head swam, my body ached; I felt sick, and my stomach lurched with every breath I took. But awareness flared within me as a pinprick of light swam into focus, a fire rising just beyond my vision. Two shadows stretched across the far wall in the low, flickering light. They scrambled as a tin cup rolled across the stone and into view, the larger of the two bemoaning the sudden quaking of the cavern floor. A tall silhouette, dancing in the light of the wavering fire.

Beck.

Beck watched like an animal at the end of a scope as I stepped into the warm light of the fire he'd made of a few bandages. I emerged from the dark, frayed rope dragging from the limp weight of my wrist. For a long moment, he merely watched as I came to a stop before the weak flame. Mallory, on the other hand, leapt to her feet at once. She slammed into me with a sharp sob, paying no mind to how I stumbled beneath the force.

I pressed a hand to the back of her head, feeling gingerly for the tender bump that had risen beneath her hair. The telltale crust of dried blood flaked beneath my fingertips, falling from her scalp like dandruff. But she didn't seem to mind the pain.

Beck's eyes fell to the rope that dangled from my wrist, heavy and sagging as I lifted my arms and wrapped them around Mallory's shoulders. The simple touch started her tears in full, a dam broken as she sobbed into my shoulder.

"*How?*"

The word hung over us all like a scythe. I met Beck's gaze and held it. He seemed so small now. Insignificant, compared to what I had seen. What I had done. The object of all his obsession had spoken to *me*. She'd tested *me*, and had freed me approvingly.

He knew it. I could see it written plainly upon his face. Relief – and maybe fear. Satisfaction coiled between my ribs like a serpent.

Icon. Only one. And there were three of us here, around the fire. I knew what I needed to do, based on what I'd seen and what I'd learned through Beck's study. I could only imagine that the Leviathan's past acolytes were more prepared for this test than me, but I'd gotten this far by winging it and I didn't plan on stopping now.

I would see Mallory through her trial. And I would take her to the heart of the cloister. Without Beck.

"You left me to die," I said, voice low. Mallory hugged me tighter, arms trembling around my neck. I pried them free and gently pushed her behind me, further from the weak campfire. Further from Beck.

He shook his head. "But you didn't! And I *knew* you wouldn't!" He started for me, arms outstretched. There was nothing but fervor in his eyes. Hunger. A desire to consume. If he could pick me apart and put me beneath a microscope he would. No love lived there any more.

I curled my fingers into a fist and swung. His jaw crunched beneath my knuckles and he reeled sideways, spilling over the loose straps of his pack and falling painfully onto his hands and knees. Beck groaned, and, with a splatter of blood and spit, a tooth clattered onto the stone.

"Get your things, Mallory," I commanded. "We're going."

"*What?*" She and Beck spoke at once, the latter's voice thick with blood. I kept my eyes fixed on him as he wiped at his quickly swelling lips with the back of his hand. I would need to take care in what I told him, how I spoke to him. Clearly there were things at play that even his years of meticulous research couldn't touch.

There could only be one. Maybe this trial was one that was meant to be taken alone. I thought back to the long table and stone chairs, to the entrance cavern in which I'd first seen the aspect of my mother. I imagined the Leviathan's acolytes gathered there, feasting in the phosphorescent light around a long table before, one by one, they went into the cloister to be tested. Those who didn't emerge would return to torment the others, a rotten limb on the body of Leviathan's flock.

In another life, I might have done anything to keep Beck from meeting such a fate. But not this one. Not now.

"You're on your own," I said, inclining my chin. "We're going."

To my surprise, Beck laughed. He tipped his head back and the sound spilled up into the open air above us, mingling with the thin tendril of smoke that rose from the pile of burning bandages. "Going?" His voice was a gunshot. "Going where, Caroline?" Too quick to mark, he reached for his bag, still sagging with the weight of the stone disc he'd taken from the cave's entrance. "This is *my* trial! You can't reach the innermost cloister without me!"

If he could have done this alone – just Beck and a flashlight – then why had he brought the rest of us? What did he gain by forcing the rest of us into a trial that *he* had started? Did he think that he was impressing this deity, this angel, this *creature* from the depths? Did he think the Leviathan cared?

I shook my head. "You may have started this, but I intend to finish it. Believe me when I say, Beck, that we don't fucking *need* you." I knew it with certainty. "*I* don't need you."

His face faltered. I could see the gears turning behind his eyes, swimming and bloodshot beneath the fire's undulating shadow. "Of course you *need* me," he hissed. "What else do you have?"

I opened my mouth to speak, but Mallory beat me to it. Despite my protest, she stepped out from behind me, hands curled into fists at her sides. "She has me," Mallory said. "I trust her more than I trust you."

Again, Beck laughed. His eyes bulged and spittle flew from his lips. "You trust – *her*?" At once, the truth of his feelings for me flooded to the surface of his flushed visage. Oil always rose to the top of clean water, after all. "What was your test, then, Caroline? Hmm? Care to regale us with the tale of your unburdened sins before you go? I'm sure it'll speak wonders to your character."

So it had always been this. He used me to whittle at the fine craft of his own ambition until I was no good for it, and only then would he turn me on others. On myself.

Fucking men.

I inclined my chin further, but again Mallory spoke before I could. "I don't care!" she barked. I could feel her trembling, the very tips of her fingers curling into my sleeve. "I don't care what you think is wrong with Caro, or what you think is wrong with *me.* All I know is that you would leave either of us to die in a second – and Caro would *not.* She's a good person! And you . . . you *aren't!*"

Beck's lips curled. He took another step toward us, the shifting of his shadows shedding light on the haphazard pile of materials he'd amassed beside the fire. More flares, a packet of rations made for astronauts and infantry. And an ice ax. Something dark coated its tip. It was *mine.*

And herein lay the quandary: I could kill him. It would be easy. Just as it had been with Hannah; it would take nothing more than a well-placed swing. I could do it in the dark. I knew the way Beck moved, the sound of his breath, how high I'd have to stretch to reach his neck. His eyes. His mouth. But I couldn't. Not only could I barely bring myself to consider taking a third life, but I understood now more than ever that I *shouldn't.* I was being watched. We all were. The Leviathan was real, and unabashedly so. She was in everything: the salt on the rock beneath our feet, the water that seeped in through the cracks in the walls, the shadows that bowed and danced beneath the weak light of the flame. I had played by her rules, and she had let me pass. Were I to cheat her of the chance to test Beck the way he desired – the way *she* desired – I wouldn't be spared a second time.

The words slipped from me, bitter and angry and heavy on the tongue, before I could stop myself. "Mallory and I are going to finish it alone," I hissed. "And we're going to get the fuck out of this place."

"I won't let you leave!" Beck flew at us, arms outstretched. "You're *mine!*" I leapt sideways and kicked out at the burning bandages, scattering the makeshift fire into embers and smoke. Beck swung for me, fingers curled into claws, and I dove for the ax, the flares, the mess of provisions and equipment that had all been ruined by the water and the cold. Darkness swallowed the cave as the fire extinguished, burnt bandages and smoldering embers scattering across the stone. As my fingers curled over something hard, and solid – *a flare?* – the rope at my wrist gave a sharp tug, and my arm was wrenched back.

Beck pulled me away from the stockpile by my wrist. His breath was loud, hot; he coughed and spluttered, heaving beneath the oppressive weight of the smoke that had settled in the airspace above the fire. I struck the flare against the rock as I was dragged across the smoldering remnants, the cap popping and rolling away. I struck it against the ground again, and it blazed to life, blinding so close to my face.

"*Fuck you!*" I thrust the flare above my head like a dagger, stomach lurching as the smell of charcoal and sulfur mingled with that of burning flesh, with a sizzle and a howl of pain. Beck fell away, howling as burnt flesh smoked beneath his waterlogged fingers.

Mallory was on him, leaping from the dark and wrapping her arms around his throat. "Get the stuff!" Mallory cried.

I propped the lit flare against a rock and stuffed the contents of the stockpile into Beck's pack. The unlit flares clattered heavily atop the seal. It was dense and burdensome, and the straps of the pack strained beneath the weight of it.

I slung the bag, heavy with the seal, over my shoulder. I wrapped the length of the rope at my wrist up my arm, tucking it in on itself like a brace, and felt in the dark for the ax. It clattered and scraped against the stone, the sound eliciting a short gasp from somewhere to my right from Mallory.

Beck's voice was everywhere, ragged and harsh as he choked on the smoke that billowed from the doused fire. "You will not ruin this!" he bellowed. I grappled for Mallory as his voice arced through the darkness, a ghost beyond the light of the flare. "You will *not* take this from me, Caroline! Little *bitch*!"

He stumbled into view, and I leapt to my feet. I spun, ax in hand, the momentum of the movement swinging my leaden pack like a shot put. I held the weapon aloft as Mallory scrambled to take up a sharp rock, holding it out like a sword at my side. The burn on Beck's arm oozed blood and ash, vermillion embers falling from the charred flesh.

"We're going, Beck." I held the ax between us. "We're finishing the trial. And we're going."

The ground rumbled beneath us, and the small hairs at the nape of my neck raised. I felt the familiar pressure of observation, as if the whole place had turned its attention inward.

He shook his head. "Not without me you aren't. You have no idea what you're doing."

"Oh, don't I?" A muscle in my jaw twitched as I tightened my grip around the ax's handle. "I passed my test, Beck. She spoke to me, told me what to do. She said I was her favorite." It was a dangerous game to play, telling him all this. His ego was as fragile as a robin's egg. "I heard the Leviathan long before I was tested. I'm supposed to do this."

"YOU?" Spittle flew from Beck's lips, his eyes bulging. "You're *nothing*!"

"Maybe so." I set my jaw, resolute. "But *nothing* is a place of possibility." It felt truer when I said it. But the Leviathan wasn't wrong. And what Beck failed to understand was this – I wanted nothing for me, and everything for Mallory. I was nothing; it was true. I had no family, and my only friend was here, at my side. If I could do one thing, make one real choice, it would be to see her out of this. And so I could be nothing. I could be everything.

As I shifted further from Beck, feeling the juncture of the wall and floor with my heel, the vein bulged in his brow and his fingers curled into fists at his sides. Even in the low light of the flare I'd propped against the rock, I could see the indentation left behind on his finger by the wedding band he'd for so long refused to take off. It was all so clear now, how stupid and blind I'd been. There was no love here. He looked at me now with only hatred. I was a toy that had run out of spark, a tool that had exhausted its use. And Mallory was just collateral.

Beck took a long step over the burnt bandages, and I swung the ax. It whistled through the smoke-clouded air between us; a warning. He stopped. Slowly, he held up his hands like he might in the face of a rabid animal. "Come on, Caro." At his side, the flare sputtered, spitting sulfur and vermillion sparks onto the stone between us. I could still smell his burnt flesh. "Let's be reasonable here. Put the ax down."

The flare hissed and sputtered again, and in a burst – with teeth bared and fists clenched – Beck turned and kicked it across the open cavern. It clattered away, rolling to a stop in the open mouth of a narrow passage. Mallory seemed to see it at the same moment as I, for she tensed at my side.

I hadn't noticed it before. And by the look of it, neither had Mallory. It was a different passage than the one I'd used to arrive here. I'd come out from the darkness closer to the rock where I'd lodged the flare. This opening in the rock was new. Provided, maybe, just for us.

This was our escape. The flare, damaged as it was, wouldn't last long. If we could just make it there, we could use the darkness to our advantage.

With my free hand, I felt for Mallory's arm. I pressed my thumb into the soft skin of her wrist, and shifted sideways. She did the same. Beck turned with us as we moved, crouched as if to spring.

"I don't care what you do here," I said. My throat ached from the burn of the smoke, from the dryness of dehydration. "I don't care if you live or die. I don't care if you find what you came here for, or if you starve to death trying and failing to decipher your stupid fucking runes. You started this when you took the seal, and you fucked us all. The kicker is that you knew exactly what you were doing. Did you come here with the intention of being the only one to make it out alive?" Another step, another turn along the cavern's circular wall.

"Tell me what she said to you," Beck said, his voice simpering and rough. The bluster seemed to have gone out of him like wind from thin sails. "You said she talked to you, yes? The Leviathan spoke to you. You're sure of that?"

I said nothing. I was here, after all. Had I failed, had she found me wanting, he would have seen me next alongside Dorothy and Oliver, reaching from within the mass of flesh sent to consume us in our failure.

"Professor Beck, *please.*" Mallory's voice was thick and wet with tears. I wanted to look at her, to comfort her, but I knew that I couldn't take my eyes off of him. "Don't hurt us. We just want to go home."

Another step. The flare began to darken, each sputtering burst of sulfuric light weaker than the last.

And then it went dead. The moment darkness swallowed the cavern, the red light of the flare dying with a final sputter, I shoved Mallory toward the passage. Beck leapt for us, a wordless cry booming in my ears. I hurtled after Mallory with arms outstretched, narrowly missing Beck's claw-like fingers.

"Go!" I cried. "Don't stop – just go!"

Beck called for us, my name echoing along the narrow passage over and over as we ricocheted off one wall, and then another. I felt the wall with one hand, fingers scraping wet rock, and pressed Mallory forward with the other. The top of my head scraped the low ceiling, feet dipping and ankles turning as we raced across uneven terrain.

And then, with a gasp cut short and a rush of air, Mallory fell away. She dropped like a stone, nothing but the scrape of her shoes on a rocky ledge to mark her descent into the open air. I scrambled, grabbing for her sweater, her jacket – but the force pulled me down, jerking me over a sharp precipice.

We landed with a crash, a carpet of loose, clattering, solid objects breaking our fall before I could even muster the breath for a scream. Something sharp sliced into my thigh, another into my palm as I struggled and failed to right myself on ground that moved, shifted, rolled like sticks beneath my every jerk and reach.

Hands grasped my shoulders. "Caro!" Mallory's voice was close, her breath hot on my cheek. "Light a flare!"

I heard my name echoed somewhere overhead. Beck was in pursuit. But we could do nothing if we didn't know where to go.

"Are you hurt?" I demanded, tugging the sharp object from the heel of my hand.

"No," she said. "I don't think so."

I pulled the pack out from beneath me. The loose flooring shifted, and I sank into the clattering coolness of whatever it was that blanketed the floor, piled so high that I couldn't fathom the ground. Rocks, or sticks; the floor gave way beneath us, displaced by our weight as Mallory clung to me. I felt blindly in the bag, fingers closing around one of the three flares that remained.

"*Caroline, come back!*" Beck's voice boomed from above us, echoing as if from far away. The floor rumbled beneath us, and whatever loose rubble had cushioned our fall rattled on the stone on all sides. I heard the grinding of stone on stone, and heard Beck curse. "We can work this out, Caroline!" he called. "Come back!"

I knew what he wanted. As my fingers scraped the smooth edge of the seal, there was no doubt in my mind that he would push me back over the edge and into the darkness of this pit the second I returned it to him.

Maybe when we got out of this place, Mallory and I could do the stereotypical thing that I always saw on television, where girls post-breakup gathered a box of their boyfriend's things and burnt them on the sidewalk. She'd do that with me. No doubt about it.

But we would have to reach the center of the maze first.

I scoffed, the sound a gunshot in the dark. "*Men*, am I right?" My voice was small. "Pick a fucking lane."

I struck the flare, blinded by crimson light. In a flurry of movement, Mallory gasped, her grip on me disappearing as she scrambled away, kicking up the debris beneath us. She cursed, her voice pitched and frantic. And as my eyes adjusted, I looked down to find—

Bones. I couldn't see the floor through the mountain of them that rose from below to meet us. The ledge we'd stepped over in the dark loomed no more than five feet overhead. In another life, the drop might have been steeper. But the floor had risen to meet us, a million tibias, and spines, and skulls, and clattering fingers loose from their sockets. Mallory scrambled for the wall, shrieking as a bleach-white crustacean skittered from the eye socket of a picked-clean skull.

"Caroline!" Rock clattered over our heads as Beck skittered to a stop at the edge over us. I turned my gaze up, holding the flare over my head, just in time to see him obscured by a scraping slab of rock. The very walls were moving, shifting; the wall slid sidelong as the floor beneath us rumbled, the rattle of bone on bone deafening. Beck struggled, pushing against the mobile limestone, but the cavern had other ideas. Just as it had done for Oliver, it changed shape to accommodate us – and to thwart him. The bones began to sink, to shift like water into a drain. Beck disappeared behind a slab of stone. I could barely hear him, as if all at once we were a thousand miles away.

The movement stopped.

I took stock of the space around us as Mallory scrambled, slipped, fell against the wall as she struggled over the bones. I could only see so far, the flare haloing us both in light that barely reached the walls. She felt at the smooth stone, muttering to herself, ". . . an exit *somewhere*," she hissed. "Got to be—"

I looked up. The circular space reminded me of the grain silo on the farm near my apartment. Tall, smooth on all the sides; each bone that shifted beneath us was nothing more than a grain of wheat.

Thanks for the help, I mused. There was no answer. Maybe it hadn't been for me after all. The help, the protection; maybe it had been a coincidence.

There, in the light of the flare, I could see what filled the walls. Like scrawls on an overfull paper, crammed and squashed between lines that bent and intersected, runes sat in deep carvings on every inch of the stone. I recognized a few of the characters from the cave's entrance, and from Beck's notes. Mallory's finger slipped over a hard edge, and blood seeped down the length of her palm.

My ears popped painfully. Mallory slapped a hand to her temple with a whimper. "Mallory," I began. My voice sounded far away, as if underwater. Up above, the sound of Beck's frenzied cries had gone quiet, swallowed by the oppressive silence. "Mallory, hang on—"

Muffled, refracting and skipping at every third note, a trilling bell-tone rose from somewhere below, blaring from under the bones. I could feel vibration far under me, rattling the loose collarbone that had settled next to me in the shifting of the cavern.

Mallory's head whipped round, eyes wide. I blinked, sticking a pinkie finger in my ear and giving a twist.

"Is that—?" I began, looking from side to side, up and down; maybe I'd hit my head. Maybe we both had.

Mallory gaped. Even in the red glow of the flare, I could see that the color had drained from her cheeks. And then, far below, a light. It shone with every vibration, rattling the bones to the familiar tune. Even obscured, it shone brighter than the flare – almost impossibly so.

"Caroline," Mallory began with a gulp. "That's my ringtone. That's my phone."

My brow furrowed. "But I have no signal. You wouldn't either."

"I know," Mallory nodded. "And besides, I lost my phone when we had to swim. It fell out of my pocket."

I looked down into the forest of jutting bone beneath us. The tone ended and began again without hesitation. I looked up. Only darkness swam above. I wondered if we were being watched. And then I turned my gaze to Mallory once more. Sweat shone on her brow, hollow bruises beneath her eyes.

No, this wasn't help. And it certainly wasn't protection. The walls had moved not to help us, but to usher us along. To herd *Mallory* onward.

She spoke again. "You said we're supposed to be tested, right?"

I nodded. Suddenly, it was obvious. But it wasn't a choice, was it? Acquiesce, or be crushed by the shifting rock. "Yeah."

"What did you see when you were tested? Was it something bad, like all the others?"

Again, a nod. "It was."

"What was it?"

The ringtone stopped and started again, the rhythmic notes warped and distended beneath us. Lying would do her no good.

And so I told the truth. "My mother was abusive," I said. "A narcissist. She overdosed." A pause, a deep breath. "I let it happen. Listened outside the door to the bathroom." She didn't need to know that I'd been the one to lock the door. She didn't need to know how free I felt, how wonderful the silence had been in the few moments of peace and solitude that followed.

"Oh."

"It was a control tactic," I said, as if that could make it any better. "What my therapist said, anyway." It occurred to me idly that this was a wild conversation to be having while trying to stay upright atop a pile of bones. But I couldn't unpack that now. "She'd threaten to do it all the time. Just to get us to do stuff, to make us feel bad, y'know. She just went too far."

"I understand." And she did. It was clear on her face. "How long ago?"

"A long time."

Heavy silence hung over us, broken only by the sputtering of the flare overhead and the ringtone below. This shouldn't be possible; this couldn't be real. And yet – of *course* it was. The unreal was possible here, probable even. There was no room for disbelief.

"Right." Mallory turned her eyes back down to the light beneath us. The ringtone looped again, each tone leaping and jolting as if it were a living thing that struggled to find pitch. "So our test would have us confront what haunts us. Guilt, fear, whatever." She asked it in a way that felt clinical, like she was parsing out a shopping list or organizing a calendar. Her fingers trembled as they splayed flat across the stone wall. Mallory gulped, then wiped at the sweat on her brow with the back of her hand.

I nodded. "That's the long and short of it."

A yelp of a laugh warbled from her. "This is insane, right? This is fucking insane."

I wasn't sure what part she meant. The phone? The bones? The cave? Or did she refer to the fact that I could feel eyes on me, watching every sliver of skin, every droplet of sweat, from every shadow? I could feel the familiarity of the Leviathan's flock, no matter how far or near they may have been. Look too hard into the dark, and I might see Dorothy, eager for the both of us to fail, even in death.

"Yeah," I nodded, breathless. "But I've got your back."

Her eyes met mine as her fingers curled into fists at her sides. Her face was pale. Again, she gulped, as if her next words tasted sour on the tongue. "In that case," she said, "I think I know who's calling."

I reached for Mallory, scrambling over loose bones and curling my fingers around her wrist. Her gaze was unmoving, fixed upon the singular point of light beneath us. It was close enough to reach for, if only we could move aside a skull here, a spine there.

"Don't run, okay?" I was surprised at the weakness of my voice, the tremble in every syllable. "Whatever it is – whatever it throws at you – I've got you."

Mallory nodded. "I know," she said. "I know."

The air was colder here, like we had descended far beyond what the labyrinth had allowed us to see thus far. Below, the phone continued to ring. As the bones beneath us shifted, so did the screen's glaring light; it almost seemed to grow, as if each time we failed to answer it saw our silence as refusal.

And then, like an audience settling in plush boxes around a grand theater, an eye flickered open above us. Another, and another; practiced by now, familiar, the presence settled into the dark over our heads like a curtain.

I tightened my grip on Mallory's wrist, crawling on my knees through the loose bones to sit alongside her, shoulder to shoulder. With a grunt, I reached across her and propped the butt of the flare in an empty eye socket. It sputtered and hissed, spilling embers onto Mallory's knee.

"Don't look up," I said, shifting my grip so that I could throw an arm around her shoulders. She was trembling, violent spasms chattering her teeth. Mallory nodded, squeezing her eyes shut.

"I need to answer the phone," she whispered.

I let my eyes drift upward again, settling for but a moment on the familiar watcher. I couldn't see it, the great, ugly body of the Leviathan's flock, but I could picture it. Pressed into every corner like putty, each eye of each remaining face watching as the atoms of this place rearranged itself to accommodate Mallory's darkest self.

Slow at first, Mallory pushed aside a clutter of bones. They rolled down the clattering slope between us and the wall, and settled in the divot of a carved rune. She dug carefully, as if the owners of these bones might emerge from the shadows and reprimand her for touching them.

But the sound of the ringing phone only seemed to sink lower. Lower, and lower, with each bone removed from the pile.

"Mallory," I began, voice careful. Clinical. "Do you have any idea what . . . well, do you think it might be helpful if I *knew* . . ." There was no easy way to ask this of her. I would have her divulge the darkest part of herself, whatever that may be. I'd already shown her mine; there was nothing that said she had to show me hers. But she hadn't judged me, and I wouldn't judge her. I would stay with her, help her – and I hoped she understood that.

She didn't slow in her digging, hunching over the small divot she'd made in the bones. In another life, we might have been two children digging a hole to China in Mallory's backyard. Summer sun, sweat, dirt beneath our nails, cicadas and pill bugs; I could imagine it. The warmth, most of all, I could cling to.

"Did you know," Mallory began, voice small, "that you can suffer from permanent brain damage if you go four minutes without oxygen?" She was looking at me, enormous eyes round as moons.

I turned my head to appraise her, a shiver dancing the length of my spine as I met her wild gaze. "No, I didn't know that," I said.

"Yeah," Mallory nodded. "And then you die after five." She'd said it so bluntly, so matter-of-factly, that I had to take a moment to understand.

The ringing bell-tone stopped, then started again. Mallory flinched, as if she'd been struck.

"Mallory?"

She said nothing as she turned her attention to the bones again, throwing them away with both hands. I watched her work for a long moment, marked each smear of blood across the bones as it spilled from her pricked fingertip. The phone rang and rang beneath us, as loud as if it sat unencumbered in an empty room. We dug and dug, not a word passing between us. Sweat dripped from Mallory's brow despite the cold, the steam of each breath puffing and puffing until it dappled our lashes with beads of condensation. Some of the bones were smooth, while others were jagged at the edge and pocked with deep divots. Bite marks. They pricked our fingers and pressed cruelly into our palms and wrists but we continued to dig.

Mallory's chest heaved, as if each breath was a monumental effort. No matter how many bones we moved, how much we'd pushed to the side into a pile against the runed wall, we didn't seem to be making any progress. The phone, the single point of light beneath us, seemed just as far away as it had when we began.

"What the fuck are we supposed to do if we can't even *reach* the damn thing?" I looked up, but only once, as if the Leviathan might materialize in the shadows above and give us a hint. The rules as I understood them were that we would be given the chance to atone ourselves, to release ourselves, with no tricks or hidden terms. It was an offering. We face the darkest parts of ourselves, unburden ourselves of the weight of it, and the Leviathan would gobble it up like communion. Unlike Beck, the creature – angel, or monster, or god – played by clear rules. Its ambitions weren't hidden to us, weren't selfish and duplicitous. It was the nature of humanity to live by pretense, it seemed. We'd all done it in coming here, hiding away our dark passengers like we could just carry them for ever. The Leviathan's rule was simple: cut out the bloated, diseased organ of our grief to make room for something new. Something good.

This was how I understood it, anyway. I understood it better than Beck. Better than Mallory. The Leviathan *approved* of me, after all. There was no pretense in that.

I cast about the bones, their shadows looming and vermillion in the light of the flare. A short distance from us, still within the upcast glare of the ringing phone, I saw a hole in the lattice of bone big enough to squeeze through.

"There!" I tapped Mallory on the shoulder. "As long as it doesn't shift over the top of us, we can crawl—"

Mallory was off, scrambling across my lap and diving into the opening without a word. She breathed through gritted teeth, each inhale belabored. The phone rang louder now, closer; it rattled inside my skull as Mallory squeezed her head and shoulders through the opening.

The very walls of the cavern shook, though the thousand eyes that watched from overhead remained immobile. And then, with a groan of rock on rock and a rattling that sounded like the chatter of teeth, bone began to fall from the sky. Wet, slick with viscera; some still weighed heavily with muscle that hadn't yet been picked clean. Hot, viscous blood sprayed down atop us from an indeterminable point above, squelching as blood and stringy, stretched-thin tendons rained down upon us.

I threw my hands over my head, curling into the hollow I'd created in the effort of digging out the phone. The blood came in a deluge, thick globules of coagulated clots splashing onto my head and arms.

The ground rumbled again. There came a great crack from beneath, like a snapping wrist—

And then we were falling. The floor fell from beneath us, the bottom of the silo buckling beneath the weight. The phone, still blazing with light and ringing so loudly that I could hear it over the torrent, fell away. Mallory's kicking legs slipped beyond my field of vision, sucked down into the wall of bones as it sank at its center and pitched downward like a spiraling drain. I threw myself toward the wall, clawing futilely at the runes for a hold, but the stone was slick with blood and condensation, and my fingers slipped easily from the carved ridges.

The mountain of bone fell through the break in the stone beneath us and into the open air. I gasped, inhaling a mouthful of blood. It ran into my eyes, my nose, over my lips and under my tongue. A curved collarbone sang through the air and clipped my brow before falling away. I was dizzy, delirious, but I had no time to right myself. We were falling, falling, pulled down by the sheer weight of the collection of bones that had broken the very floor of the cavern.

I had lost sight of Mallory. But I could still hear the damnable phone, even as the bones, the bodies, landed with a splash. I was pulled down on impact, the force of the falling bones enough to push me far beneath the surface of—

Not water. *Blood.*

I couldn't open my eyes. The blood was thick, heavy, and hot. *Fresh.*

And I could still hear the ringing phone. The same ringtone, over and over, even above the rush of blood in my ears and the deafening clatter of a thousand bones falling with a splash into the sea below.

I thrashed, struggling to the surface and gasping as I forced my face into the open air. "*Mallory?*" I called, blood spraying from my lips, the taste of rust and salt heavy on my tongue. My hair slicked to my brow, the fabric of my sweater thick and heavy with the stuff. It weighed me down, as did Beck's pack. The seal was a leaden weight, tugging me back into the pool as I struggled to keep my head above the surface. I struggled, splashing wildly toward the bone-riddled bank. There was no hint of rock or sandy shore here – everything was bone.

I pulled myself onto the shore, hooking my fingers in the eye sockets of a watching skull and dragging myself up. A red light shone from somewhere beyond my field of vision; the flare had missed the bloody pool entirely. With a heave, I let the pack slide from my shoulders and tossed it aside, immediately awash with relief at the lightness of my unburdened spine.

The phone continued to ring. Spitting blood, I crawled over the loose bones, palms slick and slipping, to the edge of the pool. The surface rippled, bones and gobs of meaty tissue splashing down from above. A trickle of fresh blood from my brow arced down the ridge of my nose, muddling my vision. I wiped it away, wincing as the harsh fibers of my sweater ground painfully into the cut above my eye.

I couldn't see Mallory. She'd disappeared the second the floor had collapsed, far beyond my reach.

I called out to her, voice weak. A part of me doubted she could even hear me over the deluge, the clattering of bones, the ringing of the phone. The heels of my hands slipped, and I pitched back into the bloody pool face-first. I scrambled back, away from the edge, cursing and spitting blood as I wiped furiously at my eyes.

"*Mallory!*" I spluttered, coagulated blood squelching between my teeth. "Where are you?"

For a horrible moment, I was alone. I could hear nothing but the persistent ringing and the splash of blood raining onto the surface of the pool. The bones had settled, some sinking further into the pool and others floating to the surface like toys. My head spun, the sound muffled by the blood in my ears.

I called out to Mallory again, the sound deadened.

And then, with a bubble of air and a ripple that clattered the bones on the surface of the pool, I saw movement. I scrambled to my feet, ungraceful and leaden in my every jerking motion, and splashed into the bloody basin. I plunged my arms into the pool, fingers jamming hard against something moving, something soft. I made a fist in what felt like fabric and pulled, slipping and sinking as Mallory's head broke the surface. She clutched the phone in both hands, coughing and spitting great clots of congealed blood down her front. The pool rippled like fresh water after us, the bones clacking and rattling at the surface as I hauled her onto the shore.

I threw my arms around her hunched shoulders as Mallory gave a cough, then a wet sob. And then she spoke, and the horrible, ragged laugh that burst from me filled the cavern: "F-found it!"

"Jesus Christ," I hissed, pressing a kiss to the top of her head.

Mallory lay the phone flat in her palms. The screen was smeared with blood, the speaker clogged with wetness, and yet it shone unbroken like it was brand new. *UNKNOWN NUMBER* flashed in bold letters over a photographic background. Mallory herself was at the center of the picture, surrounded by equally sunny-looking girls who all crowded beneath an archway made of flowers. A neon sign shaped like a rainbow hung over their heads, casting their broad smiles in shades of every color.

"This is my phone," she said. As if there had been any doubt.

Before I could say a word, she answered the call and pressed the phone to her ear. I crammed my face in close to hers, blood-slick skin on skin. At first, all I could make out was static. I could have sworn I heard movement within, like whoever was on the other line scrambled for a better signal. And then, through the static, came a deep inhale.

"*Why won't you talk to me, Mallory?*" the voice said. It was a man's, slurring and thick like whoever spoke to her now had just woken from a deep sleep. The man sobbed, then gasped, each ragged breath rife with static and gravel.

"Who is this?" Mallory whispered. By the look on her face, I could tell that she already knew.

"*Why won't you talk to me?*"

Overhead the bloody deluge trickled to a stop, leaving nothing but the lapping of the sanguine pool on the shore, and the bones, to puncture the pregnant silence. Mallory shivered violently, her shoulder knocking against mine.

"I know you're not real," she said. I watched, gaze flickering sidelong, as she struggled to school her face into a mask of bravery. I couldn't turn my eyes to the darkness above, to the audience that I knew watched with scrutiny. "I know this is all part of the test."

"*I'll show you—*" the man continued, as if he hadn't heard Mallory. "*I'll show you how much I love you. Nothing is going to keep us apart.*"

Mallory moved quickly. She startled me, arching her arm back as far as it would go before throwing the phone into the bloody lake. It sailed through the air, screen oppressively bright, before landing with an unceremonious *plunk* between a floating skull and a collection of loose finger bones.

For a long moment, we merely sat and watched the vast expanse of blood ripple and pool over the bones at the lake's edge. But then she spoke, and any moves I might have made to feel around in the dark were forgotten. "I'm going to say it out loud. If I say it out loud, it can't hurt me. Right?" She looked to me, eyes wide. "Like manifesting?"

"Sure." I nodded.

She looked down at the bones, as if expecting them to reassemble into something person-shaped. "I don't talk to my parents because they're religious. And because they're religious, they can't know what I do for money." Mallory met my gaze for but a moment, and I gave her another earnest nod. "I— I don't have sex for money, first of all. A lot of people misunderstand. But I just . . . I get on camera sometimes. I chat. Or I did, before . . . before—" A gulp, a shudder.

I reached for her, a hand on her forearm. "It's okay," I said. "No judgment."

Her lips twitched weakly at the corners, wetness gathering beneath her eyes. "And sometimes people pay extra if you talk to them in private, like in a private chat room, y'know? And people come back if they like you, and they send money and stuff just because. You're not supposed to share any personal information, and I never did on purpose, but one day there was a Cincinnati sweater in the shot and . . ." She took a shuddering breath. "They think they own you. So when they show up at the fucking Anthro exam you're proctoring, they expect something from you."

"Mallory," my voice was small, a lump heavy and painful in my throat. "You don't have to go on if you don't want to."

"No, I will." She seemed resolute. And though the tears flowed freely now, cutting thick rivulets in the blood on her face, she didn't stop. "This *guy*, who does not even *deserve* to have his name said aloud, started following me places. He followed a group of us when we went on vacation. He found us while we were skinny-dipping in the lake by my friend's cabin. Said it was nothing he hadn't seen before. And men . . . men don't like to be rejected. 'Specially not when they think they *own* you."

For a moment, I could have sworn that the bones beneath us shifted, and the darkness overhead had begun to take shape. I could hear the whistling of wind through leaves, through swaying branches. The smell of sea salt and brine gave way to the earthen wetness of soil, of pine. The smell was overwhelming, and I could taste it on my tongue. Soil in my nose, between my teeth – and then it was gone.

"I understand," I said.

"It was self-defense. And we thought he was dead."

A tremor danced the length of my spine. *Did you know that you can suffer from permanent brain damage if you go four minutes without oxygen? And then you die after five.*

I didn't know what to say. But she continued, voice almost mechanical, "He didn't . . . y'know. Didn't get the chance. I fought back. It was easy enough when he came into the lake. I'm . . . I'm a good swimmer. Strong. No one could know. We thought he'd drowned. So when we buried him—"

Mallory stared down into the bloody pool. Again, I could taste soil and silt on my tongue. I could see it plainly; she'd fought him in the water, and . . . and then—

"We thought he was dead," she said again. "When we buried him, we thought we were burying a corpse."

The idea of it came upon me as easily as if she'd been recounting the finer points of a lecture. I felt dulled, accepting and easy. Some people deserved to die. I understood that better than anyone.

"Thank you for telling me," I said. This was our pact, our own sacred ritual. There were no secrets any more. Not here.

I rifled through my pack for another flare. Mallory turned to watch me, blinking rapidly as if the movement had woken her from a trance. "I guess that's it, then. It's done. We should start looking for a way out," she said. "Keep moving – that's what Oliver would tell us to do."

I grimaced. "I don't know if I trust Oliver's judgment any more than I trust Beck's." And I didn't know if it was done. There was no way to know for sure. Surely it can't have been this simple, this cut and dried? The others had endured and failed such ordeals. Simple forgiveness didn't seem to be the Leviathan's style. But I didn't want to stick around and find out.

Even if we didn't mean it to, this was the nature of this place: there existed, now, a divide between those that had failed, and those that had succeeded in the Leviathan's eyes. We were alive, sure. And that was certainly something. But a blooming bud of satisfaction pricked new thorns into my ribs at the thought that I was somehow *chosen*. That I was *wanted* by this inscrutable thing that tested every threshold it could push us across. If I was good enough for the Leviathan, surely it didn't matter what Beck believed of me.

I was better. I was free. Mallory, too.

"That's . . ." she frowned. "He did his best."

"He failed, Mallory." My voice came out harsher than I'd meant it to. Sharper. More decisive. "He failed the second he threw me to the wolves. That man would have seen me torn apart before just accepting that he—" That he . . . what? That he had done wrong? Or that he wasn't strong enough to face the sick thing that we would all have to cut out if we wanted to be free?

Mallory's face was pale, her eyes wide and her lips pursed. "You sound like Beck," she said, voice even. "We're all just trying to survive."

It felt like a slap. I was nothing like Beck. *I* wanted to save her, to save the both of us. *I* wanted to use what I had learned here for good – because I was a *survivor*. Beck, on the other hand, was a user. A monster. Just like my mother.

I said nothing as I looked down into the bag, working away quietly as I wriggled the cap off the flare and struck it ablaze on a stretch of bone. It blazed alight, joining the feeble glow of the other that I had lost in the fall. Neither was enough to light the space from wall to wall. We were surrounded on all sides by darkness, only the low ceiling and the hole in the looming circular cavern visible in the vermillion glare.

"I made you a promise, Mallory," I said, knuckles white around the neck of the flare as I struggled to my feet. "I told you that we were going to get out of here together. And I've never broken a promise."

I extended a hand, and Mallory took it. I hauled her up, the bones on which we'd perched scattering beneath us. With a sickening squelch of soaked fabric, I tossed the bag over my shoulders again, the weight of Beck's strange disc an unwelcome pressure against every bruise that had assembled over the skin of my lower back.

But then the sound of a ringing phone cut the silence again. A pinprick of light illuminated the space beneath the lake's bloody surface, the ringtone watery and warbled as blood bubbled from the phone's speaker. Mallory ripped her hand from mine. She whirled, slipping on loose bones as she started into the bloody pool again.

"Wait!" I cried. "Just leave it!"

Mallory splashed through the blood, scrambling blindly for the ringing phone as blood sloshed up to her shoulders. "Where the hell *is* it?" she cried. "Come *on*!"

And then, from all around, from the dark beyond the low light of the flare and the lapping pool of bloody runoff, music began to play. Rife with static, as if played through an old speaker, a song I didn't recognize warbled through the cavern. Mallory froze, head snapping up from where she held it inches above the surface of the pool. Beneath her, the phone continued to ring.

Her eyes cut to me as I turned round in search of the source. The song came from everywhere, as far above as the very spot where Beck had lost us, and as far below as the bottom of the pool. I took a step from the edge of the sloshing waves, stretching the flare high.

But then Mallory spoke. "I—" She gulped, as if she had swallowed a mouthful of blood. "I know this song."

"Well, what is it?" It grew louder by the moment, rattling the bones atop the various piles scattered about the chamber.

A pause. I could see her considering, as if each word wounded her mortally. "He called it '*our song*'."

The blood rippled around Mallory's waist. It moved with purpose, thick like fingers, tugging at the hem of her sweater and soddening the loose threads there. The blood moved – but Mallory hadn't. In fact, she had gone stiller than I'd ever seen her, as if the sound of the music had paralyzed every atom, every fiber, of her very being. I felt the thin hairs at the back of my neck lift, like a trilling of electricity before the strike.

"Hey—" I began. "I think you need to get out of the—"

Mallory disappeared beneath the surface with no more than a gasp and a *plunk* as the blood swallowed her in a single ripple. Her arms flew up over her head like a ragdoll's, her mouth formed in a perfect circular gasp of complete surprise.

I whirled, tossing the bag to the floor. I ripped the zipper wide and felt in the half-dark for the ice ax, which still bore the evidence of Hannah's death at its very tip. It felt light in my hand, lighter than it ever had; maybe because I now knew how to use it. Maybe because I wasn't afraid to.

With a flinch, as the sulfuric sparks sizzled at the skin of my wrist and heated the small of my back, I tucked the flare into my back pocket. There was no telling how long it would stay alight once I went under. The best I could hope for was a few seconds. I only needed long enough to spot Mallory.

The blood was hot and thick on my face, pushing apart my lips and sliding between my clenched teeth as I dove in after her. I felt an awareness prickle behind my ear as I kicked off from the sloping pile of bones on the shore.

Leave it alone, the voice said. I knew it; it was mine, and it was not. I felt hot breath at the back of my neck, like the deer in the darkened corridor.

I wouldn't. I couldn't. I'd made a promise. There was no justice in this. Mallory hadn't done anything wrong. She and I were the same. Our demons had gotten what they deserved.

But, then, how was this trial fair? What did the Leviathan expect Mallory to do? What would, by the trial's estimations, be the acceptable outcome?

Maybe she could kill him again. Somewhere down there, in the blood – drown her tormentor a second time. Drown him for *real.* Maybe it was the nature of his death, the unnecessary suffering that came from being buried alive – deserved, as far as I was concerned – that needed to be atoned for. It was a warped and fucked-up sense of justice that outright drowning would do the trick, but who was I to question it?

At the very least, Mallory had to try. And she had to live long enough to do so.

Stifling a gag, I tucked the ax between my teeth and pulled the flare from my back pocket. Blood spilled into my mouth; over my tongue, down my throat, between my molars. Here, beneath the surface, the blood was as translucent as murky water – though not nearly as easy to move through. I swam down, fighting the pull to the surface. The phone still sang far beneath, a single pinprick of vibrant fluorescent light amid the red.

And there, a few meters below me, was Mallory. Lit by the single pinprick of light at the bottom of the pool, she thrashed against something near-indistinguishable, a black clot that kept pace with her as she descended. A formless body curled and darted like a predator, tugging at her legs, her pants. I could see the light of the phone, impossibly bright in the dark, viscous blood.

But nothing was impossible, really. Not here.

My chest ached, desperate for breath, as I kicked toward her, holding out the sputtering, dying flare between us.

I'm here! I wanted to cry. *I'll save you!*

A slip of warmth like a current in a stream wrapped around my ankle and tugged. I jerked backward, held vertical by the sliver of skin beneath the hem of my jeans, toward the surface. It startled me, and I nearly dropped the ax from between my teeth. I whirled, swiping the flare in the blood above my head – but it made contact with nothing at all. No reaching fingers, no looming body. Mallory and I were alone.

The waterlogging ringing of the phone stopped, the silence of the pool oppressive and heavy as Mallory's fingers found the light. She was too far now – I'd almost lost sight of her completely. But I could just barely make out her face, lit in stark white even through the bloody crimson.

I couldn't see the bottom. Maybe there *was* no bottom – not for me, anyway. This was for Mallory. From where I tread, kicking futilely at the viscous liquid on all sides, there was nothing. Only darkness, so thick and impermeable that the red of the blood gave way to stygian black.

Mallory's body jerked, legs outstretched. At the very same moment, I was pulled up again, the back of my sweater snagged on something solid. I swiped the flare over my head, and this time I could have sworn, as the light sputtered out, that it found something solid.

It was only the light of the phone that tethered me to Mallory. In its vibrant glare, I could see movement as it arrowed across Mallory's body; up her front, between her legs, wrapping in thick, vine-like tendrils around her ankles. No, not vines – *fingers.* Hands. Arms, hooked at the elbow. Masculine hands, prodding and tugging and reaching beneath her clothes. I situated the ax in my grasp again as I kicked down toward her, swimming and swimming but never seeming to get any closer to her.

Mallory was being touched everywhere, tugged everywhere. An unmistakable hand twirled in a strand of hair that had come loose from its tie and pulled. Fingers crept beneath the hem of her sweater, and curved along the arc of her brow. She kicked out, hit at anything she could reach, but the lecherous touches were undeterred. Everyone who'd ever wanted something from her, *taken* something from her. Everyone who'd ever used her, seen her as nothing more than a body. They were here now, and she couldn't break free of them.

And there, in the depths of the darkness beneath her, lit only by how far the phone's glow could reach, a face materialized in the blood. I could have been imagining it; I might have swallowed too much blood, or hit my head too hard on the way down from the cavern above. A man's face, and an unfamiliar one; almost a shade, something easily missed. His eyes tracked Mallory as she was pulled further and further down, his lips playing into a smile.

I'd read once, in the depths of an internet rabbit hole, that the mind is incapable of creating new faces. Even in dreams, no one is made up; every face we imagine, and dream, and conjure up was meant to be someone we'd seen before, even in passing.

But I was certain – I had never seen this man before. His broad, heavy brow; his crooked teeth and drooping jowls; his wild eyes set deep behind square glasses; all were foreign to me.

It wasn't my mind that had conjured the image, though. It wasn't my test. It was Mallory's. It was *him.*

The man conjured from Mallory's memory lifted a brow as she struggled free of the binds that tugged her farther beneath the surface. She kicked up, up, reaching for me as her eyes found mine – and then she was tugged down again.

I reached for her, and again the formless shape at my back tugged me away. This time, I was prepared. With all the speed I could muster, I spun in the bloody slog and swung the ax. Though there was no body to hit, no limb to catch, and no blood to spill, the tip of the axe made contact with . . . *something.* I felt pressure, and then release – and then the rush of blood around me as the presence at my back retreated.

She would be swallowed by it – no telling where it would spit her out. I could see no way for her to pass this test, to come out unscathed. If I could hardly breathe, my head spinning from lack of air, then I could only imagine Mallory felt the same. It *played* with her, this thing that bobbed and reached like a specter beneath her. She tried time and time again to swim up, reaching for me as she let the phone slip from her grasp, but each time she was pulled down again. Toying with her again and again; it wriggled her shoe loose from her foot, slipped up the leg of her jeans.

I wanted to call out to her. *You don't have to be sorry!* I'd say. *You don't have to pay!* I had been resolute in my decision. My repentance had been an unapologetic decision to live for myself, and for myself alone. I had reconciled with the darkest part of myself. It didn't *have* to be an ordeal. It just had to be honest.

But shame still pulled at Mallory, drowned her. She had nothing to be sorry for. I knew that. Did she?

The phone fell away, only static roaring from within. Now only the weak light of the flare I'd left on the shore lit the pool. It was too dark; I could barely see past my own fingers. But I could see movement, could feel Mallory thrashing in the waves of blood that buoyed me further up to the surface.

I had been forgiven for intervening in the grand design once before. Would I be again?

It didn't matter. Nothing mattered if Mallory died. There was no grand design, no divinity worth striving for, if she wasn't here. There was no justice in this, no lesson. Mallory was drowning; and if she wasn't now, she would be as soon as she was pulled into the depths of whatever lurked beneath the surface.

No, this wasn't right. She was going to fail. I couldn't let her. I had to stop it.

And so I went to her. I kicked at every tug on my hair, my sweater, my jeans. I found Mallory, my vision narrowing as the aching in my chest turned sharp. She clung to me, blinking against the acrid sting of the blood in our eyes. I took her by the arms and tugged her upward, kicking toward the surface but she was tugged down again. I could feel a presence here that had been invisible to me up above; like hot breath, like a gaze that lingered too long, like fingers that pressed too hard into bruisable flesh. I could still hear the music, the same song on an eternal loop.

A dark swath of blood curled around Mallory's middle, and I struck out without thinking. The tip of the ax sunk into its congealed flesh with a squelch and a spurt of cool blood – cold, almost like the salt water that wet every surface above us. Foam spilled from the wound as I wrenched the ax free and struck again, grinding the blade into the phantom limb until it loosened its hold. Mallory wriggled free. I knotted my fingers in the front of her sweater and shoved her high, sinking lower as she propelled upward.

I struck out at every reaching limb that crept toward her. Though the space around me was dark, and empty, I felt crowded. Pressure brushed against my leg, my hip, my shoulder as the *thing* from below reached for Mallory, ownership and hunger in its keenness. I sliced the ax into its limbs again and again, fighting it off as it struggled to tug at Mallory's ankles, grappling for her only to lose its grip.

Again and again, I struck out at it. I could see nothing but red; be it blood, be it rage, be it fear, there was nothing else. Cold water spilled from the insistent limbs as they formed and dissipated, bone squelching in congealed clots of salt and blood. I hooked the blade over a femur and pulled it loose, ripping free a deluge of sea foam.

A groan shook the cavern, bones dancing on the surface of the water above me. Pressure tugged me downward, like a great mouth had opened and *inhaled*, just underneath us. Overhead, Mallory kicked for the surface, bubbles spilling from her puffed cheeks. A lecherous arm arrowed past, fingers forming from the coagulated blood. Before the bones could rearrange, I struck again – and Mallory slipped beyond its reach.

And as frigid water spilled from it, like blood from a slit belly, brine and foam poured into my open eyes. In flashes, in no more than the space of a blink, I saw memories that were not my own. Just like the man's face, which had been foreign to me, images leaked into my consciousness in a trickle:

A spill of champagne onto a wooden floor; the flash of a synthetic wig across a vanity mirror; the red light of a live camera, reflected on a painted brow like a sniper's aim; a sterling-silver cross necklace shoved beneath a bed; a shadow passing across a window thick with condensation; a man undoing his belt; "why are you here?" she says; a familiar face in pursuit through the dark; the sound of a shovel as it makes contact with a skull; the sound of splitting flesh; the sound of a grown man's body falling limp into the mud; the sound of something heavy and immobile slipping beneath the surface of still water; the sound of struggle, of which way is up, of water and blood choking, choking, of letting it happen, of watching and hoping—

A cold finger traced the length of my spine. The awareness that sat perched behind my ear disappeared. It tugged at the image of Mallory – not one I knew, but one that I understood to be true – by the frayed corner, and with a rush of cold from my eyes, it was gone.

Mallory broke the surface first, gasping and spluttering for air as she scrambled ashore. She spat mud and congealed viscera onto the bones, clothes weighing heavily from every limb. She tried to speak, and failed, and then tried once more. Blood spilled from her lips, from her nostrils; she spat it onto the bones and wiped it with the back of her hand. I crawled to her on all fours, bones sliding beneath my knees and the heels of my hands.

"It's okay," I said, voice ragged. "It's okay now. Just breathe." I reached for her, and she scrambled to take hold of my fingers.

"You . . ." she began, each deep breath a pop of wetness. "You shouldn't have done that. You shouldn't have interfered!"

My brow furrowed. "Of course I should have interfered," I snapped. "You were drowning! You – you were being *pulled* down!"

She shook her head, hair slapping wetly on her cheeks. "You said it yourself. We have to play by the rules—"

"Not when the rules mean that you'll *die*, Mallory." My voice was a hiss, blood and spittle flying from my lips. The surface of the bloody pool had stilled behind us.

I wanted to tell her everything that the Leviathan had shown me. The idea of freedom, of power, of ultimate acceptance; it was a beautiful picture. The Leviathan wanted me. Chose me. Loved me, maybe, in the way a god loves its most desolate worshipers. Blank canvases to be filled with divinity; the freedom of purpose as given by another. The Leviathan offered that. But Mallory had done so first.

I looked down at the sodden socks, borrowed from her pack, that peeked from the tops of my boots. What would I be if I chose this place, this nebulous promise, over my first real friend?

Once more, Mallory shook her head. "Maybe I don't deserve to live. Maybe none of us do—" she hiccupped, pressing a hand to her chest. "M-maybe that's the point of all this."

I peered over her head, casting about for the pack I'd discarded. Even in the fading light of the flare, it was easy enough to pick out; Beck's circular seal protruded from the fabric like a beacon, sterling clean despite its surrounds.

"That's not true, and you know it."

"I did a *bad* thing, Caro!" She clutched me tighter and gave me a shake. Blood flew from the tips of my hair in cold droplets. "I'm not the good person that you think I am! Maybe this isn't really supposed to be a test for me – maybe it's just supposed to be a punishment."

"The fuck it is." I found her gaze and held it. Jaw set, eyes hard, I took her by the chin when she tried to look away and kept her there. "I don't care what you've done that makes you think you deserve to die. I saw that *man* down there. I heard his voice on the phone. And I don't care. When I was tested, I forgave myself. I chose myself. I refused to let myself be swallowed by the guilt any longer. I wasn't sorry then, and I'm not sorry now. *That's* your test. *That's* what it wants from you."

She pressed the heel of her hand to her brow. "Caro—"

"No, just shut up and listen to me. We all do things we're not proud of. But we have to do them regardless. Do you think I deserve to die?"

She shook her head, bottom lip quivering.

"Well, then, neither do you."

We had to find a way out. We had to move. Oliver had been right, despite his shortcomings – sitting around would do us no good. If we could *move*, we could – well, we could *think* of something, at the very least.

The only way out was through.

"We need to keep moving," I said, turning my attention back to Mallory. "We can't stay here. Neither of us is going to die." I felt the falseness, the flimsy nature of the promise, the minute I said it. But I had to at least try to believe it.

Mallory opened her mouth to speak, but froze as something rippled beneath the surface of the bloody pool. The bones floating at the top rattled, bobbing aimlessly away from a burbling fount of sea foam that rose at the very center of the circular stretch.

"No, *no*—" Mallory groaned. "You interfered! L-like Beck said. You *cheated* it of something. And now . . . *now*—"

Slowly, carefully, I reached for where I'd abandoned the ax, nestled among a pile of discarded bones. "There's another way," I said. "There's always another way."

Mallory rose with a clattering of bones and a squelch of blood in her shoes. I reached for her, and she shoved me away. "Let me try again!" she cried, voice breaking. "Don't be mad at Caro! Let me try one more time! Take me down again! I'll face it this time!"

"*Mallory!*" She started for the edge of the pool, and the blood splashed at the toes of her boots. She wasn't fucking *listening.* She had nothing to be sorry for, nothing to "try again." Foam spilled from the fixed point at the center of the pool, and Mallory held out her hands toward it as I crashed into her, leaping and wrapping my arms around her middle.

"Leviathan!" Mallory struggled against me, the heel of her boot catching my knee as she kicked out. "Don't punish Caro! Test me again!" She pushed at my arms as I hauled her away from the edge. And she was crying, sobbing so hard that the sound of it shook my bones.

"You have to tell it the truth, Mallory!" I cried. "You don't have to be sorry; you don't have to make it right. You just have to tell the truth!"

Her knees buckled, and she sagged against me. Weakly, pitifully, she reached for the bloody pool. But she didn't try to stand. Instead, I held her aloft.

"I was so scared, Caro," she sobbed. "I was so fucking scared."

"I know. But you defended yourself."

"I did."

"You did what you had to do."

Another sob, another futile reach for the pool. "*Please.*"

I shook her, arms barred around her so tight that I wondered if I was hurting her. But it didn't matter. She'd forgive me when we were out of here. "I need you to believe it, Mallory. *It* needs you to believe it."

Movement pressed at the surface of the bloody pool again, slick and serpentine. Waves lapped at my boots, at Mallory's . . . and then began to recede. Like a bay emptying before a tidal wave, the blood crept from us, leaving nothing but jagged bone at our feet. My boot slipped and we went pitching downward, sliding down the sloping shore. My pack pitched sidelong, the seal spilling out and into the open air.

"*Say it!*"

Her voice was a gunshot. "I killed my abuser and I'm not fucking sorry!" Mallory shrieked. Her weight was fully on me now, each word made heavy by the labor of her sobs. "He was going to kill me, or rape me, or . . . or *both*! He stalked me, and attacked me, and I killed him! He deserved it!"

I held her tighter, and beneath her wailing cries I could muster only whispers. "Forgive yourself," I said. "Forgive yourself, and come home with me. *Please.*"

She heard me. Of course she did. She was the only one who ever did. "I forgive myself!" she cried. "I don't want to feel guilty any more!"

The flare went out, throwing the cavern into pitch blackness. I felt Mallory leaden against me, her sobs filling the cavern. She slipped from my grasp, disappearing into the dark. Arctic water rushed around my ankles, winding like vines up my legs and hooking behind my knees. Like bruising fingers, it pressed into the meat of my calf and gave a tug. The bones beneath me shifted.

Mallory was torn from my grasp as I was pulled back, snatched painfully by the legs. I screamed, throat raw. She'd done it, she'd done precisely as I had. I had to save her. I *needed* her more than I'd ever needed anyone.

The seal lay forgotten on the rattling carpet of bones. This thing into which Beck had put so much stock seemed impossible to fathom now. There was only Mallory. She was all that counted. I called out to her, and she called back, water sloshing beneath every syllable. Frigid brine raced up the length of my spine, curling over my arms, my shoulder, around my waist.

At once, we were enveloped. A wave of salt water and sea foam rushed over me, choking the air from my lungs. It washed me clean of blood, seeped into my cuts and scrapes, and dragged me down from the shore. I reached blindly for Mallory, to no avail. The water was everywhere, the sea swallowing every inch of my body as it dragged me down, down, down –

I felt, in the wash of the brine, the prickling awareness at the back of my neck. For just a moment, like the hot, curious breath of the deer. I felt . . . disappointment. Disquietude.

And for the second time the Leviathan dragged me down into the sea. The blood gave way to brine, the darkness giving me no time to hold my breath or squeeze my eyes closed. I reached for Mallory one more time – and then there was nothing.

Cold water tugged at my ankle, restless and needy, until my eyes fluttered open. Humidity hung thick in the air, the ground beneath my cheek unnaturally soft and pliable. Verdant green colored my periphery as frigid water dripped rhythmically onto my temple like a persistent finger *tap, tap, tapping* until I roused.

I rose onto my forearms. Moss squelched beneath me as I moved out from beneath the omnipresent drip. Algae slicked the curve of the stone floor, as if standing water had recently drained from the very spot where I had awoken. I rubbed the salt from my eyes with the back of my hand and looked to the swath of dark at my back: a single stone corridor, straight and narrow, stretched beyond my vision.

Dark behind me, and delirious light before me. *Light!* Not phosphorous, not the sputtering crimson of a signal flare, not the weak beam of a long-lost headlamp. I was almost afraid to look at it for fear that it would disappear in a twist of half-sleep, nothing more than a dream of shore, and air, and cloud-gray sun.

And so I turned back to the dark.

"Hello?" No answer. Where I expected my voice to echo, to ring down the passage and out into whatever lay beyond, it stopped short, swallowed by the damp, teeming overgrowth. Between the patches of moss, algae, and dangling seaweed – like hair, almost, dangling from the rock like wet tresses caught in a clutching grasp – runes had been carved into the stone. I tracked them, reading from the darkest reach of my vision to as close to the light as I could stand. For the most part, they looked similar to those in Beck's notes. But some, particularly those close to the mouth of the cave, seemed truer to the Enochian script than anything I'd seen thus far.

Even in my delirium, I could spot it. Like an unsteady hand with chisel and hammer had started the script in earnest, working from the conventionally-understood alphabet and system of phonetics; the closer to the dark the symbols were clustered, the more recognizable they were. But contrary to what one might expect, the closer they drew to the light, the more mangled and indistinguishable they became. It was as if the author of these runes had lost their nerve; each rune near to the blinding light, peering out from beneath moss and dripping seaweed, had been visibly warped. Not by an unpracticed hand, but rather a precise one. Purposeful, defiant. But different. *Wrong.*

I rose on unsteady legs, peering up at the recognizably Enochian text. Only a few phrases were pure to the original language before warping, devolving, into whatever dialect of it was specific to this place. Now was most definitely not the time to be wracking my brain for the contents of my Theological Anthropology final, but it was a part of human nature to be curious, I figured.

I thought of my notes, waiting for me back at the inn. All the work I'd done, all the knowledge I'd amassed for someone else. Here, in the palimpsest of time, I could only imagine that curiosity for curiosity's sake was encouraged. If only I had something to write with.

The tips of my fingers aching, I brushed aside a curtain of seaweed and read a line of the more phonetically sound symbols. These made sense; they abided by the rules of the language, the characters, and their patterns. By the next patch of obscuring algae, they'd already begun to change beyond my comprehension. But I did recognize some of it: ZUMVI, for "seas"; EMETGIS, for "seal".

Below them were DOALIM, for "sin", and IO-IAD, which roughly translated to "that liveth for ever". Lower still read ZIZOP,

VNIGLAG, and TOH: "vessel", "descend", "and "triumph". In another life, I might have liked to record them all. This could be a completely new script, or maybe a dialect of Enochian never before seen. I was the occultist John Dee, and this was where I would hold court. Something new, something learning itself as it went along; this was the Leviathan's way, after all. Self-actualization, even if it was ugly. Even if it was wrong.

I reached for the first of the warped runes, something that might have started as TATAN, or "wormwood," much like in the entrance cavern, but ended as something completely indecipherable. There wasn't enough Enochian in my tired head to account for any spelling errors or willing changes to the text. These letters were different than those at the entrance, sloppier somehow. Erratic, like the author had been desperate for some new turn of phrase that the letters couldn't accommodate. Maybe it was something symptomatic of a more fickle understanding. Maybe whatever – whoever – had written out these turns of phrase had been bullshitting just as hard as any respectable undergrad.

Before my fingers could finish their absent tracing of the warped rune, a shadow passed across the light at the mouth of the cave. It was only in the half-dark that I could see that the curved walls and ceiling of the cave ended just beyond my field of vision, no more than twenty meters into the blinding gray light.

"Hello?" I called again, hand falling away from the rune. "Mallory?"

Again, no answer. I held my hand over my eyes to shield them from the light, squinting and blinking away the strain as I turned from the wall and started across the mossy carpet. It squelched beneath my boot, spilling foam and ruddy water out onto the stone.

A cold wind whipped me sidelong as I stepped out from the mouth of the cave. I could barely see. I fumbled blindly as my feet sank into the pliable ground. Sand, by the sound of it, shifted beneath my boots. As I emerged, I was overwhelmed with sounds that I hadn't been able to eke out from inside, as if they had all been switched on all at once. A wild performance; the slapping of waves on a solid shore, the creaking of branches, the whistling of wind.

Was I out? Had I made it?

And as my eyes adjusted, the pain of the brightness giving way to the watery light of a gray midday, I saw it all. The mouth of the cave at my back was no more than a sliver of darkness in a long stone cliff, which stretched so high above that I had to crane my neck to even imagine the top. I found myself on a beach. Slate water lapped at the pallid shore, a rolling coastline visible on the horizon. I looked up; the sun was obscured by clouds, so weak that nothing between where I stood and the water's edge cast a shadow onto the sand.

The beach was littered with debris of all shapes and shades: a pillar that looked to be made of marble protruded from the sand at an angle, propped up by what remained of a stone wall. A stained-glass window peered, half-buried, from the sand. A rusted construct, a grate that likely had once been a gate or a door of some kind, lay propped against the wall by the cave's entrance. Trees stripped of their leaves, bark bleached and smoothed by the salt on the wind, jutted at strange angles over the mismatched bric-a-brac that littered the beach, as if plucked from time immaterial and left for someone, anyone, to find.

All along the shore, thin shafts of wood stuck up like spindly trees. I went to the one nearest and tugged it free, revealing a rusted spearhead. Hundreds of spears, some broken and some intact, littered the beach as if they'd been thrown from high above and forgotten about. And among them, crosses of all shapes, sizes, and materials, sprouted from the sand. Copper, gold, wood, iron – some had fallen to pieces, and some had collected rust.

My eyes wandered to a stretch of disturbed sand, scuffed and roughened where the sea should have smoothed it flat. And there, in splinters, the door that would always keep me from my mother. The handle still shone as bright and polished as the day it had been installed. The scattered pieces of it, jagged and mismatched at every edge as if it had been bludgeoned to bits by something enormous, trailed from where I stood to the edge of the water. A lapping wave reached for a piece no larger than my hand and tugged it away, scattering chipped paint across the sand.

I had seen this place before. When I'd touched the monolith in the library I'd been shown this very beach. It was all the same.

But . . .

I turned my gaze to the horizon. There had been no visible shoreline when I'd seen this place before. Maybe the monolith had gotten it wrong. The beach, too, was uninhabited. No body. No monsters. Just me.

The ground shook. I dropped the spear as if it had shocked me, stumbling back as it rolled along the sand and clattered to a stop among the others. The surface of the water trembled, the sand shifting beneath my feet. Even the clouds seemed to warp as a great pressure filled the air, pressing at my eardrums and then releasing with a pop.

There was movement inside the cave. I could hear it: the scrambling of feet on stone, the squelch of bloody water as it was sponged from the moss. I cast about for something to hide behind, stomach sinking as I realized that the only way to get to the marble pillar and stonework wall was to cross directly across the worn path leading from the mouth of the cave – and directly across the line of sight of whatever moved within.

But then I heard "*Caro?*"

Mallory's voice was weak, watery, but I heard it nevertheless. I gasped, slipping on loose sand and falling onto my hands as I ran for the opening. "Mallory!" I cried. "I'm here!" The ground shook again and I fell against the lip of the cave, my slapping footsteps echoing into the dark. There Mallory sat, crumpled on the very same patch of moss where I had been deposited moments ago, rubbing water and salt from her eyes as she blinked madly against the light.

My knees scraped the stone as I threw myself on her, wrapping my arms around her neck and squeezing her tight. She responded in kind, burying her face in my shoulder and letting slip a single desolate sob. I took her by the shoulders and pulled back, examining every inch of her visage that I could see. There was still blood in her hair, though the deluge of seawater had all but washed it from her skin, her clothes. In the slate-gray light of the obscured sun, she looked pale and utterly exhausted. There was a cut on her cheek, red and swollen around the edges, that I hadn't noticed before.

But she was alive. *I* was alive. I was freezing, starving, thirstier than I'd ever been – but I was alive. She'd done it. We both had – we'd overcome something, absolved ourselves of something. Just as we were meant to do – as all this place's other survivors had done before us.

And we had done it together. That had to count for something.

I kissed the top of her head. "I'm so fucking proud of you."

"Are we out?" she pleaded. "Is it over?"

I nodded. "I think so," I said. Trembling, I pointed over my shoulder to the bright beach beyond the cave. Mallory squinted against the abrasive light. "Look—"

As I spoke, footsteps broke the quiet serenity of the lapping waves and whistling wind. I whirled round, throwing out an arm across Mallory's front.

There in the mouth of the cave, haloed by gray light, stood the deer. *My* deer; I knew it at once. It peered in at me, eyes keen. Its nostrils flared, and it inclined its head as if listening for something that I couldn't hear.

And then it turned and wandered out of view, away from the mouth of the cave and further along the base of the cliff that stretched out on either side. My heart sank, my stomach twisting.

"A deer?" Mallory's voice was small. "What's a deer doing here?"

So she'd seen it, too. I wasn't imagining things, conjuring ghosts born of hunger and dehydration. It had left hoofprints behind; I wasn't sure why I'd expected it to leave no trace.

No. Not out.

Maybe someplace else.

I rose, taking Mallory by the hand and tugging her up. "We should follow it," I said. "It's a friend."

I could feel her gaze on me, questioning and skeptical. But Mallory followed nevertheless, stepping from one patch of squelching moss to the next. She took my hand, and I gave her pruned fingers a squeeze. Even if it wasn't real, we could pretend. After all, the line between reality and unreality blurred here. The air was crisp and fresh, the breeze lifting the sodden hair from the back of my neck. The sound of the lapping waves was soothing, a balm for my frayed nerves. Even if this wasn't real, even if Mallory and I woke from the same shared dream to find ourselves in the dark again, I would take what I could get.

I wondered for a fleeting moment where Beck had gone. We'd left him alone, and with only one flare to light his way. I hoped he survived. He needed to live with what he'd done, to be punished for it. There was no justice in death, no matter how deserved.

When we emerged from the cave and onto the beach, the deer was gone. Its footsteps carried on, arrowing closer to the water's edge – but there was no sign of it along the unfettered coastline. As far as I could see in either direction, we were alone.

And so we began to walk. We walked until the marble, the stone, and the stained glass were nothing but a blip on the horizon. We walked until we came to the cluttered remnants of a rope bridge, draped like a table runner over a statue with no upper half. Past a tide pool in which a glass eye and two wooden ones bobbed aimlessly; through a scattering of loose pages written in Italian; past the hull of a ship that protruded from the bay and reached so high that we couldn't make out the top.

There was no end and no beginning. We stopped once, turned, and found that we could still just barely make out the glint of stained glass, a colorful speck in the low light. We walked until our legs shook, lips and tongues dry with thirst.

Dangling from the very tip of a bleached tree branch I spotted a familiar pack hung by its only intact strap. I shook Mallory wordlessly and pointed. The pack was mine; inside I found what remained of the supplies I'd pilfered from Beck's stash.

But no seal. The heavy, unblemished piece of rock that had started this whole damn thing was nowhere to be found. We cast about for it, but my head spun, and my throat ached, and I fell into the sand with a huff and a rattling exhale.

"*Thirsty*," I said. I couldn't think, couldn't pull myself together well enough to look for the rest of my belongings. How long had it been since I'd had a sip of water? How long since I'd eaten? I couldn't remember how long a human body could go without water.

The sea lapped lazily at the shoreline. I'd read once that drinking seawater was bad, that it would only make the problem of dehydration worse, but *this* water – it looked different, *smelled* different, *sounded* different as it washed onto the sand. The familiar brine I'd become so accustomed to while trapped inside the cave was absent here.

Or maybe I had simply forgotten the tang of it altogether. I was still inside, after all.

No, I wasn't imagining it. I paused, inclining my nose and inhaling deeply. Mallory looked at me like I'd lost my mind, eyes wide and lips pursed. I couldn't blame her. But I wasn't hallucinating, or forgetting; the air smelled not of brine and salt, but of . . . *herbs.* Sage, maybe mint. Bitter and green like the grass in the field behind my apartment.

"Mallory," I said, pointing to the surf. My throat was dry, my voice gravel. "I don't think that's seawater."

I didn't need to spell it out for her. We scrambled forward on all fours, tossing my useless pack aside and making for the water's edge. I cupped the water with my pruned hands and drank greedily. The smell of the water was pungent up close, like a tea whose leaves had filtered into the brew. I tipped my head back, spilling the water into my mouth and over my chin—

The bitterness was overwhelming. I swallowed as much as I could in a single gulp, but I gagged as I turned and spit the rest out onto the sand. Beside me, Mallory choked and spluttered, blowing water from her nose as she was taken aback by the taste.

"What the *fuck*!"

I pursed my lips and spat into the sand.

"Well," I said, spitting again, "I wasn't *wrong*."

It wasn't seawater; there was no hint of saline here. In fact, there was no hint of anything at all aside from the bitter herb that colored it a near-imperceptible green. My stomach turned – but it was still water. It was still necessary. We couldn't carry on if we *died* from thirst at the very end of the race.

"We have to drink," I said. Mallory shook her head violently, rubbing her tongue with her thumb and forefinger. "I don't care how it tastes, Mallory – *drink*. We have to."

"There's something wrong with this water!" Mallory moaned. "It's— It's *wrong!* Like . . . like something at the back of my mom's spice drawer went *bad*. Like really, really bad. What if it's poisoned?"

I spat into the sand again. "It's not poison, all right? It's just . . . it's just gross. Gross isn't always bad. So *drink*."

But she wasn't wrong. There were no coincidences here. The bitterness, the spinning of my head – it plucked at a long-unused string in the recesses of my memory, but I couldn't place it even if I wanted to.

Mallory did as she was told, and I followed suit. Again, I cupped my hands and filled them with the clear, bitter water and drank as deeply as I was able. Mallory and I spluttered and gagged, forcing down handful and after handful.

I was lightheaded, my fingers tingling at the tips. I'd never been this dehydrated before – was this what happened to the body when it came back from the brink of drying up into a pathetic husk? My tongue felt thick, my joints loose at every juncture. I could lay face-down in the sand and sleep for days. Be it relief or exhaustion, I felt simultaneously light and heavy, weighted into the sand and ready to take flight in equal measure.

I looked up to Mallory, and my head spun. She blurred at the edges, like heat rising from pavement in the summertime.

She met my gaze and held it, but she seemed to struggle in doing so. "I feel funny," she said. "Fuzzy."

I nodded, and the movement felt disconnected, like my head was a balloon at the end of a string. "*Drunk*."

"Yeah." Mallory nodded. "Loopy." It seemed like she was mirroring my every movement, as if she felt like nodding exactly as I had done would convince her that her head was still firmly attached to her shoulders.

I looked down, dipping my fingers beneath the surface of the water again. The greenish hue deepened with every heavy heartbeat, a drumming bird's wing just inside my ear.

"There's something . . ." I gulped, each syllable slurring into the next. "There's something in this water." Mallory had been right. Sure, it was fresh water – but it was tainted. I felt drunk, delirious and high, and unsteady with every movement. I struggled onto all fours, crawling like a child from the edge.

The sand glistened. Each blinking point of light was a dazzling star, the flock's million eyes turned upright to peer at me from below. I heard a chuckle from further up the beach, and lifted my head to find my backpack sitting upright atop the tree branch, its zipper curled into a smiling mouth.

Uh-oh, Caroline! the bag said. *You did something bad!*

"Whoa—" I squinted, lifting one hand to point. "Mallory, look. It's talking."

She was on her feet beside me, stumbling from the water. Her dragging heels drew deep trenches in the sand, each carving down into the earth until it grew too dark to see the bottom. Everything seemed to stretch, to distend, to warp and pop in a splash of over-vibrant color. I watched Mallory's back, the blood slicking from her hair in thick rivulets and spiraling up into the air over her head. She was saying something, her voice a jumble; and she was pointing, both arms outstretched for something beyond her reach. Mallory moved past my pack, which fell to hang from its branch again, swinging blithely with its zipper-mouth upturned.

The ground shook beneath me. Mallory laughed wildly, legs gelatinous. She fell hard, knees buckling, and her cackling doubled.

I'd fucked us. This was my fault. How long would we lay here high out of our minds off whatever tainted the water? At least we wouldn't die of thirst. Small victories.

I rolled onto my back and focused on a single fixed point overhead. "Lay down, okay?" I said. Had my voice gotten higher? It sounded as if it had shot up an octave or two, as if it didn't belong to me at all. My head spun as I squinted up at a single cloud, struggling to ascribe a proper shape to it. "Deep breaths." We would need to ride it out. I'd had a bad high before. More than one, even. There was nothing to do in a situation like this but wait.

And drink water. But that was moot, apparently.

I heard Mallory getting to her feet, a shuffling of sand and sodden fabric. "I think I see . . ." she began. I couldn't turn my head to watch her, though I could track her shadow as it obscured the sun just above and a little to the left. "See – I see someone—"

Scarlet diamonds sprayed across my vision. Singularly dazzling, each bead of vital color catching what little light the clouds afforded, they arced across the open air above my head. I lifted one leaden arm, hand outstretched, and reached for them as they shimmered above me. I could pluck them from the sky like stars, like ornaments, and present them to Mallory as a gift. They turned on a dime in the air above my head—

– and then they fell, and I felt warm wetness splash across my face.

I flipped onto my stomach and struggled to lift my gaze. With the back of my hand I wiped the warm wetness from my eyes. *Red.* Vibrantly so. Mallory stood stock-still; she blurred at every edge, a gown of crimson diamonds spilling down her front. Her head was thrown back, hair hanging loose over her shoulders and her visage fixed in a look of open-mouthed, wide-eyed shock. Her arms stretched wide, like angel's wings splayed for flight.

Something dark moved at the center of her, at the middlemost point. Amid the diamonds, a spot of something rotten wriggled. A worm. A snake. And then it took shape: a wooden shaft, a rusted spearhead. Blood.

Mallory slumped, held aloft like a marionette propped atop a vaudeville hook. She clawed at the diamonds down her front, and with every touch they turned liquid. Her fingers scrabbled at the wood that twisted in her abdomen, just beneath her sternum. The blood was vivid, vibrant, vibrating at every molecule—

And then a silhouette appeared at her shoulder. For a horrible moment, it was nothing but a mouth. Stretching, all perfectly straight teeth across a face blackened by shadow. Mallory's head slumped back, and she slid with a horrible, gruesome squelch down the length of the shaft. And she fell, like a lover's swoon, against

Beck's chest. His face swam into view, eyes manic and lips pulled back over a hyena's grin.

He gave the spear – the very same that I had discarded on the beach – a tug, and it squelched from Mallory's flesh with some effort. There was nothing left to hold her up; she crumpled at Beck's feet, and he sidestepped her with a curl of the lips as if she were the most disgusting thing he had ever seen.

"What have you done, Caroline?" he tutted, stepping over Mallory as he flipped the spear in his hand. The blunt end pointed between my eyes. Even now, I could hardly see straight, think straight; the shaft of the spear was a pit viper, writhing and dancing in Beck's grasp. He was impossibly tall, a forever's distance from me – and yet I heard his voice as if he screamed into my ear.

My eyes found Mallory. Blood spilled from the pinprick at her very center, blooming in fluttering petals across the sand. I opened my mouth, willing my lead-thick tongue to form her name, but the water – and the *fear* – choked me into silence.

Mallory, Mallory, Mallory. She clutched her middle, crimson cascading between her fingers. I blinked away the effects of the tainted water, struggling and failing to keep my gaze locked upon the wound, and not the dancing, effervescent spiral of smoke and blood that rose from it. This wasn't real – *Mallory* was real.

The hard heel of the spear crashed atop my head. All at once the pain was sharp and immediate. I fell face-first into the sand, her name dying on my lips.

I awoke upright. Something hard and cool to the touch propped me up, pressing into the arrow of my spine. My shoulders ached, tugged taut at a backward angle. Roughness pressed into my throat and cut at my wrists.

With great effort, I pried my eyes open. My head throbbed – both from the wound that burned hot and bloody at my hairline, and the familiar pressure of the comedown after a high. Whatever had been in the water had not been fit for human consumption; the searing ache behind my eyes was evidence enough of that.

Branches loomed overhead, twisted and gnarled fingers reaching desperately for the sea. He'd tied me to a fucking *tree.* By the throat, by the wrists – like an animal.

I made an effort to move, but the pain in my wrists, my shoulders, my neck flared at even the slightest shift. My vision cleared as I blinked away unconsciousness, drowsiness, the impairment of whatever I had encouraged Mallory to drink.

Mallory.

I found her at once, right where she'd first fallen. And then Beck, mere meters away; he had left her, still breathing and still clutching the wound in her abdomen, like she wasn't worth the time and effort it would take to drag her away from the lapping tide. He sat with his back to me, rolling the spear in his hands.

And for one fleeting moment, there was movement in my periphery – the deer. Though it would be no use, no one could help me now. Certainly not an animal, especially one I'd imagined.

Once more, I tugged against my bindings – rope, judging by the rough texture, the way the frayed fibers pricked my throat and wrists – and Beck stirred at the sound. He glanced over his shoulder as if he were nowhere more pressing than his office back in Cincinnati, like I was nothing more than a curious undergrad with a question about the previous week's pop quiz. He looked a mess, harried and soaked to the bone; the wind that whistled through the trees and the debris that littered the beach seemed to cut through him, for he shivered and clenched his teeth each time a gust passed between us. Bruises encircled his eyes, cheeks hollow. A purple bloom peeked from beneath the collar of his jacket.

The spear stilled in his grasp. "*Brandish the spear and block those who pursue me. Tell my soul, 'I am your salvation'*," he said, eyes falling to the rusted head. "Psalms 35:3. I memorized a few verses just so I could keep up with the theological masses in meetings, and in debate, but I never thought they would be of much use." He turned the spear over once, twice. "Funny how the things we think are most useless, most forgettable, come back to us when it matters most."

"What are you doing, Beck?" I demanded, voice rough. The rope at my neck pushed painfully at the bobbing in my throat. "Untie me. Let me help Mallory."

He sighed. "I can't do either of those things, Caroline. I need to talk to you, and you won't listen if I don't make you." Anger flared in my stomach. "She isn't even supposed to *be* here. It was only ever supposed to be you."

My stomach fell. "What?"

Beck rose. He propped the spear into the sand like a walking stick as he approached, leaving Mallory to the cold. "Did Mallory pass her test? Did she do it alone?"

I blinked. "What the fuck does that matter?"

"It matters because there are *rules*." He thrust the spear into the sand. "You've broken them once before, and have been forgiven for them in kind. I don't think the Leviathan would forgive you another trespass."

"I'm here, aren't I? I'm alive." Barely. And maybe not for much longer.

Beck seemed to consider this. "A fluke, maybe. Or maybe this is all for me. I did take the seal, after all. I did start this."

"I lost the seal," I said. A muscle in his jaw twitched, and I felt a short shock of satisfaction at the sight. "After Mallory's test. She passed. Fair and square, she passed. But it's gone."

"Doesn't matter," he said. It sounded like a lie. "You've bucked tradition, Caroline. The protocol, the structure. We're in uncharted territory, you and I." A laugh, like a gunshot. "It doesn't even matter, now that my notes are gone. I can't record a damn thing! All that work – just to be tested like this. *Now.* But I've prepared."

"Untie me, Beck."

Either he hadn't heard me, or he didn't want to. "In the tradition of this place, an acolyte carries the seal through their trial, through the cloister, as a show of devotion. The heavy burden of the soul made tangible, you see. They carry it to return it to the Leviathan – the *angel* – at the end of the trial, cast off the weight of their human attachments, and guilts, and burdens, and wants, and be truly weightless for the first time." He spoke like he was waiting for applause. None came. "That was, at least, what I could glean from the research." A shrug. A sigh. "Purely symbolic. There was never any map. It could have been, once upon a time. Maybe for the very first, at the beginning of it all. But certainly not now. How could it be, when this place changes to suit its inhabitants? It's supposed to be poetic."

"And you couldn't do that on your own?" I challenged, straining again against the rope that bound me to one spot. "You had to bring the rest of us?"

His lips twitched into a smile that stretched just shy of his eyes. "I had to bring *you*, specifically. The others were a proof of devotion. Belief only lasts if there are those alive – or half-alive – to participate in it." He squatted before me, gaze wild as he stared into my face.

"She's a fucking *angel.* Don't you see? Forgotten, outcast, disillusioned by and with Heaven, and we have the opportunity—"

"Opportunity? Are you fucking insane?"

"Yes, Caroline, the *opportunity* to be true believers. Imagine the gifts I'll be bestowed! You, too, in the eternity of the afterlife, of the flock! You've seen it yourself. It's well and truly alive. True believers live for ever, in a sense!"

I felt like I was going to be sick. "You knew we would all be tested, and you knew we would fail."

Beck scoffed. "I'm going to give you complete honesty here. All right? They're all horrible people, Caroline! Well . . . *most* of them. Iskra wasn't supposed to be here; that was a mistake." He spoke of her as if she were nothing more than a misspelled word. A flub. Something easily overlooked. "Dorothy is a fraud. Oliver is a coward. Hannah killed a man on the operating table because she was so high she couldn't see straight. They won't be missed."

"And Mallory? Me?"

His eyes softened. "I feel bad for Mallory. I do. The stalker, the religious family – she's had the short stick. In another life, she might have really learned something from this."

She was still alive, but only barely. I could see her shoulders moving, her chest rising and falling in a short burst of shallow breaths. I needed to get to her, to stop the bleeding, to do anything I could to get her out of this place.

"This isn't a fucking experiment, Beck! This isn't something you can go home and write about for some stupid goddamn academic journal – you're a monster!"

Beck studied my face as he drew nearer, sinking to his knees before me. He set the spear aside and reached for me, pushing away an errant strand of hair with the tip of his finger. "Well I'm hardly unique in that regard, am I?" he began, lips pursed. "I mean, you've killed someone yourself. By your own hand, even."

I jerked my face away, the rough fibers of the rope at my throat digging into raw flesh. "Hannah was an accident, and you know it."

"And your mother?"

"*Fuck off.*"

He sighed, breath hot on my face. "Come on, don't do that."

"She killed herself, and she deserved it, too."

"There's meaning, here, Caroline. Purpose, even, that you're willfully ignoring. The Leviathan doesn't care what you've done, or what was on your heart when you did it. It's about how you—"

"There's no *meaning* to my mother killing herself. It happens all the time. She was a goddamn narcissist who took it too far. And Hannah?" I shifted beneath the rope, and for a moment I felt the warmth of a bead of blood at my throat. "I just *swung* without thinking. No hesitation, no thought, so don't talk to me about 'purpose,' all right?" There was no purpose to be found here. No meaning, no higher sense of enlightenment. No matter what the Leviathan peddled – no matter what the Leviathan *was* – they were still just dead. Nothing more.

"We're alike, you and I," Beck said. "Moving through this world with nothing to guide us but our own survival instinct, our belief in ourselves above all else; it's what makes us fit to survive this place. We can't . . . rely on anything else. Anyone, even."

"You and I are nothing alike. I'm sorry for what I did to Hannah. I'm sorry for how my mother's life ended because it could have been different if *she* was different. Even if she deserved to die, even if I'm happy that she's gone, I still feel remorse. But you – you feel nothing!"

"The remorse you feel – you feel that every day?"

"Of course I do."

"Even though you didn't mean to kill either of them?"

"Yes."

Beck gestured to Mallory with the tip of the spear, as if I'd somehow forgotten. "See, I drove a spear through Mallory. I killed her with my own hands, and the rest of this sorry group with my actions by proxy, and I feel no guilt. None. No remorse. I've been spared all that." He turned the spear, then, to the sea. It carried on, lapping unperturbed against the sand, as if the world were not tilting beneath me at this very moment. "She absolved me of that. And she will continue to do so, once I've passed my own test. My success is what you're going to leave behind, and I love you for it. How does that make you feel?"

I wanted to feel nothing, to be stripped bare of all the guilt, the fear, the hunger. I had forgiven myself for what had become of my mother, and it was necessary to do. But there was no changing the chemical makeup of a soul. There was no cutting out the dead parts of it and leaving it in the water for chum. It would always be there. I didn't want to be the final piece in his divine equation. I didn't want to be anything he made me. I wanted to figure it out for myself.

Was *this* the sort of freedom the Leviathan offered? Was it a burdenless soul that Beck sought here?

"You make me feel disgusted," I spat. "*Untie* me, Beck."

"No." He shook his head. "That's not what I asked. How does the fact that I've accepted divine purpose make you feel?"

"Angry," I said. "Disgusted. I loved you, but now I look at you and I want to burn out my fucking insides. You used us all for—"

"No. Try again."

"Untie me, Beck!"

He slammed the spear into the sand again, the vein in his temple bulging. "No!" he roared. "I'm tired of you *lying* to yourself! I'm trying to educate you, Caroline, and you just won't listen. I've forgiven it time and again, carrying you – you, you blank slate, you empty vessel, you fucking needy, milquetoast *nothing* of a human being – into purpose that could *make* you something, make you *mean* something even in your last moments, but this moment is critical for us, and I am finished with it. Complete fucking honesty, Caroline! Bared soul at the end of the goddamn world!" Spittle flew from his lips, eyes bulging, face reddening. Blood flushed into the bruises beneath his eyes, and I could see his heartbeat pounding recklessly there.

This was the truth of Edward Beck: desperate, and angry, and stripped to the bones. Each word was a slap, a sliver of a knife beneath cold flesh. He was all ambition. It had never been about discovery, about the thrill of finding something new in a world so full of terrible, well-known truths. This was purely selfish. This was religion.

A horrible whimper escaped me, and I realized with a flush of embarrassment that my cheeks were wet with tears. "Beck, *stop*."

"What are you going to leave behind?" The question hung in the mere inches between us like a bullet; it could go in either direction, pierce either my skull or his.

"Nothing." The word slipped from me like it was the first time I'd ever said it aloud, foreign and heavy on the tongue. "I have nothing."

But my eyes found Mallory again, and the thought soured. I wanted to be free, yes. To be unburdened. But I wanted Mallory more. Mallory was something, a beautiful and vibrant something. A friend – a real one. Even now, the idea that someone cared whether I lived or died was foreign to me. I wanted to laugh with her again. I wanted to watch shitty television and eat junk food. I wanted to be stuck at a stupid fucking golf tournament in Bloomington. I wanted to live.

Mallory was something.

"Exactly," he said, leaning away from me at last. "You believe you have no purpose, that you exist merely as an accessory to the whims of your betters, and that *will* be true for only as long as you believe it. But understand this. You're not nothing to *me*, Caro. You're here, in this place between worlds, right now when it matters most. I love you. I do. You're here for me at the most crucial moment of my life – the culmination of my work, and of everything that's come from it. Don't ever think that you're nothing. Don't ever lie about your nature, even to yourself. You are who you are. And that is *everything*." He got to his feet, brushing the sand from his knees. "Have some courage. I chose you."

But Beck was not the only one. What he had forgotten – or had willfully misremembered, more likely – was that I had *passed*. I had earned the Leviathan's favor long before this, before him. Even if I had squandered it, thrown it away in a failed attempt to save Mallory from her own memories, it had happened. It was real.

"Please untie me." My voice was small, barely a thought. It slipped from me, lost to the wind.

Beck spoke again: "The guilt you're clinging to, that sadness you feel for Mallory – let it go. You won't need it any more. I want you to spend every second between now and the end knowing that you're burdenless."

End? He picked up the spear again, rounding the tree and propping the sharp head beneath the rope at my wrists.

My mind whirred. I had to find something, anything, to buy myself more time. Somehow, some way, I could think of a way to fight back. Beck was just as exhausted as me; all I needed was one good, strong blow to the back of the head, and he'd slump. I could pick up Mallory and . . . and . . .

And what? Where were we supposed to go?

"You still haven't been tested, have you?" I began. It was worth a try. I could talk, and talk, and talk myself blue. Maybe he'd slip, give me an out. "This isn't over, Beck. Not if you haven't been tested." His fingers paused at my wrists, hesitating before tugging the rope free. I jerked my arms to my front, tugging numbly at the rope that bound me to the tree by my neck. "I *have.*"

I knew Beck. He'd need an audience. He needed the attention, the applause. He would need to look me in the eye when he won, just so that he could see how it left me bereft of hope, of joy, of whatever the fuck he hoped to wring from me in my last moments here. So what would it be? The spear, like Mallory? The rocks? Would he choke the life out of me with this rope?

This would be his downfall. He'd needed me to primp and fluff his ego every day, every moment, leading to this one. That hadn't changed.

"That won't be the case for long," he said. "I know precisely what I have to do. I've prepared for this for a long time." Beck gave the rope a tug, and I gagged as it tightened around my throat. He lifted it, eyes on the red bulge of my cheeks as he worked at the knot keeping me tethered to the tree. And then it slackened, leaving nothing but a noose and his stalwart grip.

I slumped, feeling at the raw flesh of my throat as he gave the rope – my *leash* – some slack. Quickly, as subtly as I could manage,

I gauged the length of the rope, how far the knot at my neck was from Beck's white knuckles. There would be no fighting back like this. Maybe that had been the point. There would be no running.

And then my eyes flickered to Mallory, to the paleness of her lips and the blood that soaked into the sand beneath her.

"What are you going to do, Beck?" My voice was raw, spine aching. The spot atop my head where he'd hit me with the butt of the spear seared with pain.

"I'm disappointed that you haven't figured it out, Caroline," he sighed. "I expected more from you. You are my favorite, after all." Again, without warning, the rope that swung between us went taut. He tugged me forward, and I fell onto my stomach. "You *are* my test. I have to kill you. And it must be with my hands."

I scrambled to my feet as Beck dragged me through the sand. With a guttural cry, I wrapped my fingers around the rope and pulled, digging in my heels. Beck wheeled, pulling with both hands. The rope slipped in my raw palms.

The Leviathan had spoken to me before. Helped me, instructed me. She'd said that she *liked* me. Had it been a lie?

Please! I cried out in my mind, desperate and keening. My head throbbed. *Please tell me what to do!*

Nothing. Only silence, and the pounding of my furious heart. I felt myself dull, like a misused tool bereft of all its sharp edges. I had cheated this place of Mallory's offering – be it a failure or a triumph. I had been forgiven, accepted, cherished . . . and I had squandered it. I had, for all intents and purposes, lived beyond my usefulness.

Just like my mother. Just like Beck.

The Leviathan wasn't listening. Weren't angels always supposed to listen? Weren't gods?

Not an angel, then. Not a god.

"Beck, *please*—" I scrambled for the rope, pain searing through my hands as I gave a futile tug. I dug my heels into the sand, but Beck gave a jerk and I flung forward once more. "You don't have to do this."

"Oh, but I do," he said, voice even. He didn't even look back at me, nor did he give me a moment to right myself as he carried on toward the water's edge. "You're my test. You're my trial. You always have been – the Leviathan's been preparing me for this from the moment I discovered her. It has to be this, and it has to be you. My greatest temptation, and my greatest shame. Sacrifice has always been a part of every belief system. You, Caroline, are my ultimate sacrifice. That's why she lifted this place from the sea after so long. I'm *ready*. You should feel honored by this, given all you know."

"You think—" A splutter, a choke, a cough. "You think that all of this is for you? *About* you?" I tried again, tugging against his iron grip. I dipped my fingers between the flesh of my neck and the rope, wincing as my nails scraped the raw skin there. "You aren't special, Beck! You aren't the arbiter of some grand fucking design!"

At this, he stopped. It was always startling how easy it was to bruise his ego. Like a peach. Just a little twist of a knife, right between his ribs, and he crumbled. It had always been my job to patch the wound. No more.

And he really did believe it. I could see it plain on his face, in the way sweat beaded on his brow and over his upper lip. The vein in his brow bulged, and his lips trembled as he whirled to face me, closing the gap between us in two great strides. I didn't have time to gain ground, to tug at the sudden slack in the rope, before he was on me. His closed fist crashed into the side of my face, crunching into the already-broken cartilage of my nose. I flew, landing on my side in the sand. Here on the ground, I could see Mallory more clearly. Her breathing had slowed, the sliver of skin I could see beneath the fan of her hair much paler than it had been mere moments before.

I scrambled toward her on all fours, but Beck was faster. He gave the rope a jerk, and the wind was choked from me. With a gasp, I reached up and took hold of the rope as he dragged me to the water's edge, muttering under his breath.

"*Ungrateful*—" he hissed. "– part of something *great*—" I could hardly make out the words as I gasped for breath, clawing at the taut rope around my neck. With head spinning, I dug my fingers into the sand and threw a fistful at his back. He seemed unperturbed, with no more than a flinch as he stepped into the surf.

Beck held his chin at an incline, his spine impossibly straight as he wound up the rope like a fishing lure until it was all I could do to stand upright beside him. I dangled from the leash of his ambition, as I always had; I twitched, and choked, and scrabbled for him, as I always had. The heel of my boot splashed through the water, making contact with his thigh. He didn't budge.

I called out to the Leviathan again. *Please hear me!* My eyes wheeled; I looked for the deer, for the Leviathan, for my mother, for Mallory.

But no one came. No one answered.

And no one would know if I was gone. No one would care. My mother had seen to that. Would my father even look for me, years from now? Would he be moved when he realized that there wasn't even a body to bury?

Beck held me by the loop of rope that ran round my throat. He shoved my hands away, tugging me up until my toes slipped from the sand beneath the waves. "I need to let you go, Caroline," he said. His eyes were fast, darting from one bruised sliver of my face to the next as if he couldn't stomach looking at one part of me for too long. "I need to release you in order to save myself. You understand. Let go. You've served your purpose in this world. How many can say that?" He spoke like he was waiting for applause, like he expected the Leviathan to emerge from the seafoam like Aphrodite and crown him in a deluge of salt and pearls.

But there was nothing. There was only me.

"Beck, *please—*" I choked, clenched fists batting at his arms and swiping for his face. He craned his neck without a blink, and my fingers fell short. This was his test. *I* was his test. How long had he known that he would kill me if I made it here? How hard had he worked to keep me alive until now?

"Thank you for everything, Caroline," he said. "You've given me everything I want. Now let go."

I was plunged beneath the waves without a word. A sharp intake of breath, a shuddering halt in my chest – the tainted water prickled at my skin, burned my eyes. Sand swirled beneath us as my feet went out from under me, Beck's arms barring me beneath the surface. I flung my arms and kicked my feet, wriggling against the iron lock of his grip. I'd underestimated him; no matter how tired he'd looked, how battered and ragged, he had never been stronger. In convictions, in body – there would be no stopping him until he was the last of us, until there was nothing, no one, standing between him and whatever divine glory awaited him.

There can only be one. I'd been a fool to assume he hadn't known it. He'd known it all along. It might as well have been written in bold in his notes. He was always a step ahead, planning like a chess master at a novice's table.

Beck pushed me further beneath the waves, flattening my back onto the sandy bottom. He craned his neck, teeth gritted, as he struggled to keep his face free of the bitter water. I thrashed, kicking at his legs and clawing at his arms. I flung my arms wide again, scrabbling in the sand for a stick, a rock.

My fingers found a smooth edge, something solid and thick. The water stung my eyes as I strained, turning as far as I could to see what it was that I had found. I would take anything, could *use* anything; anything to give me a moment to wriggle free, to run.

The seal protruded from the sand as if it had been placed there, buried by a child as the crowning addition to a sandcastle. I grabbed at the smooth edge, digging my thumb into the runes and the raised, serpentine ridges that decorated it. It was much lighter here beneath the water, easier to wriggle from the sand and roll into my grasp. I took it in both hands and swung. The movement was swift and precise, as if unfettered by the water. For just a moment, a familiar awareness prickled behind my ear.

I slammed the stone disc into Beck's forearm with a crunch that reverberated through the water. He released me, falling away as the slender bone cracked, buckling visibly beneath the flesh. He reeled away as I surfaced, gasping for air. My vision swam, the tainted water stinging at my eyes and warping my vision. Even so, I could see Beck clearly: he was a black shape, a monstrous shadow that reeled and howled, clutching his arm and spitting condemnations. The keen, stinging awareness behind my ear shifted.

With a roar, I lifted the seal over my head again. Beck dodged a second too late; it cracked down onto his shoulder and he buckled, spilling into the water. He gasped, and the bitter, herbaceous water flooded into his mouth.

I ran for the shore. The seal was heavy in my arms now that I had pulled myself out of the water. It was cool and smooth in my hands, unsullied by the sand or the water.

"Come back, Caroline!" Beck's voice echoed, refracted. "I have to do this!" The edges of every surface blurred as the bitter water settled at the back of my throat. For a moment, I considered sticking my fingers down my throat – but the damage was done.

He splashed through the water after me, swaying and tipping as the tainted water took hold. I struggled to maintain focus, to haul myself onto the sand without falling. In the sand, Mallory's blood had begun to sparkle, to shimmer, lifting from her in a mist. Again, the world looked changed as I shifted the seal into one hand and rubbed my eyes hard enough to ache with the other.

I could make a run for it. I could find my way back to the cave where I'd woken, back past the moss and the runes – *vessel, sin, sea* – and into the dark beyond. I would find my way in the pitch black, find some crevice to squeeze into and wait for Beck to lose me. Or to lose himself, even sooner.

But I couldn't leave Mallory.

There was nowhere to go. This was the heart of the maze, the final cloister. The last judgment. Hiding was no longer an option.

Beck's fingers knotted in the length of rope dangling from my throat, tugging me back into the water. He scrambled for the seal as I plunged beneath a cresting wave. I squeezed my eyes shut, holding my breath as he slipped beneath the surf with me, more tainted water spilling into his mouth, his eyes. Beck clawed at my hair, my face; his nails raked across my cheek, pressing into my broken nose. I lunged, slicing through the water and sinking my teeth into his hand as he clawed futilely, blindly, at my eyes. He screamed, and the sound reverberated beneath the water. Blood and bitter herb spilled over my tongue as I bit down hard, teeth cutting into flesh and tendon.

He released me, and I was running again. I stumbled, sloshing through the surf and onto the sandy shore. The world spun, my stomach flipping and turning as my vision blurred. I fell onto the sand, spitting a hunk of pale flesh into the seafoam between my knees.

"Caroline!" Beck keened, wheeling drunkenly round as he clutched his bleeding hand to his chest. "Why are you doing this to me? Come back!"

Absolutely fucking not.

"Don't you love me?" he cried. "Don't you *love* me?"

The spear, still dark with Mallory's blood, lay by the gnarled tree. I needed to be rid of the noose around my neck, or else he'd choke me to death. Mingling blood and herbaceous water coalesced nauseatingly in my stomach as I stumbled up the beach, legs leaden. I blinked hard as the very air around me refracted, fuzzed, plunging me deeper into hallucination. My hair stretched and fractured like the branches of the tree; the break in my nose tingled and buzzed like a wasp in a glass bulb. I clutched the seal harder, the bloodied tips of my fingers scraping the stone but leaving no mark. It would anchor me; as long as it was real, so was I.

I could hear Beck behind me, scrambling and falling onto the sand in his pursuit. He was unfamiliar with the water's nature – I was not. But he was gaining on me; he was faster, stronger.

There would be no making it to the spear. And so I stopped. And I swung.

The force of the swing and the weight of the seal whipped me round, popping painfully at my shoulders. Beck wasn't expecting it; his eyes went wide as the cool, smooth stone cracked into his temple. I could hear the crunch of bone, could feel the sheer jolt of it rattling my arms and clacking my teeth. I spun in the sand on my heel, a dancer in pirouette, as Beck spilled with a splatter of blood onto the sand.

He landed on his back, eyes wheeling. Time seemed to slow as he struggled to lift his hand, feeling at the wound that grew and grew, reddening and pulsing with blood, by the second. His fingers pressed into the wound, a perfect arc according to the curve of the seal. The seal, which hung heavily in my hands; the seal, which was clean and unsullied by the spray of Beck's blood, the clump of hair and flesh that stood out atop the sand.

I swayed on unsteady legs as I towered over him. The stone disc hung heavily in my grasp. Beck met my gaze, eyes unfocused. Blood spilled from the wound at his temple, slicking his cheek and wetting his collar. He propped himself up, lifted onto his forearms, mouth hanging open.

"Caro—"

I lifted the seal again, jaw set. Breath hissed from between my clenched teeth in a spray of blood and brine. I towered over him, and for a moment Beck looked – for what I could only imagine was the first time – *afraid*. This wasn't part of the plan. This wasn't divine.

I could feel every place he'd ever touched me. Rotten, atrophying, like a long-dead limb beneath a hot iron. He had molded me with dirtied fingertips, pressed me and shaped me into what he needed of me. I'd been a good girl, a good secret. And now I was neither good, nor bad; I simply *was*.

He looked at me now and saw the face of love's rage. An empty slate, reflecting nothing but his own face.

I brought the seal down atop his head in a squelch of blood and a splintering crack of bone. Blood gushed unfettered from the dent in his scalp, a horrible gurgling sound bubbling from his lips as I slammed the seal down onto him again. And again. With each strike, each crunching blow, the stone remained untouched. Clean. Even as an eye popped from its socket; even as his skin grew so slick with blood that I could no longer count his freckles, the stone remained.

"*Fuck you!*" I was screaming, my throat tearing as hot, prickling tears spilled over my cheeks, traced the bruised dip of my jaw. "Fuck—" a moment of suspension, blood a spray of foam and mist as I arched my back, "you!"

Beck tried and failed to speak, voice garbled and imperceptible as he struggled upright, and then fell flat again. I was blind, and everything was red; the seal was impossibly light as it arced through the air over and over again. My shoulders ached as I caved in his brow, shattered his cheekbone. With each splintered piece of bone, each tooth knocked loose, each bit of cartilage spilled onto the sand, a piece of him slipped from me like an ill-fitting garment.

A wavering hand lifted, touching my ankle.

And then he was still.

His blood coated me, hot and steaming under the illusory pull of the tainted water. I let the seal slip from my grasp, paying it no mind as it rolled blithely to settle between the roots of the tree just shy of the abandoned spear and the cut length of rope.

A clump of his hair was stuck to my jeans. I swiped uselessly at it, feet still planted firmly on either side of his prone body.

His *body*.

My eyes, swimming and painted vibrant vermillion, settled upon the mangled *nothing* that had once been his face. I pitched sideways, scrambling on my stomach from him and retching into the sand. Bitter water, diluted blood, and brackish foam spilled from me.

I'd never felt so weak, so disoriented; there was too much blood on me, and I would do anything – *anything* – to be rid of it.

"Mallory!" My voice was a croak. I pushed myself up with my forearms, then onto my hands, my every joint and muscle trembling. I called to her where she lay in the sand, but she didn't answer. "Mallory, say something!"

It was only then that I realized that her shoulders had stilled. The blood had slowed in its deluge, its effervescent bloom in the sand. Even through the haze of the water's effects, I could see it. The stillness. The quiet.

"Mallory?" No answer. "*Mallory?*"

I felt a prickle of awareness at the back of my ear. The dark passenger, the omnipresent watcher. I paid it no mind as I crawled for her, spraying bloody sand as I went.

Down the shore, a shape dragged itself from the surf. A hand reached from the water and dug distended fingers into the sand. A vile squelch, a splash, a chorus of muffled groans that reverberated through the stillness; a sagging stretch of flesh pulled itself onto the shore, what once had been a face stretched beyond recognition over a limb that pulled, twisted, and took a handful of sand. A body – a multitude, an abomination, an eldritch amalgamation of eyeless faces, skin stretched over mouths, lumps of flesh and bone – emerged from the surf, too heavy to lift on its own. Limbs, too many legs and arms to count, stretched for dry land, heaving the great body of the Leviathan's flock onto the sand.

I looked once more to Mallory.

Mallory.

Mallory's body.

The flock looked past me, seeing and unseeing in equal measure. Membranous eyes flickered wide in folds and stretches of bleached, featureless skin. Each and every one, blinking madly against the gray light, rolled, and rolled . . . and fell deftly on the body.

My eyes snapped to the seal, and then the spear. I spat a mouthful of blood onto the sand. The flock watched. The flock waited.

And then it was upon us.

With a surge of energy, I threw myself at the discarded spear. I knew what it wanted, this abomination. This *thing* made of failures, and deaths, and trials never-ending. This thing made at the behest of something that was neither god, nor angel – it wouldn't have Mallory. It wouldn't take her.

The ground shook beneath its weight as the creature rushed along the sand, multitudinous arms and legs wheeling, scrabbling, kicking at the surf as it arrowed toward us. This thing, this place, could have Beck. But never Mallory.

In the light, the flock was far bigger than I had ever imagined. It towered, lifting up with the effort and strength of every body it had absorbed. The massive abomination moved awkwardly, each stretching limb unwieldy and desperate as if each soul within hungered of its own volition. Flesh slid over flesh, hands crushing spindly fingers and feet knocking into what once could have been a thigh, or a calf. Here in the open air, buffeted by the arctic breeze, I could smell it: rot, sweat, and decay. Dorothy's head and shoulders hung from it like a boil, eyeless sockets dripping black bile. Oliver's face pressed against the wide swath of flesh, while Hannah's leg dangled uselessly, kicking at the sand and missing. A tuft of Iskra's hair protruded from what might have once been a head, beside the unfamiliar eyes of a stranger. The skin sagged, like the bones within had long since finished digesting.

The faithful. The angel's prized creation.

I lurched to my feet, taking up the spear and smashing the handle over my knee. It broke into jagged halves, one bearing the blunt end and the other the bloodied spearhead. Down the beach, the first of a hundred limbs curled around Mallory's ankle, giving her a testing tug.

It couldn't have her. I wouldn't let it, even if it was the last thing I ever did.

I threw myself at the amalgam, a jagged weapon in each hand. The spearhead pierced the pliable flesh with a pop and a gurgle of blood – black, acidic, it spilled down my front. I held my breath as it splashed onto my chin, my cheek. With my left hand, I lifted the broken shaft and plunged it into what might have, in another life, been a cheek. The angle of a jawline, maybe. The horrible keening from the heart of the mass raised in pitch as it bucked and thrashed, throwing me off.

An arm stretched from within, too long and with too many fingers. It hooked into Mallory's hair, tugging her head back to expose her throat.

This was the first time I had seen her face since . . . since—

Her eyes were glassy, unseeing. Lips pale, cheeks dull, she stared out into the gray overhead with granules of sand in her lashes. The flock tugged at her almost gently, and pulled her across the sand.

A scream ripped from me, tearing my throat and filling my mouth with the tang of iron. I threw myself over Mallory, stabbing indiscriminately at anything and everything that was not *her.* I tugged her into my lap, wrapping my legs around her middle and holding her fast – but the flock gave a tug, and I, too, was shifted across the sand.

A swipe, and an errant tendon severed. Black blood and soiled sea foam spilled onto the sand. Acrid, rotten, it smelled like stagnant water. Foul. Great, open-mouthed sobs ripped from me, every scream a cry of anger, of anguish, of regret.

The spearhead punctured something wet and round; black blood, foam, and rotten viscera flooded from the wound as I carved down the creature's bloated abdomen. It seemed to deflate as a torrent of half-digested bone and sinew flooded over me, over Mallory. A formless limb shot from the creature's broadside. With strength unmatched, it whipped the spear from my grasp and flung it into the water. It slammed into my middle and sent me arcing through the air, haloed by the gray sun as the wind was knocked from me. The jagged end of the spear's shaft slipped from my grasp, rolling along the beach. I landed with a crunch, my shoulder buckling beneath me.

Undeterred, the creature reached for her, drowning her in rotten blood and curling bleached flesh over her legs, around her middle, beneath her head. I scrambled toward her on all fours as the oil coagulated, caressing her almost gently. I gathered blood-damp sand into my fists and threw it at the unholy amalgam, desperate to slow it.

Mallory's body slid across the sand, leaving a trail of blood in her wake. Vibrant red, stark against the oil and sand – and then she was gone, slipped between the folds of the creature's undulating flesh like a trinket stashed in a coat pocket.

Again, a prickle of awareness fluttered behind my ear. I swiped at it with jagged fingernails.

"*Please!*" I cried, but to whom, I wasn't sure. Anyone who'd listen. Anyone who'd hear. "Take me! Punish me!" I would do anything to bring Mallory back. Anything at all, just to ensure that she would walk out of this place. She deserved it more than anyone. And if this would be my last act, let it be one that I chose for myself.

And I *would* choose for myself. I chose Mallory.

"Please, Leviathan!" I called, throwing my head back and howling emptiness into the breeze. "If you really are an angel, *stop*!" No angel would allow this. No angel would hear my pleas, as close to prayers as I'd ever come in earnest, and turn away. The sound of a crashing wave and the squelching of the flock's slit belly swallowed my voice. The flock groaned, a multitude of voices crying out in pain as numberless hands tugged together the flesh that I had rendered in two.

It threw itself onto the sand, changing shape with every passing second as it struggled to take in the new body. I searched for Mallory in the mass, between what once had been Dorothy and what could have been Iskra, for any sign of her that I could carve out – with my bare hands, if I had to. Faces pressed against bleached skin, straining until the flesh went translucent. Wandering limbs reached for Beck, fingers opening and closing like that of a petulant child with a sweet held just out of reach.

The water had grown restless. It churned and crested as I scrambled onto my knees and tossed what remained of the spear at the body of the Leviathan's flock, at the great mass of decay and evolution that would swallow Mallory whole.

I wanted to scream and scream until its master couldn't help but listen. I wanted to *force* it to come to me. I was all that it had left. I was the only one here, alive.

My mind raced as I sank onto my heels, chest heaving. I wiped at the blood, the rot, and the bitter water on my lips and squeezed my eyes shut. Once, twice, I thudded the heel of my hand into my temple. The angel listened, and the angel refused me. It made no sense; nothing I understood of *angels* would allow such death, such violence.

The Leviathan was incomprehensible, something in between this world and a thousand others. Beck had never been able to pin it down, to understand its motives, its nature, and yet he had tried. It was human nature to try. He had done his best to understand the Leviathan's rules, but had failed to account for the fact that it called itself an "angel" or that it spoke to those it seemed to pity most. None of the others had mentioned a thing about whispers in the night, eyes at their backs, or anything else of the sort. Beck had longed for its awareness, its approval, and yet it seemed . . . it seemed obvious that I was the only one among us who had captured its ineffable attention.

It had desired the blank slate of my desperation, it said. It saw potential in the emptiness. Years and years of vomiting up filth would need to pass before I could unlearn all the things I'd been taught to think about myself. I didn't have years. I had *now*. And I would be damned if the only decision I'd ever made for myself would be to give up my very first friend. My first *real* friend.

Beck's blood had gone cold further up the sand, no steam rising from the place that had once been a face. Dead. But not gone. Anything was possible here. Beck had believed it.

The great old ones can never resist a deal, Beck had said. Gods, angels, demons; they needed human attention to survive, to subsist. Devotion; this ritual; this cloister; it was all to amass devotion. If the well dried up, and the world forgot, what would become of the gods that were neither here nor there?

Beck had believed it all. Why couldn't I?

And the Enochian phrases that I had recognized, both in Beck's notes and in the inscriptions on the cave walls. Familiar words, and then mistranslations as if done by a learner's hand. *Wormwood. Vessel. Triumph. Sin.* Again and again, "*sin*" written like a prayer in a desperate hand. A pretender's hand.

That was why Beck had chosen us all. The world would always have sin, guilt, ugliness. No matter how hard we tried, we would never be free of it. And so the Leviathan would always eat.

Not an angel – it simply wished us all to believe that it was one. What was a deity without someone to believe in it? To feed it?

And so we would make a deal. Emptiness was, after all, a place of possibility.

I scrambled for the discarded seal and crashed into the surf, frigid water sloshing up my front. I waded in until the water battered at my hips. "Leviathan!" I cried. "*Wormwood!*" The pretender's moniker, the false name, the fallen star. I'd heard the name once, when my childhood youth pastor had thought it a good idea to introduce the idea of the end-times to the third graders. A star, fallen into the sea. A star, who was not a star at all. I lifted the seal above my head. "I came, like you said! And I want to make a deal!"

There was a moment of stillness, of quiet – and then the tide began to shift. It pulled from the shore, like the swell before a tsunami wave. I was dragged further down the sloping seabed, slipping and sinking in the loose sand.

And then the world itself shifted. Far into the bay, the rolling hills and valleys that made up the horizon began to shift. They lifted as one from the sea, a great body that stretched as far as the eye could see. The sand rumbled beneath my feet as the earth lifted, peeling away from the water and turning inward.

Toward the shore. Toward *me.*

A great serpentine head arced through the surf, haloed by salt spray and gray sunlight. Her eyes shone like stars, her inky pupils long slits down the middle. Made of the very fabric of this place, each scale the size of a cathedral; as she dipped her head toward me, I could see in the far distance the whip-crack of an unfurling tail where her head had just lain.

The Leviathan blotted out the sun, the sky. I could smell the salt on her scales, each carved with runes in haphazard clusters and erratic lines. As before, some were familiar – *vessel, sin, triumph* – and others were known to me only through Beck's research. The scales moved, rippled with the sea. Verdant ocean foliage clung to her ridges, each twisting and curling in a dazzling array of impossible geometry, algae, seaweed, and herbaceous blossoms dangling from every hard angle. And beneath each lifted scale, a wild, whirling eye.

Salt and brine sprayed over me as she moved through the water, skittering over the serpent's body as if the laws of nature struggled to reconcile with the shape that cut through the air, the surf, the sand.

The hair lifted at the nape of my neck as I stumbled back, heart falling.

No, this was no angel. No God. Something else.

I met her gaze, and felt something untenable inside me slip. A trick of the mind, a loose nerve; something deep inside, like a room yet unexplored, bottomed out.

And when she spoke, her voice came to me in multitudes.

"You defy the laws of this place," the voice said, booming within and without – though the serpent's mouth never moved. "Thrice.

Unholy trinity of errors; you make demands of me that you have not earned."

"I passed your tests," I called, my voice impossibly small beneath the roar of the shifting surf. "I brought your fucking trinket! Now *take* it!" I threw the seal into the water, taking no pains to shield my eyes from the splash. The bitter water tingled at my skin, burned my lips.

A rumble shook the ground beneath me. It was bold, I knew; what was to say that this creature wouldn't simply swallow me whole and start from scratch with a new wave of hapless explorers?

"You disrespect an angel in her own cloister?" The voice rattled my bones.

I shook my head. "You're no angel." No angel, no god. "But I don't care what you are."

The Leviathan's head dipped lower. I could smell the salt on her scales, a concentrated bitterness far greater than that diluted in the water. "And what are you, then?" she hissed. "*A cheat.* I was kind to you. I helped you. *Freed* you."

"No," I shook my head. "I freed myself."

Another rumble, like thunder. Like laughter.

"You said it yourself!" I called. "What sort of god would you be if you let this place stay empty? What's an angel without someone to believe in her?" Whether she believed herself to be an angel of old, a god long forgotten, or whether she reveled in her convincing ruse, it didn't matter. I would give her what she wanted. *Be* what he wanted. As long as I got something in return. "You said that your idol would be rewarded. There can only be one, you said. I'm your *favorite*, you said. You told me not to be sorry, to forgive myself because it was what *you* wanted." It was what I wanted, too. I wanted it so fucking badly that it hurt. "So here I am. Reward me."

"You defy the rules of my cloister, spit on the memory of every acolyte that has come before you—"

"They came willingly," I countered. "We did not. We were swindled." I threw my arm wide, gesturing to Beck's half-digested body far behind me, on the beach. The amalgam sloshed black bile over his head, hair plastered to his brow. "By a man unworthy of your gifts." The words felt false as they rolled off the tongue. But if there was one thing I knew how to do, it was *lie.* Lie for reward. Lie for self-preservation. I knew minds like this creature's. Narcissistic. Needy. It was all a familiar dance. "You told me to come, and I came. I brought the seal, as is tradition. Now give me what I want."

The serpent's head tilted, like a dog listening for a whistle. "You are bold to make demands of an angel."

I shook my head. "Angels are good, and kind. You are not."

"And neither are you. You wield death for your own benefit."

"I'm a survivor."

"You have no room to bargain, Caroline Destler."

"And neither do *you.*" I took a step toward her, sinking further into the steeply descending bank. "Isn't that how gods work? You need believers. Or you simply . . . don't exist."

What is the value of a human soul? Even one was worth something.

The serpent's squamous lips twitched, and for a moment I saw the teeth behind them. My heart leapt into my throat. It took all my will to keep from skittering away, climbing up the bank and clambering to safety. Impossibly sharp teeth, spears thick with algae and salt; I would feel nothing if she changed her mind, decided she tired of the sound of my voice. She would simply swallow me.

"You have always come," the Leviathan said. "Since Babylon, since the dawn of time, you come. It is in human nature to want. Greed, sin, treachery. They find a way, flocking to my monument of stone and salt like pilgrims. And as long as humanity struggles and fails to attain the purity of soul that you so futilely strive for, there will always be *me.*"

"No angel subsists on sin." *Sin-eater.* Not of this world. "You don't have to pretend any more. I see you for what you really are."

"And what am I?" For a moment, the Leviathan sounded like Beck. Mocking, challenging, like she knew the answer and wanted to flaunt the fact that I did not. But there were some things that weren't for me to know, to understand. All there was for me was acceptance, or death.

And so I shook my head, and I shrugged. "I don't care."

"Is that so?" The rumble of her voice curled lovingly around my heart and squeezed. It peered inside me, as it had done before. Overhead, the clouds seemed to shift. They thinned, like gossamer. And for a moment, I could have sworn I saw the familiar hardness, the familiar darkness, of stone.

"Yes," I said. "I have nothing. I *am* nothing. But nothing . . . nothing is a place—"

"– of possibility." A pause. "Tell me, Caroline. What do you want?"

"Bring her back, and I'll give you whatever you want."

"But isn't it freedom that you crave? To choose for yourself?"

"I choose Mallory." Her name felt dangerous to say aloud, like it could be taken from me at any second. Mallory was freedom. Mallory was what was right and good about all of this. The future, the possibility of it; it was all no good without her.

"I tasted your sin, Caroline. I know its sweetness. You want nothing but your own freedom. Self-determination. I could have given it to you, if only you had played by the rules. I give my Icons whatever they desire; they carry my gospel into the world, plant the seeds that flourish when I return again. The works your *Edward Beck* found? The discovery that so enlivened him? It was left for him. Nothing is by chance."

She was right. For a brief, shining moment I had believed that I could reach the end of this trial, find the heart of the labyrinth, and come out on the other side a new person. I had forgiven myself, absolved myself. Released myself. I was empty – and for once, it meant that I could be anything. For *me* – not for someone else.

I could be free. But what was freedom without purpose? The only purpose, *real* purpose, I'd ever felt was with Mallory. Friendship; that was a purpose worth living for.

I curled my toes in my waterlogged boots, the ruined fabric of her socks bunching against the sole. On the shore, the flock continued to bleed. It cried, and wailed, and within I could hear the familiar voices of the expedition.

"Let me be that, then!" I cried, voice breaking at last. Unbidden tears, hot and invasive, wet my cheeks. "Take my freedom. Take my soul. I don't want it – I just want Mallory. This is the deal I want: bring Mallory back, and let us leave together. I promised her that I would save her. I *promised.*" I was crying, letting slip hot, ugly tears. I had never wanted anything like this.

"I give it all willingly!" I cried, throwing my arms wide and squeezing my eyes tight. "So take it!"

This was the way of things; where real angels subsisted on devotion, and goodness, and kindness, the Leviathan was made of sin. Disarray. Ugliness. I could be that. I had been, my whole life. I could be that again. I would give anything. Everything. Willingly, I would do it. I would give up freedom to be loved.

To die for a friend would be a wonderful way to go. To live for a friend would be even sweeter.

The tide shifted, and a great wall of spray and foam rose from beneath the serpent's body. I threw my hands over my head, but not quick enough; it washed over me, and as I inhaled sharply the foam slipped up my nose, into my mouth. I was thrown down into the bitter water and held there. As before, unbidden images flooded my mind: men and women whose faces I didn't recognize, but whose gravity I couldn't deny, kingdoms, and castles, and riches, bloodshed and war, writhing bodies crying out in pleasure and pain, and then the sea, a lash from the edge of a beach not unlike this one, dragging one body into the surf and then another. Over and over, throughout time. I understood them all to be Leviathan's, survivors of this trial and willing Icons. And one by one, they were reclaimed and dragged into the sea. Some struggled. Some accepted it willingly. But they all, each and every one, disappeared beneath the surf just as easily. Quietly. Like they'd never been there at all.

These were the terms of the pact and I accepted them. I pushed back against the Leviathan's influence, filling my mind with images of Mallory, of home, of the sun. I thought of our very first meeting. I thought of the stupid, ridiculous socks. I thought of the promise I'd made her, that I'd failed to keep. But I could make it right.

The air was cool on my face as I surfaced again, flinging my arms wildly in an attempt to right myself. I spat out the bitter water, wiping it from my eyes with the backs of my hands.

The Leviathan was gone. No far coastline broke the horizon. I turned to find the beach empty save a single door. A familiar one, with white paint and a golden handle. For once, it was quiet.

It made sense that it would end here. It was always going to end here. Here, on the other side of this door.

I went to it. The handle was warm, the hinges loose. The door swung wide, scraping across the sand. Where I had expected to find a body, a pool of bathwater, a discarded pill bottle on the other side, there was nothing but darkness. I squinted into the stygian black, and as my eyes adjusted, I saw the familiar slick of water on stone, a stalagmite protruding from the rocky floor and spiraling toward a low-hanging ceiling. Water dripped from an indiscernible source above my head, its rhythmic plunking the only source of sound in an otherwise quiet and empty cavern.

I stepped inside. The door swung closed at my back, pitching me into the dank, frigid darkness.

There, blazing to life, stood the monolith from the heart of the Leviathan's library, its sacred text alight with runes. The heart of it all. The holiest place.

Two hands emerged from the dark at my back, slipping over my shoulders and trailing up the length of my neck. Fingers dipped beneath the rope that still hung like a noose from my throat and tugged the knot loose. Lovingly, gently, they caressed my jaw, my cheeks. I felt hot breath at the back of my neck, the familiar and welcome awareness of the Leviathan's watchful eye prickling at my ear. Lithe fingers tucked the hair over my ears.

I closed my eyes.

As my neck snapped, quick and sudden, I thought of Mallory.

I looked down on myself as if from afar, my body impossibly small on the stone. I had fallen lazily, limbs splayed and head twisted at an impossible angle. Even here in the pitch, I could see it clearly. The body. *My* body.

And I was not alone.

In the shadows above, something great and serpentine slid across the stone. It spoke, and its voice shook the cavern, rattling my body as it lay prone on the rocky floor.

Your reward, the voice purred, *is a contract.*

I watched as countless runes, warped and bent celestial text that twisted into absurd configuration, seared like a brand onto my body's pale, ruined flesh. Like the Leviathan's scales, text crowded onto the slender fingers, the exposed flesh of my stomach. The membranous skin of my eyelids blackened with infernal ink, my lips pulled and prodded by the frantic calligraphy.

And my body was not alone. Bodies, naked and slick with wetness, haloed the stone on which I lay. I could hear screaming – not of fervor or ecstasy, but of fear. In the air, encircling the monolith, oblong shapes hung limp. The bodies hung, suspended in utter nothingness, heads bowed. Blood and sea foam dripped from the tips of their toes, salt crusting their eyes shut.

I recognized them – not only from the vision that Beck had forced onto me, but from what I had been shown by their master. These were all to be my kin now. Icons, beneficiaries of our shared patron's power. Would I end up here?

My awareness was neither here nor there. I watched just as easily as the sinuous shadow twisted around my limbs, leaving runes behind – and as a great stretch of bleached flesh beyond the door, deflated and prostrate on the shore at the heart of the cloister, birthed a body slick with inky blood. Pale, stretched beyond recognition; the edges were black with blood that had long since gone cold. It bubbled and roiled in the sand like molten lead, and from within the mass I could barely see a leg, an arm. There was movement from beneath.

A head, and then shoulders.

Mallory's body spilled from beneath the rendered flesh, the torn piece of the flock that I had reclaimed for myself. Her shoulders moved with belabored breaths, each expelling rotten blood from her lungs. She scrambled across the sand, eyes wheeling. And here, in the in between, I felt relief. Water spilled into the cavern that housed my body like a dam had broken somewhere deeper within the cave system, the sea level rising to swallow me – and as the surf rose, gentle as ever, to tug Mallory into the foam. She struggled against it, and I called out to her only to feel my voice choked by salt at the back of my throat.

I am the beginning and the end, the voice said. No longer my mother's voice but my own. *You belong to me.*

I was pulled down, ripped back into my own consciousness, my own body, and *squeezed.* A cold hand wrapped around my ankle, and I was thrust beneath the water again. Brackish water spilled over my tongue, rushed up my nose—

And then hands found my shoulders. Deft fingers hooked beneath my arms and hauled me up. I could feel the effort of kicking feet, swirling water beneath me as my head sagged against the pressure, the movement.

My head broke the surface of the water, and my eyes flew wide. I gasped, arms flailing wildly. The grip on my shoulders tightened as water splashed onto my cheeks.

"Caro!" Mallory's voice. Mallory – *Mallory.* My eyes wheeled, struggling against the sudden brightness. I reached blindly, fingers finding a cheek, a nose, hair. My vision shifted into focus, and for a single, terrible moment I could see nothing but the runes as they disappeared into the pale flesh at the backs of my hands.

Mallory was alive, vibrantly so – the tip of her nose blazed red from the cold, cheeks huffing and puffing from the effort of holding me up in the battering water. But her eyes were alight with relief as I came to my senses.

Mallory was alive, and so was I. I didn't want to close my eyes, didn't want to see the blazing image of her there on the beach that would be for ever seared into my memory. Her blood, her body, the horrible amalgam that had tried to *consume* her. She was here. She was alive. I had done that.

I was on Mallory at once, and though I knew it would nearly drown us both I wrapped my arms around her and squeezed. I touched her arms, her face, her hair. A horrible, ugly sob ripped from me, bubbling at the surface of the waves. Water hung from the tip of my nose in heavy droplets, ocean, or tears, or both. I pressed a wet kiss to her brow. "Oh, thank *God*!" I cried. "You're alive!"

Not God, I felt a weight behind my orbital bone, an awareness that had not been there before. It startled me, and I jerked away from Mallory with a gasping choke, spluttering on water and brine. *Me.*

Mallory seemed not to notice. She touched my cheek, my brow, the top of my head. "I lost you in the dark!" she said, voice impossibly small. "I looked, and looked – I felt like I was walking for ever!"

"What happened?" I knew. I'd seen it. But I couldn't tell her, and never would. What gentle lie had the Leviathan fed her? What singular kindness had she done for me?

Mallory blinked. I could see her thinking, the crease between her brow deepening and the corners of her lips turning down. She shook her head. "I . . . don't remember. I think I hit my head."

"You did," I countered immediately. This was neither the time nor place to fill in the holes. If she remembered nothing, she would be better for it. But only time would tell. Time, warmth, and someplace dry.

I kicked my feet against the heavy current, bobbing above low waves as rain pelted the tops of our heads. I could hear the screeching of sea birds, the ringing of bells. I tipped my head back, and let the rain sting my cheeks. Together, we struggled to crane our necks above the surf – and it was Mallory who spotted the shore first.

"Look!" she cried. Mallory thrust a finger outward, allowing herself to be buffeted by the waves. "It's the fisherman's boat!"

Sure enough, Seal Harbor unfurled before us, no more than a quarter mile from where we tread water, a sleepy collage of tin roofs and rusted boats. The very vessel on which we'd been shuttled to the cave bobbed at the dock, two rubber-clad figures milling about with ropes and buckets. They looked no different than how we'd left them, as if no time had passed at all.

We were *out*. We were *free*.

Mallory waved her arms over her head, the tip of her boot clipping my shin as she kicked wildly to keep herself afloat. "*Hey!*" she screamed, voice ragged. "Hey, we're out here!"

As Mallory called out, futile beneath the roar of the rain, I turned back. The stone skerry was gone. The great wall of limestone and quartzite was missing from the bay, leaving nothing but a slate horizon and the patter of rain. We were nothing but specks of dirt in the churning inlet, unmoored and left adrift. There was no sign of where we'd surfaced, no churning vortex or blip in the current. There was nothing.

But inside me, heavy like a leaden weight on my very soul, was something else entirely.

We began to swim, pausing every few strokes to call out to the fishermen. Joseph and Ellis heard us at last as we swam further into the harbor, limbs heavy and mouths dry. My head spun, and my body ached. With each breath, I could feel a sharpness in my neck as if each vertebra hadn't yet decided on how to rearrange itself.

But I was alive. Mallory was breathing, lungs full enough to holler proudly out into the gray.

Joseph heard us first. The moment he spotted us, the harbor exploded into a flurry of activity. It wasn't long before we were hauled up and onto the deck of the boat, wrapped in thermal blankets and shuttled back to shore. We were returned to The Silver Fisher – still empty – and sequestered in the kitchen where an assemblage of locals took our ruined clothes and provided us with new ones.

I protested when they took my socks, but the words fell on deaf ears. The sheriff and his deputy arrived, and then a man from the Navy. A number of strangers arrived to poke and prod at us, to check us for injuries and ask us questions. We were the only ones who'd come back, after all. And the great stone monolith that had occupied their bay was gone. No warning, no great shattering of earth, sea, and sky. Just us – two castoffs in the bay.

Neither Mallory nor I knew how to explain. We wouldn't know where to begin, nor how to justify all we'd seen. Later on, when we were alone, we would need to get our story straight. But that was a problem for a later time.

As we were given water and steaming soup, Mallory and I huddled together on two plastic diner chairs that we'd shoved as close together as we could manage, I found the clock over the stove. It was one of those tacky bird clocks that squawked every hour on the hour; before we'd left, we'd heard the midmorning Blue Jay singing its song. The Goldfinch followed it, the Northern Cardinal at high noon, and then the Mourning Dove at one o'clock and Downy Woodpecker at two.

The clock's hands sat just past one o'clock. My hand drifted absently to my pocket, where I usually kept my phone. Empty, of course. Lost to the sea.

"Hey—" I stopped a waitress short as she bustled into the kitchen to collect a fisherman's lunch order. "What day is it?" It couldn't be a coincidence, the time. It just couldn't.

She looked at me, puzzled. Mallory's gaze darted between us both, soup spoon poised just below her mouth. "It's April eleventh," the waitress said. "Why?"

"I think your clock is broken."

"The clock?" Both Mallory and the waitress peered up at the clock, which displayed the exact time – and date, apparently – that the cave had collapsed, killing the Grundstadts. The day was the same, and the clock had stopped – so why had it felt like years had passed down in that cave? If no time at all had passed on the shore, then what would the people of this place think of us? What had they seen? According to my estimations, they likely had seen us disappear and reappear within the time it would take the waitress to make a pot of coffee. There was no explaining that.

The people of Seal Harbor put us up in the rooms that Beck had rented for us. We were, after all, still within our booking window. Technically, they weren't doing us a favor; Beck had paid for it, after all. But they were certainly eager to frame it as such. They agreed to let us be, to let us take scalding showers and change into the clean clothes they had provided. They would have plenty of questions for us, of course. But there would be time for that.

Mallory and I took turns showering in the same bathroom, one sitting on the tile floor while the other bathed and vice versa. Neither of us could stand to be alone. I scrubbed the salt from my skin, lingering at every freckle, every joint, every errant scar for a sign of the runes that had lit me from within. My nose had been healed, the site of the break thick with brine and salt. Each of my wounds had been packed, patched, and left to soak in the sea. A gift, maybe. Or a reminder.

My neck ached, and the weight behind my eye was omnipresent. But I could will it away for a little while.

We sat beside the heater in Mallory's room in our towels, comfortable for a long while in shared silence.

Mallory was the first to break it. "What happened, Caroline?" she whispered, as if the very walls were listening. "What happened to Beck?"

I looked at her, eyes drifting to the unblemished skin of her shoulders, her arms. Whatever the Leviathan had done to bring her back to me, as promised, it had fixed her entirely. But it had left her with questions. We would need to explain away the cave's disappearance, surely. The story would be sensationalized, and soon enough every corner of the internet would call for every detail that we could drudge up. We'd hear our names on the news, on podcasts, in textbooks. Iskra's family would come calling, and so would the photographer that had been meant to accompany us.

We would need to make it good. And we would need to make it right.

And so I thought for a long while. What I told her now would define the story that we told the coast guard, the sheriff. We'd have to tell the same story again and again, to the news, and our peers. It was lucky that we had no family to tell – only each other.

"He didn't make it," I said, scrambling for a convenient lie. I could still hear the cracking of his skull, the squelch of his blood. I could feel his final touch, light as a feather on the skin of my ankle. I wondered if I would ever be able to burn it away. "He . . . some rocks fell. And . . . and—"

Mallory nodded, her hand falling onto my knee. "I'm sorry," she said. "I know you loved him."

Against my will, my bottom lip trembled. "I did," I said. This, at least, was not a lie. "I really did." Love wasn't always honest. It was always unclear, the line between love and possession. They were opposites, at the end of the day – maybe I'd never fully understood that. But here, with Mallory, it felt obvious. She squeezed my hand, straightened the crooked hem of my towel, and maybe – maybe – I got the picture.

My chest seized, a cough choking me. Mallory startled, hands fluttering over the curve of my spine as I hunched, heat flooding my cheeks. Salt water and seafoam spilled from my lungs, splattering my lips and wetting the carpet. A clot of algae squelched from deep within my throat, splattering onto the radiator.

Mallory looked on, startled. "Caro?" Her eyes were wide, face drained of all color as I coughed up seawater and brine. It spilled from my nose, and a shiver danced the length of my spine as I felt a trickle from my ear, running a single rivulet down the length of my neck. I gagged, pressing my palm to my mouth, and the heaving subsided.

"I'm fine," I lied, waving her away. A twinge of acute pain arrowed along the column of my neck. "Just swallowed some shit out there in the bay. It's just . . . just gross, is all." I took her hand and gave it a squeeze. Mallory offered a weak smile, though the gesture didn't reach her eyes. Even as we continued to sit in companionable silence, I could feel her eyes on me, watching with concern that I could never answer for.

"We won, Caro," Mallory said, giving my hand a squeeze. "We survived."

"We did," I said. "We did."

I couldn't tell her. Wouldn't. There was no telling her that I was living on borrowed time, that the sea ran through my veins now, and not blood. I wouldn't tell her what I'd given so that she could be here now. Living with that guilt, that burden, was not for her.

I was a ticking clock. I would be dragged back to the sea, called there by my watchful patron – my *master* – whenever I was needed. My life did not belong to me. But it never had. Not really.

The Leviathan had given me a gift, after all: *time.* I looked to Mallory, linking her fingers with mine. I was free despite the weight, and despite the sea. Despite the promise, and the time, and the knowledge of what awaited me – I was free. I could choose on my own. Even if I knew that she would miss me when I was gone, that she would mourn the loss of me when I was called back to fulfill my end of the bargain, it was mine. This life, this chance. No matter what I carried with me, no matter the dead I'd buried at sea.

Whatever I did, whatever I chose, I would do it myself.

On the anniversary of my mother's death, I woke to the smell of baking bread and the sound of music. I had dreamed of her, as I so often did. My mother, Beck, and the sea – though they all felt one in the same most days.

I stretched and wiped a seawater tear from the corner of my eye. It wasn't unusual to wake this way, halfway between a sob and a sigh. But I woke to the sun more often than not, to warmth, and so I could excuse the sea-brine that pooled in constant reminder at the corner of my eyes.

My tears become the sea, I'd been told. Once. By an old friend. Or an old enemy – only time would tell.

Today, I was inclined to call the dark passenger a friend. She had given me time, after all. Time to wake in an apartment I shared with my greatest friend, my dearest companion; time to eat eggs and bacon in the sun; time to heal old wounds with new care, to spend a day that had once been dark and unhappy painting over the scuffs and filling the cracks with new life.

Today, I had time. Mallory sang along to the radio, an old, tinny thing we'd thrifted that lived on what little counter space we had to spare. She'd made her bed, her door swung wide open to let in the fresh morning air that spilled from the living room window.

I padded down the hall in my socks, sweatpants, and overlarge t-shirt. I rubbed at the lingering salt at the corner of my eye and eddied in the kitchen doorway. Outside, there was nothing but color. Grass, verdant and thriving; sun, warm and blinding. A gaggle of children played on the playground at the heart of the apartment complex. Their mothers sipped iced coffee on the benches that the very same children had been allowed to paint just months before.

And Mallory – wonderfully, beautifully alive.

She turned as I leaned against the doorframe, stretching my arms above my head. "Got time for breakfast today?" she chirped, voice ever cheery. Mallory knew what day it was, though she'd never say it aloud unless I brought it up first. She was mindful like that. Thoughtful. She took note of things that no one would ever expect her to think of, to notice, to remember. The world could stand to be more like her. And I was trying. I would find it someday.

Everything yields to time. Even the soul. When it came time for mine to return to the sea, as promised, I would go willingly.

A smile tugged my features wide as the last of the omnipresent brine fell from the sleep-crusted corners of my eyes. For Mallory, I'd do anything. Even if it meant eating burnt bacon.

"Yeah," I said. "I've got time."

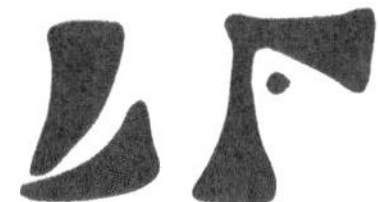

Enochian script

A STAR WHO IS NOT A STAR

Acknowledgements

The fact that there are so many brilliant, talented, genius people who believe in this book is absolutely mind-boggling to me. There was a time when I couldn't even bear to sit with this book because of how deeply personal it was and is. I didn't even realize at first why I felt so uncomfortable with this thing that I'd created, but when I shared it with my indomitable agent, Clara Chuiton, she helped me see that the discomfort was what made it something important. The topics handled in this book, like narcissistic abuse and self-harm, are difficult. That difficulty, that uncomfortability with the idea of acknowledging them, is and was the point of the story. I remember so distinctly emailing Clara with an apology for the book. It felt like I was apologizing for myself, for everything that was inherently wrong with me, and everything I was afraid of. But she refused to hear it. She believed in it from the jump. And she made me believe in it (and in myself), too. Clara has always been the best advocate a person could ask for, and I feel incredibly lucky to have someone like her in my corner.

I also have the distinct honor of working on this with Nadia Saward and Alyea Canada. I've never felt so supported and so empowered by a team. They, too, made me think that this book –

and what of me is in it – could be something really, really special. They made the work fun, approachable, and doable. Publishing can be so opaque and insular, and a lack of security kind of comes with the territory. But they always made me feel rallied around, valuable, and capable. I am working with what is truly the best team in the business, and I'm looking forward to telling many, many more stories alongside them. Nadia and Alyea, who took one look at my terrible TSHID-related meme collection and said, "Oh yeah, *that one*" – thank you for helping me tell such an important story.

A big part of this story is the idea that friends, too, can help you find yourself. No matter what you've been through (though not many people can say that "what they've been through" includes fighting an eldritch abomination in a sea cave), friends can fix everything. So of course, I have to thank the friends that made me want to write a duo like Caro and Mallory in the first place. The Bob Mob, who started as a bunch of nerds at a DnD table and have since blossomed into an unstoppable force of laughs and stories, you're all why I feel like I can do this at all. Rosa, Julie, Chloe, Therese, Darran. Your stories keep me sane, despite the inherent angst of what happens at our tables. And you all refused to let me *not* believe in myself. That's what real friends do. And I hope you all know that I believe in you just as hard. It's very easy to do, frankly. You're all rockstars.

To Grace, who is my forever first-stop beta reader – thank you for sifting through the garbage whenever it comes. You are a wonderful and patient person, and you deserve to meet Oscar Isaac one day. You're also stupidly talented, and now you can't argue with that fact because it's in print.

Carly, my oldest friend – we may live far from one another, but you're still close to my heart. Thank you for supporting my stories at their weirdest, and for making me feel like a superstar. I can't wait to see you again so that we can talk books for real.

And, of course, to the stalwart rock of a human being who made sure I ate, drank water, and occasionally touched grass while working on this book: Hunter, my wonderful husband, you are the coolest and best person I know. You're my best friend in the whole world. When we met, you pulled me out of the darkest depths and took me ashore. I love you for ever. Thank you for encouraging me to be the best version of myself, no matter what came before. And thank you for answering all the medical questions I'm too afraid to google.

I would also like to take this opportunity to suggest some reading that I've done on my own time regarding narcissistic abuse and people-pleasing. This is by no means a comprehensive list, but these texts have been really useful for me in the past. I've done a lot of work (and therapizing) where these topics are concerned, and I want to encourage anyone struggling with narcissistic abusers to do the same. I see you, I hear you, and I promise you that there's a light on the other side. You are your own; you are worthy; and you are ready to break free of it.

- *Adult Children of Emotionally Immature Parents: How to Heal from Distant, Rejecting, or Self-Involved Parents* by Lindsay C. Gibson
- *When Pleasing You Is Killing Me: Setting Boundaries With the Controllers in Your Life* by Les Carter PhD
- *Boundaries Workbook: When to Say Yes, How to Say No to Take Control of Your Life* by Dr Henry Cloud & Dr John Townsend
- *Enough About You, Let's Talk About Me: How to Recognize and Manage the Narcissists in Your Life* by Dr Les Carter

Last, but certainly not least, thank *you* – the reader – for coming on this journey with me. I'm looking forward to going on many, many more. Now stay out of sea caves!

About the author

Megan Bontrager is an author of SFF and horror currently based in the UK. She received her MA from Johns Hopkins and BFA from the University of Central Florida, and is currently a PhD candidate at NUI Maynooth where she studies Shakespeare. When she isn't frantically scribbling down her next big idea, Megan enjoys playing TTRPGs, seeing musicals and volunteering with animal rescues. She is responsible for two furry and four-legged children, and hopes to support their lavish lifestyles with her books.

Find out more about Megan Bontrager and other Run For It authors by registering for the free monthly newsletter at orbit-books.co.uk.

Dear Reader,

We'd love your attention for one more page to tell you about the crisis in children's reading, and what we can all do.

Studies have shown that reading for fun is the **single biggest predictor of a child's future life chances** – more than family circumstance, parents' educational background or income. It improves academic results, mental health, wealth, communication skills, ambition and happiness.[1]

The number of children reading for fun is in rapid decline. Young people have a lot of competition for their time. In 2024, 1 in 10 children and young people in the UK aged 5 to 18 did not own a single book at home.[2]

Hachette works extensively with schools, libraries and literacy charities, but here are some ways we can all raise more readers:

- Reading to children for just 10 minutes a day makes a difference
- Don't give up if children aren't regular readers – there will be books for them!
- Visit bookshops and libraries to get recommendations
- Encourage them to listen to audiobooks
- Support school libraries
- Give books as gifts

There's a lot more information about how to encourage children to read on our website: **www.RaisingReaders.co.uk**

Thank you for reading.

[1] OECD, '21st-Century Readers: Developing Literacy Skills in a Digital World', 2021, https://www.oecd.org/en/publications/21st-century-readers_a83d84cb-en.html

[2] National Literacy Trust, 'Book Ownership in 2024', November 2024, https://literacytrust.org.uk/research-services/research-reports/book-ownership-in-2024